# BROTHERS OF
# THE SNAKE

A WARHAMMER 40,000 NOVEL

# BROTHERS OF THE SNAKE

## Dan Abnett

*For Rachel Saunders*

*The author would like to thank Graham McNeill for his good counsel,
and editors Andy Jones and Christian Dunn for watching over the
Snakes on the way to this book.*

## A BLACK LIBRARY PUBLICATION

First published in Great Britain in 2007 by
BL Publishing,
Games Workshop Ltd.,
Willow Road, Nottingham,
NG7 2WS, UK.

10 9 8 7 6 5 4 3 2 1

Cover by Clint Langley.

A CIP record for this book
is available from the British Library.

ISBN 13: 978 1 84416 475 2
ISBN 10: 1 84416 475 6

Distributed in the US by Simon & Schuster
1230 Avenue of the Americas, New York, NY 10020, US.

Printed and bound in Great Britain by
Creative Print and Design Group, Harmondsworth, Middlesex, UK.

See the Black Library on the Internet at
**www.blacklibrary.com**

Find out more about Games Workshop
and the world of Warhammer 40,000 at
**www.games-workshop.com**

IT IS THE 41st millennium. For more than a hundred centuries the Emperor has sat immobile on the Golden Throne of Earth. He is the master of mankind by the will of the gods, and master of a million worlds by the might of his inexhaustible armies. He is a rotting carcass writhing invisibly with power from the Dark Age of Technology. He is the Carrion Lord of the Imperium for whom a thousand souls are sacrificed every day, so that he may never truly die.

YET EVEN IN his deathless state, the Emperor continues his eternal vigilance. Mighty battlefleets cross the daemon-infested miasma of the warp, the only route between distant stars, their way lit by the Astronomican, the psychic manifestation of the Emperor's will. Vast armies give battle in his name on uncounted worlds. Greatest amongst his soldiers are the Adeptus Astartes, the Space Marines, bio-engineered super-warriors. Their comrades in arms are legion: the Imperial Guard and countless planetary defence forces, the ever-vigilant Inquisition and the tech-priests of the Adeptus Mechanicus to name only a few. But for all their multitudes, they are barely enough to hold off the ever-present threat from aliens, heretics, mutants – and worse.

TO BE A man in such times is to be one amongst untold billions. It is to live in the cruellest and most bloody regime imaginable. These are the tales of those times. Forget the power of technology and science, for so much has been forgotten, never to be re-learned. Forget the promise of progress and understanding, for in the grim dark future there is only war. There is no peace amongst the stars, only an eternity of carnage and slaughter, and the laughter of thirsting gods.

*Fear not the Snake for his guile, nor his silence,*
*Fear him for his speed at striking,*
*The clenching strength of his coils,*
*The armour of his scales,*
*And the sharpness of his bite.*
*Fear the Snake, oh enemies of Man,*
*For his coils encircle us*
*And his bright eyes, unblinking,*
*Watch over us forever.*
                                    – from *The Lays of Proud Ithaka*


*In those days, there was a circle of brothers,*
*warriors of a mettle unsurpassed in all the worlds of*
*the Reef Stars, and they were called the Iron Snakes*
*of Karybdis. And an oath they swore, a great undertaking,*
*that for as long as their circle endured, they would stand*
*watch over all the Reef Stars and, by force of arms,*
*protect them from all the manifold powers of Ruin.*

*And they would know no fear.*

                                    – from *The Karybdiad*

# PART ONE
# GREY DAWN
## Undertaking
## to Baal Solock

# I

IN THE LAST days of the Ripening Season, in the northern cantons of Pythos, harvesters working late one hot, thundery evening in a field of swinecorn and eating lily, saw a piece of lightning fall down onto the world behind the Pythoan Hills.

They knew it was a piece of lightning, for what else could it have been? It made a streak of white light across the soft, blue evening clouds that was so bright that it left a memory of itself on their vision when they closed their eyes. When it landed, far away and out of sight, it made a crack like thunder. In the warm, sultry hours of those late days, summer storms regularly rumbled in and out of the sky and sometimes broke with great violence. And now a piece of one had torn loose and fallen out of the air. So the story passed from village to village.

In due time, a day or two after the event, the story reached the court of Samial Cater Hanfire, First Legislator of the Pythoan Cantons, brought into his zinc palace on the hill, along with a box of berries, by a talkative fruiterer delivering from the produce market. It came to Hanfire by way of a kitchen boy, two gossiping maid-slaves and a dutiful butler. Legislator Hanfire was a wise and

11

educated man, as one might expect a man of his station to be. He had been schooled in the Academy at Fuce and had travelled widely in his day, once as far as the thistle forests on the Western Tip. He was educated enough to know that lightning was not a solid commodity that simply fell from the sky from time to time.

A slave was sent down to the produce market, which was by then closing its shutters for the day, and the fruiterer was summoned back to the palace. There, he retold his story to Hanfire. He was a small, humble man, cowed by the presence of authority, and unduly ashamed of his hands, which had been stained almost blue by the juices of the fruit he traded in. He tried to keep them concealed in the folds of his patched apron.

Hanfire listened carefully, and then made the man repeat the story while the little metal golem at the foot of the First Legislator's wooden throne recorded the account on a clattering hand press. Hanfire then thanked the fruiterer and offered him some wine and a plate of food, which the fruiterer refused, and three electrum coins, which the fruiterer hastily accepted before fleeing the zinc palace.

Hanfire dined alone, reading back through the ink-impressed sheets that had rolled out of the golem's hand press, and by the time his steward brought the fruit posset and the small, crystal thimble of amasec, he knew what was now expected of him.

A rider was sent, without delay, to the High Legislator at Fuce, bearing a report written in Hanfire's own hand, requesting that the official Receiver of Wreck attend Pythos with all haste.

The Receiver of Wreck, a tall, hard-boned man called Hensher, arrived by fleet coach with his entourage two days later. After consultation with First Legislator Hanfire, the Receiver went up-country into the hills to make his survey. Hanfire accompanied him. This was not usual, but Hanfire was an educated man, and wonderfully curious about out-worldly matters.

The rising country was hot and dry. Summer storms lingered about the high places, and the sky was bruised with clouds like the skin of a windfall fruit. The string of coaches made good progress up the winding trackways, stopping at villages along the way to gather news. At each place, the locals came out in great crowds. They had never seen such important men in the flesh before, nor such finely garbed soldiers or such magnificent vehicles. They had never seen tailored clothes, or laslock rifles, or anything as inconceivable as the little metal golem.

They humbly told the First Legislator and the hard-boned Receiver everything they knew, as well as many things they didn't. The story had grown and it had been embellished, and trimmings of the very finest rumour had been attached to it. Yes, a piece of lightning had fallen from out of the sky. A great, splitting noise it had made when it fell. Where? Well, beyond the hills there, towards the vale known as Charycon. Now it rolled about there, grinding and grumbling, lost and bewildered, sometimes lighting up the sky at night with firework flashes.

Hanfire listened attentively. The Receiver of Wreck had his own golem make careful notes, and seemed little impressed. At the hamlet of Peros, beside the tumbling headwater of the Pythoa, the locals solemnly swore that the piece of lighting had set fire to great spaces of wilderness wood behind Charycon, an inferno that had raged for days and nights, until a storm downpour had quenched it. At Timmaes, a tiny place of low stone crofts, the inhabitants told of noises after dark and strange figures seen at a distance by shepherds on the hill pastures.

The hamlet of Gellyn, when they passed through it, was strangely empty, as if it had been vacated in a hurry.

'Simple folk fear things,' the Receiver told Hanfire as the coaches rattled onwards. 'It is their way, as we might expect.'

Hanfire shrugged, sitting back in his suede upholstered seat to feel the cool breeze of the coach's air fans.

'They would flee their homes? Run off into the night?'

'A piece of lightning has fallen from out of the sky,' the Receiver said, smiling the first smile Hanfire had seen cross his face. 'It could be dangerous.'

'But it's not?' asked First Legislator Hanfire.

'You wouldn't have summoned me if you thought so,' replied the Receiver, going back through the pages of the report his golem had produced during the day. 'You did the right thing, of course by sending for me. I admire your worldliness, sir.'

Hanfire knew he had just been complimented, but he wasn't quite sure how. 'I'm sorry?'

The Receiver looked up, peering through his half-moon spectacles. 'It's quite clearly a ship. A vessel that has foundered and crashed, just as you surmised. In the name of the High Legislator and the God-Emperor who preserves all, we must locate the site and secure it.'

'Is it dangerous then?' Hanfire asked.

The Receiver took down a zinc box from the luggage rack. It was a measuring device of some type and it had been clicking like a cricket for the past day and a half.

'See?' said the Receiver.

'I'm not sure…' replied Hanfire.

The Receiver adjusted a dial and the clicking became louder and more intense. 'Residue,' he said. 'Contamination. It has permeated this landscape. Probably the spill from a drive system. Once we've found the site, the area should be confined.'

'You've done this before?' asked Hanfire.

'I am the Receiver of Wreck,' the other man said. 'This is my job. Things fall from the heavens all the time, and thanks to men such as yourself, they are brought to my attention. There are fabulous treasures to be secured, in the name of the High Legislator. Technologies. Devices. Precious metals. And if it is a vessel of our Holy Imperium, there may be good human people in dire need of rescue.'

Hanfire had been very much enjoying his journey into the hills with the Receiver. It was a welcome change for him to spend time in the company of a learned, finely educated man, but now he felt some alarm. He was out of his depth. The Receiver was so much more cosmopolitan than he was. He knew such things. He knew of wonders beyond the mortal sphere. He knew of space and its mysteries. He spoke of them matter-of-factly, as if they were commonplace.

'Have you ever…' Hanfire began.

'Have I ever what, sir?' the Receiver asked.

Hanfire felt rather silly asking the question, but he needed to know. 'Have you ever been… beyond Baal Solock?'

The Receiver of Wreck smiled again. 'I was born on Eidon, sir, and came here as a child.'

The full, dizzying burden of that confession silenced First Legislator Hanfire for an hour or more.

When he spoke again, in the rocking, bouncing carriage, it was to ask the other question that had been gnawing away at the edges of his thoughts.

'What if it isn't?'

The Receiver of Wreck had been annotating the pages of the golem's report with a silver quill. He looked up at the First Legislator.

'Sir?'

Hanfire took off his gloves and rubbed his hands, though the night was warm. 'What if the vessel is not ours? What if it is... other?'

The Receiver of Wreck sat back and put his papers aside. 'The term we use is *xenos*, sir. Alien in origin. It may be, but such occurrences are very, very rare.'

'But what if it is?' asked Hanfire. He scolded himself inwardly for being so silly. It was just that he had never considered the idea before.

The Receiver reached up and pulled the communication thread. The fleet coach came to a halt, and the entire procession stopped around it. Hensher raised the window blinds and called out a command.

The retinue of twenty men-at-arms hurried forward and assembled outside the coach, snapping to attention. Receiver Hensher had brought them with him from Fuce. They were very excellent men indeed, tall and strong, plated in quality field armour of khaki metal. They bore the finest and most modern laslocks that Hanfire had ever seen.

'Ordinate Klue,' the Receiver called from the coach window, 'what is the principal order of the detachment?'

'To make safe the wreck and exterminate anything that is xenos,' the master-at-arms barked from behind his visor.

The Receiver looked around at Hanfire. 'These are good men. The best. Specialists, you might say. I pity the alien scum that meets with them in dispute. We are quite safe.'

'They are splendid indeed,' Hanfire said. He took his seat again.

'Carry on, Klue,' Hensher called, and the procession began to roll forward again.

'I haven't allayed your fears, have I, sir?' Receiver Hensher asked after a while.

Hanfire smiled. 'I have heard such things, sir: stories, murky rumours: warning tales of the Ruinous Powers, and the dread greenskins. They say they fall upon worlds and slay them utterly. I have been told, especially, of the thin, dark ones–'

'Ah, the primuls. They are just a bad memory now.'

'Stories say that they have stripped many worlds in the Reef Stars with their cruelty.'

'The primuls may once have been fact. But they are not here. I don't believe they exist any more. They are legends, stories, First Legislator.'

Hanfire couldn't let it go. 'But if they were… your fine detachment would be no match for them, would it?'

Receiver Hensher sighed. 'No, sir, not if the stories were true. But there is always ultimate salvation.' He leaned forward, and showed Hanfire his signet ring. It was curiously wrought, and marked with a double-looped serpent symbol.

'If doom ever came to Baal Solock, this would be our answer.'

Hanfire looked at the signet ring for a moment and then burst out laughing.

'Now you're telling me stories, sir! The sign of the snake? That's a folk tale! Children are taught that the coils of the snake enfold us and that its eye watches over us, unblinking… but that's just nursery talk.'

'Why?'

'Because it is, Hensher! Just a myth! Supreme warriors in grey armour, waiting to sweep in and guard us? A child's tale!'

'Is the God-Emperor of Mankind a myth too, First Legislator?'

'Of course not!'

'Have you ever seen him?'

'No!'

'Yet you believe in him?'

'Upon my life, sir,' said Hanfire.

'Do not dismiss the Snakes of Ithaka, then. They are real. They have made an undertaking to guard us, until the end of time. I believe this and so should you. If we find calamity here, if my fine detachment of guards cannot cope… if, if, if… then I will send instruction to Fuce and a petition will be made to the Brotherhood of the Snake. They are honour bound to answer.'

'Has that ever been done?' Hanfire asked.

'Of course,' said the Receiver of Wreck.

'When?'

Hensher frowned as he thought. 'If memory serves, it was last done six hundred and thirty-three years ago, in the time of High Legislator Ebregun.'

'And the Snakes of Ithaka came to Baal Solock's aid?'

'So the annals say.'

Hanfire shrugged and sat back. He didn't believe a word of it.

THE NIGHT WAS warm and light. Thunder rolled like a rock around the drum of the sky, and gentle sheet lightning lit the hills with an almost constant radiance, like a flickering twilight. It was high time they stopped for the night and rested the teams of quadruped servitors drawing the coaches. First Legislator Hanfire informed the Receiver of Wreck that a hamlet called Tourmel lay just another half an hour away up the track. There, they might find lodging, or at least a space to pitch their dormitory tents.

'The Vale of Charycon is less than an hour away beyond Tourmel. We can be on it at first light.'

This plan met with the Receiver's approval. The procession rattled on, its lanterns lit now, through the fragrant groves of musk trees and sandalwood.

And then it stopped.

Hanfire climbed down out of the fleet coach after the Receiver. The men-at-arms stood by the trackside, peering out into the dark woodland beyond the road. They had their weapons raised. Thunder rolled. In the shivering glow of the sheet lightning, they looked like statues.

'What is it?' Hanfire asked, and the Receiver shushed him. Hanfire swallowed. His unease returned. His pulse began to race.

'Ordinate Klue?' The Receiver whispered.

'Something in the trees, sir,' the soldier replied quietly. 'It's been following us for the last ten minutes.'

'Probably a lost goat or a–' Hanfire began lightly.

'Please, sir,' Hensher whispered. 'Quiet.'

One of the other soldiers suddenly raised his hand and pointed out into the dark. Klue nodded, and gestured for his men to move in. In a wide line, they stole forward into the trees. Hensher followed them.

He glanced back at Hanfire. 'Stay with the coaches, First Legislator.'

Hanfire obeyed. In a moment, both the men-at-arms and the Receiver of Wreck had vanished into the thickets. A silence descended, stirred only by the grumbling storm and the wheezes of the servitor teams. Hanfire walked back to the fleet coach. Coachmen and servants had climbed down from their seats, and stood around in small groups, quietly watching the woods. Hanfire could tell many of them were scared.

In an effort to display the sort of composure that ought to distinguish a man of high office, Hanfire went back to his coach, got in, and sat down to read some tithe returns he'd brought on the trip. He took his zinc quill out of its case, and determinedly began to make annotations in the margins of the forms by the light of the coach lamps.

After a few minutes, he heard a pop from off in the distance. It sounded remarkably like the plosive sound that corks made when pulled from flasks of effervescent Fucean wine. There was another one shortly afterwards, then two more in quick succession.

Hanfire put down his quill and climbed out of the coach. The footmen and drivers were still staring into the darkness.

Two more pops. Then an odd rattle, like pebbles rolling down the swaying blade of a push-pull saw. This was followed by another sound, muffled and far away.

'That was a man,' one of the coachmen said.

'Be quiet,' said Hanfire.

'It was a man, sir,' the coachman insisted. 'He cried out.'

Hanfire turned and looked sternly at the coachman. The coachman's name was Petters, and he had been the First Legislator's team driver for eight years. Hanfire couldn't bring himself to reprimand such a four-square, faithful retainer.

He didn't have to. One look at Hanfire's disapproving expression and Coachman Petters bowed. 'My apologies, First Legislator.'

Hanfire smiled. 'There's nothing to be scared of,' he told the people around him. 'Did you not see the fine fellows Receiver Hensher brought with him? I doubt the High Legislator himself boasts a troop so formidable.'

Some of them smiled. Hanfire was pleased they'd been even slightly soothed by his remark. Inside, once again, he didn't believe a word of it.

They waited a while longer. Over the low mumble of the thunder, they heard more pops and more rattles. Then a cry again, unmistakable this time.

The retainers looked at Hanfire. He could taste their fear.

'Take your places,' he told them. 'Get ready to proceed. Kester, unlock the gun chest and issue weapons to the coach riders.'

The retainers hurried to their places, some calling out orders. Hanfire turned back to look into the black thickets. More pops, four or five in a rapid, almost frantic series.

Then a smell came to Hanfire on the night air: a curious smell, dry and dead. He couldn't place it. Years before, he'd visited Marblevault, on the edges of the Old Desert. There, the hot wind had blown out of the empty quarters, filling the city with the desiccated, mineral stink of the desert.

It was like that, but not quite.

'Sir, we are ready to proceed,' Petters called down from the driving board of the fleet coach. Hanfire raised his right hand.

'Wait. We should wait a moment longer.'

They waited. The quad-servitors snorted anxiously, pawing the turf. Behind him, Hanfire heard a rapid clicking. He thought it was one of the coach riders slotting shells into a repeating rifle.

It was the Receiver's zinc box up in the luggage rack, the measuring device. It was clicking as fast and loud as the finger cymbals the houris of Marblevault clattered when they danced.

Hanfire cleared his throat, swallowing hard again. 'We will proceed!' he called out.

'Sir!' Petters called from his vantage up on the fleet coach. 'Look! Look there!'

Hanfire looked. Something was moving out in the trees. Something was approaching them – a figure. A running figure.

Hanfire heard weapons cock.

'Hold your shots!' he cried.

The running figure came closer, tearing and clawing through the underbrush in its haste. It came into view.

It was the Receiver of Wreck.

His clothes were torn, and his hard-boned face pricked with blood by passing brambles. He ran towards Hanfire and the fleet coach.

'What is it?' asked Hanfire.

'Get the coaches moving,' Hensher said. 'Quickly now.'

'What's going on?'

The Receiver didn't answer. He ran to the rear of the fleet coach and dragged the canvas travel cover off the vox-caster set secured on the luggage rack.

'What is going on?' Hanfire demanded, hurrying after him.

'Run, First Legislator,' the Receiver said, urgently throwing switches to power up the vox-set. 'Everyone here must run. Now! Tell them. Order them. Run south in the name of the Golden Throne.'

'You are scaring me, sir,' said Hanfire.

'Good. I mean to. I've seen what's out there. Holy Terra, my men. All my men…'

Hanfire glanced back at the dark woods then looked at the Receiver. 'What about your men?'

'They're dead,' said the Receiver.

The First Legislator felt a cold, stony weight sink into his gut. 'What precisely do you mean?' he asked, very clearly and carefully.

'I mean precisely that they're all dead!' Hensher barked. 'Have you shit for brains, man? Are you stupid? I'm using simple bloody words–'

'There's no need to be offensive,' Hanfire said, smarting.

The Receiver of Wreck looked at Hanfire and sighed. 'I'm sorry,' he said. 'I'm truly sorry for those words. My temper got the better of me. We're in trouble, sir, very grave trouble. I'm asking you to command the company to flee. On foot. As quickly as they can. They have to lose themselves in the woods right now. Tell them to head south. Please, sir.'

As he spoke, the Receiver carefully tuned the active vox-caster to a particular channel, and then flipped open the optical reader mounted on the caster's fascia. It blinked as green light fluttered inside its cowled lens.

The Receiver took off his signet ring and pressed it into the reader's slot.

'Oh my lord,' stammered Hanfire. He stumbled away from the rear of the coach and raised his voice, wishing desperately that it wasn't so tremulous. 'All of you!' he cried. 'All of you! Run! Run now! Into the woods! Be quick about it! Run! Head south! Run!'

The coach crews and servants exploded off the stationary vehicles like a flock of startled crows and began to run. Hanfire watched as they scattered into the trees behind the coaches, panicking, disappearing from view. He heard fearful cries and rushing footfalls retreating into the darkness.

The Receiver of Wreck took his signet ring back out of the optical reader and slid it onto his finger. He keyed the 'repeat/send' toggle on the set. Monitor lights flickered and pulsed. He turned around and found Hanfire behind him.

'Are you still here?' he asked. There was a tight sadness in his voice.

'Of course,' said Hanfire. 'I am First Legislator of these cantons. I'm not about to run like a common fool.'

'I wish you had, sir,' Hensher said.

'I'm staying here,' Hanfire said. 'This is my land, my territory. I hold it in fealty to the High Legislator himself. I'll be damned if I flee from the soil I am elected to protect.'

'Then you'll be damned,' said the Receiver. He climbed into the abandoned fleet coach, and pulled a strongbox off the luggage rack. It had been sitting beside his clucking zinc device. The Receiver opened the strongbox and took out two matched firing pieces, gold-inlaid bolt pistols that had been nested in the red velvet slots within. He loaded both, quickly and surely, and handed one to Hanfire.

'You are a brave soul, First Legislator Hanfire,' said the Receiver of Wreck. 'I wish I could have got to know you better.'

'There's still time,' Hanfire began.

'No. I'm afraid there's not,' said the Receiver of Wreck. 'I'm so sorry, sir. I have misjudged this. We are in trouble.'

'You mean… you and I?'

'I mean Baal Solock.'

First Legislator Hanfire sighed and nodded. He took his place beside the Receiver of Wreck, in front of the empty fleet coach.

The primuls appeared. One or two at first, forlorn and rake-thin figures in the soft flicker of the lightning. Then more, a dozen, two dozen. They were very black and hard: spiked figures that stepped quietly out of the thickets, gleaming in the storm light. They seemed to Hanfire to have the character of hooks or thorns about them. So very glossy-black and sharp.

The Receiver of Wreck raised his pistol. Samial Cater Hanfire did the same.

'I really am so sorry,' the Receiver of Wreck said.

'No need to be,' replied the First Legislator.

They began to fire.

Behind them, drowned out by the roar of their pistols, the zinc device continued its furious clicking, and the vox-caster continued to pulse.

## II

It APPEARED TO be a joke, though the punchline wasn't obvious.

Perdet Suiton Antoni, primary clerk to the High Legislator of Fuce, read the wafer again, and saw no structure to the humour. Just thirty-three, a nimble-fingered woman with a nimble mind, Antoni took her job seriously, so seriously that it had already cost her a marriage and most of her circle of friends. Women were only just beginning to advance in the Legislature of Baal Solock, and no female had ever held a post so lofty or so ambitious as Perdet Suiton Antoni. It took tenacity and drive to overturn the old, hide-bound attitudes to gender and profession. A woman had to work twice as hard and be twice as good as any male counterpart to win advancement, even now the rules had changed, and suffrage was recognised by law.

Antoni was a slight woman, who looked much younger than her actual age. On state occasions, she seemed swamped by the brocade and fur of her ceremonial garments, and, many said – most of them male – by the stature of her office. For her, every day was a battlefield to get men to take her seriously.

'This is a joke,' she said.

The duty rubricator in the palace's communiqué chamber shrugged ruefully. 'It is authentic, as far as we can see, dam. You'll note the thread line that declares the authority of the Receiver of Wreck.'

Antoni already had. She had an eye for such things. She didn't need to be told. 'But it's a request for–' she stopped and laughed. The rubricator laughed too, soullessly, just trying to keep her company.

Antoni stopped laughing, and so did the rubricator. 'This hasn't happened before,' she said.

'Please you, dam, it has.'

'When?'

The rubricator shrugged. 'Ah… I'd have to consult. Maybe five hundred years ago?'

'This is a joke,' said Antoni again.

'I would hope so,' said the rubricator. 'So much paperwork to fill out if it's genuine.'

Antoni looked at the wafer again. She knew she could simply ignore it, that was in her power. She could ignore anything she didn't want to bother the High Legislator with.

But she'd not won her position in the world by ignoring the rules. No one knew the Legislature statutes more thoroughly than Perdet Suiton Antoni. She was a woman of process, a woman of letter. This wafer, however ridiculous it seemed, carried about it the seal of urgency and proper procedure. Antoni knew that some protocol simply couldn't be ignored, even if it seemed daft. Just because something happened once every few thousand years didn't mean it wasn't still important.

'Be advised,' Antoni told the rubricator, 'I have to treat this as genuine. Inform your staff. If it's a hoax, we'll find out who's behind it. Until then, stand ready. I have to take the authority at face value. I have to take this to the High Legislator.'

'Rather you than me,' the rubricator said.

Antoni nodded. 'Carry on,' she said.

As she hurried away down the long, draughty corridor, the rubricator turned to his staff, clapped his gnarly hands, and urged them to meet emergency conditions.

FRA QUESH AZURE, High Legislator of Fuce, was watering his high garden with a little, green, spouted can. The high garden was a long terrace on the roof of the palace, marvellously festooned with weeds and scrubby plants that the High Legislator would not allow to be pruned or cut back. He fancied himself a botanist, and this was his collection of precious samples. He had written several heavy books on the subject, all of which had been dutifully published, all of which sat, unread, in the palace library. Years before, the high garden had afforded a fine view across the roofs and chimneys of Fuce. Nowadays, it was hard enough to locate the edge railings in all the undergrowth, let alone see out.

The High Legislator was dressed in a housecoat, a long robe of silk. The tie-sash had long since been mislaid, and the High Legislator pulled the robe shut around his portly frame with one hand. Princeps, his attack dog, a black-satin beast of hard muscles and slavering snout, trotted behind him through the weeds, leash-less.

'My Lord Azure,' Antoni called from the doors of the garden room. The High Legislator was invisible amongst the sprouting moss worts and climbing dreddle. 'Uh, my lord?'

Princeps stiffened and growled, hulking his back like a fighting bull.

'Stay now, Princeps, my good boy,' muttered the High Legislator, setting down his watering can. 'That's just Antoni. You know Antoni, don't you? Yes, you do. Yes, you do.'

The hound stopped growling and padded off through the overgrown garden to meet their guest. Antoni stiffened as she saw the dog approaching. It circled her twice.

'Let him sniff you!' a voice called from out of the spidery green. 'Antoni? Let him smell you. Then he won't harm you.'

Antoni held out a fist. The attack dog came to it, sniffed it, and licked it.

Antoni shuddered.

With a grumble like distant thunder, the attack dog padded off into the garden room, and began fidgeting with a bone.

'Antoni?'

'My lord?'

Azure emerged out of the weeds. 'Hello, my dear. What's the matter?'

Antoni gave the wafer to the High Legislator. 'A joke, I believe,' she said, 'but I am constrained by protocol to take it seriously.'

Azure peered at the paper slip. 'Hensher sent this?'

'It seems so, sir.'

'From where?'

'The Pythoan Cantons, sir.'

'Never been there. I'm told they're horribly rural. Horribly rural. Who's our man up in that neck of the woods?'

'Hanfire, sir.'

Azure paused, thinking. He shook his head. 'No, don't know him.'

'He was here last winter feast. Smart fellow, very proper.'

Azure shrugged. 'Still nothing.'

'Should we take this seriously, sir?' Antoni asked.

'If it was from this Hamfer–'

'Hanfire.'

'Well, whatever his name… then no. But Hensher solicited this signal.' The High Legislator paused, and glanced around his garden. His robe fell open. Antoni looked away at some nearby sunflowers.

'The official Receiver of Wreck ought to know what he's talking about, wouldn't you say, Antoni?'

'Yes, sir. Could you maybe pull your robe, with respect, closer to you–'

'What?'

'I was saying, the high garden's looking particularly lovely, sir.'

'I'm happy you think so.' The High Legislator looked again at the wafer. 'This is a protocol matter, Antoni.'

'Yes, sir.'

'I mean, fake or real, this is a matter of protocol.'

'It is, sir.'

'How long has it been?'

'I checked, sir. Six hundred and thirty-three years.'

Azure nodded and dead-headed a few tuberoses. 'If this is a scare, I'll have heads on pikes for it.'

'Yes, sir.'

'If it isn't… Antoni, you know what to do.'

'Sir, do you really want me to–'

'The Receiver of Wreck is no idiot. He wouldn't have done this unless he expected us to take proper action. If it turns out to be his idea of foolery, then I'll flay him alive and use his skull as a goblet.'

'Hensher never struck me as a man fond of games,' Antoni said.

'Me neither. Go and set things in motion, please.'

'I will, sir,' said Antoni.

\* \* \*

THE ALARUM CHAPEL was actually a basement room underneath the Holy Cathedral in the heart of Fuce. Time and circumstance had layered buildings above and around it.

The door to it was locked. Antoni had to wait for several minutes while the beadle found a key.

'Been no call for it in such a long time,' the beadle said, blowing dust off the key. He regarded the primary clerk with eyes rendered dull by cataracts. 'Begging your pardon, dam, but is this–'

Antoni cut the beadle off. 'I'm certain.'

The door swung open with a drawn out, lethargic creak. Antoni walked alone into the cool, dark crypt, and ancient glow-globe systems, sensing either her body heat or motion, slowly came alive, growing in radiance until the chapel was bathed in a pearly, green shimmer.

On the stone shelves and alcoves around her, Antoni saw urns and amphorae, thick with dust, painted with the figures of warriors. Grey-clad warriors, from the sky. Six hundred and thirty-three years earlier, they had come to Baal Solock's aid. As she wandered forward, Antoni studied the stylised, painted figures, legs splayed, lances lifted to strike.

'This is all so much nonsense,' she said to herself.

The plinth was made of ebony, or some black stone that was warm to the touch. It was surprisingly small, and gave off a faint scent of energised heat, like an astropath enclave. Old systems, still ticking over. Antoni felt the surfaces of the plinth carefully, wiping away the accumulated dust with the corner of her cuff.

Antoni had brought the codex with her. She took the small, brass-clasped volume out of her coat pocket, opened it, and began to read. No one had performed this action in a very long time, and nobody had even practised it. Some court procedures were rehearsed on a regular, formal basis, but not this one. For a moment, Antoni felt a brief connection to the last person who had taken this codex out of the palace library and opened it: another primary clerk, his name (without doubt, he had been a he) now lost, six hundred and thirty-three years before.

The instructions were fairly simple. Antoni laid the codex open on the top of the plinth, and saw how the leaves naturally fell apart on the right page. Fabric memory. Her predecessor had pressed the book open, and laid it just where Antoni had now done, so as to be able to consult it.

She took off her signet ring, and fitted it into the seal reader. The double-headed snake motif locked in and turned like a key. A rectangular panel slid open in the front face of the plinth, allowing more warm air to escape, and revealed a small, finger-touch keypad and several other small controls.

The codex contained a list of numeral sequences to type in, with their corresponding meanings. Antoni spent a moment deciding which was the most appropriate. She settled on a general request for assistance, and nervously tapped in the designated code. Then she carefully followed the rest of the instructions.

The final touch. A simple, recessed button, edged in brass. Antoni hovered her index finger above it for a long time, and then pressed it.

She wasn't sure what to expect, though she anticipated something impressive. There was a click, then a silence, then a low groan that gathered force until it became a lingering murmur that hung in the air. Heat radiated from the black plinth. The chapel lights dimmed for a second, ever so slightly. Then there came another sound, so deep she felt it rather than heard it. She backed away from the plinth, slightly alarmed.

The sounds all died away and silence returned. The plinth went dead, except for one, slow, blinking blue light.

Antoni picked up the codex and read on. There was nothing else. She was done.

She walked out of the chapel, the lights fading in sequence behind her. The beadle was waiting by the door.

'When do you start, dam?' the beadle asked.

'I'm finished,' said Antoni. 'Lock the door.'

### III

Two MONTHS LATER, a star appeared in the western sky.

For three hours, it glowed against the curdled, grey, dawn clouds, and those citizens of Fuce who had not by then fled for the south, leaving their properties boarded and locked, regarded it as an ill omen.

A tardy ill omen, at that. All the bad things an omen like that might presage had surely come to pass already.

The star grew brighter and larger. It divided into three points of bright light, then came closer still, and revealed itself to be a dark shape upon which three bright lights were mounted.

It was a ship.

One of the palace guards woke Perdet Suiton Antoni and the primary clerk hurried to the high windows along the west wing of the palace to look. Her feelings had changed a great deal in the previous two months. What had been puzzlement and suspicion had turned into dismal fear.

And now, suddenly, to hope.

'Assemble a retinue!' she yelled. 'An honour guard, now! Quickly!'

Her voice was drowned out as the ship passed over Fuce with a roar like rushing wind.

Antoni left the palace grounds in a two-wheeled gig, goading the servitors. She'd barely had time to put on her formal robes. Her men-at-arms rushed out after her on foot, clattering shields and weapons. They left the marching band behind. It was taking the players too long to assemble their instruments.

'Where did it go?' Antoni shouted to her troop master. 'Did anyone see it land?'

'The lights came down on the water meadows,' the troop master replied. 'Down beyond the state park.'

They hurried that way. The ground became too boggy for the gig, and Antoni dismounted, picking up the hem of her robes so she could run with the men-at-arms.

She saw a shape through the trees ahead, a fog of water vapour slowly dissipating in the dawn. She smelled a curious perfume of heat and chemicals and mud.

'Quickly now!' she called to the men strung out in the muddy grasses around her. 'And look smart! You there, straighten that tunic!'

'Yes, dam.'

Antoni was brought up sharply by the steady hand of the troop master on her arm. 'What?'

'This could be *anything*, dam. This could be... *more* of them. Let me lead the way.'

The thought hadn't occurred to primary clerk Antoni. It chilled her. She nodded, ashamed of her sudden cowardice. The troop master moved forward, calling orders to his men to spread out. Antoni followed them.

The steam was clearing. A few old willows stood limp along the edge of the water meadow, and beyond them lay the ship. Fierce, sleek, its galvanised hull was scored and pitted, its landing stanchions half sunk in the soft earth.

Antoni frowned. It seemed to be a very *small* ship.

The advancing men-at-arms came to a halt well shy of the landed vessel. They aimed their weapons at it. The grey dawn was very close and still, except for the croaking and fluting of waterfowl in the meadows and the estuary beyond. Strands of mist unfurled themselves out through the air like gauze.

A hatch opened. A ramp extended with a loud whirr. Water birds wading close by broke and fled aloft in a panic of beating wings.

A lone figure came down the ramp, just a silhouette in the misty air. It crouched down at the foot of the ramp, busy with some task. Antoni peered forward. What was it doing? Anointing itself? Drinking?

The figure rose to its feet again. A voice suddenly rang out of nowhere and everywhere, amplified.

'Unless you mean to be my enemy,' it declared, 'stop aiming your weapons at me.'

The men-at-arms slowly, nervously, lowered their firearms.

Antoni pushed forward, past the troop master and approached the figure.

'I am Perdet Suiton Antoni, primary clerk to…' she trailed off and came to a halt. The craft ahead of her was certainly small, but the figure at the foot of its ramp was not. He was a giant, cased in armour that was gunmetal grey, edged in red and white. His head was bare, a heavy skull on a broad neck, black hair pleated in coils around his crown. He seemed two or even three times the mass of an ordinary adult male, and even the tallest men-at-arms in Antoni's retinue would only have come up to the giant's chest.

'Oh god…' Antoni murmured.

The giant took a step off the end of the ramp towards her. With a gasp, Antoni sank to her knees, squelching in the mud.

'There's no need for that,' the giant said. His voice was so deep, so immense, Antoni felt it quiver her diaphragm.

'Please, get up, primary clerk.'

Antoni looked up, but did not rise. She stared into the giant's face. It was massive and angular like a mountain cliff, but the eyes were sharp and alive.

'You sent for me.'

'I... I mean, we... I mean the people of Baal Solock... we sent... I sent... a signal, just a signal... according to the old law of undertaking... a signal to the Iron Snakes of Ithaka. For... for help...'

'I am Priad of Damocles, of the Iron Snakes. Your signal was heard, and I have answered it. Where is the enemy?'

Antoni got up, her robe tails wet with mud. 'In the north. North of here.'

'Number and disposition? Type?'

'I don't know. All I know is that the primuls have attacked our world.'

'Primuls? That's an old term. I haven't heard it used in years. Come with me, please.'

The giant gestured for Antoni to follow him back into the ship. Antoni hesitated.

The giant turned back. 'I'm sorry. I was getting ahead of myself. There's some ceremony, I suppose? Your local leader wishes to feast me? Something like that?'

Antoni shook her head. 'Our High Legislator went into hiding six weeks ago when the primul attacks became more intense. We... we have no proper welcome for you, sir. I only hesitate because...'

'What?'

'I'm afraid of going into your ship. I've never–'

'I see. That's all right. It's perfectly safe. It's just like a regular sea boat. Please come with me. I need to know what you know, if I'm going to help you.'

Antoni nodded, and scrambled forward to join the giant. Near the foot of the ramp, she slipped in the mud, and the giant shot out a hand to grasp her arm and steady her.

The grip was like a bear trap. The giant's huge gauntlet entirely enclosed Antoni's hand.

'All right, primary clerk?'

'Yes. I was wondering...'

'What?'

'You are a Snake?'

'Yes.'

'You are alone?'

'Yes.'

Antoni smiled and nodded. 'I understand. The ship seemed so small. When do the other Snakes arrive?'

'What others?' replied the giant.

## IV

Antoni followed the giant warrior up the ramp into the belly of the ship. Their footsteps pealed echoes off the metal decking.

'I don't understand,' Antoni said.

The interior of the ship had a strange, musty smell of hot metal, scented oils, bleach and ozone. They were in a kind of hold space with a black grille floor and harsh, greenish lamps recessed into the verdigrised walls. All the surfaces were scuffed and worn, utilitarian. A steady, throbbing click and gurgle came from behind the wall plating as the ship's systems cooled and shut down.

It neither looked nor smelled anything like Antoni's idea of a space vessel. The giant strode across the grille floor and attended to a row of machine units with glowing screens mounted along one side of the hold space.

'What don't you understand, primary clerk?'

Antoni cleared her throat. 'You are... alone? You come to us alone?'

'Yes,' said the giant. 'That is the standard way. If a client world solicits Ithaka for aid, the Chapter Master traditionally authorises one warrior to respond. And one warrior usually suffices.'

'But if the problem is grave?' she began. 'Surely one man is not enough...?'

'I can make that assessment. Others can be summoned. I don't think they will be needed on this occasion.'

'With respect, the territories of the Legislature are under assault. There have been raids, quite barbaric raids, and many deaths. Towns and villages have been burned. We have sent in our best troops. None have returned. None have ever been seen again. The primuls-'

'Are fiends,' said the giant. 'I know. I am acquainted with their handiwork. You were lucky, in fact.'

'Lucky?' she echoed.

'In the last six months, my company has been engaged in a sporadic contest with the dark el– with *primul* factions in this stellar neighbourhood. A number of skirmishes on half a dozen worlds. We scattered them, and now my battle group is occupied hunting the remnants of them down and mopping them up. The Chapter House relayed your signal to my battle-barge. We were just a few systems away. It was deemed convenient to drop me off as we came by. Primary clerk, how do you suppose we answered your signal so quickly?'

'Quickly?' she replied. 'It's been two months!'

The giant looked at her with a faint, forgiving smile. 'What did you say your name was, primary clerk?'

'Perdet Suiton Antoni,' she said.

'Well, Perdet Suiton Antoni... you are clearly an educated woman. How far away do you suppose Ithaka is?'

'I don't know,' she confessed.

'To the nearest parsec, maybe?'

'I don't know what a parsec is, sir.'

The giant nodded. 'Ithaka is a long, long way away, primary clerk. It would take the Iron Snakes ten or twelve months at the minimum to get here from there. We were in the neighbourhood. Count yourself lucky.'

'I didn't–' she began.

'Didn't what?'

'I didn't realise space was so big. Ithaka *is* in the Reef Stars, isn't it?'

'Yes, it is.'

'And the Reef Stars alone are so vast that it would take a year to cross from Ithaka to Baal Solock?'

'No time at all, where space is concerned. It would take three and a half years to cross the Reef Stars group, and that is just a small part of the whole Imperium. Galactically speaking, Ithaka is close by. A bright, yellow star, which you might see in summer time, close to the western horizon.'

'You know where Ithaka is in our sky?'

'It was the first thing I checked when I arrived. I like to know where I am in relation to it. A foible, you might say.'

Antoni felt slightly light-headed. 'I'd like to sit down,' she said.

The giant clanked over to her and wrenched down a foldaway seat built into the corroded wall. She perched on it.

'Thank you. Could I also trouble you for a cup of water?'

He paused. 'I don't have... I mean, we don't need supplies... rations. We can operate for a long time without...'

She nodded. 'I understand. It's all right.'

'No,' he said. 'It's not. A drink of water.' He reached down and took out a flask from a sheath strapped to his armoured thigh plate. The flask was tubular, copper, banded with straps of dull zinc. He unstoppered it and handed it to her. 'It will be brackish, I'm afraid.'

She sipped. It *was* brackish, but the water was welcome anyway.

'Thank you,' she said, handing it back.

The giant just nodded again, re-stoppered the flask, and put it away. He stepped across the hold space and pressed a series of heavy, wall-mounted pressure switches.

On the left side of the hold, a section of wall retracted, revealing equipment, armour and weapons hung from secure brackets. Antoni saw long, copper lances, a pair of shields, and an enormous firearm that she knew, just by looking at it, would be too heavy for her to lift.

On the right side, a section hatch furled up to expose a secondary hold in which a craft of some kind hung in a supporting frame. To Antoni, it looked a little like a row-boat, but grey and armoured, with seats for two, and heavy weapons mounted on the prow. The giant threw some switches, and power began to pulse through to the small craft, charging its engines.

The giant returned to his bank of monitor screens. 'They've milked out,' he said.

'What?'

'My scanners. I'd hoped to get a decent topographic scan as I came in, and fix a position for the hostiles. But they've milked out, blind. Radiation, that's my guess.'

'Radiation? What's that?'

'I think the primuls might have crashed here, primary clerk. It's not an invasion, it's a forced landing. Their drive core has leaked, perhaps even exploded, polluting hundreds of square kilometres. The return is so harsh, I can't get a decent track.'

'I can show you where they are,' Antoni said. 'In the palace. I have maps.'

'I'd appreciate that,' the giant said.

THE MEN-AT-ARMS fell back as she led the giant up through the water meadows from his ship. She chatted all the way, and the giant made little response. He simply trudged after her, towering like a high man from the old stories, occasionally steadying her when she slipped or stumbled.

As they walked in through the arches of the palace, the giant said, 'It's unusual, isn't it? For a female to hold such status?'

'Yes, it is,' she replied. 'I am the first woman to achieve the rank of primary clerk. I earned it.'

'I have no doubt of that.'

'On Baal Solock, we are proud of the way we have recognised gender rights. This is a modern, enlightened age.'

'Yes,' said the giant, smiling again. 'I rather suppose it is.'

'THERE,' SHE SAID.

The giant studied the charts Antoni had rolled out.

'High country, then?'

'Up beyond Charycon. Hills and vales. Most of the villages there have been razed. The entirety of the Pythoan Cantons is considered a no go.'

The giant considered the maps, blinking from time to time. Each blink was matched with a click.

'What is that?' Antoni asked.

'I'm simply storing data.'

'Your eyes are like a camera?'

'Yes. I suppose you could think of it that way.' His eyes clicked again. Now he was looking at her.

'You recorded my pict?' she asked.

'Yes, primary clerk. Target recognition. I'd hate to shoot you by accident.'

'Why would you?' Antoni asked.

'Because I know what you're going to ask of me.'

'When?'

'Tomorrow.'

## V

IT WAS, AGAIN, a cold, grey dawn. Mist, heavier than the previous day's, draped like swaddling around the precincts of Fuce, making all sounds strange and hollow.

Antoni came out into the damp chill of the palace yard. Sentries stood around in attendance, and somewhere, a drill master was ordering a change of guard shifts. The bellowing voice was twisted and transmuted by the levelling mist.

Antoni put down her small travelling case. She was dressed in a woollen winter roving suit of shirt and trousers, with waterproofed leathers worn over. She waited.

Princeps, and three of the High Legislator's other attack dogs, roamed the yard. The High Legislator had insisted, before his departure, that his trusted hounds should remain behind 'to safeguard the palace'. Antoni stayed well out of their way.

A new sound throbbed through the mists, an engine sound. Antoni looked up. So did the sentries in the yard, and the dogs too. The engine note came closer, then died away outside the palace yard gate. A moment later, heavy footfalls crunched in through the yard entry. The giant, in his hulking armour, appeared through the mist.

The dogs immediately ran towards him, growling, hackles up. 'Stop them!' Antoni called to the nearest sentry, but he just shrugged, helpless.

The giant came to a halt as the dogs came for him. He sank to one knee and let out a swift, sharp whistle, a sound that Antoni couldn't imagine a human mouth making.

The dogs immediately dropped onto their bellies and put their chins flat on the wet cobbles. One of them let out a little whine. The giant, still kneeling, wiggled his metal-gloved fingers and Princeps got up, ran forward with his head low, and allowed the giant to pet him. Princeps gurgled and rolled over, legs splayed.

The giant rose again, pointing a finger at Princeps. The attack dog settled down on its belly once again. The warrior stepped past the supine dogs and came over to Antoni.

'Fine dogs. War dogs?'

'Yes.'

'Very fine animals.'

'How did you…' she began, then thought better of it.

'You're dressed for travelling,' he remarked.

'I intend to come with you. There are, I believe, two seats aboard your travelling machine.' She looked up at him. 'This is the question you knew I would ask.'

'Yes,' he said. 'I won't make an argument. You have summoned me to accomplish a task, and you wish to see it done. It is normal for client states to require a witness or inspector to oversee our actions.'

'So you will take me with you?'

'Primary clerk, we have learned from experience it's better to say yes than to refuse and have someone like you tail us. I need to know where you are so I can keep you safe. There are basic conditions, however. You will do as I say at all times, without comment or question. You will accompany me only so far. Once we reach the tactical edge of the operational area, you will stay put and allow me to continue alone.'

'Now wait, I–'

'These conditions are non-negotiable, primary clerk. You may come with me to the edge of the fighting area, and then wait for me. I am very capable, but I cannot guarantee your safety once we are in a shooting zone. You will wait for me at the tactical edge. Once I'm done, I will return for you and allow you to review the scene and assure yourself that I have been thorough. Do you agree to these terms?'

'I suppose so.'

'You do or you don't. If you don't believe you can abide by them, then you're staying here.'

'Very well.'

'Are you armed?' the giant asked.

'Can't you tell?' she asked.

He looked at her, and there was another click as he blinked. 'Battery source, upper left hand pocket. A communicator or a recording device. Pict recorder, hip pocket. Battery source, collar and spine of overcoat... a heating element, I'm guessing. Charge pistol, lower coat pocket. Las?'

'Yes?'

'Show me.'

Antoni took out the small laspistol she'd checked out of the palace armoury that morning. She handed it to him. He looked at it for a moment. It seemed like a child's toy in his massive gauntlets. Then he tossed it away to the nearest sentry, who caught it neatly.

'No firearms, primary clerk. I must have absolute say over weapons discharge. Apart from the enemy, of course. I can't permit you to carry a handgun. In an emergency, it could confuse things far too much.' He paused. 'I smell black powder, and trace fyceline from ignition caps.'

'The sentries here are armed with solid-slug side arms.'

'That's not it. Please.'

Antoni sighed, and removed the percussion pistol from her trouser pocket. He took it, disarmed it, and threw it to the sentries.

'Nice try, though,' the giant said.

'How am I supposed to protect myself?' Antoni asked.

'You're not. That's my job. That's the point. Anything else? Speak now.'

'I have a blade. A sheath knife.'

'Show me.'

She pulled up the cuff of her right trouser leg. The blade was strapped in a scabbard to her calf.

'I'll allow that. But hook it to your waistband where I can see it and you can reach it.'

Shaking her head, she did as he told her.

'Anything else?' he asked.

'No.'

'I can still smell black powder.'

'Spare cartridges, in my case. It will take me a moment to unpack them.'

'Never mind. We ought to be going.' He turned away, then swung back. 'I want your word, dam, as a servant of the Imperium of Man, that you will obey my instructions at all times. I say this only because I want you to remain alive. Disobedience will likely result in your death.'

'Is that a threat?' she asked candidly.

'Not at all. But I know what I'm doing and you don't. As I said, I want you to remain alive. Disobeying me will likely cause an accident. Are we clear?'

'Perfectly.'

'I have your agreement?'

'You do.'

'Then let's go.' The giant walked away across the yard and began to disappear into the mist. Antoni looked at the waiting sentries standing nearby. She shrugged.

'Emperor protect you, dam,' one said nervously.

'As I understand it, he already is,' she replied. Then she picked up her case and hurried after the giant.

THE GIANT'S TWIN-SEATED vehicle was parked outside the gate in the lingering mist. Antoni approached it, and found the palace attack dogs sitting in an obedient line beside it. The giant was bending down, ruffling their ears and talking to them in a low voice.

They growled as she approached, case in hand.

'Be still!' the giant said, and they were.

Antoni stared at the travelling machine. It emanated a stink of lubricant oil and heat. The thickness of its sturdy armour and the power of its mounted weapons was self-evident. The giant had strapped further equipment onto its rear cargo cage. Antoni blinked and looked at the vehicle again.

'What?' the giant asked.

'Why...' she began.

'Why what?'

'It has no legs or wheels, but it doesn't touch the ground.'

'Skimmer technology. It's a speeder. Anti-grav.'

'It floats?'

'Yes.' He walked over to her until he was towering above her, face to face. 'Look, primary clerk, I think it would be best if you stayed here at the palace after all.'

'No.'

'I can't...' he trailed away and corrected himself. 'I won't have unnecessary distractions. You're unsettled even by my machinery. Culture shock, it's perfectly understandable. Stay here.'

'No,' she insisted.

'If the sight of my land speeder alarms you then, Throne knows what–'

'I'm fine,' she said. 'I was merely... impressed. Skimmy technology. A marvel.'

'It's *skimmer*. Skimmer technology.'

'I'll be fine. I am primary clerk to the High Legislator of Fuce. I can take this in my stride. I will be fine, and I will be no hindrance to you. Now, sir, how do you get into this thing?'

'Just climb up. Like a boat. No, the other side. That's the driving position.'

'I knew that.'

'You were going to drive?'

'I was just looking. Here? Like this? Will it... sink under my weight?'

The giant shook his head. 'No, dam. It won't sink.'

'Because it's skimmer technology,' she announced confidently. She sat down in the seat and folded her arms. 'See? I'm utterly fine. Look at me, sitting here in your land speeder.'

'All right, then...'

'I forgot my case,' she said suddenly, trying to dismount.

'I've got it,' he said, picking up her case and securing it in the rear cage.

'Thank you.'

He came across to her side of the floating vehicle. 'Now do up the harness.'

'Yes.' Antoni hesitated. 'The what?'

'The harness. The straps here. Secure them across your body, and your waist. The metal tongue fits into the buckle mech like so. See?'

'I can do it. What are these for, precisely? Prisoners?'

'No, safety. It's a land speeder,' he said, laying emphasis on the final word.

'Very well. I see.'

The giant walked round to the other side of the speeder, where the dogs were waiting. He said something, and they all looked up, eager, wagging their tail stumps. 'You,' said the giant, and Princeps leaped up onto the bodywork of the speeder.

'You intend to bring a dog?' Antoni asked.

'In my experience, it could be useful. Where primuls are concerned.'

'I see. I will be led by your experience. Is the dog to ride up there?'

'No, he'll have to travel in the cargo cage, seeing as you've taken his seat.' The giant led the tail-stump wiggling Princeps back down the bodywork of the speeder and got him to sit down in the cargo area.

The giant clambered his huge bulk up into the driving seat. The floating speeder actually wobbled like a rowing boat in slack water as he got into it. He secured his harness, and threw some switches on the dash. The drive system began to whine as it powered up, the same engine note Antoni had heard earlier.

'Ready, primary clerk?' he asked.

'When you are,' she nodded.

The speeder began to pull forward through the grey dawn. Antoni stifled a sob.

'Are you afraid, primary clerk?' the giant called out over the engine roar.

'A little.'

'I assure you I can deal with these primuls.'

'I wasn't thinking about them,' Antoni admitted. 'I was merely owning up to fear about this form of unearthly locomotion.'

'You'll get used to it.'

'Never in a million years!' she squealed as they began to increase speed.

They were leaving the palace gardens and the park behind them. The three attack dogs left behind galloped after them, yowling and yapping, like hounds following the hunt. Princeps stood up in the cargo space and began to bark back at them, leaning his snout out of the cage, letting his tongue and ears flap in the slipstream.

Increasingly, they left the chasing dogs behind.

'One thing, primary clerk,' the giant called out above the roar. 'Your arms are supposed to go *outside* of the harness.'

'Really,' Antoni replied, her teeth gritted into the wind, trussed up like an escapologist, 'I'm fine as I am.'

* * *

## VI

IN JUST A few hours, they undertook a journey that would have taken a week, even in a fleet coach. Roadways and country tracts flashed by so rapidly, Antoni thought she might be sick, and she hated being sick. They passed through villages and hamlets, orchards and roadside groves, in the passing of a moment. They flew up-country, into the sunlight. The late season land around them baked under the hot sky. Dry fields were harvested and bare. There was a smell of chaff and burned stubble in the racing air.

Princeps seemed to enjoy the rush. He laid down in the corner of the cargo cage and stuck his head out of the mesh, trailing his tongue like a bannerole in the rushing wind.

Antoni gagged and choked, coughing. She spat.

'All right?' the giant asked.

'Bug.'

'Keep your mouth closed.'

UP THROUGH TIERMONT, Rakespur, Dionsys. Little, flitting hamlets in the sunlight that were gone before they were there. Peros, beside the tumbling headwater of the Pythoa, was empty, the thatch cotts burnt to the ground.

They stopped and got out. A smell of dead fire hung in the air. The cotts and outbuildings had been terribly reduced by flame. Just black stumps and twisted clay, deformed by a furnace heat.

Antoni surveyed the scene. The giant strode away into the wilted undergrowth in search of something. Princeps ran off from the parked speeder, rootling in the ashes.

Crickets and lacuna bugs ticked in the sun-cooked thickets. Antoni put her hand on the warm handle of her knife. She saw a basket of eggs that had been dropped and left in some commotion. The sun heat had half-cooked the broken whites. Flies buzzed around.

Princeps began to woof. He was busy with something in the ashes, caking his black pelt with grey dust.

Antoni wandered over to the busy dog. Pinbills called from the trees across the road. White larksfoot blossom shone in the hedgerows, nodding in the breeze. A dragonfly, arched and immaculate, swooped by her face, hovered and zipped away.

'What are you doing?' she asked the dog. It ignored her, and roo-
tled some more.

'Stop that.'

Princeps carried on with his rummaging. Antoni bent down and
shoved the dog aside. She scooped down into the piled dust. She
touched something smooth and hard and warm.

She dug deeper, smoothed the dusty earth and ash aside, and
exposed it.

It was a jaw bone, a human jaw bone. It had been burned clean
of meat and fat by some infernal fury.

'Oh,' she said.

Princeps, with whom she had never knowingly understood any
connection before, looked at her, eyes wide, tongue out, blinking
away flies.

'I think we might have found something awful,' she told the dog.
Princeps turned and began to dig again, chuffing dust out under its
paws.

'What have you found?' she asked. 'Princeps, what have you
found?'

She reached her hand into the dirt pile the dig was exposing, and
then drew it back immediately, in pain, Something had sliced the
ball of her thumb, so deep, so sharp, black-ruby blood came up
out of an invisible slit.

She licked it, and took out her knife, using the tongue of the
blade to excavate instead. In less than a minute, she'd dug up a
sharp, shiny object, angular and no bigger than a coin.

'Did you cut yourself on that?' the giant asked suddenly, looming
behind her.

'No, no. I'm fine.'

'You sure?'

'Yes. What is it?'

The giant bent down and picked up the sharp, shiny object. He
examined it.

'What is it?'

'Barb from a splinter rifle.'

'That doesn't mean much to me.'

'It means an awful lot to me, primary clerk. Eldar. Dark eldar.'

'Who?'

'Primuls. It's proof.'

'Proof I wasn't lying?'

'I never thought you were, primary clerk, but I had to know what I was up against. Did you cut yourself on this?'

'No, it's all right–'

'Did you cut yourself on this?' the giant demanded. His voice was suddenly intimidating. Antoni recoiled. Princeps quailed back. She held out her hand. 'On my thumb. It's nothing.'

He studied her dirty hand. The deep, invisible slit was still weeping blood. 'It's something. They can smell it.'

'Who?'

'Who do you think?'

The giant went over to the travel machine, opened a pannier, and took out a small metal flask. He came back over to her.

'Hold your thumb out.'

'Like this?'

'Yes.'

He squirted a spray of filmy lacquer from the flask which coated her thumb.

'Skin-wrap, in aerosol form. Let it dry.'

'To stop me bleeding to death?'

'No, to stop them scenting you.'

'Oh.'

He helped her to her feet. 'I think more than sixty people were murdered here.'

'Why...? Why do you think that?'

'I've done a tactical scan around the site. I read hot bones in the ground. This place is a riot of colour to me: weapons discharge, heat-spill, burned bones.'

'Heat-spill. You mean blood?'

'Yes, primary clerk. Come on.'

They got back aboard the speeder. The giant clapped his hands, and Princeps came bounding over and leapt up into the cage.

'Secure your harne–'

'Already done,' she said.

THEY PASSED UP through the hills, into Timmaes and then Gellyn, both dead and empty.

'It was from about here,' Antoni said, reading off her sensor paddle, 'that the Receiver of Wreck went missing. First Legislator Hanfire too.'

The giant nodded. 'I think we're coming up on the tactical edge of the operational area now. It's probably time you got out, primary clerk. Let me drop you here.' He began to slow the speeder down. 'Walk back to the nearest township and let me do this.'

'Alone?'

'I'll send the dog to watch you.'

'I'd rather stay with you.'

'I'd rather you didn't. My orders, remember.'

'Frankly, I don't trust that dog.'

'He's fine.'

'He's a bastard.'

'When it comes to anything, I'm a bastard too,' the giant said. He smiled, but there was no warmth in it. 'Time for you to go, primary clerk. Please. From here on, it gets interesting.'

'I'm interested.'

'All right, that wasn't the right word. Please, dam. Get out here and go back to–'

The giant was interrupted by a whine from the back. Princeps was up on his feet, his hackles rising. With a final, woeful bark, he jumped out of the slow-moving speeder and ran away down the track.

'Damn,' said the giant. He slammed the speeder forward in a rapid acceleration.

'What's happening?' she asked in some alarm.

'Duck down, stay close to me, and do exactly what I say.'

## VII

WHAT HAPPENED NEXT happened rather faster than Antoni could follow, but it was probably a blessing she didn't quite appreciate what was going on. By the time she did, it was too late to scream.

The speeder accelerated so rapidly that she was thrown back into her seat, the harness pulling tight. Hot sunlight, strobed by the overhanging trees, flashed across her. The giant's left hand shot out and adjusted a control box on the console, and a loud, clattering machine noise rattled out of the vehicle's nose right ahead of her.

Then came an even louder noise, a series of violent, booming reports that drowned out both the clattering and the pitch of the straining engines. The sounds slapped her like solid punches, and hot smoke stung her eyes. The speeder seemed to stumble and chug, as if its advancing speed was being arrested by a series of hammer blows.

A line of trees on the bend of the road ahead shredded in a huge, splintering concussion.

The giant slammed the speeder to a rough halt that threw Antoni forward against her restraints, and then rotated the vehicle through ninety degrees on its vertical axis until it was facing the trees and scrub on the left-hand side of the track. The speeder's prow-mounted cannons unloosed again, and blitzed the roadside to tatters. The gunfire's roar was extraordinary.

As soon as it ceased, there was a buzzing sound, as if a swarm of bees was billowing past them. The giant put his hand behind her shoulder-blades and forced her down as low as she could get. She heard scraping, pinging impacts, sharp metal on metal, the sound of split-peas flicked at tin. Some of the impacts gave off curious, screeching notes. The speeder was moving again, the vents of the racing ramjets vectored so wide that it was virtually advancing sideways up the road, the giant keeping his side of the vehicle facing the storm of impacts. To shield her, she realised.

Abruptly, he swung the speeder face on again, and unloaded a third, withering salvo from his cannon. Antoni glimpsed a line of dusty impacts stitch away up the track, and then she winced as a stand of old maple and furze dead ahead disintegrated in a spray of fire and dirt and smoke.

She thought she saw a figure on the sunlit road. A man, but not a man. Too tall, too thin, too glossy-black, running with a long, almost capering gait that no human could have mimicked.

Then it was gone.

The speeder lurched again. The violent changes in velocity over the previous few seconds had made Antoni deeply nauseous and served only to baffle her senses. She swallowed back the nausea. She so hated being sick.

They seemed to be racing directly towards the roadside, towards the undergrowth of thorny hedge and bracken.

The speeder tore through that barrier without hesitation, ripping the undergrowth aside. Antoni heard thorns and tough twigs squeal and scrape off the bodywork, and heard branches and tendrils twang and crack as they snapped.

They came rushing out into broad sunlight, over a field of swinecorn that had been left, unharvested, to grow heavy-headed and golden brown in the late season. The expanse of crop was as dry as dust, and the downdraught of the speeding machine kicked up a tumultuous cloud of chaff and loose husk into the air behind them like smoke, or spume from a crashing breaker.

She wanted to cry out, to demand he halt, but the ramjet noise was too loud, and chaff dust prickled into her face and forced her to keep her mouth tight shut. They veered around, turning out across the wide, parched field.

There were figures in the corn. They were half-concealed, but yet distinct, so black were they against the bright, golden staves. They were running, loping through the tall crops, fleeing before the speeder. Antoni had hunted from the saddle in her time, and knew what quarry looked like when it was run to ground. The black shapes seemed almost pitiful in their flight.

The vehicle's cannons blurted again, gushing streamers of hot, sweet smoke back into her face, and a tract of corn vaporised, taking a black shape with it. The giant banked them around, and razed another explosive trench through the tall, swaying corn. Another black shape twisted and fell, and a third was lifted briefly into the air.

It was airborne for only a moment before dropping out of sight, but it was an image her mind would store forever: a slender, black humanoid shape, contorted and broken, limbs bent by traumatic force into positions that were all *wrong*.

Something burst behind them with a force that shook and dazed her. The speeder began to vibrate horribly, and the note of its engines changed from a whine to a hard, labouring rasp. They peeled away left, over the corn, and when Antoni glanced backwards, she saw they were trailing scuds of dirty brown smoke.

'What?' she cried out. 'What happened?'

The giant didn't reply. He put the nose down towards a grove of olive trees on the western edge of the field. They flew in low under the arching branches and came to a juddering halt.

Smoke fumed and boiled out of one side of the engine mount.
'What?' Antoni asked again.

The giant leapt out. 'Get into cover,' he told her, pointing towards
a nearby ditch hemmed in wiry sedge. 'Stay down.'

'But–'

'Do it!' he ordered.

She undid her harness and climbed down. Now she could properly see the damage some projectile had done to the speeder. The
plating was buckled and fused, charred black. The giant fitted himself with equipment from the cargo cage: the heavy firearm she'd
seen in his ship, which he slung over his shoulder by its strap; a
small, plated shield for his left forearm; a sword with a short, heavy
blade.

'Go on!' he growled. His voice made her shake. He had put on
his helmet, a weighty, slit-eyed thing with a snarling grille for a
mouth, and his voice issued from the helmet's speaker, hard and
metallic. She ran for the ditch.

By the time she was down in cover, brambles pulling at her
clothes, insects humming in the still, close air about her, the giant
had turned from the parked speeder and was striding out of the
olive grove and away into the sunlit cornfield.

## VIII

ANTONI LAY STILL in the scratchy gloom of the undergrowth for
what seemed like several lifetimes. The encounter on the roadway,
and the hunt across the open field that had followed, had gone by
too fast, just a blur of unpleasant and violent sensations rather
than a proper sequence of events that her mind could set some nar-
rative to.

Now she was still, now she was alone, time began to decelerate
to a clammy creep. She could smell dry earth from the field, damp
soil from the ditch. She could smell her own sweat, a realisation
that made her blush. She could hear insects chirring and clicking
in the grasses around her and, somewhere, a bird cooing. At least
her nausea had relaxed. For that, at least, she was grateful.

The giant had disappeared. The speeder sat where he had left it
in the olive grove, smoke still leaking from its wounded engine. Its
drive unit shut off, it ticked and muttered to itself as it cooled.

Beyond the gloom of the grove, the golden corn was dazzlingly bright in the open sun. The ripe corn heads nodded in the slight breeze. Corn flies billowed like chaff above the crop.

After a very long time, she heard distant noises. A trembling crash, like a trestle table being overturned, a crunch. Three or four loud, quick bangs that she assumed were shots. A pause. More bangs, then two more jarring, echoing impacts, like a hammer being taken to an iced drinking trough in the dead of winter.

Finally a howl of undiluted, drawn out pain.

Antoni shivered.

A few minutes later, she heard more shots, from much further away.

Then there was nothing, except insects and birdsong.

When she could finally stand it no more, Antoni slid out of the ditch and looked around. Apart from the ugly, warlike land speeder, lurking under the olives, there was no sign that the scene was anything but a late season day in the rural Pythoan Cantons.

She decided she ought to do as the giant had instructed her. Not his last instruction – to lie in the ditch – but his original one, spoken just before the ambush, to quit the 'operational area' and make for the nearest village back down the road. All the while she was here, she was an encumbrance to him, a distraction he didn't need.

She went over to the land speeder, and retrieved her case from the cargo cage. Then she got her bearings and began to walk what seemed to her like south.

The path led down through a series of olive groves and field margins. The sun was hot, and the air was busy with flitting beetles and flies. She walked along, case in hand, for all the world like a traveller in search of lodging. It became so warm that she had to loosen her heavy travelling clothes.

After a while, she became convinced that something was following her, something, she was sure, that could smell the blood of her slit thumb and the sweat of her body. At least once, she was certain she heard a growl from somewhere in the underbrush nearby. She began to dearly wish the giant had allowed her to bring a weapon.

Then an idea struck her. She sat down in the shade of a mature beech, and opened her case. She took out the spare black powder cartridges that she hadn't had time to unpack. There were ten of them, each a measured load for her discarded handgun. She searched her case and found sheets of vellum writing paper, and a tinder-striker.

Carefully, she laid out a sheet of the writing vellum, and emptied out the ten charges into it, piling the fine, black powder in a heap. Then, taking care not to spill any, she wound the writing paper up around the powder in a tube, sealing the ends by screwing the paper up in tight little twists. It was makeshift, but she was pleased with the result, even though she couldn't say for sure what might happen once she'd lit one of the twisted ends.

She got back on her feet, slung the case over her shoulder by the carry strap, and began to walk on, the parcel in one hand and the tinder-striker in the other.

She walked for another five or ten minutes, down into another olive grove.

Then she paused. There was no tell-tale sound, none at all, but some sixth sense informed her, and she turned with a start. Ten paces behind her, part of the deep shade pooling in the olive grove detached and became a figure.

Antoni froze.

The figure was very tall and very lean, like the shadow of a man cast long by a sinking sun. Its form was black and sharp, like an ebony knife. Its face was as white as bone, utterly hateful, entirely inhuman. It smiled, and its teeth glittered.

The primul made no sound at all as it stepped towards her, long legs pacing like callipers across a map. It moved with great poise, like a dancer. There was no way she could have known it was following her unless – and this thought terrified her most of all – unless it had meant for her to know. The primuls were insanely cruel things, she knew that much, and they delighted in toying with their prey. And now she was this one's prey.

She fumbled with the tinder-striker, but her hands stopped moving when she noticed one final, awful detail.

The primul wore a decoration on its skinny breastplate, something pale and soft that had been stretched taut and pinned in place to the glossy black metal. It was a face, a mask of flesh that had been peeled away from a human skull.

Even though it lacked the form and structure of the hard-boned face that had once worn it, she recognised it.

It was the Receiver of Wreck.

## IX

ANTONI SHIVERED AT the horror of it. She began to back away. The primul suddenly ceased smiling and came at her, faster than anything had a right to move.

Something slammed into it from the side and brought it to the ground. There was a terrible scrambling and growling. Princeps, as lean and black and warlike as the thing he wrestled with, had the primul by the throat.

With a savage, indignant cry, the primul lashed out with one long arm and the High Legislator's favourite attack dog was hurled away through the air. Princeps landed hard with a sharp whimper of pain. The primul leapt up.

But by then, Antoni had lit her makeshift fuse.

The vellum burned quickly. She barely had time to throw the parcel before the black powder charge ignited.

The force of it hit the lunging primul in the chest. There was a blinding flash, a whizzing hiss that ended in a deafening bang, and the creature was thrown backwards across the grove. Antoni ran towards it, ears ringing. It wasn't dead, not even close, but Princeps dashed in again and seized it by its pale throat once more before it could rise. Dog and creature thrashed around, whining and growling. Antoni knew she simply could not allow it to get on its feet again.

She took out her sheath knife and, after a moment's hesitation, plunged the blade straight down into the primul's neck.

The primul went into convulsions. Antoni stumbled clear, alien blood spotting her hands, and Princeps backed away too, growling and whimpering.

The primul took a while to die. At one point, Antoni was sure it was about to wrench the blade out and get up again but it shuddered and spasmed on the ground, and finally its heels began to stamp and kick at the earth like a drum beat.

It stopped. It flopped over, still.

Antoni, shaking and pale, looked over at Princeps. The dog, blood on its teeth, turned big eyes back on her.

Antoni took one step towards the thing's body and then halted. She hung her head, almost in shame. She had been a fool to think it would be that easy.

She turned around.

They came out from behind the trees around her, two, then three, then five, all told: five primuls in a circle around her, their eyes like murder for what she had done to their kin.

They threw themselves at her.

For many years afterwards, for the rest of her life, in fact, Perdet Suiton Antoni often wondered how none of them heard him coming. He was just there, suddenly. How could something that big move so fast and so silently, and appear without notice?

Between the moment when the primuls began to spring and the moment when they would have fallen upon her, the giant appeared and interposed himself between her and the foul, pouncing creatures. It was almost as if he had stopped the flow of time and edited himself into that particular frame of it.

What followed lasted about three seconds.

The giant had his combat shield locked on his left arm and his short, heavy sword in his right fist. As he arrived, he was swinging the shield out, and smashed it flat into the nearest, leaping primul, shattering bones and deflecting the thing away. Wheeling, he hacked his sword clean through the neck and shoulder of the second, casting out a shower of dark red blood, and then ripped backwards low, cutting through the corpse's thighs even as it toppled, so that the whole mass of the primul folded into a collapsed heap. The third, coming in at the giant's left flank, held some kind of pistol weapon, an ugly, spiky device that spat hard, sharp bullets of buzzing metal. The giant turned, raising his left forearm upright from the elbow, and guarded his face with the combat shield in time to switch the buzzing projectiles away. They struck the shield with loud, angry cracks. One embedded itself there. Another bounced off and decapitated a nearby sapling. As the third bullet hit, the giant deftly tilted his arm very slightly, and ricocheted it off sideways straight into the face of the fourth primul. The creature's head split like a blood-fruit and the primul was savagely thumped backwards, off the ground, its legs wide. It landed, spread-eagled, on its back.

Before the third primul could fire its pistol again, the giant whipped his right arm over and threw his sword like a lance. It struck the primul through the chest, lifting it off its feet with the force of the throw, and impaled it to an olive tree's trunk, its feet dangling and twitching.

The remaining primul, wicked blades in both hands, was dancing round behind the giant. With his free right hand, the giant grabbed the heavy firearm that had been knocking at his hip on its long strap, and shot the primul twice, in the face and the chest. The double boom of the massive gun was so loud it made Antoni cry out and cover her ears. The force of the shots tore the primul apart, and slammed its mangled body across the grove. It bounced sideways off a tree trunk and fell into the bracken.

Silence, except for the gurgle of leaking blood. The giant raised his firearm, now gripping the underbarrel with his left hand. He turned slowly, aiming into the trees, covering the area point by point.

'We–' Antoni began.

'Quiet!'

She shut up. The giant continued to circle, weapon aimed. Antoni fancied she could hear discreet whirrs and clicks as the giant's helmet sensors hunted and probed.

Finally, he lowered his weapon and looked at her.

'Are you unharmed?' he asked. His voice still carried that deep, metallic grate.

'Physically,' she said.

'What does that mean?'

She sighed, shaking. 'I don't think I'll ever… I mean, that was… I… I don't suppose I'll ever sleep well again.'

The giant said nothing. He strode over to the body of the primul he had smashed with his shield and, without hesitation, put a round through its head. Antoni winced at the brutal noise of the shot.

'You killed them all. Just like that,' Antoni said. 'It was so fast. I mean, so terribly fast, I couldn't really… You killed them all.'

The giant wrenched his sword free from the split tree trunk and let the pinned corpse flop limply to the ground.

'Not all of them, it seems,' he said.

He crossed to the creature that Antoni and the dog had bested.
'You did this?'

'Yes,' she said.

He plucked out her sheath knife and wiped the blade clean on a handful of bracken. 'I'm impressed,' he said. He handed the knife back to her. 'There aren't many souls in the Reef Stars, outside the Chapter, who can claim to have slain a primul.'

The giant sheathed his sword, reached up with both hands to disengage his collar lock, and removed his helmet.

'I told you to stay put,' he said. His voice was still stern, but at least it lacked that dull, metal edge.

'I did, but before that, you told me to leave the area and let you work. That's what I was doing. I was doing what you told me to do.'

For the first time, Antoni noticed new dents and scratches marking the giant's armour.

'Are *you* hurt?' she asked.

'No,' he said, as if surprised she should care.

'Is it over?'

'Pretty much,' he said. 'I've killed a number today, the best part of a clan team. I doubt a ship of that size would have carried many more.'

'So... it's over?'

'The crash site is in the next valley. I got a decent fix. Once I've checked that, then it will be over.'

'What should I do? Wait here?'

'No,' said the giant. 'Come with me. I can protect you best if you're close by.'

## X

THE GIANT CROSSED the bright cornfields and marched up into the wooded slopes beyond, tailed by the woman and the dog. The day was still maliciously hot and close, and thunder made its threat in the west. Striding steadily, the climb took two hours, through dark glades and open banks of harsh sunlight. Tired and overheated, Antoni stripped off her jacket and tied it around her waist. Every now and then, she looked back at the quiet valley and slopes they were leaving behind, the threads of woodlands, the wild spinneys in the open fields. The air was a clear blue and the white radiance of the sun cast an almost pulverising light. She shielded her eyes.

Once in a while, as they trekked upwards, the giant halted and raised his weapon, sweeping the sloping glades around them. At such moments, Antoni would wait, anxious and tense, the dog at her side. At each all clear signal, Princeps looked up at her, tongue waggling.

They crested the hillside at the very end of the day, as the sun began to sink heavily. What lay beyond was a stark contrast to the land they had left behind. It was as if two entirely different worlds had been spliced together along the crest of the ridge.

The vale before them was dark and shaded, blinkered to sunlight by the bulk of the hill they had scaled. It seemed like a miasmal depth, mysteriously wreathed with combs of misty vapour. The air smelled of cinders and ash. Below them, the woodland had been stripped and burned for many acres in all directions. Blasted black tree trunks lay like rods of coal on the ash-white, dusty ground. There was no sign of life at all.

As they picked their way down into the gloom, Antoni realised that all the dead trees lay angled in the same direction, as if they had all been felled by a single, surging shockwave. A residue of white ash caked the black trunks like ice. As they walked, their feet lifted paper-dry dust from the cindered litter on the ground.

They went deeper into the burned, misty world. It was eerily quiet, robbed of birdsong or insect noise. When their feet broke dead twigs underfoot, the pistol cracks echoed loudly in the gloom. Princeps's black coat became grey, dusted with white powder.

Antoni saw trees ahead of them, bare trees that were still standing in the haze. Then she realised they weren't trees at all. They were metal ribs and broken stanchions, the wrecked framework of some large vessel that had augured into this hillside and torched the landscape with the heat of its impact.

They walked in through the scattered wreckage. Antoni gazed up at the charred hull sections and bent bulkheads embedded in the earth. Small pieces of metal and strange, polished machine components glittered in the thick soot underfoot.

The air was very cold, but Antoni felt warm, almost feverish. She loosened her shirt again. She was perspiring.

The giant stopped, and walked back to her. He opened a compartment on his back and produced a small injector.

'Expose your arm,' he said.

'What for?'

'I need to give you a shot. This area is irradiated very badly. You need this, or you'll suffer the consequences of exposure.'

Antoni wasn't sure exactly what that meant, but it sounded grave, so she rolled up her sleeve. The shot felt like a pinch. She rubbed the tiny bruise it left on her pale skin.

'Don't you need it?' she asked.

'I'll be fine.'

'But you carry it because–'

'I'll be fine. My body is… made differently to yours.'

'What about the dog?' she asked.

He smiled slightly. 'Dogs are resilient.'

They walked a little way further.

'I should warn you,' he said, 'about the shot. It might make you a little sick.'

'Sick?'

'Just woozy, probably. That'll pass. If you feel too ill, tell me. It affects people in different ways.'

Antoni felt perfectly fine, but the thought alarmed her. She so hated being sick, especially in front of anyone.

'Look there,' he said abruptly.

Ahead, through the mist, a large shape loomed, like the buttress of a castle. Antoni blinked, finding it hard to focus suddenly. It was part of the ship, some section or compartment pod that had remained largely intact. It looked like half a dozen giant seed cases fused together.

'The main habitat section,' said the giant. 'Well armoured, self-sealing. That's why they survived the crash.'

Antoni nodded. She was rather more concerned that there was something wrong with her balance. She stumbled slightly.

'I think–' she began.

The first stomach cramp took her off guard. She gasped and fell to her knees. The pain ebbed away, but she was too dizzy to get up again.

'Primary clerk?' the giant said, coming back to her.

'Away! Look away! Look away!' she gurgled, realising what was coming next. A hot rush of vomit hosed out of her. She gagged and retched.

'Don't look at me!' she cried, and was sick a second time.

'That's normal…' the giant said.

'Not for me! Look away, Throne damn you!' Frowning, he obeyed. She was sick several more times until her insides were empty. That left her feeling weak and shaking. The force of the vomit had been so great that it had splashed onto her shirt. She was seized with embarrassment.

'Let me help clean you–'

'No!'

She got up, then sat down hurriedly on a heat-folded stanchion. She was mortified by the mess she had made, and the smell of the mess. She opened her case, took out a water bottle and swigged from it, trying to rinse her mouth and throat. A second later, the water came up too.

'Oh Throne…' she groaned, head bent forward. 'What have you done to me?'

'Saved your life,' the giant said, studiously standing with his back to her, 'from tumours and leukogens and a number of other abominable things that would have made your latter days unbearable. But I appreciate this moment is unpleasant.'

Antoni would have retorted if she hadn't been so busy dry-heaving. Princeps looked at her, head on one side, worried and confused.

'Can you move on?' the giant asked.

Antoni half articulated a sound that she had intended to be an angry 'No'.

'Well, I have to. Dog–'

The giant looked at Princeps. He said nothing, nor made any gesture, but the dog immediately trotted round and sat down at Antoni's side, head up and alert.

'I'll be back in a short while,' the giant said.

'Unarmed!' Antoni moaned, clutched her cramping stomach and looking up at him.

'What?'

'I'm unarmed!'

The giant paused, then came over to her. He produced a large, heavy object from his kit and held it out. 'This is all I can give you. All that I have that you might even manage to lift. Treat it with respect. It's a grenade.'

'Show me how it works,' she gasped.

'Push in the nipple here. See? Then throw it. You'll have three seconds. Throw it hard and get down anyway. This is not a subtle weapon. Do you understand?'

Involuntarily, she threw up again, this time on his massive boots. 'Sorry...'

'Do you understand?'

'Yes.'

'Best of all, don't use it. Don't use it at all. This is a last resort. All right?'

She nodded and took the heavy munition, clutching it to her belly.

'A last resort.'

'All right, all right! Go away before I'm sick again.'

'I'll be five minutes,' he promised.

He vanished into the smoky vapour. She sat on the piece of wreckage, hugging her stomach and rocking back and forth. Bilious waves washed across her and made her gag.

Princeps stayed at her side, head cocked.

Suddenly, the attack dog got up, staring at the main section of the wreck. A second later, the sound of shots echoed from the vast hulk. Two or three shots at first, then several sustained bursts that reverberated like a rock-drill. Princeps whined. Through the intermittent shooting, Antoni could hear blunt, buzzing noises, like a flaring rip-saw eating into soft lumber.

She wanted to get up, but her legs were jelly. Head spinning, she sat back down and was sick again. By now the retching was painful.

The sounds of warfare ceased. Silence returned to the gloomy, burnt valley. The sky was growing dark overhead, adding to the forlorn sense of doom and desolation.

Princeps growled.

Something was moving, off to their left. It was coming towards them. Blinking, trying to clear her head and her vision, Antoni tried to make it out.

'Iron Snake?' she called, her voice hoarse.

A figure came out of the dark towards them, drawn by her voice. It wasn't the giant.

The primul was limping, blood streaming from a puncture in its glossy black thigh armour. It was labouring with a heavy casket, an open strongbox that it needed both hands to support. When it saw her, it dropped the casket into the ash on the ground. The casket rocked over as it landed, and spilled out its contents. Antoni simply stared at what had slid out into the soft, white powder. It was a jaw bone, a huge, stained jaw bone, caked brown with a lho-smoke sheen. It reminded her at once of the jaw bone she had dug out of the burned soil at Peros, but this was so much bigger. It had belonged to a giant, not a giant like the Iron Snake, but a real giant, a monster. The teeth, those which remained in their rotting peg-holes, were broad and flat, like chisel blades, broken and discoloured. Pieces of rusting metal plate were screwed into one side of the jaw, around the hinge.

Antoni looked up slowly from the strange treasure and met the piercing, malevolent gaze of the primul. It leered at her, hungry, excited. Perhaps it saw a chance here, a hostage, a bartering piece for its own miserable life.

'What is that?' she asked.

'Whar tizz hhat?' it replied, echoing her sounds without understanding them. Its voice was like a knife on a whetstone. It took a limping step forward. 'Whar tizz hhat?' it giggled. With its right hand, it slid a hooked blade from a sheath at its waist.

'No closer, you hear?' she called out. She tried to stand.

It said something back at her in its own tongue, something brittle and sharp.

'Damn you, no closer, I said!' she cried. Princeps had sunk low, growling, his back ridged.

She got up, intending to show the fiend her weapon, but the grenade tumbled out of her weak hands and landed in front of her with a thump.

The primul raised its eyebrows as it saw what lay on the ground. It cocked its head, like a dog.

Antoni dived for the grenade, and the primul did too. She got there first, but it smashed into her, scrabbling. She could smell the animal stink of it, the body heat, the strange, musky scent of its alien flesh. It was fast, and vicious, and dreadfully strong. Its armour was like silk, impossible to grab. It punched her hard, and she cried out as she felt a rib snap. The primul grabbed her by the hair, wrenched her head back, and raised its hooked blade to slice open her throat.

Princeps's powerful bite closed around the raised wrist and the primul yowled. Princeps was making a fluid throat noise, a growl-rattle, his mouth full, his jaws vicing. The primul kicked at him, pulling harder on Antoni's hair, drawing her round. She shrieked as her broken rib twisted and ground. The pain made her lose all control. She threw up again, a violent spatter of acid bile, right in the primul's face.

The primul let her go, spitting and cursing. Antoni rolled clear. The primul kicked Princeps off him and got up, wiping his face.

Antoni ended up face down in the ash. She realised she had the grenade in her hand.

She got up, holding the grenade out in her left fist, her fingers clenched around its heavy form.

'Get back!' she warned the creature.

It spat again, wiping flecks of her bile off its alabaster cheek.

'No closer!' she cried again, brandishing the grenade, squeezing it tightly. There was a tiny click.

Antoni realised that she had squeezed the trigger. The primul had heard the click too. Its eyes went very wide.

She hurled the grenade right at it, even though it was standing in front of her. The primul dodged, cat-like, and the grenade sailed past its left shoulder and landed in the open casket behind it.

Antoni began to turn and dive.

The world unfolded, like a blooming flower. Light hit her, solid like a wall, and carried her far away.

## XI

SHE CAME TO. The blast had thrown her several metres, and the back of her clothes was scorched. There was a wretched smell of fyceline and burned flesh in the air. Smoke gusted around her.

She rolled over. Princeps licked her face.

'Stop that,' she wheezed, her throat seared by the heat.

Princeps nuzzled her instead. She could smell the wet dog smell of the High Legislator's apartments and singed fur.

'Are you all right?' she asked the dog, sitting up and suddenly feeling stupid that she'd asked an animal a question.

Patches of his coat were burned, but Princeps was intact. So was she.

She got up.

The primul lay on the ground, mangled and torn. It had lost the better part of both legs and one arm. Fused bones protruded from the shattered armour and blistered, tattered meat. The white ash around was stained almost black with its blood. Weakly, it raised its narrow, lean head and looked at her. Its white flesh was spattered with crimson blood. One of its leering eyes had burst.

It looked around, its head unsteady, and saw the casket. Nothing remained of the box itself – just a wide, smouldering crater in the ground where the ash of the forest inferno had been blown back to expose a bowl of seared, raw earth. The jaw-bone had also been destroyed. All that remained were a few of the chisel teeth, littered on the ground, steaming.

The primul began to laugh. It was a screeching, baying sound, broken by choking rattles as blood filled its throat.

'What are you laughing at?' she demanded. 'What?'

It didn't answer. It just continued to laugh, the sound echoing up into the darkness of the dead valley.

It was still laughing when the giant reappeared and silenced it with a shot to the head.

## XII

ANTONI DIDN'T REMEMBER much about the journey back to Fuce. The giant had given her some drug to dampen the pain, and it made her drowsy. Fatigue did the rest. She remembered the motion of the land speeder, the back-echo of its damaged engines rattling off the twilight woods they passed. The giant said nothing.

Once, she woke, and saw a huge sky full of stars like sequins. One of them was Ithaka, she supposed.

When she woke again, it was cold. They were no longer moving. Voices were calling for a doctor, and by the light of jostling lanterns, she saw the stone walls of the High Legislator's palace.

SHE DIDN'T WAKE again until dawn, though which dawn, she couldn't say. She was in her own bed in the palace apartments. Her torso was tightly wound with bandages. A nurse in a starched white wimple, who had been sitting watch at her bedside, got up and went to fetch the doctor.

The doctor told her that her injury was troubling, but not critical. He was generally concerned for the state of her health. Her blood-work had shown curious levels of various substances, and–

'Where is the giant?' she asked.

She was told that he was making ready to depart. Antoni felt a little aggrieved that he hadn't seen fit to speak to her before leaving. At her insistence, a messenger was sent down into the state park.

'YOU SENT FOR me?' asked the giant.

'And you came,' she replied. Despite the doctor's protests, she had risen from her bed and was sitting in a high backed chair in the Legislator's solar. 'And now you're leaving, so I presume the matter is done with.'

'It is, primary clerk,' he replied.

'Will you sit?' she asked, gesturing to another chair.

'I would break that,' he admitted.

'So the matter is done with?'

'As I said. The area is cleansed to my satisfaction. I have left instructions with the troop master here, however. The area must be contained. No one must go there. It's not a matter of superstition.'

'Contamination?'

'Just so. I have noted the proscribed region on your charts. It must be a civil edict, well enforced. The rural workers must not be allowed to venture back into that place, for the sake of their lives.'

'It may not be a matter of superstition,' she said, 'but superstition will help. How long must the region remain closed?'

'Forever,' he said.

'Surely–'

'The contamination will linger for a long while, longer than you can measure or judge. Forever is the simplest way to consider it.'

'The Legislature of Baal Solock is indebted to you. We should mark this occasion with a feast day or a pageant–'

'There's no need. Besides, your city is empty. It will take a while, I should think, for the people to return to their homes from hiding. I thank you for the thought, but I must go.'

Antoni looked crestfallen. 'If you must, then. But I will have to compose a report for the High Legislator. He will want to know everything about these events, in all detail. You said your name was Priad?'

'Yes.'

'And what rank are you? A general? A warmaster?'

The giant shook his head. 'I hold the honourable rank of brother.'

'Brother? Like a monk? I see. But you are a commander of men, surely?'

'No, primary clerk. I am a brother-warrior, an Iron Snake. I am proud to be a member of Damocles squad.'

Antoni was confused. 'You are just a warrior?'

'Just an ordinary warrior. A year ago, I was simply a petitioner. working to prove my worth for inclusion into the phratry. I won a place in Damocles, and with them I have seen action three times. My squad sergeant, Raphon, selected me for this mission. He saw it as an opportunity to test my abilities on an individual undertaking.'

He saw the look in her eyes. 'I'm sorry if I disappoint you, primary clerk. The Chapter certainly intends Baal Solock no slight by sending a junior brother such as myself. It is the way we do things.'

'And one warrior usually suffices,' she said. 'That's what you told me, wasn't it? I'm not disappointed. I think it will make my report rather more exceptional. If just one "ordinary" warrior can accomplish what you have done, then what must...'

Antoni let the thought hang. She adjusted the way she was sitting to make her aching ribs more comfortable. 'What was that thing? That jawbone?'

'I didn't see it. From the description you gave to me, some trophy of war, something precious to the primuls. It's lost to them now.'

'Not quite,' she said. A small dish sat on the side table at her left hand. In it lay two dirty, peg-like teeth. She had picked them up from the ashy ground and saved them.

He nodded. 'They are your trophy now, then, primary clerk. A trophy for a killer of primuls.'

'I hardly think–' she began, with a laugh.

'Be well, primary clerk. May the Emperor protect your world and your people.'

'Well, if he chooses not to, I know where to come.'

THE NEXT DAY, in a foggy grey dawn like the one that had greeted him, the giant took his leave. The roar of his vessel's engines echoed out across the water meadows and the state park, and rattled casements in the palace of the High Legislator.

Dressed in a long gown, and leaning heavily on a knurled cane, Antoni stood at one of the high windows in the west wing and watched the white-hot star of thrusters rise up, pearlescent, through the grey mist and slowly disappear into the sky.

Then she limped away down the empty hallway with the black dog padding obediently at her heels.

# PART TWO
# BLACK GOLD
## Undertaking to Rosetta

# I

THE FLASK IS tubular, copper, banded with straps of dull zinc. Brother Memnes draws it from a sheath strapped to the thigh-plate of his Mark VII power armour.

This is the Rite of the Giving of Water, and none will look away. Nine armoured warriors, the entire assault squad, surround the kneeling Apothecary as he unscrews the stopper, then tips a few drops out onto his segmented glove. Their armour is gunmetal grey, edged with white and red, and the desert has coated them all with a film of white dust. The threads of water make stark black streaks on the dusty metal of his gauntlet's fingers. As the brothers intone the sacred rite, voices toneless as they rasp out through visor speakers, Memnes dribbles the water onto the rock he has chosen. In a second, the suns have baked it away to nothing, but the rite is nevertheless made. Water has been given, precious drops from the raging salt oceans of their homeworld, Ithaka.

They were born from a world of seas, raised from it like the great horn-plated water-wyrms they name themselves after. To them, it is the embodiment of the Emperor, who they voyage space to serve. Wherever they go, they make this offering, the life-water of Ithaka, the blood of the Emperor. This place – called Rosetta on the arcane charts shown to them at briefing – this place is now consecrated. Water has anointed this vast landscape of heat and dust.

They are Iron Snakes. The double-looped serpent symbol stands proud upon their auto-responsive shoulder plates. They are Tactical Squad Damocles, charged with this holy duty. They stand in the ring, as Brother Memnes rises to join the circle, ten warrior-gods in the form of men, armoured and terrible. They sing, a slow ritual tune, and beat time in deadened clanks, slapping right hands against their thigh plates.

Their weapons have been made safe for the Rite of Giving of Water, as ready weapons would be disrespectful. The chant over, they move with smooth precision, clicking sickle-pattern clips into bolt pistols. Brother Andromak connects the power feeds to his plasma gun. Blue lightning crackles into life around Brother-Sergeant Raphon's lightning claw. He nods. The circle breaks.

The salt-pan glows like milk in the sunlight. Visor tints and nic-titating bionic eyelids dim the glare to a bright blue translucence. The brothers are silent as they skirt the littered rocks along the edge of the depression, moving single file through the shadows.

Two suns have risen: one dull and fuzzy like an apricot, the other vast and sizzling and too white-bright for even their visors to negate. The third, a tiny spot of heat like a melta-flame, will be over the horizon in four minutes.

In line then, Brother-Sergeant Raphon, Brother Andromak, Brother Priad, Brother Calignes. A break of ten paces, then in file Brother Pindor, Brother Chilles, Brother Xander, Brother Maced. Another break, then Brother Natus and Brother-Apothecary Memnes. Brother Andromak carries the Chapter standard: the snake crest, double-looped, pinioned above his shoulder blades.

No words are spoken or needed. Visor arrays are matched by sharp senses. Ranges are judged and logged; terrain is assessed and scanned. Brother-Sergeant Raphon uses his auspex to watch ahead. They know why they are here and what they must do. And when they must do it.

A low wind rises in the east, shivering across the pan. It picks up salt dust as it goes, brushing the fine white powder into eddying cones. The dust seethes, flicking like foam off rock outcrops or churning in lines across the flat. The dust ripples look like snakes, Brother Priad thinks, or like waves breaking on a rocky shore. He nods at Brother Calignes: a good portent.

At the head of the snake of men, Brother-Sergeant Raphon sees it too. He knows the dust has been stirred up by a solar wind, precursor of the third sunrise. The third sun is small, but its radioactive force on Rosetta is fiercely powerful. Triple dawn is almost upon them.

With a gesture of his hand, he double-times them. They crunch on through the indigo shadows of scattered white rocks, bleached like teeth. The Iron Snakes pass into a canyon, starkly black and white with its division of shadow and light.

Shadow and light. The key to this.

Beyond, below, in a dimpled basin scoured from the pan, lies the target. Raphon sees it for the first time. Rosetta Excelsis Refinery Nine: a ten kilometre-square edifice of riveted black metal and orange pipe work, looking like a wasp crushed into the desert by a great heel. Oily girder work laces the structures and pouting, soot-mouthed stacks vent dark fumes and the occasional flame-bellied belch of smoke into the crystal-blue desert sky. Raphon looks at it for a while – a few seconds probably, but for him an eternity of contemplation. He knows, for he has been told, that this is a vital facility, sucking black fluid out of the porous rock buried deep beneath the salt-pan. Ten weeks ago, the pipelines that run from here to the cargo port at Alpha Rosetta sputtered dry. The precious supply of fuel had been staunched. Without its flow, the armoured battalions of the Imperial Guard on half a dozen neighbouring worlds had ground to a halt.

Raphon opens his comm, selecting the command channel. 'Damocles, I witness to you the target. We will begin on my word.'

Liberate, they were ordered. Brother-Librarian Petrok, great Petrok himself, had given the briefing. Liberate the facility and the fuel supply. Exterminate any who oppose.

Such simplicity. Raphon smiles again, feeling the hungry weight of his bolter in his right fist, the warmth of the lightning claw that encases his left.

The third sun rises. A brief and extraordinary phenomenon striates the desert salt-pan. The three opposing suns, with their trio of conflicting intensities and directions, fill the stark whiteness with a startling criss-cross of shadows. The desert becomes a chequerboard of darkness and light, grey sidelong slants, fathomless pools, intersections of harsh glare as stark as snow. It is called the Risings, Raphon knows. Librarian Petrok was quite specific. At this hour, for four and three-quarter minutes, the conjunction of sunlights make a shadow maze of the landscape.

'Damocles: move!'

Their window of opportunity.

Ten armoured warriors descend the dimpled slope at a run, crossing shadow and light, lost like sifting sand in the complexity of the flickering cross light.

## II

BROTHER RAPHON REACHES a sloping wall of iron-buffered siding. He scales it, ripping hand-holds with his claw, sliding over the top to bring his bolter to bear.

Two men guard the parapet, two men dressed in refinery overalls augmented with sections of body armour. The backs of their tunics are marked with sprayed stencils showing the vomitous sign of the Ruinous Powers, of Tzeentch. The skin of their faces is dark and knobbed, like the hides of crocodiles. They have injected fluid tars under the skin to taint it, and buried metal piercings, girder rivet heads, in the flesh. A mark of honour, so Librarian Petrok said, of membership to their foul cult. They stand by their pintle-mounted autocannon, watching the sun rise, feeling the warmth on their lumpy, black faces.

Raphon fires twice. One drops without a head; the other reels, his spine removed in an explosion of blood, gristle and bone shards.

Brother Andromak reaches another part of the perimeter. The alternating light and dark flicker of the three suns is confusing him, but Sergeant Raphon explained how this would be to their advantage. He kicks open a shutter door and enters the gloom, squeezing the grip of his plasma gun. Things with bright eyes set in black faces look up for a second and then die, screaming.

Brother Priad leads the assault over the north wall. Grenades loop from his hand and scatter like seeds across the grilled deckway. Explosions rattle the length of the wall line. Somewhere, an alarm starts to whoop.

They are in.

PINDOR CROSSES AN open space between derricks, blasting freely. Huddles of bleary enemies stumble outside in confusion, and are cut down as they flee. Calignes enters a service vault by the north wall and finds three cultists struggling with the tripod of a storm bolter. He saves ammunition and butchers them with his knife.

Chilles and Xander catch a dozen of the enemy as they panic. They impose a crossfire that pulverises all. More emerge, firing back with lasguns and autocannon. A searing shot marks Xander's shoulder guard with a denting scorch. Memnes moves in around them, setting up a third part to the crossfire. Like the three suns with their inescapable shadows, the three tracing lines of their bolter fire pummel into and explode corrupted bags of flesh. Memnes chuckles as he does the Emperor's work.

Calignes moves from bunker to bunker, slaughtering. Through one doorway, he turns to face the stained features of a screaming heathen who opens up on him with an autocannon. Thumped backwards three paces by the succession of impacts to his carapace, Calignes grunts. His boltgun has been blown from his fist and his smallest finger has been vaporised. The autocannon cycles suddenly on empty, and as the cultist gropes for a reload, Calignes rushes him, exploding his head with a clap of his augmented fists.

The Iron Snakes move deeper into the facility. Between two low concrete blockhouses, Maced is rushed by twenty cultists who stream over him like ants, bludgeoning him with girder strips and wrenches. He laughs as he kills them, crushing necks, splintering limbs, punching his fists through bodies. His battledress now dressed with blood, he churns through the gore into the control room and tears the cultist he finds at the primary console into two twitching pieces.

His laughter rolls through the comm. The other Snakes rejoice in it. Raphon kills as he laughs with a shot from his bolter. Priad fires on full auto. Andromak scorches. They kill and kill again.

Something stops Chilles in his tracks. He pauses, almost thought-ful, trying to make sense of things, struggling to overcome his clinically trained battle hunger. He stands on a derrick walkway, with a good view of the control centre. He looks down.

There is a hole clean through his torso, a hole that passes right through him. As his legs give out, Chilles screams in rage. He was not finished. His face hits the grille deck, denting it.

They all feel his death. Through the rapport of inter-fed life signs, they all feel it. The Iron Snakes mourn Chilles even before he has fallen. And they see his last sight: the Traitor Marine. The hulking, pustular form of a Dark Tusk warrior, cackling over the smoking muzzle of his weapon.

Eyes wet with anger, Priad turns to find another Dark Tusk mere paces from him, charging with a rusty, barbed lance. Priad can smell the rot in the air, the foetid stench of corrupting matter.

A bolter is not enough to cleanse this filth. Priad bowls the primed grenade in his hand with such fury it smacks the Dark Tusk off his feet as it strikes him in the gut. He falls, almost comical, spread-eagled around the impact. Then the grenade ignites.

Priad is drenched in mauve fluid. It clogs his vents for a moment and he falls, choking with the stench. As he gags, he sees the feet beside him, the great steel-bound boots of another Dark Tusk who is standing over him, whooping and sucking with liquid laughter, about to fire.

Raphon kills it. He squeezes the trigger of his boltgun until the entire sickle clip is empty and a hurricane of rounds have ham-mered the Chaos Marine into a heap of organic and metal wreckage wreathed in a mist of blood.

Raphon pulls the choking Priad to his feet. 'More than we thought,' he rasps.

'Is it not the way?'

'The way of killing?'

'Just so... give me more, make them lethal, make the fight worth fighting.'

Raphon clips Priad on the shoulder in respect and encourage-ment as the younger brother reverses the cycle of his helmet vents to expel the ichor clogging his intakes.

They turn. There is another scream. Maced is dead. Poisonous splinter barbs from some inhuman Dark Tusk gun have blown his legs and lower torso to shreds. A dirty, toxic knife has silenced his screaming rage.

Vengeance burns in their throats, making them as dry as the salt-pan. As he strides forward with Priad, Raphon uses his auspex to judge the deployment of Damocles. The surgical precision of their strike is melting as the men turn back to avenge their fallen brothers. The assault is hesitating.

Raphon will not allow this. Keying open his comm again, he barks off a string of orders that redirects and fortifies the ebbing wash of his men's advance. He quotes the motivational sermons on the use and abuse of vengeance in battle that they all heard during tactical indoctrination on the fortress-moon, Karybdis.

Memnes supports him, cutting in on a sub-channel, singing the battle dirge of Ithaka that glorifies the dead in the Emperor's name.

Raphon and Priad meet with Andromak and Xander at a railed walkway by one of the facility's well-head arrays. There is a fog of liquid oil in the air. Xander finds Maced's corpse, sprawled in pieces in the shadows of a ductway. He signals Memnes to it.

The Apothecary arrives, opening his belt pack for the reductor and the other tools of removal. Maced himself is beyond the help of Memnes's narthecium. The bright steel tongs of the reductor are already slick with Chilles's blood. With deft but reverential hands, Memnes strips open Maced's chest armour and begins to dig the flesh apart for the sacred progenoid gland. Such rare treasure, the genetic wellspring of a Space Marine's power, cannot be abandoned. He pulls it free, a glistening thing, drops it into a chrome bowl, cleans it with a spray from a sphyxator, then places it carefully into a self-locking, sterile tube. He stoppers the tube and slides it back into the rack in his narthecium, next to the one already holding Chilles's gland. There are eight empty tubes just like them.

Bestial wails and calls reverberate the ironwork. Andromak and Xander have cornered a Dark Tusk. The exchange of fire is brief but intense. Xander takes a hit that rips a thermal waste dissipater off his backpack. In return, he puts a bolter round in through the Dark Tusk's left visor socket. As the Chaos servant falls, thrashing, Andromak roasts him slowly with his plasma cannon.

Raphon and Priad skirt the vaulted bunkers a hundred metres west. Sharp slabs of sunlight interlace long shadows thrown by the buttresses. Priad sees where the etched inscriptions on the Imperial iron facings, eulogies to the Golden Throne, have been defaced and overwritten with dripping blasphemies. He starts to repeat the dirge to soothe his mind.

Raphon silences him. Drips of something like tar soil the white sand in the sunlit openings. They think they have another of the Tusks, gone to ground between two pump station units but the pulsing machinery is fogging Raphon's auspex.

The Tusk comes on them from the rear, grabbing Raphon from behind with great armoured limbs that lock around his throat. It drives a barbed and rusted spike through his left hip. Priad turns and dives into them, so that the three sprawl, locked, armour grinding and scraping together. The Tusk is half as big again as either of them, ancient armour black and shiny like a great scarab, dressed with filthy loops of chain. Priad twists, fighting to get his bolter close to the vile thing's face.

Blood in his mouth, Raphon fights the Tusk, fights the grip, fights the pain. He writhes to give Priad a clean shot. The spike breaks. It shatters inside Raphon. He blacks out.

The Tusk gets a hand around Priad's wrist and hauls him over, but this is a mistake. It has cleared the shot. Though still gripped, Priad fires twice, the point-blank shots shattering the Tusk's helmet and skull and igniting its power pack.

The blast lifts Priad and Raphon and tosses them ten paces. By the time Priad is on his feet again, they are lying in a wide pool of blood which is streaming from the spiked hole in Raphon's armour. The wound is huge. Blood drizzles out from under him, through the buckled puncture in the plating. Wordlessly, for to speak would be to scream, Raphon shudders and uncouples his lightning claw.

Priad wants to argue, but knows this is not the time or the place. Raphon has been grooming Priad for command responsibilities since Priad's induction into Damocles five years earlier. Priad has always hoped that such an inheritance would be a long time coming. He pulls off his own left gauntlet and arms himself with the claw.

He plugs the power lead into a rune-shaped socket on his elbow. Gold leaf traceries etch the knuckle backs of the ancient weapon, recording its history and uses. The commander of Damocles squad has always worn the claw. Priad flexes its fingers as the electrical charge shimmers around it. On the ground, a stiffening island of metal in a lake of blood, Raphon opens his command channel and begins his eulogy, his passing over, instructing them all to answer to Priad.

He is finishing, his voice fading, when Memnes arrives. The Apothecary clasps Raphon's naked hand once as a gesture of honour. He opens his narthecium for medical tools.

'No time,' Raphon murmurs.

Memnes scans, concurs. Raphon's pelvis is shattered and his lower abdomen is laced with metal fragments from the shattered spike-haft still impaling him. With a ship's infirmary, care, time, and bionics it would be repairable but there is no time, and the spike was venomed. Filth and toxins permeated the Traitor Marine's weapon, plague spores that blister and chew their way through Raphon's body, despite his superhuman, implanted metabolism. Soon he will be a tainted slab of decaying flesh, the progenoid gland too.

Memnes removes the gland. He doesn't wait for Raphon to die. Despite the pain of the extraction, Memnes believes that all Marines would rather die knowing their legacy had been saved. The surgery wounds, rending and deep, kill Raphon. They are perhaps a blessed relief from the toxic wave that sweeps over him.

Another tube for the rack.

### III

PRIAD OPENS THE command channel and speaks to his men. They hail him with grim solemnity and utter devotion. Raphon will be mourned later. Natus reports the southern perimeter secure, and Pindor and Calignes add that all opposition has ceased. In thirteen minutes, they have killed three hundred and eleven of the foe, including the Dark Tusks. For the loss of three. It has been a costly victory.

The Iron Snakes regroup at the main gantry as Memnes and Andromak torch the corpses of the foe, and lay out the three dead

Iron Snakes with honour and ceremony. Working from stored instructions in their helmet memories, Priad and Natus toil to re-engage the pipeline so that fuel pumping may recommence.

Calignes searches the scrappy and incomplete log entries of the refinery's control personnel. He draws Priad across and shows him what he has found: listings of anomalous core samples and petro-leum spectrographs. Three months before, to the day, Rosetta Excelsis started to suck something other than oil up from the desert aquifer.

'There is something down there,' Calignes says. 'Something foul and ancient that has slumbered in the oil reserves for...' He does not finish his sentence. Time passages of that length are beyond his ability to guess or articulate.

Priad is silent, numb perhaps. Their mission here, the directives of which he has inherited and intends to carry out with loyal pre-cision, were to recapture this valuable well-head. It was assumed that the forces of the enemy had overtaken this place to disem-power the Imperial Army.

That is shown to be a lie, and the deployment of the Dark Tusks to bolster the cult's troops now makes sense. There is something valuable to the Ruinous Powers here. Some artefact, perhaps, some icon, some thing of power, perhaps even an entity, buried deep below in the lightless lakes of oil.

Damocles has won: won the facility, discharged its mission at great cost. And yet it has lost. They have won a place that is worth-less, seized back precious Imperial territory, only to find it now tainted and despoiled. If they had known, from orbit, they could have...

Priad pauses. He clears his mind with slow intonations of the focus chant. Disappointment is a mind poison. So is the thought of failure or the loss of belief in either cause or purpose. Calignes knows it too and follows Priad's lead, casting out the negative senses of loss and error gnawing at him. He needs no cue or com-mand to do this. They are Adeptes Astartes, Iron Snakes Chapter. There is no failure, there is no defeat. There is only victory and death, and both are to be savoured when they come.

Priad looks around, imagining the moment when the refinery first spewed up the taint from deep below. He feels a tiny stab of pity for the workforce, men he has helped slaughter this day. Loyal servants of the Emperor turned to the ways of Darkness by something that they began to exhume from the depths. There is no choice now. They must do what should have been done first of all.

Priad orders Natus to stop work on the reconfiguration of the pipeline pumps. He summons Pindor and Xander, and makes them assemble all the explosives they can find. They take the full complement of grenade munitions from each Space Marine, then search the weapons stocks of the enemy for more.

Memnes enters the gantry and Priad quietly tells him of the discovery. Memnes thumbs open the neck seals of his helmet and removes it. His scalp is shaven and beaded with sweat. He wipes a gloved hand right back across its stubbled dome, his old face dark and serious.

'Your decision is correct. You do as Raphon would have done.' Though second in the chain of command under the squad leader, the old Apothecary has seniority on his side and his assent is always noted by the leader. Memnes knows that is what Priad, a Marine barely half his age, is looking for.

'We have not failed. It is simply that the nature of the victory has changed,' Memnes says.

'I know it. We will make true victory from this spoiled triumph, and celebrate both in the Emperor's name.'

Pindor reports that the munitions are collected. They load them into a cargo cart and push them to the well-head. Natus and Andromak take drill weights off one of the main bores and strap the explosives into place, lashing them into mesh ore sacks.

They are half-finished when the counter-attack comes: a bombardment from the east that fractures the perimeter wall and flattens two derrick towers in a frenzy of sparks and shrieking metal. Roses of fireballs bud into the sky. Priad has signalled their egress to the east and now he countermands, asking for a western extraction. The change will add four minutes to the Thunderhawk's flight-time.

Pindor works to complete the stowage of the explosives. He is stripped down to the waist to allow him access to the cramped space under the bore-head, his armour stacked nearby. Fluid-heavy feed lines cross his naked carapace from the belt mount, held in place by flesh staples. His shoulders bear the old scars of punishment rituals carried out on Karybdis. Pindor always scored low on morning firing rites, but his expertise at close-fighting and explosives have made him indispensable. Scar tissue, puffy and pink as coral, bunches and twists as he works.

The enemy advances from the east. More long-range bombardment, and then the first signs of troops. Dark Tusks, in two assault teams, with Razorbacks in support.

Damocles have no long-range weapons, nothing with reach like the Razorbacks. Resistance at this point would be futile. Priad orders midday prayers, and they circle around him, kneeling, helmets off, heads down, as he chants the litanies of devotion, the psalms of destruction and fortitude. He does it so they will not even consider the idea they have failed. No one voices such a thought. He asks each man in turn to speak a word for the fallen.

Calignes remembers Chilles, a moment of bravery on Paradis Antimony. They all nod, remembering. Xander shows a scar that would have killed him on Basalt Ignius III, but for Maced. Maced is remembered too. Natus celebrates Brother-Sergeant Raphon's tactical skill and his bravery. Andromak recalls the day Chilles slew a water-wyrm on beloved Ithaka. Naked on a rock-tower, with a sea-lance braced. He took the horn-hide. The polished scales were still looped in his belt when he died. Memnes speaks well of Maced, reminding them of his brute strength against the grisly H'onek on Parlion One-Eleven. Chapter legend, a legend that has died today in flesh but which will live in memory. And not, Priad reminds himself fiercely, in vain.

Pindor joins them, still half-stripped, dripping sweat and oil. He kneels and tells a short, gutsy story of Raphon at the gates of Fewgal, blinded by mud and killing all the foe he could find, cursing all the while for 'a good sea-lance' to test them. Pindor draws their laughter: honest, forthright, uplifting. No hint of defeat or failure in them now.

As is should be, thinks Priad. We have won; the Snakes have won, no matter what.

'I have done the work,' Pindor tells Priad as the laughter subsides.

They help Pindor redress his armour, while Calignes cycles the rock-bore to dig and sends it down. Oil waste flushes up around his feet like a black tide and then seeps away down through the mesh of the gantry deck.

The foe is at the gates. A tumult of voices and gunfire. Helmets in place, the seven Iron Snakes withdraw in close file down the main cargo avenue, under the shadows of lifters and skeletal cranes. They fire as they go, lacing bolt-traces and plasma fire into the buildings and niches.

At the west cargo gate, they form into a spearhead as the Tusk advance guard rushes them down the avenue. Blisters of light mark the air, exploding metal bulkheads, breaking girders and digging white powder from the ground. A descending hellstorm, chasing after them. The Snakes drop two of the foe with concentrated fire before Priad orders them out of the gate. He himself pauses in the archway long enough for the first Tusk to reach him. Priad disembowels the disgusting creature with the lightning claw.

In Raphon's name.

A saved grenade brings the cargo gate down after him and they are moving into open desert away from Rosetta Excelsis with the Chaos advance momentarily halted. The stark light of the midday suns burns the landscape white and shadowless, and there is no longer a horizon between bleached land and colourless sky.

The gunship awaits, hazed by heat and dust, in a narrow arroyo. Its entry ramp is down like a tongue in the soft dust. Bolter rounds whine after them as they board. The Dark Tusks have broken through in pursuit. Memnes and Priad, in the rear, turn and engage for one last time, killing as if to underline the undeniability of their victory.

## IV

FROM SPACE, THE surface of Rosetta is hard and white and sharply scored, like the back of a dry skull. They are just making transitory orbit when the munitions fire, nine hundred metres down in the oil reserves. There is no visible sign from up here. Almost an hour later, the surface turns dark and puffy, like wet-rot, the patch extending for three thousand square kilometres around the focus of the refinery. Sub-crust fires, linked to magmatic disruptions and fuelled by some unknown source of exploding power, burn out Rosetta a day later.

In the dank belly of the gunship, their discarded helmets rolling on the metal floor in little circles as the ship pitches and yaws, the survivors of Damocles sit in silence. They are tired, blank, parched. They mourn. Now, and only now, do they allow themselves the thoughts. They have lost. Yet they have won. They have taken a victory, the right victory, but not one they expected or were sent to achieve.

Memnes takes out his flask. It is tubular, copper banded with straps of dull zinc. He draws it from a sheath on the thigh of his armour.

This is the Rite of the Sharing of Water, and none will look away. Six armoured forms, the remains of the assault squad, watch as Priad takes the flask. He wants for cool, slaking water, but he knows this must come first. A sip of the salt water of Ithaka. He swigs it. It is sharp, warm, saline, bitter.

He looks up at them all and they pound their thigh armour in approval. The ceremony is over but the bitterness in his mouth remains.

Whether it's from the water of his homeworld or the mission, Priad isn't sure.

# PART THREE
# WHITE HEAT
## Undertaking to Eidon

# I

GREEN ROCK, AMBER sky, white heat. It was all revealed in a lurid glare that slanted in through the widening aperture of the whining hydraulic landing ramp.

The tip of the armoured ramp crunched into the mica glass dust of the landing circle. The oily piston struts hissed to a halt. Steam dissipated, and there it was. Eidon. A precious, ancient world, and one possessed of a savage, natural beauty.

So thought Petrok, Chapter Librarian, as he stepped down out of his landing shuttle and surveyed the open majesty of the land. He was framed for war, bareheaded and clean-shaven, his black locks bound up behind his deep skull, a towering form tall and broad even for a Space Marine. The edges of his gunmetal grey power armour were lined with white and red.

But he did not lack a soul. Eidon was starkly beautiful. The rocks in the landscape around the blasted landing circle were vivid green, semi-crystal, glittering in the warm, clear air. Along the skyline, jagged vents spat white fire into the air. The phosphor fires, burning up from deep seams and faults in the earth beneath, powered the foundries and smithies of venerable Eidon City.

White heat, the flames that kept the smelters and manufactories of Eidon turning in the Emperor's name.

Petrok remarked upon the majesty of the place to his lexicanium, Rodos, as they walked together down the cinder path from the landing circle, under shattered rockcrete arches, towards the main Imperial staging post, their bearers in procession behind them. Rodos looked at him as if uncertain as to whether Petrok was joking or not.

Petrok decided to drop it. If the man couldn't see it, then there was no point explaining. Some Ithakan hearts, he knew, were too ironclad to see anything but war. Petrok wondered if the fact that he could see the beauty was his weakness or his greatest strength.

Doom had come to Eidon the year before, when the dark eldar had taken it in a single night. The action had marked the start of a renewed period of primul raids, as the foe launched out of their shadowy fastnesses and hiding places to strike into the Reef Worlds. Due to the strategic position of its base world, it was the Chapter's blood privilege to bear the brunt of all incursions into this part of the Imperium, and it had been so since records began.

Imperial Guardsmen – a massed force of three hundred thousand, mainly Leoparda stormtroops and Donorian light armour – had been deployed to Eidon in the first months to effect a liberation. They had failed, ground to a standstill.

Freeing six squads of the phratry from the ongoing reprisals against the dark eldar incursions elsewhere in the Reef Worlds, mighty Seydon, Master of the Chapter, had sent his Snakes to succeed on Eidon where the Guard had foundered. The force was led by the veteran Hero-Captain Phobor, and by Librarian Petrok.

Petrok's landing had been delayed by an orbital bombardment. By the time he and the young, tonsured lexicanium marched into the Imperial staging post, Phobor was already leading an assault on the southern walls of Eidon City.

Petrok could hear the crack and volley of the distant fighting rolling across the gritty, green slopes, and he could see the smoke pall rising, three kilometres away. The white phosphor vents on the skyline continued to rasp and blur the amber sky with their primordial heat.

The staging post was all but empty. Half a dozen sculptural white awnings, discoloured slightly by months of exposure to the heat sear, swayed in the breeze. There were rows of smaller habitents made of a darker, coarser canvas, and stacks of munitions under netting in sandbagged dugouts. Several armoured vehicles were parked nearby. They had been painted with a lime overcoat to mask them in the green landscape. Behind the main command tents, on the lee of the hill, rows of infirmary tents stood all the way down to the roadway in the valley. Petrok could smell the rot and disinfectant drifting up from them.

Guardsmen in the livery of the Leoparda saluted as the great Librarian approached, his quite formidable lexicanium a step behind, carrying the casket containing the Librarian's holy tarot deck on a padded, satin rest. Behind them came the bearer of Petrok's ornate helmet and the bearer of the power sword Bellus. Behind that strode two more bearers swinging censors and holding fluttering pennants of the Karybdis phratry aloft. And behind them walked four more, carrying the sacred Book of Lives in its litter-like hardwood chest. All the bearers were robed, hunched homunculus figures.

One of the Guardsmen pointed at the main tent. Petrok saw how he was trembling, his face pallid and dank despite the midday heat. Without speaking, Petrok advanced towards the tent. His bearers snuffled and growled sidelong out of their cowls at the Guardsman, making him dart back.

'Enough of that!' Rodos barked at them.

Inside the tent was a vast, round table, the surface of which was a glass plate illuminated from beneath by moving lights that showed the contours and arrangement of the city and the disposi-tion of the troops. Guard officers stood around it, and they all looked up and stepped back solemnly as the distinguished warrior and his retinue entered.

'I am Petrok of the Iron Snakes,' he said, as if any here could not know who he was.

One, a Leoparda general by his sleeve bars, stepped forward. 'Major General Corson. Welcome, great sir. Your worthy com-mander has already begun his assault. He requests that you make your strategic assessment as soon as possible, so that–'

Petrok held up one huge, armoured hand. 'I am well aware of what my commander expects of me. Show me the dispositions.'

Corson led Petrok to the table. The Librarian looked down at it, his sharp eyes clicking as they took in every detail, every flickering unit light-point, every drifting rune. Those eyes fed the data back into his brain, his greatest weapon, where they could be composed, considered, analysed, dissected.

He smiled.

'Master?' Rodos asked, noticing the expression.

'Three point fluid dispersal along two insertions. Typical of dear Captain Phobor. Just as he did on Tull.'

Rodos gazed at the tabletop for a moment, trying to discern the pattern. 'I see,' he said.

He did not, and Petrok knew it. Rodos had a long way to go before he would master the techniques of memory and comparison that allowed a great tactical mind to take in all battle assessments at a glance.

But the real reason Petrok had allowed himself to smile was not his immediate recognition of Phobor's favourite tactic. It was a simpler thing. The table reminded Petrok of the strategium board where he had learned his craft long ago from his old, beloved master, Nector. It was a whimsy, but it pleased him to enjoy it. He had, as he liked to remind himself, a soul.

'These here?' he asked, tapping the table-plate with his fingertips.

'Three battalions of Leoparda, in reserve.' The major general's voice was hollow and scared.

'Why?'

'Y-your brave captain wanted them... out of the way. He was quite insistent. He didn't want them to... to...'

'Confuse his aim,' said a Donorian officer smugly from behind, clearly enjoying the Leoparda's discomfort. Petrok smiled again. He could just imagine how Phobor had roared in here, accusing the Imperial Guard officers of weakness, cowardice, incompetence, and every other sin under the suns. They had failed to discharge the holy liberation, and Phobor would make them sweat now and repent in punishment details later. No wonder the camp was terrified.

There was some muttering in the officer ranks, and Petrok frowned, still looking at the table.

'Silence!' Rodos growled, noticing his Librarian's furrows. Hush fell again.

Even the bearers had stopped their growling.

Petrok put his hands on the tabletop and leaned down, looking deeper, no longer making a tactical, forebrain assessment. He was reaching out with the darker, more profound parts of his mind. He was using his gifts to see beyond the now, into the when and the if, to sense the fortunes of the battle.

A chill fell on the tent enclosure. Frost formed on the tabletop glass around Petrok's hands. One of the junior Guard officers fainted and was bustled away out of sight. The bearers began to murmur and bark, until Rodos quieted them with a savage look.

Petrok ignored them all. He was locked with the patterns of past, present and future. He was seeing behind reality, watching the way the structures moved and meshed.

It was… perfect. Phobor's ploy had been entirely appropriate. The vanguards and support lines were placed correctly. Eidon City would fall within four hours, with minimal losses on their part. His report would convey little to Phobor except to bolster his confidence.

Except… something. Something small and awry. Something persistent and nagging. Like a tiny pebble lodged inside the cuff of a Terminator glove, niggling away.

What? *What?*

'Master?' Rodos asked.

Petrok stood back.

'This,' he said, pointing to one light on the eastern side of the illuminated chart.

Rodos consulted the key. 'Damocles squad, master. Captain Phobor sent them round to ensure the foe would not break from the city when it fell.'

'A sound move, but it troubles me. There is heavy fighting there.'

'The chart doesn't show it.'

'I feel what glass and electrocrystal patterns do not. Damocles is in danger.'

'They're but one unit,' said another Leoparda general, speaking up. 'Surely the overall victory is paramount? None can be spared or freed from the main assault to support them. Losses are… inevitable.'

The general fell silent as he realised he had said too much.

Petrok looked up, but there was compassion in his eyes. He knew how hard the Guardsmen had been driven to conquer the superior foe, and he knew how bitterly Phobor had railed at these men.

'You're right, sir,' he said. 'Lives must always be secondary to victory. But I will not see Ithakan souls wasted where waste is unnecessary.'

He turned, abruptly, and tugged his great power sword from the sheath the waiting swordbearer held. The bearer started in surprise. The blade, great Bellus, glowed and hummed as it breathed air again.

'What are you doing, master?' Rodos asked.

'What I must. Wait here. I will render my tactical survey to Captain Phobor when I return.'

Despite their fear and their awe of Petrok, the Guard officers began clamouring to a man. Phobor had left them with one task: to greet the great Librarian and speed his assessment to the front-line. Fear for their lives made them question the huge, armoured figure in the doorway of the tent.

'Shut them up, lexicanium,' Petrok said softly as he strode outside, beyond the baying chatter of the soldiers.

As the Librarian made off across the green rock, towards the white heat, he could hear Rodos shouting 'Silence!' over and again.

## II

IN A GREEN rock defile on the eastern edge of Eidon City, washed by the stink of the phosphor vents so close nearby, Brother Andromak of Damocles squad cursed Eidon in the name of every spirit he could remember as he blasted away with his plasma gun. In reply, enemy shots whickered down the gully and blew one of the biting-snake finials off the Chapter standard he wore over his shoulders: the snake crest, double-looped.

'Back! Back!' snarled Brother Pindor from behind, half dragging Andromak towards the cover of the gully wall. 'There's no way through there!'

'You think I don't know!' bellowed Andromak, fussing at his hot weapon, replacing a feed line that was about to melt out.

'Commander!'

Brother-Sergeant Priad heard Pindor's cry over the vox-link as he sheltered from a blistering enemy salvo behind a green boulder.

He tried to make sense of the terrain and find some gaps in the enemy fire. Curtly, he called Calignes, Illyus and Xander forward. They made a few metres before a round tore through Xander's shoulder plate and they dived for cover. Too heavy, too much!

Priad cursed. He'd rather be back home on Ithaka, hunting water-wyrm than caught in a dead end like this.

He had cursed too when Captain Phobor had sent them east to act as a guard in case any of the dark foe tried to break out of the city as it fell. Priad had felt Damocles had been cheated of sharing the victory. He'd wanted his squad to join the main assault.

Now they were sidelined and all but forgotten and none of them could have predicted the fierce fighting they would encounter. Priad couldn't explain it. It was as if the dark ones had already recognised their defeat and were fighting to retreat east out of the smeltery city. Damocles was the only unit in position to quell the retreat. Splinter-fire lanced around them.

Apothecary Memnes was beside Priad suddenly, dropping into cover from the rapid dash he had made. The faceplate of his helm was burnt and dented by a glancing shot.

'Memnes,' Priad growled. 'Explain this!'

'I can't, brother-sergeant,' the elderly warrior replied gruffly. 'We were meant to be a safeguard. So Phobor said. It feels like we're meeting the main force of the enemy.'

Priad fell silent. He surveyed the blistering firefight through the enhanced optics of his helmet. None had fallen so far. Andromak and Pindor were buffered in the gully. Calignes, Illyus and Xander were pinned in the open. Natus, Scyllon and Kules were ranged out behind the position he and Memnes shared.

A hail of gunfire rained down from the steep, stone slopes of Eidon City before them.

Apart from local vox-traffic between the members of the unit, communication was down, drowned out by the static of the erupting phosphor vents. Even through his respirator, Priad could smell the heat-stink of the fire wells.

They could no longer even tell how the main assault was going. Perhaps Phobor and his squads were strewn dead across the western bulwarks of the city. Perhaps they were alone.

Priad slowed his breathing to clear his mind. He looked across at Memnes, and though he saw nothing through his visor lenses except Memnes's buckled faceplate, he could sense the old, wise face beneath it, the compassion, the support.

You will make the right decision. We trust you. Damocles trusts you, brother-sergeant.

Priad flicked out the data-slate from his thigh pouch and checked again across the detailed light map of the city's eastern approach. He studied the ground's swell, the access points, the fortifications. The Imperial planners had built it well.

And these dark eldar had taken it in a night.

Curse them! Damocles would do the same in an hour!

He slid a stud on the side of the slate and overlaid the structural data. It showed the density and thicknesses of the rock walls, the hard points and pilings of the defences. It betrayed the actual physical weaknesses of the land and buildings they fought for.

Something… something…

There was indeed something. Priad switched the overlay back and forth, matching and rematching. According to the old charts, there was a section of the east wall built of compacted rock shards rather than ferro-concrete as an expediency during construction.

Priad felt his palms dampen with anticipation inside his gauntlets. He rolled onto his backside, his shoulders against the rock, and began to copy the data from the slate into a vox-message for Andromak. Dark eldar splinterfire stitched the green rock around him and covered Priad and Memnes with a fine, lime green dust.

'Andromak!' Priad rasped over the helmet vox to the squad's standard bearer. 'Open your data-link and stand by to receive!'

Andromak responded, a clipped atonal bark over the metallic vox. A red light on Priad's armour cuff glowed darkly to show that the link was open, and Priad sent the vox-pict.

'I see it, brother-sergeant!' Andromak's tinny voice came back. 'You want me to hit it?'

'Count of four, Andromak. You have the plasma gun. Bring that wall down at its weak point. Damocles, stand ready to go on five. As soon as Andromak lays in, move out and follow through.'

His voice was a robotic, emotionless growl through the comm, but the other Marines' voices responded as one, unfaltering. Even Apothecary Memnes, who was right beside him.

Priad checked his bolter and his lightning claw. The claw sizzled in the dry air, hungry for blood. Priad prayed to the lost soul of Brother-Sergeant Raphon to watch over Damocles from his place high up in the Lost Heavens where the oceans surged forever, and the Emperor knew each man's name, and the wyrms rose eternally for the Great Hunt.

Let us be sharp and true and fast as a harpoon, Priad thought. Raphon, help us take the foe as we would a wyrm rising from the seas, without flinching, without balking.

Make our thrust the victory thrust.

Priad made the count.

On four, Andromak swept up out of cover and sent a blazing blue spear of plasma energy down the gully with pinpoint precision. Green rock exploded in a vomit of flame, brighter and louder than the white heat crisping and fountaining along the horizon.

Damocles moved. The Space Marines broke from cover, firing as they went, gunning up at the walls.

Smoke washed across them.

They made ten metres, twenty.

Then Priad saw the wall. It was unbuckled, unbroken, still standing despite the oozing, molten burn Andromak's plasma gun had inflicted upon it.

The dark eldar, invisible in their positions above, renewed their fire.

A splinter shot clipped Scyllon's leg and spun him down.

Kules faltered as glancing shots whipped around him.

Natus went down, crying out, as his left arm came away raggedly at the shoulder in a spray of fire and blood and armour shreds.

'Cover! Cover!' Priad yelled.

They fell into cover, Memnes dragging the crippled Natus into safety behind a rock. Enemy shots filled the air around and over them, or chipped and shattered the rocks they clung behind. Crystal dust and weapon smoke washed across the approach.

Twenty metres. They had made just twenty metres, and still the wall stood.

The available cover was so slight that Priad was forced to lie face down in the green dust. He turned his head sideways and saw Illyus lying on his back next to him. A smoking hole had laid Illyus's visor open, and blood was dribbling out. Illyus had lost an eye and a cheek to a rebounding splinter round. Priad crawled over, pulling out his medical field pack, spraying jets of wound-sealing skin-wrap into the helmet hole. Illyus was still conscious. His fortitude was astonishing, even for a Space Marine. He mumbled some poor joke to his brother-sergeant, though half his face was gone.

Priad could smell blood. He thought it was Illyus's until he realised that was impossible. He glanced down and saw the raw, black-edged hole in his thigh. A splinter round had punched right through his armour and through the meat of his leg. There was no pain. Adrenaline was washing the agony away – that, and the augmented systems of his body.

Later, there would be pain, but that was not his chief concern. He hoped his Astartes physique would be enough to fight the venoms and filths with which the Dark Ones coated their weapons.

But the wound had self-cauterised. He would not bleed out, at least.

'I smell the blood of a hero,' said a voice through the vox-link.

'Who's that? Who speaks?'

Priad rolled over, daring more volleys of enemy fire from the fortifications above.

'Who?'

There was a figure behind them on the green rockside: an Iron Snake, tall, bare-headed, swathed in a cloak, stalking forward, oblivious to the rain of fire that doused the ground around him but miraculously left him unharmed. He held a sword aloft, a power sword that sang like the shrill keening of a water-wyrm.

Petrok! It was great Petrok himself!

### III

PETROK DROPPED INTO cover beside Priad. 'Well met, brother-sergeant!' he grinned.

'Well met indeed, master!'

'Your leg wound, does it pain you?'

'No, sir. I can move and fight if I have to, and I know I must.'

'You honour Karybdis with your bravery, leader of Damocles. Your men?'

Priad gestured sidelong to the nine Space Marines sheltering from the storm of fire.

'Natus is crippled, his arm gone. Illyus, there beside you, has been injured gravely. The rest are more or less intact.'

Petrok rolled over next to the sprawled Illyus. He looked down into his face. 'You'll have a noble scar, Illyus.'

'Thank you, sir.'

'Don't thank me. I didn't do it. The wound-wrap is holding and the blood is stemmed. You're strong. Your body will fight any venom or taint. I'll personally ensure you get the best new eye if you'll fight with me.'

'Eye or not, I'll fight with you anywhere, any time!' Illyus said, fury in his voice. He wriggled over and grabbed his fallen weapon.

Petrok looked across at Priad.

'A fine squad you have here, brother-sergeant.'

'Thank you, master,'

'Call me Petrok. It's quicker and simpler in the heat of battle. And I like my friends to know me by name.'

'Sir... Petrok...'

'Better, Priad. Now advise me of your situation.'

Priad gestured across at the insurmountable fortifications. 'Captain Phobor sent us back here to watch for a retreat.'

'Typical of the captain's textbook moves,' Petrok mused with a grin that made Priad smile involuntarily.

'I didn't expect much. Truth is I thought we had been given a secondary role. But the resistance is huge, as if they are already breaking... or guarding something important.'

'A good assessment, Priad. I... felt as much. So you know, Phobor is taking the city as we speak. But this here is unwarranted. I came personally because it troubled me. I hate to lose any of our iron-clad brotherhood. You're a first cast wyrm-killer yourself, aren't you, Priad?'

Priad started at the recognition and felt a flush of pride despite the tumult around them. 'It was my honour to take a wyrm first cast, sir.'

'Petrok.'

'Petrok. Yes, in the summer of my admission to the phratry. I took a wyrm with my first harpoon in the channel ways beyond the Telos archipelago.'

'So I know. A proud achievement. It took me three harpoons before I took my first. You should teach me sometime.'

'Sir… Petrok.' Priad was laughing despite himself.

'What do you think they're guarding?' Petrok asked directly.

'I don't know,' Priad replied, suddenly serious. 'Something of value. Great value to them.'

'Indeed. Your tactics so far?'

Priad flexed his aching leg and checked his bolter clip. 'We assaulted, as simple as that. When we ran foul, I tried to get Andromak, my plasma bearer, to take out this section of wall, where a weakness seemed to be.'

Priad showed the slate to Petrok.

'But the gambit failed, and so we are dug in.'

Petrok regarded the slate Priad had given him for a moment, as further splinter rounds cracked into the green rock around them. When Petrok put the slate down, it was covered in frost.

'You were right, Priad.'

'Sir?'

'Petrok, Petrok,' the Librarian smiled at Priad. It was unnerving to see an unarmoured face. Priad almost shuddered.

'How was I right, Master Petrok?' he asked.

'You took your wyrm with the first cast, didn't you?'

'I was lucky.'

'How many others have done the same?'

'Very few, I suppose.'

'The water-wyrm is armoured and fierce. Sometimes you must expend several harpoons, despite the strength of your lance arm, to kill the beast. So it has been in my experience.'

'What do you mean?'

Petrok rolled over again and adjusted his vox-link so he broadcast to the whole of Damocles.

'Wyrms are hard to kill. You may know where to strike them but still it may take many casts, Brother Andromak. Prepare your plasma gun and repeat your strike on my command. Damocles, let us repeat our cast.'

Petrok looked back at Priad. 'With your permission, of course.'

'I grant it gratefully, but I'm not sure–'

'Any who are brave enough to take a wyrm with the first strike have not the benefit of knowing it is wise to strike again.'

'Sir?'

'Now, Andromak!' Petrok bellowed.

Brother Andromak swung back out of cover again and sent a boiling spear of plasma fire across at the wall. It blistered and scorched the Eidon City fortifications. As soon as the blast stopped, the enemy renewed its shooting. A blitz of splinterfire and las-rounds hosed the approach. Rock and earth threw up in thousands of individual impact geysers. The green boulder sheltering Xander fractured and exploded, sending him scrabbling for better protection.

'Again, Andromak!' Petrok cried over the vox-link. 'Strike again.'

Andromak did, staying on his feet and taking a glancing deflection to the shoulder as he triggered his massive weapon.

Something shivered as his plasma fire touched it. A split low down branched up into jagged cracks. It was like watching a leafless tree grow. Andromak blasted again for good measure.

A section of wall buckled and tore down, spilling dark, shattered bodies with it. A further explosion blew the wall out. Debris rained down, and a tidal wave of green dust choked its way down the approach.

'Now! For Karybdis!' Petrok cried.

Enhancing their optics against the wall of smoke, Damocles squad advanced behind him towards the breach.

Crushed, broken bodies lay in the rubble: black, lean, hooked things, or burst pallid fleshy things with gaping mouths. The Marines chose not to look at either. They scrambled up the rubble after Petrok and Priad, bolters barking up into the darkness that welcomed them. The city's eastern flank was open to them, and they were biting into its innards.

Petrok led the way, his power sword shrieking in the air. Priad kept his distance from the charging Librarian, blasting with his bolter, fanning the men into the breach.

Within ten minutes, they had captured the first section of the wall. Petrok was pressing on, his sword cleaving through the defenders: shadowy, flickering beings who darted around him quickly, but none so quick as to avoid his blade. Bellus drank well of the dark kind's blood. Petrok left a trail of pieces behind him: severed scissorhands, cloven horned helmets, split torsos.

Damocles closed in after the great hero, following the trail of destruction. They moved wide in support, edging around into side corridors and chambers, flanking Petrok. The city had been raised centuries before, built from local stone cut into huge blocks and smoothed into almost seamless walls. Ornate light globes ran along walls or were suspended from the ceilings, and the white light reflected off the green stone, making everything lambent and pale. It reminded Priad of the waters of Ithaka, of the times he had dived down beneath into the green, into the silence.

There was no silence here. Rumbling blasts, screams, shrieks from the fallen foe, the chatter of bolters, and the wail of the plasma gun. Vox-traffic snapped back and forth between the Space Marines, and they could all hear the angry hum of Petrok's power sword. Priad ducked back as a salvo of rounds tore the corner off a wall before him, flaking green stone in all directions. Then he was on top of the foe, a gibbering thing in segmented red armour, its eyes yellow slits in its visor. It reeled at him with a bi-form blade weapon, raising a bladed firearm in the other clawed hand. Priad hit it with a bolter round that exploded in the middle of its chest and blew it across the chamber where it dropped, squealing, limbs thrashing in a death frenzy. Its blood painted semi-circles across the wall above it.

Andromak burned corridors and hallways out with his plasma gun, chanting the Hymn of Karybdis as he went. Any movement, any twitch of dark limb or slender blade, and he boiled the air of the chamber, scorching the stonework.

Calignes and Pindor found a way to the right held fast by piled furniture and flak boards. Single splinter shots stung down at them from the makeshift strongpoint. They rushed it together, their power and weight bringing the entire barricade down over the dark eldar defending it. There was a brief, confused hand-to-hand fight in the jumbled wreckage. Pindor shot one at close range and then smashed the head of another into the wall with his right fist. Calignes throttled the third.

They pushed deeper. Parted from Calignes briefly, Pindor found himself in a wide, featureless vault where enemy assassins leapt out from the shadows. He slew them all with his bolter and his knife, in a frenzied combat that lasted five or six seconds, but which he would remember all his life.

Xander, Kules and Scyllon drove forward into a munitions bunker and butchered forty dark eldar in a straight fight. Kules's spent bolter was glowing white-hot as he used it to cudgel an assailant before throwing it aside and laying in with his blade.

Natus, despite his wounds, kept up position outside with his bolter held in his remaining hand, picking off the dark eldar as they ran, one by one.

Memnes half-carried Illyus forward, and the two of them laid down a crossfire that slaughtered the eldar things in a haze of thermite smoke and blood.

Priad was with Petrok, advancing into the depths of the eastern fortifications. The sergeant's lightning claw, eager for victims, smote dark eldar into smouldering pieces as he advanced. His bolter rattled out its funereal beat. Primuls exploded all around him, fell back and fell down, weeping bloody matter onto the tiled floor.

Petrok's power sword scythed through stone and brick and armour and flesh and left the sliced remains of the enemy as smoking meat debris behind him. He sang the hunting song of the Ithakans as he fought. It was the old lay, the custom-verse of the wyrm-hunters as they rowed out to find their prey. Priad found himself joining in, singing along with the great hero, rejoicing in the slaughter and the blood fog.

At last, Petrok bowed forward, sinking over, his bloodied sword set with its tip on the Eidon City stone. He sighed.

'Master Petrok?' Priad asked, blasting at the last of the scum who flickered and reared out of the stone shadows about them.

'Phobor has taken the wall. Eidon City is ours. The Snakes have won the place.'

Priad faltered. 'Then why do you look so pale, master? Why so anguished?'

Petrok rose again, wiping blood from his cheek and raising the mighty power sword so that it sang in the air over his head.

'Because they are coming. The dark ones are coming. Fleeing in bloody panic, they move this way, abandoning the west of the city. Can Damocles handle a real fight?'

'On my oath, they can!' Priad snarled.

Forty seconds later, Damocles squad got to prove that boast.

Shrieking and fleeing from the city breach, the vast forces of the dark eldar retreated east and met the lone warriors of Damocles squad. The eldar were frenzied and keening, their senses of self-preservation entirely subsumed by their overwhelming need to escape. They gave no quarter, no sign of surrender or submission. They came as a black armoured torrent of thick, spiked evil that rushed out of the city like rats from a fire, or water through a shattered dam.

Overwhelmed, Priad killed and killed again and went over in the tide of barbed fiends until Petrok hauled him up by the collar and set him back on his feet.

Side by side, Petrok and Priad, with blade and claw, levelled the eldar into a pile twenty deep.

Blood was clogging the corridors now: rich, ruddy, stinking. Behind the eldar, the warriors of Damocles squad closed the trap. Andromak was beside his commanders, lancing his plasma beams into the choked confines, slaughtering dozens of the foe as they charged and panicked. Now Xander, his bolter coughing. Now Calignes and Pindor, smashing with their blades. Illyus, his face half gone, his weapon punching into the dark. Scyllon, Memnes, Kules. A slaughterhouse. A killing field. Ten Iron Snakes damming the tide of the dark eldar. And fallen Natus outside, singing the lay, shooting down each and every straggler who got past the deadly blockade.

Priad was washed with blood, and his bolter was dry-firing as Petrok steadied him.

'It is done, Priad. We have slain a thousand over and again.'

Priad pulled off his helmet and cast it to the ground. It floated away a few yards on a stream of enemy blood that gurgled down the hallway. The air was too close, too full of smoke and blood vapour. They had expended virtually all of their ammunition and most of their physical strength, but they had killed infamous numbers. But for the evidence of the bodies around them, the scale of their victory was unimaginable.

'This day will be remembered by Damocles,' Priad whispered in the dampness and the dark. He began a small prayer of thanks to the Emperor.

'There is something else,' Petrok replied curtly, moving ahead. 'We're not done.'

## IV

THEY ADVANCED AGAIN through the corridors, clambering over the heaps of the slain, firing their bolters into the heads of anything that twitched. Occasionally, the fierce heat of Brother Andromak's plasma gun seared down the tunnel.

Memnes, old and trusted Memnes, came to Priad's side. 'This is wrong, something is wrong.'

Priad began to shake his head in reassurance, his lightning claw extended into the dark, but a voice echoed back to them.

'Memnes is right. Well felt, brother.' Petrok's voice in that dim place was loud and penetrating.

Priad formed Damocles up behind him and moved towards the voice of the Librarian. He found Petrok looking down over a chasm from which the white heat of the phosphor vents belched up unstintingly.

'Look,' Petrok said, pointing down with his great sword.

Priad craned and looked.

There were charges below, alien packets of explosives strapped to the vent walls. That was the dark eldar's final legacy. They had mined Eidon City and the phosphor vents. What they could not keep, no one would have.

'That explains the concentration of their strength at the east, and my... suspicion. The Dark Ones knew that we would best them today. They kept us fighting long enough to be able to set this trap.'

'Can we stop it?'

Petrok shrugged. 'Their materials are exotic and strange to us. I cannot guarantee understanding their explosive mechanisms.'

'Then what?' Memnes asked.

'We take them off,' Priad said directly. 'They've been placed here in order to trigger the phosphor seams. If we can't stop them exploding, we can at least ensure they explode away from their intended target.'

Petrok looked at him with clear, frank eyes. 'You're right. The only way. Even if these things have been made tamper proof or rigged to explode if touched, this is our duty.'

Petrok leaned down into the vent and reached for the nearest charge packet. He had to use the tip of his sword to loosen its metal claws from the rock. He raised it slowly. A spiked black cube with a winking red tell-tale.

'Who's first?'

Memnes took it carefully, directly, and began to pace steadily down through the body-strewn corridors and out towards the breach in the wall. By the time he had disappeared from sight, another two charges had been pried loose and Xander and Scyllon were also on their way, nursing their deadly burdens.

Another came free and Andromak took it. Then one each for Illyus, Calignes, Pindor and Kules.

Petrok looked back from the open vent at Priad. Sweat coursed down his face, the sweat of stress perhaps, though Priad knew the up-wash of heat from the vent was huge. 'Four left,' Petrok said.

'Two each, then. We can't wait for any to return.'

'It'll be tricky managing two.'

'We'll do it.'

Petrok nodded as he reached lower to grab the last few. Priad had to hold onto Petrok's waist and legs so the Librarian could get hold of the lowest-set charges. The four came out one by one.

Priad lifted his two. They were heavy, and he had no desire to treat them roughly. As it was, he was sure the red tell-tales were flashing faster than they had on Memnes's explosive.

Petrok hooked his sword in the loop of his belt and picked up the last two packets.

Priad was already walking.

Concentrating on keeping the bombs level and unshaken, it was difficult to remember the route immediately. Confusion had led them there, and the battle-scarred halls all looked the same.

Priad reached a junction and heard Petrok behind him urging him to go left. He did so. At another turn, he nearly slipped on the slick blood covering the floor.

The tell-tales were definitely flashing faster now. Light showed ahead through the green gloom. White heat, amber sky. The breach in the eastern wall of Eidon City where they had come in.

Priad and Petrok scrambled outside, trying to remain upright in the sloped rubble and slurry, trying to keep the packets steady. The rest of Damocles had fallen back down the gully approach into the cover of the escarpment, leaving their packets scattered on the hillslope away from the city wall. They cried out encouragement, urging haste, greater haste!

The sergeant and the Librarian put their packages down alongside the others that the rest of Damocles had borne gently out of the captured city. They looked like a strange crop of dark fruit planted out in the desert dust. The lights were almost strobing a continuous red.

'Run,' Petrok said.

Priad needed no encouragement. They raced together down the slope, crunching hard on the crystal rock, armour clanking, hydraulics buzzing. Priad heard the great Librarian start to say something.

The charges exploded, an almost simultaneous ripple of air-splitting detonations. A flash of white heat brighter than the vents. A solid wall of shock-force that hurled them both like harpoons.

## V

FINGERS OF BLACK smoke and a huge pall of dust stained the amber sky above Eidon City. Air support and the blocky dark shapes of supply vessels and troop-landers cut low through the haze.

At the staging post above the western approach, the Imperial forces were celebrating their victory, and the massed Iron Snakes were hailing their Captain-Hero Phobor. Great voices were raised in chanting song, gauntlets slapping against armour plate. The Rite of the Sharing of Water had been made, and the Iron Snakes rejoiced in their triumph.

Petrok and the men of Damocles squad returned when the revelries were in full swing. Night was falling, and patterns of stars were winking in the clear sky above the veil of smoke. There were great lights up there too, the running lights of orbiting Imperial battleships and escort vessels. Already, news of the successful reclamation was speeding through the warp to the Chapter House on Ithaka.

Below, in the camps, braziers were lit, and drums were beating. As their men broke camp and headed for the troopships and the next warzone, small groups of pale, fearful Guard officers were being marched away under escort, bound for the punishment ships. Phobor's orders. They had failed. They would pay.

The noise of armoured vehicles and artillery units preparing to disembark filled the smoky evening. On the dark roadways below, lines of torches and vehicle lamps wound in snakes. Above, the clouds thundered as support ships brought technicians and workers back in to re-man the foundries.

'Master! I had become most concerned for your well-being!' began Lexicanium Rodos as Petrok reappeared. He clapped his hands, and the midget things scurried out of the darkness to take Bellus and the Librarian's blackened gauntlets.

'I'm well enough,' Petrok said. 'Call up more staff. See to these men.' Priad led Damocles squad into the camp. Andromak and Xander were half-carrying Natus, and Memnes supported Illyus. Before accepting any help or acknowledging anyone else present, Priad formed Damocles into a circle and had Memnes conduct the Rite of the Sharing of Water to mark the end of their fight. Then they could rest, celebrate, be tended to.

Rodos observed the rite, waited until it was over, then barked more orders for surgeons and Chapter servants. Figures darted out of the awning tents, some carrying supplies or medical tools. Illyus and Natus were taken to the healing tents immediately.

Petrok watched, making sure the squad was well attended.

'He was looking for you,' Rodos told the Librarian quietly, from behind.

'Phobor?' Petrok asked, turning.

Rodos nodded. 'He wasn't pleased. It seemed to take the edge off the victory for him that he didn't have you running around, heeding his every order.'

'There were other things to do, more important things.'

Rodos nodded. 'I do not question you, master, but he will. Now it looks…'

Rodos's voice trailed off. Phobor had appeared, powerful and dark against the fires. His scarred face had a grim set to it. The flames flashed off the double-headed snake crest on his shoulder-plates.

'Petrok! I wondered where you had damn well got to. My directions were clear enough, weren't they? I wanted an appraisal of my tactics.'

Petrok took a drink from a goblet one of the midgets offered him before replying. 'Your tactics were perfect. You proved that by taking the city, for the love of the Emperor. You had no need of me.'

Phobor shrugged. He was one of the iron-clad warriors, Petrok knew. Total discipline, total courage. No imagination. No... soul.

'You have commended your men for the victory?' Petrok asked.

'Aye, all of them,' Phobor nodded.

'Perhaps not all. Let me tell you about Damocles and what was achieved on the other side of the city today. Let me tell you of another war, of steadfast courage, and of white heat.'

# PART FOUR
# RED RAIN
## Undertaking to Ceres

# I

FOR AS FAR as any of them could see, the place looked like a vast open wound. The soil of Ceres was rich in iron ore, which gave it a deep, red cast. The climate circulated particles of the ore into the atmosphere, so that when it rained, it rained crimson liquid.

It was raining now. It had been for weeks. Drizzle, bright as oxygenated blood, streamed down from low, dark clouds, turning the russet soil into soft, scarlet, wet folds that looked like raw flesh.

Through the wounded land, the Rhino crawled, heavy tracks slipping and thrashing in the red mire. Its grey, white and red livery was washed a watery pink from the rain, and the Chapter banners hanging from the rear frame were as dark as soaked bandages.

Ahead, lay Hekat, and death as bright and bloody as the rain.

DETACHMENTS OF PHRATRY warriors from the Chapter, beloved of the Emperor himself, had arrived on Ceres two weeks before to prosecute the sudden uprising of a Chaos cult. Ceres was an agricultural world with a sparse population that accreted around small farm townships, each one separated from its neighbour by thousands of square kilometres of arable land. The uprising had engulfed Nybana, the main township and landing field, a dejected place of shanty habs, grain hoppers, threshing mills and freight yards. That had been the Chapter's first port of call. Four full squads of towering armoured forms, forty warriors, had disembarked from their drop-ships at dawn and scoured the township, incinerating the cultists without question or quarter. The fighting had been intense but brief, lasting only until noon. Armed with autoguns, crop-scythes and fanatical zeal, the cultists were ruthless and formidable, but no match for the boltguns and superhuman power of the infamous Space Marines. By noon, the Iron Snakes' banner and the Imperial eagle had been fluttering over the main guildhall of Nybana.

Captain Phobor, the venerable and much-decorated commander of the Iron Snake mission, along with his squad officers, had then met with Inquisitor Mabuse, who had spent some months on Ceres uncovering the cult before contacting the Chapter for aid.

In the atrium of the guildhall, the phalanx of giant warriors stood in a semi-circle around the robed, white-haired inquisitor in dutiful silence as he appraised them of the situation. Mabuse began by praising their work in liberating Nybana. From outside came the thump of bolters as the assault squad finished its cleansing. The bodies of the fallen cultists, some six hundred or more, had been stacked in an outlying granary and torched with flamers. The pungent scents of burning filled the air, despite the heavy rain.

'They call themselves the Children of Khorne,' Mabuse had said, his lofty voice faltering just slightly as he was forced to pronounce the dark name. 'We can presume the pun is lost on them. My investigation has shown that the taint was brought in from off-world. Nybana is the main lift-port, and a large proportion of the population are indigent freight handlers and cargo-men from a dozen other planets. Some vermin coven, practising the foul ways secretly in their midst, carried the poison here and set it loose into the population.'

'Is it restricted to the main habitation?' Phobor asked, his voice metallic and expressionless as it filtered through his helmet speakers.

'No, captain, I don't believe it is.' Mabuse got to his feet and wandered over to an ornate side table.

Standing to the left of Phobor, Brother-Sergeant Priad of Damocles squad watched the inquisitor with curious eyes. He had served with the Iron Snakes for nine years, and for the last four had commanded that decorated detail. He had seen things of such horror and such wonder in that time that no amount of training in the Chapter Hall of Karybdis could have fully prepared him. But he had never seen an Imperial inquisitor close up before. He knew that no two were alike, and he knew that all were feared, perhaps as feared as the Space Marines themselves. Inquisitors were singular beings, braving both the physical dangers of the galaxy and the mental torments of limitless evil as they struggled and probed to uncover the taints of the Great Foulness.

Mabuse was a tall, lean man in his forties with a shock of white hair and a face angled and sculptural, as if the pale skin clung tightly to his skull. His robes were black and edged with golden braid, and his right hand, now Priad saw it, was a mechanical prosthetic of intricate golden callipers and gears.

Mabuse lifted an object from the table in his artificial hand. It was a figurine, about thirty centimetres high, woven from straw.

'A corn-doll,' Mabuse told them, holding it up for them to see. 'A votive object, common on so many rustic and agricultural worlds. Here on Ceres, they weave them at harvest time, one to represent each of the outlying harvest towns, and they are displayed here in the main guildhall during the Time of Celebration.'

He lifted another from the table. There was something hideous and twisted about this one, even though it was only a doll woven from straw.

'I found this… and six more like it. Khorne-dolls, if you will. I see the pun is lost on you Marines too. Whatever. Each one has been made according to the practices of various harvest townships, but the designs have been perverted to make them symbols of the cult.'

Mabuse let the thing drop back onto the table top as if he had no wish to touch it any longer, even with a hand made of metal.

'And from that, we may infer that at least six of the outlying townships have been polluted by the cult. Though the main uprising here in Nybana has been quashed, it is vital that these outlying offshoots also be checked and, if necessary, burned and cleansed.'

'You can identify the relevant townships from the dolls?' Phobor asked.

'Yes,' Mabuse said, as if such an arcane act of divination was child's play. 'You must send teams out at once, captain. Send them out to purge these places. Until that is done, Ceres must be considered unclean.'

There were eighteen farmships on Ceres outside Nybana. Mabuse and his aides had identified six positively from the loathsome dolls, but he insisted that all should be checked in turn. Phobor kept one squad with him to hold Nybana firm, and sent out the other three to undertake the purge.

Damocles squad had been sent north-west. Four townships lay in that direction: Nyru, Yyria, Flax and Hekat. Of these, only the most distant – Hekat – had been positively marked by a doll.

It took Priad and his squad a full day's hard drive across the rain-swept land to reach Nyru, and a further day to confirm it was free of taint. Another day's trek brought them to Yyria, which also proved to be clean, though the fear and resentment of the towns-folk kept them suspicious and prolonged the search.

Another day and a half's drive through fallow uplands followed, and the wet season greeted them with low storms, squalls of bloody vapour and hard, red rain. They approached Flax on the seventh day after leaving Nybana. By then, reports had drifted in from the other two roving squads. Pliades squad had found cultists in the township of Broom, far to the south, and had been engaged in a running street battle for a day and a night. Manes squad had uncovered another nest of evil in a township called Sephoni, and had been forced to put it to the torch.

Damocles reached Flax farmship.

Flax was dead. A week dead, Priad estimated. Damocles squad moved out from their Rhino transport and fanned through the blood-wet streets, finding nothing but burnt-out habitat sheds, ransacked grain hoppers and rusting harvesters. Brother Calignes finally found the townsfolk. They had been harvested. Four hundred men, women and children, butchered with corn-scythes, their bodies and body parts piled in a corn silo to rot. The place was crawling with crop weevils.

Priad voxed the news to Phobor at Nybana. Inquisitor Mabuse himself came on the line and questioned Priad closely. Was it a cult centre that had chosen suicide? Was there any sign of true corruption? Had the place been sacrificed by cultists from another farmship, Hekat perhaps?

Mabuse relayed simple instructions as to what to look for. Priad listened carefully, and then dispatched his men to search. An hour later, he climbed into the back of the Rhino, removed his helmet, and spoke to Mabuse on the vox-link again. Outside, the bloody rain drizzled.

'Lord, I think it is the work of outsiders. There is no trace of a shrine or a cult fastness in Flax. The only signs we can find are the blasphemous sigils daubed in blood on the sides of the granary where they piled the bodies. My men have found tracks trampled in the cornfields around the township. I thought at first it might be the signs of the murderers' escape, but the tracks wind and overlap. From the top of the granary barns, you can see they make a pattern. The trampled lines are quite deliberate. They form a vast, unholy symbol in the corn, hundreds of paces across. Inquisitor, I pray I never have to look upon such a sign of the Ruinous Powers again.'

'You have done well, brother-sergeant. From your reports, I am sure that Flax was a sacrifice. A force of cultists, large enough to overwhelm four hundred humans and slaughter them, is loose in your region. They made a statement out of Flax, a declaration. You must hunt them down. From the evidence as it presents to us, I'd hazard Hekat is the most likely place to start.'

DAMOCLES MADE READY to move on to Hekat, two days away. Priad had Brother Pindor take a flamer from the Rhino and torch the cornfields, obliterating the crop-mark. They also burned the dead, and made blessings over the vast pyre, consecrating the innocent and the fallen in the name of the Emperor.

## II

HEKAT FARMSHIP NOW lay before them, and the Rhino puffed and wheezed its way up the muddy trackway towards the cluster of barns, crop-silos, habitats and mills.

Brother Scyllon drove the armoured transport. In the rocking, bucking rear section, the men of Damocles squad began a final weapons check and murmured private prayers of salvation and forbearance to themselves.

Priad sat in the chain-seat near the rear hatch, adjusting the fit of the hefty lightning claw around his right hand. The claw was the symbol of leadership for Damocles squad. Sergeant Raphon, hallowed be his memory and his rest, had worn it before Priad, and had bequeathed it to the young Snake on Rosetta when he fell four years before.

Before Raphon, it had decorated the fist of Pheus, heroic in battle. Before Pheus, it had honoured the might of Berrios, mighty Ithakan. Before that, great Sartes had made it wet with Irdol blood. Before that, Dysse had carved his way to the sleep of champions with its electric majesty, ripping his way through the cruel hordes of the pirate eldar scum.

And before that, a line of heroes whose every name and every deed Priad knew, and who were with him every time he donned the claw. Right back to Damocles himself, great Damocles, greatest of the great, generations before, who had first raised the claw and given his name to the fighting team.

Priad flexed the long, segmented fingers of the metal glove, and watched as blue sparks hissed from digit to digit. The claw weighed close to seventy kilos and was three times the size of a human hand. But even without the strength-enhancing mechanics of his Mark VII power armour, Priad would not have been tested by the weight. He was of the Adeptes Astartes. He was a post-human titan, gene-forged to serve the Emperor of Terra from birth to death. Stripped of his armour, he was still a force of destruction, many times a man. Armoured, his face hidden behind the expressionless visor of the Space Marine helm, his limbs encased in electric-motivated ceramite plates, his senses magnified a thousandfold, he was a god-killer.

Let the Foulness spew up its dark deities! He would face them and slay them!

Priad looked down into the open palm of the gleaming claw. He saw the nicks and dents of war that it wore as badges of valour. He knew them all. This deep scratch earned by Raphon in close combat with a daemon-thing on Brontax. This jagged scar made by Pheus when he killed a Chaos dreadnought. The missing digit tip

Dysse had left impaled in the chest of the warlord Grondal when he had torn out that fiend's heart.

Then he saw something else, looking back at him from the mirror surface of the steel glove. A face: pale, dark-haired, dark-eyed, resolute. Himself.

For a scant moment it looked far too mortal and vulnerable. Priad took up his helmet and locked it into place. What he saw now, through the lenses of his battlevisor, reflected back up from the polished claw, was a great deal more reassuring: a Space Marine.

'Ten minutes from the township,' Scyllon called over the trooper to trooper headset.

Priad acknowledged and looked around at his men. One by one, he took in their power.

Kules, shortest of them all at just over two metres, was thickly set like a barrel, his long black hair braided up against his scalp as he put on his helmet.

Illyus, his handsome face scarred and sutured around his artificial eye, was loading his bolt clips.

Xander was the youngest and tallest, his eyes golden and faraway.

Pindor, with his deep-set eyes and hawk-look, was resetting his armour links.

Natus was easing the pistons of his bionic left arm and sliding his boltgun into its thigh pouch.

Andromak, smiling as ever, was adjusting the weight of the massive plasma gun on his back-harness.

Calignes, sharp-faced, black-eyed, roguish, was cleaning the spine plugs in his neck before setting his helmet in place.

Memnes, the Apothecary, preserver of life, minister of death, grey-bearded and solemn, checked the contents of his narthecium before snapping it shut.

Scyllon was at the helm, stripped to the waist so as to manhandle the controls better, his taut, muscled torso blistered with plug-ducts and link implants.

Damocles squad, Priad thought. Praise be. God-killers, world-smiters, Space Marines, as great and as doughty as any band of Iron Snakes to use that name.

Priad looked over at old Memnes. The grey-beard took the sign and raised his voice, beginning the Litany of Approaching War,

which the other men joined. Memnes took them through the Call
of Ithaka and the Loyalty Oath of Karybdis, and each man
answered the returns without hesitation.

All of those who had not yet donned their helmets now did so.
Kules took the helm of the Rhino as Xander and Pindor helped
Scyllon to armour himself. Each lock and twist of the armour seals
was praised and blessed.

Captain Phobor had conducted the Rite of the Giving of Water,
the old Iron Snakes custom, at Nybana when the force had first
arrived, but now Memnes solemnly carried out the Rite of Sharing,
as was appropriate before a battle. The tubular copper flask containing precious water from the endless seas of their homeworld
Ithaka was passed around, and each man anointed his winged
snake chest-symbol with a drop or two as Memnes intoned the old
words.

Brother Andromak took out the Iron Snakes standard – the snake
crest, double-looped – and fixed it to his shoulders. Brother-
Apothecary Memnes anointed it with water too. The water was
clear, like liquid glass. How unlike the blood that rains on us here,
Priad thought.

The Rhino churned into the open main square of Hekat and
Kules slewed it to a halt.

The place looked deserted.

Priad popped the rear hatch, and Damocles squad fanned out in
formation, weapons armed and raised, hunting for movements.

Nothing.

So very ominously like blood, the rain washed down over them all.

### III

THE FAN OF Iron Snakes spread down the main street of the
farmship, scanning to all sides with their auspex units, weapons
braced ready in armoured hands. Eight of them were on foot, with
Priad at the head of the fan. Kules rolled the Rhino along after
them, turbines idling, the main rig of floods and searchlights
ignited to probe the stormy darkness of the place. Rain sleeted in
dark stripes through the beams of hard light. Scyllon rode on top,
in the open turret, his hands on the grips of the pintle-mounted
storm-bolter.

There was no sound except the crunch of their footfalls, the low rumble of the transport and the beat of the rain.

Priad held up his left hand, showing three fingers, circled his hand and pointed.

Calignes, Xander and Pindor moved ahead on the left sweep, checking doorways and the dingy breezeways between building units.

Calignes signalled back 'clear' and the three Marines took up firing positions on the left side of the street.

Priad gestured again, his right hand this time, power-gloved. Another three fingers, crackling electricity.

Andromak led Illyus and Natus down the right side. There was a longer wait, as Natus checked an open side barn that the farmers had used to store broken machinery and trash. He emerged and shook his head in a clear, over-emphatic gesture.

Andromak checked the main entrance of what appeared to be the town hall. He turned back and made a gesture of clasping his hands together that Priad knew meant 'locked' or 'chained'.

Priad strode across to Memnes, who was gazing around the dismal place speculatively. Priad's massive armoured feet splashed through puddles of gore-like rainwater that had accumulated in the gouged tracks of the muddy street. It was like being in an abattoir that hadn't been cleaned in decades.

'Like Flax, you think, Brother-Apothecary?' Priad asked, his vox-burst punctuated at start and finish by a click of static.

Memnes shook his head. 'Something feels different, sergeant. Oh, we may find the townsfolk butchered in some corner, as Calignes did in Flax, but there is something else...'

Memnes snapped open the faceplate of his helmet and slid it up so that the red drizzle flecked his bare face. Had any other member of Damocles done such a thing without permission, Priad would have reprimanded him for presenting a target. But Memnes, old Memnes, had more experience than the others put together, and he could breathe in signs of danger. Sometimes, Priad knew well, it paid to let him scent the location.

'Fear, anticipation, anxiety... the air is heavy with it. There are living souls here, even though our auspexes don't show them.'

'Hiding?'

'I would think so…'

Priad wondered if he should open the Rhino's tannoy and hail the hidden people with a declaration of support and rescue. He decided against it. The quiet was unnerving but somehow he had no wish to break it.

Priad crossed to where Andromak and Natus stood by the doors of the town hall. Pausing only to allow the pair to raise their weapons ready, he smashed the doors in with one savage kick. A broken trailer chain dragged across the floor from the splintered doors. Someone had locked themselves in.

The trio entered, guns chasing for targets. The room, a huge hall with wooden pillars, was dark, and the floor was scattered with debris. One massive skylight far above was shattered, and rain streamed in, flooding the floor. Natus tried the wall lever for the lights, but the power was out. They switched to night vision and saw the place in a ghostly green phosphorescence.

'The floor is flooded. Rain,' Natus's voice crackled over the link.

'Not all of it,' answered Andromak. He had reached a far corner that was slick with red liquid though it was far away from the hole in the roof lights. 'That's rain. This is blood.'

He was right. It was impossible to tell where the rain ended and the blood began, but by any standards, there was a lot of blood. It splashed and smeared the walls, and there were smudges and occasional hand prints, but no sign of corpses.

Priad moved through to a council chamber behind the main hall. There was more blood here too, soaking the hessian rugs and the soft furnishings of the rows of seats. The far end wall was covered in framed placards listing the names of the town's mayors and the annual harvest yields in proud gold leaf. The boards were peppered and riddled with small-arms fire, punctured, holed and splintered. Priad realised there were thousands of spent shell cases littering the bloody floor.

'Quite a fight,' said Andromak beside him.

'What were they shooting at?' Natus asked, moving forwards past them. He pointed, and to their expert eyes it was clear that the gunfire damage made distinct arcs and sprays across the wall, as if sustained automatic fire had been trying to chase and catch targets that had moved with frightening speed.

Andromak kicked open a door to the left, off the council room, and found store closets and filthy cloakrooms. Blood covered the grimy blue tiles in here too, and the wooden latrine stalls had been shot apart by frenzied automatic fire.

Behind the council room, down a long, onyx tiled hallway, they found a chapel dedicated to the Emperor depicted as the provider of bounty and fruitful harvest. But the statue of the Emperor, holding a sword in one hand and a ploughshare in the other, had been decapitated, and the altar rails blasted into matchwood by more gunfire.

One of the loathsome daemon-form dolls, what Inquisitor Mabuse had called, as if it was some wry joke, a Khorne-doll, had been nailed to the statue's chest. Words composed of letters and symbols so foul they made Priad sick to see them had been daubed across the plinth.

Beside him, the sergeant heard Natus cough and gag in his helmet, choking on his rising gorge.

'Brother Natus?'

Natus, over the link, made a mewling noise. Even the strongest of the phratry could fall prey to the insidious horrors of Chaos, and this abomination had them all stunned and revolted. To desecrate the image of the Emperor with these marks...

Priad knew he needed Natus sharp. Despite the horror that was in him too, he turned on his brother Snake.

'Natus!'

Natus couldn't form a coherent word. Priad raised his left fist and smashed the back of his hand across Natus's armoured face plate. The warrior reeled, his visor dented.

'Compose yourself, brother! This is precisely what the Darkness wants! This is why they performed this sacrilege! To un-man the likes of you!'

'I-I'm sorry, brother-sergeant,' said Natus, stunned back into rational thought.

Priad raised his bolter, swung around and blasted the deformed statue and the corn-doll into fragments with a burst of explosive rounds. The noise was deafening.

The vox-links exploded into urgent life.

'Weapons fire! We heard weapons fire!'

'Brother-sergeant? Respond?'

'What's going on in there?'

'Stand easy,' Priad replied, exchanging the clip of his boltgun deftly. 'Just a little cleaning up. No targets. But the enemy is here. Be vigilant.'

OUTSIDE, ACROSS THE street, Xander heard his brother-sergeant's words. With Calignes and Pindor, he held the positions on the left side of the thoroughfare.

A small white dot showed on his auspex suddenly, moving and jinking in a disordered pattern. Fifteen paces off, behind the row of agri-shops and smithies.

'Contact!' he reported.

Calignes and Pindor saw it too, and the trio swung around to address the buildings on the left side. Memnes crossed to them, readying his boltgun. Kules moved the Rhino up a little, with Scyllon sweeping the storm bolter.

Xander looked back at Memnes. 'Do we go in?'

'Brother-sergeant?' Memnes queried.

'We're coming out,' Priad returned over the link. 'Move in.'

Xander and Memnes moved off the street down a littered breeze-way, a side alley that took them along behind the store barns and smithies into the back yards of shanty habitat terraces. Calignes and Pindor broke open the door of a tractor shed and advanced through the gloomy interior, passing farm vehicles under tarpaulin wraps. Rusty chains dangled from the low beams of the roof. The pair made a parallel course to Xander and Memnes, marking the blue dots of the Space Marines on their auspex scanners. The white dot blinked ahead, between the two fronts.

Xander and Memnes pushed through a back gate made of rain-warped pulp board and slid along a crumbling brick wall, thick with black moss and lichens. They were in a narrow back ditch behind the habitats where they backed on to the farm shops and the tractor shed.

The light was bad and the rain heavier. The swirling black clouds seemed to be right down low over their heads. Even with night vision optics, visibility was poor.

'There,' said Memnes, his visor still raised, pointing ahead. 'It's in that outbuilding.'

The structure was a single storey lean-to of corrugated iron. Xander and Memnes advanced and approached the entrance at the western end, furthest from the main street. Calignes signalled that he and Pindor were approaching the other end from the back of the tractor shed.

Xander tried the door, easing the handle down, testing for locks.

Something came out of the lean-to, taking the door off its frame and slamming it into Xander. The force was so great that the massive armoured warrior was thrown backwards and through the mouldering wall on the other side of the ditch. He took down a section of rotting bricks and ended up on his back in the yard of one of the terraced habitats.

Just behind him, Memnes braced and fired, raking a bright line of explosive bolts through the air that blew out the framework of the lean-to's left side. He tried to track the shape that had exploded out of the shed and floored Xander. It was all he could do to see it.

He glimpsed a quadruped, long and lean, twice the size of a man, it seemed. It was as blood-red as the rain. Memnes saw a suggestion of teeth, huge as scythe blades; of claws; of a whipping tail, as long and knobbed and gristly as a length of human spine.

All his shots missed, but they drove the thing back into the lean-to.

He charged after it. 'Calignes! For the love of Terra! It's coming your way!' he bellowed into his link.

At the far end of the shed, Calignes and Pindor tensed and trained fire, but were still too slow. A red blur, something they couldn't even see but knew must be there, burst out of the shed and leapt up over their blasting guns.

Calignes felt a hard impact and lurched away, winded and dazed, falling sideways and hard into a stack of tractor wheels. He heard Pindor exclaim over the vox. An utterance of surprise, roughly cut off.

Priad, Andromak and Natus, with Illyus close behind, came out of the rear of the tractor shop at a run. They found Calignes slumped against the rusting wheel hubs. Something had ripped through the front of his chest plating, making three jagged stripes in the ceramite. Blood leaked out of the torn armour.

There was no sign of Pindor except his fallen bolter.

\* \* \*

## IV

THEY REGROUPED AT the Rhino. Scyllon and Natus carried Calignes in and tended to his wounds. The rents were deep and refused to clot. Blood wept out of him like rainwater. Xander was dazed but intact.

Priad tuned up the Rhino's main auspex and hunted for Pindor, chasing the tell-tale trace of his armour, the identifying signal. There was nothing. It was as if Brother Pindor had simply vanished.

Memnes could see how black Priad's mood was, and how spooked Damocles was as a whole. They were all used to the superiority of being Adeptes Astartes, and on the rare occasions they encountered something more formidable, it left them dazed. For himself, Memnes couldn't begin to account for the speed of the thing. It had moved so fast, so powerfully, he hadn't even seen it clearly.

'I must find him,' Priad told Memnes quietly. 'Alive or dead, I will find Pindor.'

Memnes nodded. He expected no less of his brave sergeant.

'I simply won't accept that he's just vanished.' Priad cast a dour look at the Rhino's auspex unit. 'You felt life here, and we haven't found that on our scopes either.'

'I felt something, brother-sergeant. It may have been that thing.'

'You felt fear, old friend. That thing faced down four Iron Snakes and took one of them as a trophy. It was not afraid.'

'True. So we cannot trust the auspex.'

'No, indeed!' said Priad. 'Something's blocking it – something that's hiding Pindor, the locals… and that thing.'

'Except at close range. Xander drew us to it when he got a fix.'

Priad mused. 'Adamantium sometimes blocks auspex scans.'

'There's none of that here, I fancy. Nor do I know of any local substance that can kill Imperial scans. If the auspexes can't be trusted, it's because of… of witchery. The talents of the dark to lie and befuddle.'

'Aye, I thought as much. All our instruments are blind. You were the only one who even glimpsed it.'

'My visor was raised,' noted Memnes.

Priad opened his own visor and turned to the men. 'We hunt a great evil that is invisible to our instruments. Open your visors. Use your eyes well.'

It was… unheard of, but they all obeyed. They opened their helmets and made themselves vulnerable, so as to be less vulnerable.

'Search teams!' ordered Priad, his voice sounding strange and raw, unfiltered by the vox-link. 'Section the town and take it apart!'

THE EIGHT REMAINING active members of Damocles squad searched Hekat, basement by basement, attic by attic, barn by barn, silo by silo. They worked in pairs. Calignes, whose wounds had at last been staunched by skin-wrap sprays from Memnes's narthecium, stayed with the Rhino, watching the streets from the turret.

As he searched, partnered by Kules, Priad wondered if he should report in to Phobor and Mabuse at Nybana. He didn't know what he could tell them or what advice he could hope they would offer. In the end, he settled for a simple battle code message, saying they had engaged the cult and were pursuing its destruction.

Several urgent responses came from Nybana, promising reinforcement. Some were from Mabuse, demanding to know the nature of the cult.

Away from the Rhino, Priad ignored the chime of the vox messages. He would do this his way. He would find Pindor and salvage the situation.

In the Rhino, Calignes heard the beep of the vox-caster, demanding response. It would involve a great deal of pain to climb down into the cabin, so he screened it out.

Like Brother-Sergeant Priad, he was sure there was nothing the power of Damocles squad couldn't overcome. Besides, by the time help came, it would be days too late.

## V

ILLYUS AND SCYLLON found them in the basement crypts of the Ecclesiarchy temple at the north end of the main street. Three hundred and fifty farmers and family members, cowered terrified behind locked and barricaded doors.

Why the auspexes hadn't sensed them, none of Damocles could say.

Under Memnes's supervision, the civilians were brought out and taken to shelter in the farmstead's mess hall, a long, low building full of trestle tables and crude metal chairs. Medical aid was provided by the Apothecary, and Scyllon and Xander were set to guard them while Natus broke open the stores and made food for them on the mess hall's ranges.

Priad and Andromak questioned the farm leaders, three scared and emaciated men.

'We heard what happened at Flax, so we decided to hide. Some… thing came, killing dozens. That's when we hid in the crypt.'

'This thing… what is it?' asked Priad.

'For the love of the Emperor, my lord, we didn't even see it!'

'It came in! It slaughtered!'

Priad looked over at Andromak. 'So Hekat is to be made a sacrifice like Flax?'

'It seems so, brother-sergeant… and therefore the cultists are hiding out there in the corn fields.'

Priad got up and stalked the room. Something wasn't right. He could feel that as plainly as he was sure Memnes felt his 'scents'.

The doll back at Nybana clearly marked this place as a cult centre, or at least a place were cultists were active. Yet there was nothing here but townsfolk driven underground by some beast, and an attempt made to bleed the populace for the worship of some otherness deity.

Which was it? A cult centre or an innocent place? It couldn't be both.

And if it was innocent, what of the doll at Nybana? What had been its purpose?

To… bring them here?

The leader of the farmers broke off his reverie. 'You will save us, won't you, brave Space Marine? For the love of the Emperor! Please!'

Priad nodded. He would. He swore it.

ILLYUS AND KULES were searching the grain silos at the eastern edge of Hekat when the rains came down in a torrent. Flash floods of grain and squirming weevils burst from the sodden hoppers and washed around their feet. Illyus kept wanting to close his visor to shut out the blood rain, but Priad's instructions had been clear. He moved forward into the pelt, his gun ready.

Illyus had lost an eye on Eidon, and his bionic implant twitched and irked him. When he glimpsed the red shape flashing through the rain, he first thought it a ghost image, a phantasm conjured by his artificial organ.

Then he realised he could only see it through his real eye.

All that they had surmised was true. The thing that stalked Hekat was only visible to naked sight. Mechanics and bionics, auspexes and scanners were worthless.

Illyus began to fire – and to cry out.

Kules ploughed over to join him, his own gun blazing, in time to see the great bestial thing, with its whipping spinal chord tail, flying out of the rain to take Illyus down.

Kules emptied his clip into the monster. It was busy killing Illyus and thus formed a stationary target for an instant. If it hadn't paused to rip Illyus asunder, it would have been moving too fast for Kules to see.

He blew it apart with a dozen placed shots. Tissue and bloody matter exploded into the downpour.

Kules's sense of triumph was short-lived. Illyus had been decapitated and eviscerated by the thing in the blink of an eye. The dead Iron Snake lay sprawled beneath the exploded carcass of the daemon.

Kules opened his vox-channel and reported in.

'We have slain the beast!' Priad exclaimed to the farm folk around him.

'Damocles, with me! You people stay here until we return. Your nightmare is at an end.'

Damocles squad formed up and left the mess hall.

None of them noticed the disquieted looks the farmers gave them.

KULES WATCHED OVER Illyus's body and waited for the others of Damocles to arrive. He tried to imagine what the thing's purpose had been. To kill and terrify the township, that was certain. But what else? Why had it been here? What had it been protecting?

Despite his orders, Kules crept forward and entered a silo to the left of the alley. What he saw chilled him to his soul.

In the open metal bin of the silo's base, an altar had been arranged. Candles fluttered and hideous patterns had been inscribed on the walls.

Pindor hung, upended, on a crucifix made of baler twine and wire. He had been tortured and abused, his armour stripped off. The Children of Khorne, twenty of them, resembling those Kules and his Iron Snakes brethren had slaughtered in Nybana, stood around, performing a ceremony.

Pindor was clearly close to death.

One of the cultists turned and saw Kules. He cried out in alarm. In an instant, the twenty ritual heathens turned and pulled out automatic weapons, blasting up at the silo's entrance aperture that framed the Iron Snake.

Kules slammed down his visor and waded into the chamber, percussive rounds pinging off his power armour. He opened fire, swinging his boltgun, exploding one cultist after another.

When he reached the crucifix, he used his blade to cut Pindor down and pulled his naked, limp form into his embrace.

'I'll get you out of here, brother,' Kules said.

It wasn't going to be that easy.

## VI

As INQUISITOR MABUSE later concluded in his summation of the Ceres outbreak, the main cult centre was Hekat township, and not Nybana at all. When the main uprising in Nybana was overthrown, the cultists had left deliberate traces to draw the Iron Snakes to the remote harvest town, where they intended to perform a sacrifice.

The beast that Kules had killed… that had just been a diversion, a guardian force summoned forth from the warp to keep the Marines busy. Hekat and its people, all converted to the Khorne belief, wanted an Astartes as a sacrifice. If they could ritually spill the blood of one of the Emperor's own, they could vouch a spell that would crack open the heavens and let loose an avatar of damned Khorne himself.

PRIAD LED HIS detail through the streets to support Kules, and they found themselves attacked from all sides by the very farmers they had sworn to save. For the first time in his life, Brother-Sergeant Priad realised he was going to have to break a sworn pledge.

The cultists, who but minutes before had seemed to be ailing farm workers eager for help, came at them from all sides. They were feral, insane.

'Kill them! Kill them all!' Priad told his men as they fought towards the silo.

Their armour and their bolters were a match for the superior numbers of the cultists, but barely.

Andromak lost a finger to an auto-round.

Xander fell and was beaten half to death with ploughshares before Natus pulled him free.

Scyllon took a scythe blade in the arm and bled for weeks.

The rampaging cultists overwhelmed the Rhino in the main street. Calignes, weak from blood loss, had almost passed out. They set it ablaze and ripped him limb from limb.

Memnes fell, without a sound, a bullet through his exposed face.

Priad reached the silo and slaughtered the cultists around them. He was as red with blood as with rain. He reached Kules and helped him drag Pindor clear.

Then, with his power claw blazing, he set about finishing the grim business, revoking his pledge and killing the traitorous farmers rather than saving them.

At dawn the next morning, he was done.

Memnes, Calignes and Illyus were dead. So were four hundred and seventy cultists.

A VICTORY, OF sorts. It didn't feel that way to Priad. He ignored Inquisitor Mabuse's attentions as he led his battered squad into its departure shuttle.

'You have done a fine job, Priad. The Emperor will laud you.' Mabuse's voice was lofty as ever.

'I walked my men into a trap you should have seen, inquisitor,' Priad replied as the hatches closed. 'Next time Emperor willing, you will do better.'

The hatches slammed. Bearing their noble dead, Damocles left Ceres and returned to the void of space.

Below them, unceasingly the blood red rain fell.

# PART FIVE
# CRIMSON WAKE
## Ithaka

# I

ITHAKA. PROUD ITHAKA. *Ocean world. Cradle of Snakes. The armoured drop-ship turns like a comet in high altitude, streaming fire like a falling star. On its white-hot hull, the double-looped serpent insignia of the Iron Snakes Chapter glows, incandescent…*

PRIAD UNLOCKED HIS seat restraints and lumbered in full armour to the nearest porthole. He stood with his hands braced against the hull wall either side of the port. Beneath him, through the luminous streams of re-entry fire, he saw the oceans, the dark tumult of vast, cold water, the thrashing frenzy of the deep, Ithakan seas.

The drop-ship swooped, levelled and ceased to burn. It skimmed low over the ocean face, assailed by hurricane salt-winds and kilometre-high waves. Seunenae, the folding wall of iron, bane of every wyrm-hunter.

Priad saw the bright reflection of the racing drop-ship flashing off the dimpled, roiling darkness below. He saw marysae, the white water foam. He saw the boiling cauldrons of ulbrumid, the wyrm-spoor.

Ithaka. Proud Ithaka. Ocean World. Cradle of Snakes.

They would be making planetfall soon, in a minute or two. Time for the squad leader to unscrew the copper flask and make the Rite of the Giving of Water.

Priad had not been home for ten years. And this was home. This was Ithaka.

Salt-water ran from his eye corners. The Rite had begun. Removing his glove, Priad wiped the tears from his eyes and marked the emblem of the Iron Snakes on the bulkhead. His men watched him do it.

Sometimes the Rite was special. Sometimes, you didn't need the flask.

The drop-ship streaked west across the sky like a tracer round, over the fishing villages and orub-groves of the archipelagos, basking in the sun, out towards the stilt-rocks of the Primarch's Causeway. These great towers of rock rose from the water like spines in a two hundred and eighty-eight-kilometre curve where the archipelagos met the open ocean.

Priad had already given the drop-ship's pilot instructions. The ship slowed, adjusted and hove down towards Sulla's Rock, a thirty-metre stack dominating the trailing western lines of the Causeway. Ocean faring hookbeaks and smaller littoral scale-birds burst from their roosts on the stack at the shrill sound of the dro-ship's downjets. They mobbed and circled, clacking bills and crying into the wind, the sunlight flashing off their grey flight-scales. White water boomed and erupted around the stack's base.

The drop-ship shuddered and settled on the flat top of the stack, its three landing claws extended and firm. The hatch opened with a clank, flooding the cabin with cold sea-air and the boom of the ocean.

They felt it on their faces. All of Damocles squad were un-helmed. Priad led them out into the buffet of the stack top. As one, they breathed in the clean metallic stir of the open water. It was overwhelmingly intense.

For long periods of time, their senses had been siphoned through the relay systems of their armour. Now they were exposed, raw, in the wind. The olfactory receptors built into their skulls amplified the scents of the place a millionfold. Priad sighed. He could smell the ozone in the fleeting wind, the lime-stink of the scale-birds guano.

He could detect the aroma of saline mucus in the bivalves clamped to the stack's base, the oil slick of a sounding rocaloe shoal ten kilometres out and the citrus in a glass of grain alcohol poured twenty kilometres away in a waterside tavern in the archipelago.

Too much.

Priad crunched across the salt-crusted rock to the lip. Below him, at his toes, a giddying drop to the water. Hookbeaks turned and banked in the rising spray, cutting through the brief rainbows the vapour made.

He looked back to his men: Kules, Xander, Pindor, Natus, Andromak with the snake-standard flapping between his shoulder blades, and Scyllon. The pilot and his assistant had also emerged from the drop-ship, kneeling a little way behind the main group to show their respects.

'In the name of the primarch who sired us, in the name of the Chapter which binds us, in the name of the God-Emperor who rules us, in the name of Ithaka... let this which was Ithaka's be Ithaka's again.'

Priad unstoppered his copper flask and let the last of the water trickle out. The spattering droplets fell away down the side of the stilt, twinkling in the sun. This was the Rite of Returning. Every Iron Snake carried a flask of sacred life-water from his homeworld to anoint his actions across the galaxy, for the life-water comes from the ocean and the ocean is the blood of the Emperor. Now, on returning, what little remains must be given back.

One by one, the men stepped to the brink and poured the contents of their own flasks away. When all had finished, Priad, Andromak and Xander returned to the edge and emptied three flasks whose owners had not made it home. The life-waters of Calignes, Illyus and beloved Memnes. Then Kules, Scyllon and Natus stepped forward, bringing the eusippus, the copper urns. As the oldest of Damocles, this last duty fell to hawk-eyed Pindor, not the sergeant.

As Priad intoned the Lament of Dysse, Pindor unscrewed the lid of each eusippus in turn and shook out the grey ash. Soft, loose, light, it sieved away into the wind and returned like the water to the sea. They could smell it. Microscopic motes on the wind. The smell of death and glory.

Calignes. Illyus. Memnes. Fallen to the archenemy on Ceres. Gone, but never forgotten. In his armour's hip-pouch, Priad had the prepared statement of their lives, actions and deaths, sealed and ready to be placed into the archive of the Chapter House.

'Look!' said Pindor, catching Priad's arm. 'Look, there!'

Out beyond the stilts, barely a kilometre distant, the ocean boiled and seethed. Ulbrumid. Wyrm-spoor. The great whirl was midnight black under the churning froth of white water. Thousands of sea birds wheeled and spiralled above the massive upsurge.

For a moment, one great serpent coil broke the froth, horn-plate dazzling as it caught the light. Then it was gone, the ulbrumid fading, and the sea birds dispersing.

'A good sign, a good omen,' said Pindor.

Priad nodded. The great snakes of Ithaka had taken back their own.

## II

'You HAVE PERFORMED the due rituals?' asked Lexicanium Phrastus. Priad nodded.

'Sir, the Rite of Returning is done. This morning, on the home-world below. We went there directly before coming here.'

'I see.' Phrastus walked round to his writing lectern and took a holoquill from the energy well. 'Their names?'

Priad had been gazing out of the tower chamber's pressurised window, looking across the rockcrete fortifications and the barren crags of the moon to where Ithaka, green-white, was rising over the horizon.

'Names?'

'Of the fallen, sergeant.'

'Ah.' Priad sighed. 'Calignes, Illyus, Memnes.'

The lexicanium wrote the names down.

'Any record of deeds?'

Priad took the sealed scroll from his hip-pouch and handed it to the lexicanium. 'Full orders of merit, in detail and all particulars. They all have my highest commendation.'

'These will be catalogued.'

Priad unslung the narthecium from his shoulder and placed it on a side table. Inside, in self-locking sterilised tubes, lay the precious progenoid glands taken from the fallen. With Memnes dead, Priad had been forced to cut the glands out himself.

Phrastus rang a bell and summoned Apothecaries to take the narthecium away.

'You will need new blood,' said Phrastus, setting aside his quill and coming to join Priad.

'Yes.'

'Captain Phobor has asked me to personally assist in your selection.'

'I am honoured, sir.'

'I have prepared a list of phratry petitioners, all of them new recruits of the highest quality. They are itching for selection into an active squad. And Damocles has a worthy reputation.'

'I'm glad of that, sir.'

'You lost your Apothecary, didn't you?'

'Memnes. Yes, sir.'

'That is the hardest choice, in my experience. There are two promising candidates, both newly raised to that rank. Sykon and Eibos. I'm sure one or other will suit your needs.'

'I'm sure, sir. But I was hoping for Khiron. I heard what happened on Cozan. I thought–'

'Khiron? Oh no, no. I'm sorry, brother. That just won't be possible.'

Priad looked around. The scent of the Chapter House seemed suddenly intensely sterile and cold.

'Not possible?'

'The Emperor grant you grace,' said the lexicanium. 'Welcome back to Karybdis, brother.'

KARYBDIS. FORTRESS MOON. Chapter House. Barefoot and dressed in a loose white chiton, Priad stood on the marble deck of the observation platform at the summit of the Chapter House's fortress. From here, he could see out across the mighty defences of the Iron Snakes' bastion, across the sloped turrets of the primary emplacements, the massive curtain walls, the hardpoint blisters of the void batteries like sea urchins. He could smell stone, promethium, fyceline, oils. The crude power. This was where the Iron Snakes' legacy took flesh, and from here they marched out to conquer the stars in the Emperor's name.

Priad had spent two hours in the armour-drome with his men as Chapter functionaries slowly removed and blessed every segment of their Mark VII battle plate and took it away for overhaul and repair. Then an hour soaking in the warm baths of the balneary, in deep dishes sculpted from the polished coil-plates of great wyrms. Then the plunge pools and the cold scrubs, the brusque ministrations of the wooden thryxus to purge and scruff the skin and exo-skeleton, the application of warm, glossy orub-oil, the salving of sore body plugs and inflamed bio-link sockets.

Their hair had been oiled, combed out and coiled; their faces shaved and smeared with depilatory wax. All Iron Snakes in the regular troop levies were clean shaven. The wax treatment kept their faces smooth for years at a time. The irritation of bristles and whiskers growing under a full-face helmet that might be worn for months at a time was considered a distraction from the focus of combat.

Washed, oiled, scrubbed, anointed. Priad felt cleaner and rawer than he had in years. His skin tingled. The perfume from the oils and unguents adorning him seemed noxiously sweet. They assaulted his armourless, superhuman senses, sickly, invasive.

And he felt light, superhuman. Like he could jump up, break through the sky with his hands and never come down.

He hadn't realised what a weight the armour had become, no matter the strength and invincibility it gave him in battle. He had become used to its burdensome weight, and the focusing muzzle it had put on his senses. In truth, he had not been out of armour for any real length of time in ten years.

Ten years. Ten years ago, he had stood on this very deck, similarly robed and similarly cleansed. He had gazed out over the fortress of Karybdis and rejoiced. He had been Troop-Brother Priad, newly selected for Damocles by Sergeant Raphon and Apothecary Memnes.

Now he was back again. As Brother-Sergeant Priad, in Raphon's place. And Memnes too was dead.

Priad was painfully aware of the way honour had passed into his hands. He looked down at them, surprised to see them human and bare. It felt wrong that the great power claw wasn't clenching as he closed his hand.

He had held the squad together well since Raphon's death. They had taken victories on Ceres and Eidon, though Ceres had been especially bitter. Now he had to remake it. Almost a third of the squad had to be reselected and inducted.

Priad looked up at the stars, as he often did when in search of guidance, no matter what part of the galaxy he found himself in. He didn't know even half the names – that was the job of a Librarian or an Apothecary – but he usually found meaning in their display and formation. The God-Emperor of Mankind was in the stars, in every one of them, after all.

Directly above him was the tight band of the Reef Stars, the linear constellation to which Ithaka belonged. Though the Iron Snakes travelled far and wide in the service of the Emperor, this cluster was their particular battleground. Since the start of Imperial time, the Chapter had policed the Reef Stars and undertaken to keep them safe, especially against the influx of the dark eldar, their oldest enemy.

'Sometimes the great, old wyrms will submerge for years at a time,' said a low voice, 'but not so deep as your thoughts now, boy.'

Priad turned, and immediately dropped to his knees. There was a sudden, saintly odour of power and electrical machines.

'Chapter Master!' he gasped, making the sign of the aquila.

'Get up, boy. The Emperor in his wisdom gave you sturdy legs, so use them.'

Priad rose slowly, his head down.

'Look at me, Priad.'

Priad gradually raised his head.

Chapter Master Seydon was just a shadow: robed, mysterious and towering. His cloak was made of broken, polished wyrm-horn pieces linked together like a jigsaw puzzle by gold wire. Slow respiration throbbed from the exchanger tanks under his cloak. His head was cowled, but there was a suggestion of inner light coming from where his eyes should have been.

He was a good metre taller than Priad.

'Master...'

'There are many things an Iron Snake might be allowed to fear, boy: the massed legions of the Archenemy... the hordes of the greenpigs... the swarms of the accursed hives... but I am not one of them. Slow your pulse and your breathing, Priad. Be calm.'

'I had not expected to see you, lord.'

'I make it a point to see those Snakes who return after a long absence, especially those I am fond of. Damocles squad – now, I've been fond of that ever since I told Damocles to form it. One of the finest war-squads this Chapter has ever produced. One of the Notables, right up there with Thebes, Veii, Parthus and dear, brave Skypio. And you, Priad, you're Damocles now.'

'Yes, lord.'

'Petrok spoke well of you. On Eidon, you impressed him, and it takes a lot to impress my illustrious Librarian.'

'I am not worthy, lord.'

'They tell me Memnes is dead. I will lament that in the temple. A great loss.'

'Lord.'

'Who else?'

'Calignes. Illyus.'

'Calignes… I always liked him. Had an air of old Pheus about him, the way he carried himself. Illyus… now he had the mark of a leader on him. Might have led a squad of his own, one day.'

Priad was quietly amazed. Though the phratry numbered a thousand Marines, the Chapter Master spoke as if he knew every one of them personally.

'You'll miss the men most in the long run,' said Seydon.

'Sir?'

'A great man like Memnes, everyone will mourn. That'll make the loss easier. But Calignes, Illyus… in my experience, a squad leader will miss the common troopers most. No one mourns them in quite the same way as a squad commander who misses their nuances and moves.'

'I'm sure, lord. But Memnes is a great loss to me.'

'Naturally. You've thought about a replacement?'

Priad nodded. 'I was bold, lord. I wanted an experienced man as Apothecary. Khiron–'

'Not Khiron, boy. Forget about him. Khiron won't be joining a squad again.'

'Lord, I… I heard what happened on Cozan. All of Ridates squad lost except for Khiron the Apothecary. It surely wasn't his fault.'

Seydon turned and looked out across the moonscape.

'No, it wasn't. Men die in war, and Ridates squad fell valiantly. Khiron was lucky to survive, and I know for a fact he wishes he hadn't. I'd have liked to have him back in a squad quickly. But it is more recent events that bar him from consideration.'

'Lord?'

'Look elsewhere, Priad. Look to your heart. I know you'll make a good choice.'

'Thank you, lord. I will try, but...' Priad's voice trailed away.

As silent as a phantom, the ancient Chapter Master had gone.

BROTHER NATUS GRUNTED and shifted his weight onto his left leg as the petitioner put his full force into the swing. The cnokoi he wielded whistled over Natus's right shoulder, and Natus pivoted around and brought his own staff up skilfully into the petitioner's ribcage, doubling him over and dropping him onto his backside on the straw mat.

Xander and Andromak laughed broadly and applauded. Natus grinned, and leaned over, reaching out with his augmented left arm to pull the gasping petitioner to his feet.

'Nice try,' Natus said, 'but your reach was wide and it left you open.'

'Sir,' the petitioner nodded, limping back to the edge of the mat where the other petitioners were waiting. At least three of them were sitting, nursing bruises and contusions.

Priad stood with Pindor, Kules and Scyllon on the far side of the sparring hall. Like all the Iron Snakes in the chamber – Damocles veterans and aspiring initiates alike – he wore a flexible bodyglove of dark grey hide, his feet, hands and head bare. The bodyglove was form-fitting, sculpted to the contours of the powerful physique beneath. Rubberised studs covered the lumps of cutaneous plugs and dermal implants.

Only Lexicanium Phrastus was robed. He wore a long grey euchoi of silk, edged with white and red beading and sat on a stone vaulting block, making notes on a data slate.

'Next man!' he called, flicking his fingers.

The next petitioner in line stepped onto the mat and picked up the discarded cnokoi. Two metres long and made of bronze, the cnokoi was a practice weapon designed to simulate the weight and balance of a sea-lance. There was no blade tip, but one end flared slightly into a blunt, spatulate flatness.

'Name?' asked Phrastus.

'Dyognes,' said the petitioner. He was tall and slender, his hair tied back behind the crown of his head in a short knot.

'Begin,' said the lexicanium.

Natus settled into a casual crouch, legs planted wide, the classic laoscrae or deck-stance that kept a man upright on a wake-rocked boat. He held his pole across his chest, upper tip angled out to deflect, lower pulled back ready to snap out an underhook from the waist when it was least expected. Dyognes, the petitioner, took up a similar but less stooped stance and they circled. He'll soon be knocked off his feet, Priad thought, his centre of balance is too high.

Dyognes swung his pole tip down at Natus, who deflected it with his own raised tip, immediately pushing out the underhook in response. But Dyognes blocked the hook with a bell-like clang of metal, swept in with his upper tip and, as Natus parried that, deftly slid both his hands to one end of his cnokoi and hooked it like an oar behind Natus's knees.

Natus landed on the mat hard, his breath barked out of him. Now it was the petitioners' turn to clap. Andromak and Xander laughed again.

'Good,' said Natus grudgingly as the petitioner helped him up.

'Again?' asked Dyognes.

'My turn,' said Scyllon, stepping forward onto the mat and taking the cnokoi from Natus as he withdrew. Next to Priad, Scyllon had the best record of any in Damocles when it came to wyrm-hunting, and he was a master of lance-craft.

Priad wandered over to Phrastus's side as the bout began.

'Interesting,' said the lexicanium. Dyognes was the first petitioner to have won a bout against the members of Damocles since the session had begun that morning.

Scyllon moved in without formality, barely seeming to prepare himself. He spun in with a flurry of blows, high and low, that had the younger man lurching back across the mat. The air rang with the strokes of bronze on bronze.

Just when it seemed he was going to be driven across the red out-of-bounds border around the edge of the mat, Dyognes rallied and threw a series of thrusting strikes that forced Scyllon to first duck and then back off. What marked the petitioner's ability particularly was his unorthodox style, Priad noticed. Dyognes frequently changed grip, so that many blows were readdressed and swiftly reversed, and he wasn't afraid to swing the cnokoi one-handed, increasing its reach.

Taking one hand off the staff in a bout was frowned upon, of course. Half as much grip... twice as much likelihood of having the weapon knocked from your grasp.

Dyognes blocked three expert thrusts from Scyllon, and then tore in with an underhook so well-timed Scyllon had to leap back to avoid having his ribs broken. But he was wrong-footed. Dyognes drove on the advantage, scything his pole out one-handed to clout Scyllon around the head.

But Scyllon had feinted. He brought his pole up and intercepted Dyognes's wrist. The petitioner's cnokoi went spinning away through the air. Scyllon then butted Dyognes in the chest with the tip of his pole and dropped him onto the mat.

There was general applause.

'Bout, Scyllon,' said Phrastus.

'No,' said Priad. The applause died down. Priad pointed to where Scyllon's left foot was squarely planted in the red border.

'Out of bounds. Bout, Dyognes.'

Scyllon cursed at his own error good-humouredly and helped Dyognes up.

'There's one,' said Priad to the lexicanium. 'Mark him down.'

### III

'HE KILLED BROTHER Krates of Phocis squad.'

'He what?' Priad snapped in disbelief.

'Lower your voice, brother. It's not a popular topic in the Chapter House these days. Khiron's disgrace has astonished everyone.'

Priad couldn't believe what he was hearing. He stood with his old friend, Brother-Sergeant Strabo of Manes squad, in the atrium of the Chapter House temple just at the end of twilight prayers. The columns of the portico rose above them, entwined with acanthus and bas-relief wyrms. In the alcoves stood proud kouroi statuary hewn from marble and faience. Priad was almost choking on the scents of the smouldering incense. His nose just wasn't used to such broad, unfiltered odours.

'Ridates, Phocis and Thebes were deployed on Cozan, so I heard,' Strabo whispered. 'The Archenemy was there in force, protecting some foul shrine or other. Ridates squad was wiped out, except for Khiron, and Phocis took some casualties before Thebes managed to turn the day and destroy the foe. They shipped back here with the wounded.'

'And?'

'Two days after they got back, Khiron walked into the apothecarium and put his boltgun to the head of Brother Krates, one of the wounded from Cozan. Just like that.'

'But... why?'

Strabo shrugged. 'They say Khiron claimed Krates was an instrument of the warp, and that he was protecting the Chapter. But there was no proof. It seems more likely that Khiron's mind had gone. The loss of his squad and everything. He's been locked away, raving, so I heard. There may be a trial, but more likely just... *oethanar.*'

Priad shook his head. It all seemed so unlikely. Khiron was one of the most level-headed and respected Apothecaries in the Iron Snakes. To lose his mind...

'You wanted him to take Memnes's place?'

'Yes,' said Priad.

'I'd leave it alone, brother. Look elsewhere. Khiron is no longer of the phratry.'

AFTER THE EVENING bell and a brief break for nourishment, the routines of combat practice recommenced. Damocles squad returned to the sparring hall to put some more petitioners through their paces.

Dyognes was a certainty in Priad's mind, and there had been two others with promise. Now, in the evening session, two more performed well, especially a thickset youth called Aekon.

Lexicanium Phrastus had also brought one of his suggestions for Apothecary, a blunt, grey-haired man called Sykon. Priad didn't take to this Sykon much, though it had less to do with the man's bearing and more to do with Priad's state of mind. Khiron was going round and round in his thoughts.

He'd known and admired Khiron since his own days as a petitioner, and indeed had been intending to try for Ridates squad when Raphon called him to Damocles. The selection to one of the Chapter's most prestigious squads, one of the Notables, had shocked and honoured him. Priad had not then recognised his own worth. Only afterwards did he discover that he was one of the top petitioners of his year and that several squad commanders had argued over him. Priad had been unusual in that he had not joined the Iron Snakes with any burning ambition for advancement. Many of the petitioners dreamed of induction into Skypio, or the Terminator elite. For Priad, it was enough just to be an Iron Snake. A place in one of the standard tactical squads like Ridates would have been more than enough for him. With hindsight, he wondered if that very lack of ambition had got him to where he was. Perhaps the Chapter commanders noticed him because he had been more concerned with solid warcraft and service than on promotion or glory.

It was certainly what he had seen as appealing in Dyognes and Aekon. They came to the mat with none of the strutting bravura of others. And those others usually left the mat on their hands and knees.

Priad conducted the last few bouts of the session himself. He tried not to take out his exasperation on the poor fools who came up against him, fumbling with the cnokoi as if they'd never held one before. He tried to remind himself that every one of these men had taken at least one water-wyrm single-handed. They were Ithaka's best. Priad left them gasping and spitting blood on the mat.

'That's it,' Priad called, and the group broke up. He handed the cnokoi to one of the petitioners to return it to the wall rack. Phrastus came over.

'I don't think I have to ask...' the lexicanium began.

'Unless you've got something better to show me tomorrow, sir, my choices are Dyognes and Aekon.'

'Good choices, I believe,' said Phrastus. 'At your word, I'll confirm the selection with Captain Phobor and then prepare the induction rites. They will be Damocles by the end of the month.'

He paused. 'About the Apothecary. His induction should take place at the same time.'

'Let me meet both candidates here tomorrow at seven, and I'll give you my choice after that. Bring the inductees too – Dyognes and Aekon, and the others we have marked as possible. I'll review them all one last time to be sure.'

'There is still time tonight, brother-sergeant.'

'Tomorrow, sir, please.'

THE THOLOS LAY beneath the Chapter House, founded deep in the rock crust of Karybdis. A punishment blockhouse it was, thanks to the meticulous discipline of the Chapter, seldom used. Its most common residents were prisoners of war, held pending interrogation under the watchful eyes of the Chapter Wardens.

Phybos, the night's duty-Chapter Warden, was a grizzled veteran who had lost both legs and an arm on Kinzia five decades before. He wore a long, grey beard and tied back hair, and his mechanical carriage grumbled as it carried him down the cold stone passage.

'This is irregular, brother-sergeant,' he complained.

'But permitted?'

'Yes. I suppose. Do you have a reason?'

'Do I need one?'

'You're the leader of Damocles squad, brother. No, you don't.' Phybos paused and tutted, shaking his head at something.

'Has he said much?'

'You're joking!' Phybos replied. He tutted again and yelled, 'Shut up, in the name of the primarch!'

Priad frowned. He had heard nothing.

'He's raving, raving night and day,' Phybos said, moving on. 'You hear that?'

Priad couldn't.

'You won't get any sense. And don't get too close to him, either.'

Phybos stopped in front of a heavy bronze door and slowly unlocked it, using the chain of keys around his scraggly neck. The door swung open to reveal an inner cage door, and beyond that, a gloomy cell containing Apothecary Khiron.

'There,' said Phybos. 'Raving, like I said.'

Khiron wasn't raving. He was seated at the back of his cell, silent, staring out at the open door with intense eyes. His face was bruised and purple around the nose and cheek.

'Leave us,' Priad said.

'Don't be too long, brother,' Phybos answered, and trundled away.

'Priad.'

'Brother Khiron.'

'No brother now, I'm afraid,' said the older man. 'I am cast from the phratry.'

'Why did the Chapter Warden say you were raving?' asked Priad, approaching the bars.

'Am I not raving? Am I not hurling abuse and torrents of blasphemy at the cage?'

'No.'

'I see. That's what most men think I'm doing.'

'Why?'

'Because th–' Khiron paused. 'It doesn't matter. I'm grateful you see me and not a deranged monster. But there's no point trying to explain it to you. It wouldn't do any good, and they'd just claim I was trying to deceive you.'

'I–' Priad began, but didn't really know what to say.

'Let me ask you a question,' said Khiron. 'Why have you come?'

'I couldn't believe the stories. I wanted to see for myself.'

'I'm a curiosity now, am I?'

Priad shook his head. 'I didn't mean it like that. Damocles lost Memnes on Ceres. I was hoping to induct you as a replacement. My choice has been… blocked.'

'Memnes… dead?' Real sadness clouded Khiron's wise, swollen face. 'Then we have both suffered our losses this season.'

'Ridates will be mourned. Brave brothers all.'

Khiron rose to his feet, but did not approach the bars. 'Crossfire. In a gully. Dead, all of them, in less than six minutes. Only some cruel chance spared me. Stray shots brought down the gully wall and I was buried in rubble. The impact broke my cheek and nasal bone, as you can see. The Archenemy thought I was dead too.'

He fixed his stare on Priad. 'I wish I could have done more for them. More than just dig their progenoid glands out of their cooling bodies, one by one.'

'You did all you could.' Quietly, Priad was trying to goad Khiron. If the loss of his squad really had snapped his sanity, these raw questions might expose that and convince Priad. But Khiron remained calm.

'Have they decided on a trial?' Priad asked.

'No. I have asked for oethanar. It is set for two sunsets hence.'

Oethanar. Trial by wyrm. The worst fate a man of Ithaka could undergo. Left alone and unarmed on a stilt rock, he would face the wyrms as they were summoned. If he was alive at the end of six hours, his guilt was determined. The water-wyrms would not touch the tainted. If they took him, he was one of Ithaka's and his innocence would be celebrated in funeral songs and grief rites.

'May they take you cleanly and quickly,' Priad said.

'Thank you, brother.'

Priad turned to leave and stopped. 'If you are facing oethanar anyway, tell me.'

'Tell you?'

'The truth of it as you know it.'

'The truth of it, eh?' Khiron sat down again. 'Aren't you afraid I'll taint your mind?'

'Just tell me.'

'A daemon, Priad. A thing of the warp. It was on Cozan, in the air, in the foliage, haunting us and directing the enemy beasts. It orchestrated the massacre of Ridates squad. But it was a cowardly, feral thing. When Thebes squad overran its minions, it fled and it hid.'

'Where?'

'Where? In Brother Krates. It was inside him when they brought him back, wounded. No one could see it. No one knew it was there. It blinded them all with its daemon glamour. But I knew it was there.'

'How?'

'I could smell it. I'd been close to it, remember. It had passed right by me after the massacre, believing me to be dead under the rockfall that smashed my face. I will not forget the smell.'

'What smell?'

Khiron looked up at the cell roof for inspiration. 'It has no equivalent. Once you smell it, you know it.'

'And that scent was on Krates?'

'Yes. It wasn't Krates any more. It was that thing, cackling and jubilant to have been brought inside the Chapter House, ready to strike at our heart. That's why I took my gun to poor Krates.'

'At least you can go to the wyrms knowing you stopped it.'

'No, Priad,' said Khiron, his face alarmingly serious. 'It's still here. I killed Krates but I didn't kill it. Like a fool, I used a gun instead of flames. It's moved on, into another host.'

Now Priad felt uneasy. This did seem like mad-talk to him. 'I haven't smelled anything.'

'Of course you haven't. It's gulled the whole Chapter House. But it's still here, be sure of that, tricking you all.'

Phybos reappeared suddenly and slammed his baton against the bars. 'Cease your raving, scum!' he shouted, though Khiron's voice had been low and soft. The old Chapter Warden turned to Priad. 'Haven't you heard enough?'

'I think I have,' said Priad.

THE HALL OF the balneary was quiet and dark, lit only by the lamps along the inner kolonos. The main bath pool was fifty metres square and filled with sacred sea water imported from Ithaka.

Priad stripped off his bodyglove and dived into the water. He swam a lap or two hard and then floated on his back, looking up at the starlight filtering in through the circular window in the domed roof.

He suddenly realised he wasn't alone.

Above the soft lapping of pool water against stone, he could hear the faint pat of bare feet on the kolonos.

He waited for a call of greeting or a splash, but none came. After a minute or two, he folded at the waist and cartwheeled down under the water. Submarine noise roared in his ears. In the low light, he saw the legs of men moving through the pool towards him on all sides.

Priad surfaced. Six men surrounded him, standing where the pool was shallow enough, confidently treading water where it was deeper.

They were the surviving members of Phocis squad.

'Priad of Damocles,' said one. 'You injure us.'

'I what?'

'We are wounded by Chaos and you take Chaos's side.'

'No! Why would you think that?'

'We know you spoke with Khiron,' growled another. 'That bastard is warp scum! He slew Krates! He did a daemon's work!'

'Why would you show him pity and talk with him?' asked yet another.

'I showed him nothing. I wanted the truth.'

'The truth?' snarled a man to his right.

'You would scorn Phocis squad so?' asked the warrior next to him.

'Brothers… I have nothing but respect for Phocis squad. Why have you come here like this? What is your intent?' Priad tensed. Inter-squad fighting was unheard of in the Iron Snakes, but he knew that in some rowdy Chapters, rivalry sometimes led to brawls between brothers.

Was Phocis's honour so damaged they had turned on him now? At the least, this was intimidation.

'Speak!' Priad persisted. 'What is your intent, brothers?'

'Enough!' A strong voice echoed from the pool side. Priad squinted, and made out the tall shape of Captain Skander, leader of Phocis squad.

'We've said what we needed to say,' Skander announced. 'Do not insult my squad again, Priad of vaunted Damocles.'

The members of Phocis withdrew, climbed out of the pool, and followed their commander out of the balneary.

Priad was left alone in the shadowy water.

### IV

IT WAS JUST after seven, three hours after dawn bell. Priad had rested badly, his mind more troubled than ever. Now he stood in the centre ring of a combat mat in the sparring halls, a cnokoi in his hands.

'Sir?' asked petitioner Aekon, edging out onto the mat to face him.

'Aekon?'

'You seemed to be elsewhere, sir.'

'As you were.'

Priad set the pole down and paused for a moment. On the mat next door, Xander was sparring with Dyognes. Near the arched doorway, Lexicanium Phrastus was introducing the Apothecary candidates Sykon and Eibos to Andromak and Pindor.

Down away, down the length of the sparring halls, Priad could see Captain Skander leading the men of Phocis through hand combat drill. Beyond them, Sergeant Strabo was conducting flamer practice with the men of Manes squad, and paidotribae were exercising other petitioners.

Priad's superhuman senses could smell burning promethium, sweat, furze and, from Phocis, the background taint of salt water from the pool the night before.

He had almost told Andromak and Pindor what had happened in the balneary, but didn't want to be responsible for a squad feud.

Shaking the thoughts off, Priad swung his cnokoi up.

'Let's begin,' he told Aekon.

They exchanged a few, paltry pole-to-pole hits. Priad knew he could block everything the youth hooked at him.

'You'll have to do better,' Priad said, adopting the laoscrae. His attention was caught by Captain Skander, yelling at one of his troopers while looking Priad's way.

Skander glowered.

'Sir?' Aekon asked, faltering.

'Let's begin, I said!' cried Priad and brought the bronze pole up at Aekon's face. The boy turned, and deflected Priad's follow-up.

Priad circled again, and blocked with his cnokoi.

He glanced sideways, and saw Skander was staring at him, as if he wanted Priad dead.

Priad fumbled.

Light and pain exploded behind his eyes. Taking advantage of the sergeant's momentary distraction, Aekon had struck him squarely across the nose with his cnokoi.

'Sir! Sir, I'm sorry!' he could hear the petitioner gabbling. 'I thought you'd block, I thought–'

Priad got up onto his knees, his head swimming. The boy had got a sound blow home. Priad's vision was fogged, and blood was pouring from his cracked nose, spattering across his chin and chest. There was a fuss of voices around him, and beyond them he could hear scornful cat calls and jeers from the men of Phocis and Manes squads.

He put his hands to his face. His nose was broken, and his left cheek bone too. The blow would have crushed a normal human skull.

'It's all right, Aekon,' Priad slurred, spitting blood. 'It was my fault for not concentrating. You saw an opportunity and took it. I'd have been more offended if you'd pulled the blow. There's no room in Damocles for men who show quarter to the enemy.'

He got up, blinking tears out of his eyes, feeling the soft tissue of his face beginning to swell as his enhanced metabolism dealt with the injury. Now he could smell nothing but the iron scent of blood, potent and stifling.

'Golden Throne, brother! The boy's hurt you worse than all the scum on Eidon ever managed!' chuckled Andromak, steadying his arm.

'Let me attend the wound,' said Sykon.

Priad shook them all off. 'Stop fussing over me like pack-mothers! Enough!' He could see better now and the self-sealing mechanisms of his augmented blood-vessels, along with the genetic clotting agents in his blood, were already staunching the flow. 'I'll go to the Apothecarion when this session is finished. Right now, Aekon and I are conducting a bout.'

He wiped his face with the back of his fist and left a smear of blood across his knuckles. Apart from the stink of blood, his sense of smell was registering nothing. Aekon's blow had probably damaged the olfactory augmetics too.

'Go, go!' he snapped, waving the anxious Aekon back to his starting place on the mat.

Blood. And more than blood.

Priad realised it suddenly. There was a smell, a strong scent behind the lingering dominance of his own blood. Sweet, yet stale. Soft, yet strong. It was…

It was like nothing he'd ever smelled before.

*It has no equivalent. Once you smell it, you know it.*

The smell of murder, of obscenity, of insanity. The smell of the warp.

'Brother-sergeant?' Aekon was staring at him, puzzled.

Priad ignored him, turning to scan the chamber. Close, so close by…

He could hear his own pulse beating in his temple like a drum. Where? Where?

Priad started to move, to run. He left Aekon standing on the mat. Over his shoulder, he yelled, 'Damocles, form and cover, Hades spread!' Stunned, reacting, the men of his squad broke from their bouts and conversations and leapt to follow him.

One bound took Priad onto the practice platform where Phocis squad was drilling. He shoulder barged one of the men who had intimidated him in the balneary and sent him sprawling. Another half turned, and Priad elbowed him aside.

'Skander!' he bellowed.

Captain Skander's eyes were wide in surprise.

Priad's cnokoi smashed him to the floor.

Dazed, Skander had wit enough to roll as Priad's next blow clubbed down. The bronze pole made a dent in the wooden platform.

The men of Phocis howled in rage. One made to grab Priad, but he wheeled and smacked the man backwards with the flat of his practice lance. Two more moved in, but suddenly the rest of Damocles were there, striking out, grappling, covering their leader's back.

Damocles were all dressed for cnokoi drill in grey bodygloves, carrying the metal poles. Phocis were all in half-armour, exercising with small oukae batons and small bucklers. Priad's men had the advantage of reach and hitting power, but Phocis were much better protected.

Andromak and Scyllon laid in with their poles, breaking shields and forearm guards. Natus smashed a baton from one man's hand and then caught him neatly on the chin with the head of his whirling pole. Xander, Kules and Pindor were wrestling with opponents of their own. One of Phocis cracked Natus hard across the clavicle with his baton and was about to do so again when Dyognes dropped him with a cnokoi-flat to the forehead.

Priad's attention was entirely on Skander. The captain expertly kicked away Priad's footing, and they crashed together over the edge of the platform and into the practice area occupied by Manes squad. Priad could hear voices – Strabo's amongst them – shouting for them all to desist. Men from Manes put down their flamers and ran to try and break up the fight. Several found themselves drawn into it.

Priad would not desist. Struggling hand-to-hand with Skander, he was almost suffocating in the warp stink oozing from the man.

Skander threw Priad over onto his back and heaved in with his oukae. The short hardwood pole shattered against Priad's cnokoi, but Skander followed in with a savage kick that broke two of Priad's fingers and sent the pole skidding away across the decking.

Priad ducked back and threw a punch that cracked Skander's head sideways. Pain flared up Priad's arm from his broken fingers. Skander undercut and punched Priad in the throat and then broke the edge of his buckler across Priad's reeling head.

'Enough! In the name of the primarch, enough!' Strabo screamed.

Breathing hard, Priad paused. For a moment, he wondered if he had indeed gone mad. Rage was pounding in his head. He glared at the bloody-faced Skander.

If this was all madness, then he would lose his command. Lose his place in the Chapter most likely.

Skander was raving at him, oaths and abuse. Priad couldn't smell the warp any more. He had made a fool of himself and disgraced the squad. He had–

He looked into Skander's eyes. There was something there. An after glow. A shadow. A corona of darkness around the pupils.

*Like a fool, I used a gun instead of flames. It's moved on, into another host.*

Priad stepped back and bumped into Strabo. His old friend was trying to hold him back and pin his arms. Priad wrenched free, and tore the flamer unit from Strabo's shoulder.

He swung back. Thumbed the toggle.

A cone of flame engulfed Captain Skander. He twisted and screamed as he was engulfed.

Alarms started ringing.

All the fighting had stopped. Damocles, Phocis and Manes alike, all the petitioners, the lexicanium, the paidotribae, stood in utter shock, staring at the collapsed human fireball.

And at the man who had burned him.

'What... what in the God-Emperor's name have you done...?' Strabo stammered.

'Look,' said Priad weakly. 'Look.'

Something disengaged itself from Skander's burning corpse. A small thing, leathery, flapping smouldering bat wings as if it hoped to fly away. It shimmered, as if it was made of smoke. Its fingers were tendrils of articulated bone and it had nothing but a hundred blinking eyes for a face.

The sound it made chilled the souls of every one present.

'You see it?' asked Priad.

'Y-yes...' murmured Strabo.

'Good,' said Priad, and hosed the daemon-thing with flame, annihilating it.

V

'I SAW IT with my own eyes,' Lexicanium Phrastus was telling Captain Phobor. The veteran Iron Snake was glaring at Priad, who sat on the edge of the practice platform, dabbing at his nose.

'I thought Sergeant Priad had gone mad at first, assaulting the captain like that,' Phrastus continued. 'But I saw it. A thing of the warp. A thing from inside Skander.'

'Priad!' growled Captain Phobor.

'Sir,' Priad said, getting to his feet. The men of Damocles fell in behind him, bruised and bloody-lipped from their brawling. Priad was impressed to see that Aekon and Dyognes took their place in the line.

'There will be questions, Priad. A lot of questions.'

'Sir.'

'From what the worthy lexicanium here says – and the other men besides – you may be exonerated, praised even.'

'Sir. I hope that what has happened here might assist in the case of Khiron too.'

Phobor paused. 'It's too late for him.'

'Sir?'

'At Captain Skander's personal request, Khiron was taken to Ithaka at first light. I'm sorry. Oethanar is already under way.'

THE SEAS AROUND the Primarch's Causeway were raging. White water marysae bloomed around the line of the stilt rocks, and a fierce storm was rolling in from the ocean.

Retyarion. Wyrm-storm. The ferocious squalls that seemed to follow the movement of the marine serpents. Soon, the seunenae, the folding walls of iron, would rise out in the deep waters and come crashing in, kilometres high.

'I can't go in any closer!' the shuttle's pilot wailed. 'The wind shear will break us on the rocks!'

'Damn you!' Priad snarled. 'Lower then! Drop height!'

'You're mad!'

'Do it!'

'Look at the auspex, in the name of Seydon!' the co-pilot shouted above the noise of the wind and the rain. 'Hard returns, coming up from the depths! *Kraretyer!*'

Priad saw the swirling green shapes on the scanner's dished screen. They were big. Perhaps not kraretyer, the giant bulls. But big. Three, four. Maybe five of them.

'Drop height!' Priad demanded again.

The shuttle's turbines shrieked as it came down over the water at less than ten metres. It was a hunting ketch, sleek and long-bodied, that Priad had virtually stolen from the Chapter House dock.

Priad scrambled back into the cargo bay where two lancing skiffs lay in hydraulic cradles. He ordered Scyllon, Xander and Kules into one, and leapt into the other himself. All of them were still clad in their grey bodygloves.

'Pindor! Andromak! With me! Natus… man the releases!'

Natus hurried to the aft position, pushing past the agitated and bemused petitioners Aekon and Dyognes. Priad wanted a good man at the release clamps. A clean clearance was a key part of a hunt run. And Natus knew that craft well.

Andromak caught Priad by the arm as he was unlashing the fore-tethers. The squad's standard bearer held out his right wrist. It was twisted, broken in the brawl.

'Stand out, brother, you're no use to me. You!' Priad pointed at Dyognes.

'Sir?'

'Can you hand lances?'

'Yes, sir!'

'Take his place!'

Dyognes helped Andromak out of the skiff and took his place midships, pulling the covers off the lances racked under the gunwales.

Priad looked up at Andromak, Aekon and Natus. 'Make sure our brother-pilot doesn't fly clear away. We'll need extraction.'

'Sir!' the trio chorused.

A bell clattered.

'Drop height!' sang out Natus.

'Prepare!' ordered Priad. He dropped down on one knee in the prow of his skiff and looped his hands into the side ropes, pain throbbing from his broken fingers. Behind him, Dyognes did the same, and Pindor braced himself at the slim vessel's aft.

In the other boat, Scyllon, Xander and Kules duplicated the stances.

'Go!'

'Belly open!' cried Natus, raising his voice to yell over the engine noise and sea thrash that boomed in through the opening hold doors.

'Hunt with the gaze of the primarch and the grace of the Emperor!' Natus yelled. With an experienced, unruffled eye, he watched the wind speed indicator and the shuttle's yaw.

'Brace, hold... now!'

Natus threw the release lever. The skiffs dropped out of the shuttle and fell towards the water.

Impact. A swirl of bubbles, and a rush of water noise. Priad held on as the skiff inverted, drowning them, and then slammed upright again as the thin, helium filled buoyancy tanks self-righted them.

Kneeling at the back of the craft, Pindor cued the engines and they lurched forward, lifting out of the swell and skipping across the breaking waves like a flying fish. The slender nacelles containing the anti-grav plates extended out from the skiff's sides.

'Turn in! Turn in!' Priad yelled, his voice lost in the roar. But Pindor, at the helm, read his gesture.

Still crouched at the prow, Priad looked back at Dyognes.

'Draw a lance,' Priad said.

Dyognes crouched with his legs wide to ride out the buffets and slid a sea-lance from the rack. Two metres of polished bronze with a long spine of razor-sharp adamite projecting from the tip. He passed it deftly to Priad.

'Draw another and wait,' Priad said. He settled in the prow with the lance against his hip, the tip projecting out across the bows.

They circled in around Oullo's Stilt, kissing the edge of the marysae that slammed up around the rock tower. Priad had ridden retyarion before, worse than this. But it was gathering force. And the sky out to sea had gone a fulminous dark yellow. The iron waves were close.

'Around!' Priad cried, circling his fingers so his helmsman Pindor could see. The skiff took off left, bouncing through the incoming breakers, nacelles shuddering.

Priad looked aft. The other skiff was following them in, Scyllon at the bow with a lance in his hands, Xander behind him amidships ready to pass more lances forward, and Kules, sitting low, at the helm.

'Wyrm-spoor!' Dyognes yelled.

Dark, thrashing ulbrumid broke the water two hundred metres to their port side. Priad's hand clenched on the haft of his lance. He was no longer aware of the pain in his damaged fingers.

The ulbrumid calmed and faded. A sub-surface rising. They're down there, but not breaching yet, Priad thought.

'Auspex!' he yelled.

Dyognes was already on it, wiping flecks of spray from the screen. The auspex scanner was built into the deck just in front of the lance-giver's position in the middle of the boat.

'Deep! Two of them! One below at ninety metres!'

'Others?'

'Three more, out at a space of six hundred metres.' Dyognes adjusted the rangefinder's water-proofed brass dials.

'And anoth– God-Emperor!'

Priad felt the lurch. He grabbed the side ropes automatically. Foam broke around them, an explosion of white water. He caught a glimpse of coiling horn plate sliding under them.

Dyognes had taken a mouthful of seawater. He coughed and spat.

'Sorry! Sorry! That one came from nowhere!'

Right underneath them. But it hadn't surfaced. They were still turning and rising.

'Left!' Priad indicated with his hands. Pindor swung them.

They passed objects floating in the water. Brontoie, the summoning drums, automatic percussion buoys dropped by the shuttles that had brought Khiron down here at dawn. Their steady but erratic beating mimicked the sound of struggling prey in the water and brought the wyrms in. One brontoie could bring a hunting wyrm from a thousand kilometres away.

Priad looked back. He saw his own shuttle hanging off near Splinter Rock, and another hunting ketch swooping down after them. It dropped its skiffs half a kilometre behind him.

Over the vox, Priad heard the battle chant of Manes squad. Brother Strabo had brought his men in to join the hunt.

The skiffs of Manes closed up, powering in, and all four vessels cut a wide crescent of white wake as they circled around Boethus Tower and the minor stacks that huddled nearby. Captain Phobor had told Priad that the oethanar duty ships had left Khiron on Lacres Stilt, a thirty metre-high column right at the edge of the Primarch's Causeway.

Priad could see it now, a finger of rock rising from the white water. There were dozens of summoning drums in the water, beating out their enticing rhythms. Perhaps they were already too late.

'Wyrm! Wyrm sounding!' Dyognes hollered.

It came up out of the ocean fifty metres behind the squadron of hunting skiffs, pluming sheets of spray from the edges of its interlocking horny plates. Twenty metres out of the water, barely a third of its whole length. A maturing sub-adult. Its bone-armoured skull, the size of a drop-ship, opened to expose a white maw and articulate translucent fangs that were longer than a sea-lance. It called. The sub-sonic note blasted them with ultrasound. Then it writhed and fell back into the sea with the detonating force of an Earthshaker salvo. Tidal waves smashed out from its impact.

But Priad wasn't looking at it.

He was gazing ahead at Lacres Stilt. Ulbrumid was boiling at the base of the rock stack. And high up, on the flattened top, stood a lone figure: Khiron.

The ulbrumid broke and a wyrm coiled up around Lacres Stilt. A mature female by its silvery plates, one hundred and forty metres long. Horn plates glistening, it wrapped around the rock pillar, rising. A second wyrm came up, a juvenile male eighty metres long. It locked around the female, writhing up around her, trying to constrict her into the rock with its coils.

The wyrms snapped and sounded at each other, snouts banging against snouts. The ultrasound of their calls percussively dimpled the sea swell, causing back waves and eddies. The skiff wobbled, but Pindor steadied them, and curved them in.

Priad raised his lance and made the hand-down sign to Pindor that meant slow.

Ulbrumid boiled in the water ahead, rocking the skiff. In a surge of foam, the flat arrow-shaped head of a wyrm broke the surface, jaws open. It was another juvenile, but big enough to swallow them whole.

Priad rose on the casting deck in the broad, braced stance of the laoscrae and cast his lance. It tore into the beak-bone before falling away into the sea.

The wyrm broke the water and went down out of view.

'Draw me!' Priad cried.

Dyognes reached a fresh sea-lance into his waiting grip.

'Auspex?'

'It's running under us! Ten metres!'

'About! About!'

Pindor turned the skiff hard. Priad watched the water, braced, the lance ready. His arm was pulled back and the tip of the sea-lance was beside his ear.

The wyrm broke again, running the surface. Priad saw the horn-plates slicing through the chop as it slid under.

He cast again.

The sea-lance went right into the wyrm's side between the plates. The water went dark around them.

'Hold on!' Priad yelled, grabbing the side ropes.

The wyrm's death frenzy stormed the water into a chaos. They were lifted clean out of the sea by a blow from the writhing tail.

'On! On!' Priad cried.

Pindor pulled on the helm to correct and powered them out of the death froth.

Priad looked back in time to see one of Strabos's skiffs thrown up out of the water and splintered to kindling by a mature female. He saw bodies flailing, falling. The wyrm lunged and took the lance caster out of the air like a feline snatching a dangled treat.

Hurling lances from his casting deck at the prow, Strabo turned his skiff back desperately to assist his wyrm-taken boat.

'Scyllon!' hissed Priad over the vox. 'In!'

'Aye!'

The two skiffs of Damocles ran in towards Lacres Stilt. Dyognes passed a fresh lance to Priad. There were three left in the other rack.

Priad looked up at Khiron, forlorn on the top of the stack. Below him, the mature female and the juvenile male were locked in mating combat, cracking the stone as their coils tightened. The smaller, fatter male bit its fangs deep into the female's back. In response, she shuddered and swung her sinuous head around, ripping out the male's throat with her vast blade-teeth.

Dead, the male collapsed back into the sea, its ropes of coil slackening. The weight of its impact threw up a swell that capsized both Damocles's skiffs.

Priad spluttered as they righted. He was still holding the third lance.

The female had gone.

Priad looked around. There was no sign of her. Had the juvenile injured her so badly she had withdrawn?

Priad looked up at Khiron. The Apothecary was standing at the lip of Lacres Stilt, looking down.

He disappeared for a second and then reappeared, running.

Khiron threw himself off the stilt top and closed his body into a perfect diving shape. He hit the water like a missile.

A thirty-metre dive into marysae, into white water. Not even the best... Priad thought.

'Brother-sergeant!' Dyognes called.

'What?'

'Hard return, twelve metres, rising...'

Priad scanned the water. There was a flash of foam. Khiron surfaced, spluttering and coughing, fifty metres ahead of them.

'Pindor! Swing us in!'

'Brother-sergeant!' Dyognes called again. 'Hard return! Huge echo, six metres astern!'

Priad looked back. He saw the ulbrumid. Saw the size of it. This wasn't the female returning. This was why the female had fled.

A mature male. A giant bull. Kraretyer.

## VI

PRIAD LEANED OVER the bow and grabbed the floundering Khiron by the arm. Struggling, he heaved the half-dead Apothecary up over the gunwale. Scyllon's skiff closed in to assist.

The kraretyer broke the surface behind them.

Even old Pindor cried out in alarm.

It was an old, old bull. A three hundred-metre monster. Its girth matched the widest rock stack. Its huge skull seemed the size of a battle-barge. It towered above them, cascading water from its ancient plates, opened its maw and exposed five metre-long fangs.

It sounded. The surface water was blitzed into drizzle. Both crews fell down in agony, holding their ears. The hardwood casting deck of Priad's skiff cracked.

The bull surged forward, forepart raised out of the water. Scyllon threw a lance that bounced off the plate, and then snatched a fresh one from Xander.

He threw again.

It was a perfect cast.

The lance punctured between the third and fourth plates and lodged fast.

The old bull didn't even seem to feel it.

Priad dragged Khiron onto the casting deck and turned to pick up his lance. The vast wyrm was right on them.

Priad seized another lance and cast it hard.

It struck the bull's nose scales and quivered away.

'Draw me!' Priad yelled.

But Dyognes was leaning back to throw the next lance himself. Cursing, Priad stooped and pulled the last remaining lance free from the rack.

Dyognes cast. The lance went clean into the bull wyrm's right eye. It shuddered and writhed back.

Priad had the final lance in his hands. He pulled his arm back and threw.

It went right down the wyrm's gaping throat.

As it fell, as it died, the bull wyrm blasted up vast wakes of water that smashed the skiffs aside and broke them on the stilts.

The plume of wyrm-blood spread and marked the water for a kilometre square. The hookbeaks and scale birds rioted down to feed in their thousands.

## VII

ITHAKA. PROUD ITHAKA. *Ocean world. Cradle of Snakes. The Apothecary kneels in the surf on the beach as the moon rises between the stacks of* the Primarch's Causeway. Waves break around his bulky armoured form. He fills the ten copper flasks with the lifewater of the homeworld.

It is time to ship out. The battle-barge awaits to carry them to a new undertaking. This is the last act before leavetaking, the Rite of the Claiming of Water.

The Apothecary intones the litany, and the men of Damocles squad, each one in full armour, circle around him at the waterline, making the ritual responses. He hands each one his flask of lifewater. The last two go to the newest inductees, standing proudly in their polished war-plate. Dyognes. Aekon.

The Rite is done. The Apothecary stands, screws up the stopper of his own flask, and slides it into his thigh pouch.

'Ready, Brother-Apothecary?' asks Priad.

'I'm ready, brother-sergeant,' says Khiron of Damocles.

# PART SIX
# BLUE BLOOD
## Undertaking to Iorgu

BRIGHT AS A serrated knife, daylight winking off its ridged bows, the Imperial barge fell away behind them until it was just a dwindling star beginning to set in the western sky. Far below, the shadow of their landing ship jittered and skipped as it pursued them across the parched, pink wilds of Iorgu.

The land was cracked like scurf-skin, or like beach sand that had baked and crazed in the sun after the tide has withdrawn. Priad knew enough about Iorgu to understand that these seabeds had been dry for aeons and no tide would ever return. Every few dozen kilometres, they overflew a desert town or settlement: little clusters of white domes like brooches of pearls pressed into the pink dunes, or strung out along the lips of red-rock canyons, bone-white as crusts of air-dried salt.

The lander shivered as altitude thrusters crimped and fired, nudging them northward. As the angle changed, rungs of golden sunlight stole in through the portholes and washed like slow liquid across the faces of the men on the starboard side.

The warriors of Damocles squad were seated in restraint-thrones, back to back, five looking to port, five to starboard. They wore full

Astartes wargear, except that their heads were bare. The ten, grim-visored helmets were suspended in hydraulic clamps above their thrones. Their weapons were locked in racks underneath their arm-braces.

Priad slowly tore his gaze away from the desiccated landscape flashing by below and consulted the luminous red screen of the data-plate above his window. Bearing, height, airspeed, time to set-down...

'Two minutes,' he said. 'Activate armour.'

A series of low whines answered him as ten M37 dorsal-mounted power units woke up. Priad immediately felt an enervating vigour throb in his ceramite-sheathed limbs; the reassuring surge of inhuman strength.

'Is vital monitoring satisfactory, Brother Khiron?'

'I have ten steady life-beats, brother-sergeant,' replied the squad's Apothecary promptly.

'Ninety seconds,' said Priad. 'Lock armour.'

Hydraulics hissed and clanked. The ten helmets lowered onto the heads of the Marines. Most of the men wore their hair tied back or braided over their scalps, ready for helmet-fit, but Priad noticed how young Dyognes deftly scooped his glossy mane of black ringlets up under the lip of the descending helmet before it met the neck-seal and secured. Priad's own helmet clicked into place and abruptly he was breathing cool, internal air-supply and seeing everything through the bright green display of his visor optics.

'Auto weapons check,' Priad instructed, his voice an electronic murmur carried by the intersuit vox. The individual data-plates before them scrolled with diagnostic reports fed from their racked arsenal.

'Run auto-sense target trial,' he said.

The plates flickered with rapid test patterns that measured and calibrated each Marine's targeting systems. Through his visor optics, Priad locked up six vari-range practice icons as they appeared on his data-plate, freezing each one in turn with a hard, white graphic cross. Satisfied, the plate responded by displaying a default aquila symbol. He muttered a prayer of thanks.

'Set-down positions,' Priad said finally.

The thrones tightened their grips, clamping limbs, torsos and necks and rotating slightly into the lock-up position so that each

Space Marine was firmly cradled and tilted back. As the thrones reclined, segmented blast shutters closed like eyelids over the window ports, shutting out the light.

Thirty seconds. Priad switched his visor display to access the view through the lander's forward pict-readers. He saw emerald crags and a lime-green sky rushing past him, overlaid with rapidly changing graphics of trajectory, contour and flight path prediction. A column of numerical data crawled up the left side of the panorama. Priad knew the emerald rocks were really pink, and the lime sky really smoke-blue, but when the city came into view at last, he longed to know what colour that truly was.

Outposts at first. Wide-spaced lines of towers set in the ragged basalt like fangs rising from a meatless jawbone. Thin ribbons of highways radiating out from the city. An outer ring-wall, tall and crenellated, then a great, shadow-filled ditch that the highways crossed on stilted stone viaducts. Steps of stone-built walls forming irrigated terraces teeming with lush doum trees.

Then Iorgu City. Five hundred metre curtain walls, sloping gently inwards, smooth as ice. Defence towers sprouting like stalagmites from the wall's upper levels. Beyond the cyclopean wall, the hazy vista of the inner city: towers and steeples and domes clustered around the gigantic landmarks of the Imperial Basilica, the Royal Palace, the steeple of the Astropathica and, in the distance, the Sacred Mound, the only soft, organic shape in sight. The city was so vast that Priad was soon unable to take it all in with one look, despite the one-eighty degree sweep of his scope.

A jolt. Braking jets. A rolling sensation of weightlessness as they decelerated hard, swinging south on a sustained burn of vertical thrusters. Now some of the towers were climbing past them, dwarfing them. Down below, on a wide platform of rockcrete ninety metres above the city floor, a star of landing lamps began to strobe-flash, the lights pulsing along the arms of the star towards the centre.

Another judder of jets. A lurch.

Fifty metres. Twenty. Ten. Two.

There was a noise like an iron shutter falling, a violent jarring, and they were down.

'Damocles! Disengage and deploy!' Priad cried.

The thrones slammed back to vertical. Power feeds, monitor plugs and restraints disengaged in a series of pings and clangs. The hatches opened, lifting like trapdoors, five along each flank of the lander, and daylight flooded in.

Sliding their weapons from the throne-side racks, Damocles squad strode out into the bright heat on the landing pad.

This wasn't a combat zone, and they weren't expecting trouble, but even so they dismounted from the lander in standard assault pattern, covering each address with their bolters, sweeping and hunting for targets until Priad gave the word and they locked off their weapons and slung them up.

The five men on each side turned and marched around behind the lander, coming together like the teeth of a zip to form a precise double-file.

Dust swirled around them. They waited a moment as Brother Andromak raised the Chapter standard and fixed it between his shoulder blades so that it fluttered above his head. Then Khiron performed the water rites.

'Advance!' said Priad, as soon as the ritual was done. Ceramite-shod feet, marching in perfect synchronicity, rang on the rockcrete. The great brass iris hatch on the edge of the pad opened as they strode towards it. A tall, white-bearded man in an ornately braided dark jacket and white jodhpurs came out to meet them, flanked by an escort of sixty heavy guardsmen in patterned silk, spiked helmets with silver aventails, and salute-raised linstocks. The guardsman immediately to the officer's right held up a massive parasol of white canvas and rosewood to provide shade for his commander.

'I am Seraskier Duxl of the Interior Guard,' the bearded man said. His face was lined from years in the sun, and nictitating augmetic filters of smoked plastic had slid down over his eyeballs. 'It is my honour to welcome the hallowed Astartes Iron Snakes to Iorgu City.'

'The honour is mine, seraskier,' Priad saluted, switching his suit-vox to speaker. His voice rumbled across the open pad. 'We have come to do homage to your king.'

\* \* \*

## II

'I HAD WISHED for more,' Priad had said in the dim, tranquil vaults of the Chapter House on Karybdis. 'Ten months have I spent, reforging Damocles into a fighting unit, and we are ready. But the inductees, Dyognes and Aekon, have never seen actual combat, and Khiron, though I count myself blessed to have him as Apothecary, has not worked with the squad in the field. I had wished... I was hoping... for a combat mission.'

'I trust, brother-sergeant, that every Iron Snake hopes his next task will be a combat mission.' Profoundly deep, and without the merest glimmer of light, the voice of the Chapter Master had welled across Priad like the deep, oceanic volume of proud Ithaka.

'Of course, my master,' Priad had said hurriedly. He had not intended offence.

'We are sworn to duty, the duty of the Astartes, enfranchised to us by the God-Emperor of our race. We undertake each duty as it comes, and we do not question it.'

Priad had bowed his head. 'No, of course not, my master.'

For a long moment, Chapter Master Seydon of the Iron Snakes had remained silent, a gigantic shadow in the dim light of the temple.

'Our duty is to serve the Emperor,' Seydon had intoned suddenly. 'Our specific duty is to protect the Reef Stars. Iorgu is a principal world in that region. A proud bastion of Imperial power. I lament that the long, wise rule of Queen Gartrude has come to an end. It is appropriate for our Chapter to send an emissary guard to attend the coronation of her successor. It would be disrespectful for the Iron Snakes to ignore the event.'

'I realise that, my master.'

'I have chosen Damocles to perform this duty. To march in the coronation train. To witness the crowning of the new king. To represent our interests and demonstrate both our unswerving loyalty and the permanence of our vigil. Do you question that choice?'

'No, my master. I was only saying that I would have wished for something less... ceremonial.'

'I would have tasked you to combat, Priad, but the Reef is quiet for now. I know how you yearn to baptise and test your squad in fire. Do this for me now and I will find you your crucible. How say you?'

Priad's pulse had been thudding in his temples. He had managed a smile. 'Damocles will go to Iorgu, my master,' he had promised.

'WE WILL GET fat and slow,' Brother Xander blurted, dropping his helmet and then his gauntlets onto a chaise. Until Dyognes and Aekon had been inducted, Xander had been the youngest of Damocles, and he still liked to act the firebrand.

'Fat and slow?' echoed Brother Pindor as he disengaged his own helmet. 'Really?'

'Figuratively,' snapped Xander. 'Pageants. Pomp. Feasting. This isn't what we were made for.'

Scyllon and Andromak growled their agreement.

'I tell you what, Xander,' said Khiron, disconnecting his gauntlets and flexing his bared hands thoughtfully, 'this is precisely what we were made for.'

Xander frowned at the Apothecary. Khiron had an excellent reputation, and no one in Damocles squad questioned his ability, but he was still a newcomer, a stranger in the place of beloved Memnes. They were still getting used to his straight-talking wisdom.

'How so?' Xander asked.

'I suppose,' said Khiron, 'that you long for battle?'

'That is our calling,' Xander nodded.

'When the God-Emperor wishes it. It is our forte but not our calling.'

Khiron turned to face Xander. The young, dark-braided warrior had a proud, glacial face and towered a full head's height above the grey-haired Apothecary with his narrow eyes and jut-jawed, bear-trap frown.

'Our calling is the Emperor's service, brother-boy. He wills that we fight, we fight. He wills it that we stand respect to a coronation, we stand respect. He wills it that we support a toppling temple on our shoulders, we brace and take the weight. And if he tells us to strip naked and stand on our heads, that we do too. That is what we were made for. To serve the will of the Emperor.'

Xander looked away. 'I stand chastised, Brother-Apothecary Khiron.'

Khiron chuckled and smacked the warrior's arm plates. 'You just stand, Xander. That's all he asks.'

'The area is secure,' Natus reported to Priad. The sergeant nodded. The area was secure. The area was also dripping with opulence. Five communicating private apartments on the sixtieth floor of the Iorguan Palace, draped in silks and coshiori embroiderwork, lit by glow-globes and glass-fluted wick-lamps. Every item of furniture was gilded and carved. Vast windows of tinted glass overlooked the city sprawl below.

'We are their honoured guests,' Priad murmured.

'What is... this?' asked Brother Aekon, regarding with some confusion a soft heap of cushions and silk-cased bolsters.

'A bed,' replied Priad.

'For sleeping?'

'Indeed. There are ten of them, two in each room.'

'Salt of Ithaka...' Aekon said. 'I would drown in that softness.'

'The Iorguans don't really understand what we are, do they, brother-sergeant?' said Khiron. 'They give us beds and fine state rooms.'

'And food,' said Priad, gesturing to a long side table where platters of fruits, breads and sweetmeats were arrayed. The bio-engineered metabolisms of the Astartes warriors could go without conventional rest or regular food for weeks. If pushed, a twenty-minute restorative nap, which could be taken upright with armour locked, and an intravenous nutrient pack, could prolong their operational capacity.

'We are gods to them,' Priad said. 'Legends from the stars. Most citizens of the Imperium go their whole lifetimes without seeing one of our kind in the flesh. They presume us to be men, yet fear us as deities of war.'

'I would not disabuse them of either notion,' said Khiron.

'Maybe you see now why our attendance here carries so much weight,' Priad said to Xander. 'Why even ten of our Chapter coming here and paying homage to the new king is a significant event. The folk of Iorgu will remember this time. The day the Adeptus Astartes set foot on Iorguan soil in person to acknowledge their king.'

AT NIGHTFALL, A nervous troop of palace guards came and summoned them to audience. The sky outside had turned purple and the golden towers of the city glimmered in the last rays of the setting sun.

Damocles had polished their armour to a sheen and wiped away the last traces of dust. A terrible hush fell on the huge audience hall as they marched in, three abreast, with Priad at the head. Five thousand people – nobility, dignitaries, city lords and servants – gazed at them in awe. Trumpets suddenly blared a fanfare and many people jumped.

Led by Seraskier Duxl, a royal party approached to inspect them. Various silk-wrapped nobles with tall, soft hats; beautiful concubines in costumes made only of precious stones; brute bodyguards who looked like youths next to the towering, immobile Space Marines.

And the king elect: Naldo Benexer Tashari Iorgu Stam, by the grace of the Golden Throne. A boy, Priad noted with disappointment, just a chinless, excited boy with a too-long neck and watery, inbred eyes. The furs and gold that clad him were worth the annual economy of some frontier colonies, and were so heavy, teams of silver-painted children had to carry the train. Naldo himself floated on a suspensor plate that surfed him across the tiled floor.

'I am honoured,' he said, his voice nasal and reedy, 'that you… mighty warriors attend me here.'

'Lord king,' Priad said, tilting his head to look down at his majesty. Priad's words rolled like distant thunder from his suit's speakers, and some of the guests shivered or gasped. 'In the name of Seydon, master of the Iron Snakes, in the name of the God-Emperor of Mankind, and in the name of my beloved Chapter, I greet you and do you homage.'

He knelt, power-armour joints whirring softly. Even on one knee, he was at eye-level with King Elect Naldo. His majesty's face was a pale green blob in Priad's optics. Unbidden, automatic target graphics framed Naldo's visage with white crosshairs. Priad dismissed his visor's treasonous suggestion and the icon vanished.

Naldo was looking up and down the ranks of Damocles with adolescent delight. 'You are all the stories speak of… and more! Giant warriors, all identically cast from the same great pattern!'

Priad hesitated. Identical? How could this child not see the differences? Dyognes and Xander tall like oaks, Kules short and broad, old Pindor and the noble bearing of Khiron, Aekon thick-set, Natus with his bionic arm, Scyllon whip-thin and supple as a lance, Andromak sturdy like a sea cliff.

We are meaningless, he thought, a cipher. That's how they all see us. Interchangeable giants, replications without character. The wargear masks us so.

'Rise, warrior,' Naldo said, relishing the opportunity to give a Space Marine an order. Priad got up.

'Join our festivities. Mingle freely.'

The king elect and his entourage moved away. Conversation began to start up again, and musicians began to play.

'Mingle?' Priad voxed suit-to-suit. 'What in the Emperor's name does that mean?'

### III

THEY STOOD ATTENTIVE and still for two hours as the gala swirled around them. Some guests ventured close and admired them as if they were statues. A few stole closer and risked touching their armour for good fortune or simply on a dare.

Damocles didn't move.

Priad spent his time fixing and logging faces. His optic gaze wandered through the thickets of the crowd, blink-recording and tagging each face and figure he saw and adding them to his suit's internal memory. Not only persons, but the structure and dimension of the hall, the number and site of the exits, the position of the band. A warrior of the phratry was taught to assess and catalogue his location for tactical purposes wherever possible, usually a quick matter of key points. Now he had time to waste.

The number of valves or strings on each instrument. The number of frets. The number of buttons on a jacket or gemstones on a gown train. The number of facets on a wine glass. The number of beads on the chandeliers.

He logged and identified the robust commander of the local PDF, flamboyant in red satin robes. Five subsector governors and their staffs. Lord Militant Farnsey, two Navy commodores and a cluster of Guard officers who, like Damocles, had been sent to the coronation to represent their institutions. The Princess Royal of Cartomax, a beautiful young woman with a surgically perfect face framed by the gauzy fields of a personal force-veil, and perfect breasts pushed up and out in a balcony of diamonds. The Imperial Hierarch, Bishop Osokomo, his bulk supported on grav plates, his extravagant mitre three metres tall. A ranking emissary of the Navis Nobilite wearing a holographic face to hide his unseemly third eye. Nine senior adepts of the Guild Astropathicus. The chief clerk of the Administratum Iorgu, with sixteen higher recollectors. Six merchant princes.

A man in black robes which did not completely hide his golden prosthetic hand.

Priad jolted.

'Andromak.'

'Brother-sergeant?'

'You have charge here.'

'Yes, sir.'

Priad strode across the packed room. Men and women, the cream of Iorguan society, fled out of his path, aghast that one of the statues was now moving. Priad ignored their whispers and exclamations, and headed for the rear exit of the great hall. The man in black robes had made a hasty retreat in that direction.

The outer passageway was dim and quiet, though Priad's optics saw into the shadows as if it was day.

He drew his bolter. An ammo load tally immediately appeared on his visor display, alongside a floating target cross. He stalked along the passage, studying every centimetre of the lime-cast view, from the dark teal of the coldest, deepest shadows to the fizzling white flares of the lamp reeds.

A tall figure in black stepped out from behind a pillar to face him. Hands – one gloved, one gold – came up and pulled the hood of the black robe down. White hair, an angular, pinch-skinned face.

'Well met, brother-sergeant,' said Inquisitor Mabuse.

'You make no attempt to hide from me?' Priad said, disconcerted, wondering if he should prepare for some ordo trick, some ordo magick.

Mabuse smiled, revealing small, neat white teeth. 'I am an inquisitor, Brother-Sergeant Priad. My business is looking and finding and revealing... and knowing how well others do the same. There is small point in a mere mortal trying to conceal himself from an Astartes warrior.'

'Yet you fled the hall as soon as I saw you.'

'When we last met, on Ceres, we did not part on cordial terms. I suspected perhaps that, seeing me, you intended me some harm.'

Priad was insulted by the idea. 'I am a servant of the Golden Throne, inquisitor. I do not indulge in spite or petty retribution against another of the Emperor's servants... despite what I might think of them.'

Mabuse nodded. 'Yet... your weapon is drawn and armed and pointing at me.'

Priad realised it was. Annoyed with himself, he locked the safety and holstered the bolter.

'What are you doing here?' he asked bluntly.

'In this passageway? In truth, brother, I withdrew from the hall so that we could speak privately.'

'I meant–'

Mabuse held up his delicate golden hand to interrupt. 'This is important, Priad. Only you know my true name and calling. The court of Iorgu knows me as Sire Damon Taradae, a sericulture merchant. I would like to retain that disguise a while longer.'

'No one will hear the truth from me, or from my men.'

Mabuse nodded again, pleased. 'That is good. Thank you, brother-sergeant.'

'Now will you answer my question less literally?'

'Of course. Come...'

Warily, Priad followed the inquisitor into an alcove between thick basalt columns where light reeds fizzled and glowed. Mabuse raised his golden hand again, and the little finger detached with a tiny click and hovered beside them at shoulder height on a beam of repulsor energy. Priad's visor-view suddenly fogged and scrambled.

'Open your visor,' he heard Mabuse say, his words dulled by Priad's armour.

Priad undid the magna-lock and removed his helmet, looking down into Mabuse's eyes.

'Don't worry,' Mabuse said, gesturing lightly to his hovering digit. 'It's generating an anti-vox/pict field around us so we can speak openly. There is danger here, Priad.'

'Danger? What danger?'

Mabuse shrugged. 'I don't know. Not yet. I've been here six weeks, since the old queen died. It is standard practice for the Inquisition to send a representative to investigate the death of any significant Imperial potentate, and Queen Gartrude, may the Emperor gather her to himself, was certainly that.'

'Foul play?'

'Oh, most certainly. She was murdered. But in such an exquisitely subtle way, it looked like the action of old age.'

'Murdered?'

'Yes. The Medicae Royal missed the signs, but I am certain.'

'Then it must be reported! It must–'

Mabuse reached out with his golden hand and rested it on Priad's armoured sleeve. It was a curiously bold yet informal gesture and Priad fell silent at once, out of surprise more than anything else.

'Knowing she was murdered is not the point, brother-sergeant. Knowing why and by whom is the job of the Inquisition.'

'The boy… the new king. He would have most to gain,' said Priad.

Mabuse chuckled. 'You are a greater warrior than I will ever be, Brother-Sergeant Priad. But you are no detective.'

'I–'

'Hush. King Elect Naldo is not the culprit. Of that, I am assured. I had considered that possibility. No, the regicide is down to someone else. Person or persons as yet unknown. I have suspicions. I may be able to act on them soon. For now, I simply wish to broker peace between us, Priad. Indulge me and keep my mission secret. When the time comes, I may have need of the mighty Iron Snakes.'

## IV

THAT NIGHT, ONCE the duties in the great hall were done, Damocles went without rest. In the lamp-lit gloom of the apartments provided for them, they waited and loitered, wargear loosened or partially stripped off. Some talked into the night. Others ate and drank from the rich fares provided, just for the novelty. Xander hand-wrestled with Aekon and Andromak. Old Pindor played a game of regicide with Scyllon.

Priad watched them move the pieces across the inlaid board. How inappropriate, he thought to himself.

He opened a glazed brass hatch and let himself out onto the balcony that terraced their apartment level. The night was warm, with the scents of dune-orchids and exhaust fumes on the dry desert air. Straits of silvery cloud barred the moon and shone against a sky as dark and purple as fresh heart muscle. Lit by a soft amber radiance, the city lurked beneath him. Dots of light, the running lamps of air traffic, muddled along the canyons of streets below. Occasionally, a higher altitude transport hummed past, soaring between the gilded spires.

Priad rested his bare hands on the balcony rail and looked down. The lights of the traffic made a long glittering river, like a kraretyer, a giant bull-wyrm, rising to bask.

'Brother?' It was Khiron. The noble Apothecary had teased out his mane of grey hair so it fell around his wide shoulders.

'Khiron. We must be on our guard for trouble.'

'I knew there was something on your mind. What kind of trouble?'

'We'll know it when it comes.'

There was a low rumble. Priad wondered if Khiron had growled something. Then a distant flash and another grumble.

Thunder.

Priad heard a tapping sound.

Rain, heavy drops of it, was beginning to fall.

THERE WOULD BE, Seraskier Duxl explained, four days of celebration. Four daily rituals and observances leading to the full coronation. Damocles would walk in the van of the great procession on each of those days as the rites were performed. On the first day, the king elect would march to the Imperial Basilica at the head of an entourage of ten thousand worshippers and there his suitability would be judged using the ancient treasures of Iorgu. Ten million citizens would line the streets and praise him.

Priad asked about the rain. Unusual, the seraskier admitted. The rains only came once every few decades. But a good portent, nevertheless.

The uproar of the procession was worse than any battle. Horns and trumpets blared and cymbals clashed. The millions cheered and strewed their way with palm fronds cut fresh from the doum trees. Glittering regiments of Imperial Guard and PDF flowed down the main boulevards of the city, escorting nobles in lift-litters and motor limousines, columns of tracked war machines, bands of painted dancers, and packs of glabrous sand-sloth, swinging their massive heads and barking as their jockeys cropped and goaded their wrinkled flanks.

During the long and tedious ceremony at the Basilica, thunder rolled again, and a fume of aurora lights flushed the darkening sky. The citizenry moaned and howled in awe at this great sign. By the time Bishop Osokomo got to the verses where the treasures were to be brought forth, rain was hammering on the roof-dome and streaming like molten glass down the multi-coloured windows. The stained light in the Basilica shifted and danced.

The treasures were unimpressive. A crown, an orb, a sceptre, a torc, ancient things that were only brought out for coronations. They were the heirloom legacies of the first monarchs of Iorgu, pre-served for all time in the Sacred Mound where the founding colony had built its original fastness.

Apparently, they possessed arcane power, and would react in supernatural rebuke if presented to a ruler elect who was not fit. The treasures did not stir on their silk cushions as they were waved under Naldo's face.

He was, so it seemed, fit to rule.

The crowd cheered, drowning out the thunderstorm. The caval-cade withdrew to the Palace. The next day, they would process to the Astropathicae for the subsequent round of mumbling rituals.

THE STORM DID not let up. Rain pelted into the evening, and more flamboyant auroras marked the heavens. Tense and unnerved, Priad withdrew Damocles to their apartments.

At midnight, an aide from the staff of Lord Militant Farnsey came to them and requested a private interview with Priad.

'My lord wishes it known that there is some alarm in the visiting dignitaries,' said the aide.

'I see,' said Priad.

'The weather, the lights in the sky… they seem to be more than portents. Omens, perhaps.'

Priad shrugged.

'Great war-brother,' the aide said uncomfortably, 'there is disquiet in the city. In the low quarters there has been some rioting. Also, reports of apparitions and visions stalking the streets. Murmurs in the warp, unsettling the Guild Astropathicus. Unrest is growing.'

'I have noticed as much,' Priad said.

'It is feared the forces of fate do not wish this coronation accomplished,' said the aide. 'If it continues – if it grows – the lord militant and all the off-world guests will be forced to withdraw from Iorgu. My lord trusts that the acclaimed Iron Snakes will escort them to safety, if that becomes an issue.'

'I serve the Emperor and his vassals,' Priad said, remembering his Chapter Master's instructions.

'Good,' said the aide. 'The lord militant will be delighted to know that.'

BY DAWN, IT was very much worse. Panic-induced riots had scoured through the city's suburbs in the night, despite the brutal response of the Magistratum, leaving several wards in flames, smashed and unpoliced. The vast crowds now filling the avenues and boulevards of the central quarter had become protesters, not worshippers. They chanted for help, and for release from the curse that had fallen on Iorgu, even as the Magistratum's riot-trucks hosed them off the streets with their water cannons. Lightning had struck the steeple of the Astropathica, killing forty-two adepts and injuring scores of others. Unextinguishable corposant flickered and burned around the pylon tops of eighteen city towers. It was said the silk-makers' quarter had been entirely abandoned after a terrible phantom had been glimpsed roaming there.

On Priad's behest, Kules had made contact with their orbiting battle-barge. The transmitted picts he had received in answer were troubling. Six satellite towns around Iorgu City showed signs of rioting and civil unrest. Whole stretches of desert had bloomed with unseasonal foliage and bright flowers, turning the pink landscape green and white for thousands of hectares.

The deluge had washed fresh, shallow tides into the basins of the old dry seas.

* * *

## V

Lord Militant Farnsey didn't send an aide this time. Surprisingly, he came in person.

'Rioters and common filth snap around the palace and rise in numbers. We are departing the planet.'

'We, lord?' asked Priad.

'The nobility, sergeant. The worthy guests. Augurs say that Iorgu is about to fall in fire and damnation. We must not be here when that happens.'

'Indeed not,' Priad replied. He stood at the head of Damocles facing the lord militant and his gaggle of assistants and bodyguards. All of Damocles were now in full wargear, battle-ready. Only Priad had his head exposed, his helm under the crook of his arm.

'I trust then you will escort us to the landing field and see us off planet.'

'The Imperial Guard…'

'Is occupied supporting the local Magistratum in putting down the riot. They have their hands full.'

'You'd leave them here?' Priad said.

Farnsey glared at him. 'Get some notion of priority, brother-sergeant. They are dog-soldiers and fighting is what they do. We are nobility and we will be afforded every respect. See to your duty and get us out of this hell-hole.'

'Of course,' said Priad, turning to his squad and preparing to issue them with instructions.

A tiny, gleaming missile flew into the apartment, low enough over the heads of the lord militant and his entourage to make them duck in consternation. It came to a halt and hovered in front of Priad.

It was a perfect human index finger, machined in gold.

A soft focused hologram, tiny enough to cup in the palm of one hand, materialised in the air above it. An image of a man in a black robe.

'Brother-Sergeant Priad. The hour is nigh,' crackled the voice of Mabuse through miniaturised vox-relay speakers. 'I call on you and Damocles. I have found the why and the who.'

'Can you proceed without us?' Priad asked quietly.

'Yes, brother. But without you, I will not succeed, and Iorgu will perish.'

'Are you exaggerating for effect, Mabuse?'

'No,' replied the little hologram. 'I am underestimating.'

'Damocles stands ready.'

'Follow where I point and find me,' said the hologram as it dissolved. The golden digit swung around in the air and waited impatiently.

'Damocles! Arm up and set for combat! Follow me!'

There was a loud clatter of readying weapons.

'What are you doing? Where are you going?' Farnsey bellowed as Priad led the squad out of the apartment past him.

'I have a real duty to perform, my lord,' Priad snapped.

'You'd leave us to the mob? How dare you, Astartes? I am a lord militant! You will conduct me to the landing field in safety!'

Priad turned back for a moment. 'I suggest you dig in and lie low, my lord. Damocles cannot assist you at this time.'

'What the hell do you think you're doing?' raged Farnsey.

'Getting some notion of priority, lord,' said Priad.

Farnsey's curses followed them down the hallway. He would report them, discredit their name with the Chapter Master, ruin them and ruin their reputations.

The threats bounced off Priad's armour as harmlessly as raindrops.

THE GUIDING DIGIT led them down through the sprawling bulk of the Royal Palace. Some rooms and hallways lay deserted, some showed signs of ransack. In the corridors, they passed servants and aides who had pilfered what they could take and were busy getting clear, or the halted baggage trains of departing nobles, stewards calling out for servitors that were unlikely to respond. On one colonnade walk, PDF troopers were fighting a losing battle to secure shutters across window spaces blown in by the storm. Lightning splintered the darkness outside, and rain drenched in through the opening. They passed a hall where hundreds of palace inhabitants were kneeling in terror as agitated hierarchs led them in desperate prayers for deliverance.

The spinal elevators were choked and occupied, so they made their way to a service lift in the western side of the palace spire and commandeered it. The palace staff waiting to use it fled the moment the great Astartes appeared.

The service lift deposited them in a deep-set garage bay of slimy rockcrete. The wall-set lights flickered as the main power source fluctuated.

'Secure transport,' the little holoform of Mabuse said.

Most vehicles had gone. Laden, overcrowded transports were queuing up the exit ramp. The majority of the remaining vehicles were too small to take the whole squad.

'Here!' cried Scyllon, reading off his auspex. In a private side bay sat several of the lift-litters and repulsor barges used in the coronation procession. Amongst them was a long-hulled land-yacht of luxury-build. Liveried servants were struggling to load travel caskets and baggage aboard it.

'Vacate the vehicle!' Priad barked on speaker. Some of the servants ran, dropping the luggage they were handling. Others froze and gazed at the approaching Space Marines in blank dismay. Pindor and Natus shoved them out of the way and boarded the yacht.

'Powered up and set to go!' Pindor voxed back after a moment.

Priad gestured Dyognes and Xander forward to throw off the baggage already stowed.

'What the devil do you think you're doing?' wailed a voice.

Priad turned. The Princess Royal of Cartomax, clad in a floor-length fur, her face pale, was rushing towards them, flanked by half a dozen less-than-eager bodyguards.

'That's my vehicle!' she declared, glaring up at the brother-sergeant. She barely came up to his elbow. Priad was amazed at her brazen outrage. She seemed to have no fear of the towering warriors. Or maybe, he considered, her fear of the situation outweighed her fear of the Astartes.

'We need it,' Priad said simply.

'Damn you!' she cried. 'It's mine! Mine!'

'Lady, please…' one of the bodyguards whimpered, keeping his eyes fixed on Priad and his men and his hands very obviously away from his own sidearm. 'Please… they are Astartes…'

The princess slapped the man so hard he fell over.

'You will not take my transport,' she told Priad.

'I have already taken it. Calm yourself and return to the palace compound.'

'You will escort me to safety then! You serve me!'

Ah, now, that was it, Priad realised. She wasn't afraid of them, because she didn't understand them. Raised in the rarefied atmosphere of a high court, she had been educated to think of the Astartes as servant-warriors. Servants of the Imperium. She was royal-born, so undoubtedly they had to serve her.

Such marvellous arrogance.

'Go away. Now,' he said.

'Do you know who I–' she began to say.

'Go away *now*,' Priad repeated.

She gave an indignant shriek and shot him. Point blank, with a micro-laser from under her furs. The blast scorched his chest plate and flashed warning sigils across his visor-scope. Scyllon and Aekon had their bolters aimed at her in a heartbeat.

She gasped and backed off a pace, incredulous.

'Go away,' he repeated as calmly as he could manage, trying to ignore the urgings of the target cross that filled his view and framed her face.

'Lady,' a voice boomed. The golden digit now hovered between Priad and the Princess. Mabuse had boosted the volume of its vox-speakers. 'I advise you to run away now. Right now. Do as the brother-sergeant instructs you.' The little holoform glared at her.

'Why? Why?' she choked.

The holoform of Mabuse shivered and dissolved. It was replaced by the hard-light of a crest-insignia. The rosette emblem of the Inquisition.

'That's why.'

She ran, wailing.

A salutary lesson, Priad thought. Even someone haughty and thick-skinned enough to be unafraid of the Astartes hides in terror from the Inquisition.

## VI

PINDOR RAN THE yacht out of the garage bay into the streets. Xander and Dyognes had been forced to walk in front of it to clear the jumble of transports from the ramp. Once they were through, the two warriors reboarded, and the yacht sped clear down the boulevard.

Monsoon rain was falling in swirling curtains. Weird electrical effects underlit the low, sinister sky and Priad saw at least five city towers struck by lightning in as many minutes.

The road was littered with the detritus of rioting, and overturned vehicles burned in the rain. Dim figures flashed by in the shadows, fleeing down the pavements and walkways. At one junction, the bodies of nine Magistratum officers lay broken on the roadway. Priad's sensors detected sporadic gunfire from neighbouring streets.

For one fifty-metre section, the street-level windows of a tower showed not their passing reflection but a clamour of open-mouthed ghosts, screaming at them from the rain-streamed glass.

'Golden Throne!' cried Andromak. 'Did you see that?'

'No,' Priad lied.

The yacht swooped east, along the main city highway, up and over a hump-backed bridgeway that ran across a stately park. The doum trees in the park were on fire, but the leaves weren't burning.

'Turn east,' Mabuse voxed. 'Head for the Sacred Mound.'

Pindor struggled with the yacht's controls. They were unfamiliar and his massive, gauntleted hands were too big to manage the dainty, knurled levers and throttles. He tried to steer the yacht onto the wide avenue that rose through the mid-town towards the area of the Mound, and ran them a glancing blow along a section of crash barrier. The impact showered sparks into the air and left an ugly weal down the side of the luxury transport's hull.

In quick succession, three lightning strikes brutally stung the roadway nearby, one to the front, the other two to the left. They left scorched blast holes smoking in the rockcrete. The electro-magnetic pulses left them dazed and blind for a second, and the golden digit fell to the deck, dead and inert. A second later and it rose drunkenly back into the air, the holoform reigniting.

'Come on!' Mabuse voxed.

'Dear God-Emperor...' Pindor mumbled.

Priad looked out. A human skeleton, its bones made of polished ebony and its socket-eyes glowing with a ghastly yellow radiance stood on the roadway ahead of them. It was forty metres tall.

Damocles threw open the top hatches and started to blaze at the monstrous thing with their bolters, white tracers ripping the wet air. Andromak fired an incandescent blue blast from his plasma gun.

Undamaged, unflinching, the skeleton thing took a step forward.

'Stop wasting ammunition!' Mabuse all but screamed, his voice tinny and shrill. 'Go through it! It's just a glamour... an apparition!'

'Do it!' Priad ordered.

Pindor threw the throttle lever to full ahead and drove the yacht at the nightmare's black, tree-trunk tibia. They all braced for impact.

None came. They were clear and gone, heading up the avenue. The gigantic phantom had vanished into the storm.

THE SACRED MOUND was massive, its apex crackling with corposant. Damocles abandoned the yacht at the base apron and advanced at double time up through the lashing rain onto the old stone causeway that crossed the perimeter ditch to the main entrance.

Mabuse was waiting for them under the lintel of the wide doorway. He held a laspistol in his real hand, and the fused unrecognisable remains of several corpses sprawled on the flagstones around him.

Mabuse raised his golden hand and the roaming digit flew up and snapped back into place.

'Come on,' he said, turning to move into the Mound. Priad saw he carried what seemed to be a heavy knapsack on his back.

'Would you care to tell me what's going on?' Priad asked.

'There isn't really time,' Mabuse replied curtly.

'Those bodies... who did you kill?'

'I mean it, brother-sergeant... there isn't really time.'

As if to underscore his words, a salvo of autogun fire whipped down the entrance tunnel from within, the large calibre shells ricocheting off the stone floor and low roof. Natus cursed as several rounds struck his armour.

Priad ran into the gunfire, his bolter juddering in his fists. On his visor, the ammo tally dropped. The target cross jumped and flickered as it searched the green gloom for a body.

A flash of muzzle discharge, hot white against the emerald background.

The cross locked.

Priad fired and a human figure tumbled out of cover with such force it bounced off the wall behind it.

To his side, Khiron and Xander cut down two more ambushers.

In seamless formation, Damocles swept into the inner atrium. Natus and Aekon covered the back, Xander and Scyllon the exit ahead. Pindor and Andromak advanced into the centre of the hall.

Priad knelt to examine one of the bodies.

A human male, a local. Nothing especially significant about him apart from the fact that thirty seconds before he had been brave or foolhardy enough to open fire on a squad of Space Marines. Priad's bolter fire had all but turned him inside out.

'A looter?' he asked.

Mabuse leaned over Priad's shoulder and reached out with his golden hand. The ring finger projected a thin, searing fusion beam almost a metre long that grotesquely peeled the corpse's flesh away from his forehead. Priad shuddered as he saw the rune branded into the front of the skull.

'Cultist,' Mabuse said, switching off the fusion beam. 'The inner brand, the bone-burn. In all my years of hunting these devils, I've never found out how they do that. How they brand the mark into the bone without blemishing the skin over it.'

'I've never seen its like,' Priad admitted.

'It's the mark of a powerful and ancient cult,' said Mabuse matter-of-factly. 'I've terminated their activities on three other worlds. I was dismayed to find them at work here.'

'And how did you find that out?' Khiron asked.

Mabuse turned to the Apothecary and smiled.

'Don't tell me… there isn't really time.'

'Indeed,' nodded Mabuse. 'Besides, there are some things you don't need to know. To keep it simple, a notorious and well-backed cult is active here on Iorgu. They carried out the murder of the old queen for one simple reason. They wanted a coronation.'

'What?' Priad snapped. 'Why?'

'Because only during a coronation would the stasis locks of the Sacred Mound be disengaged and the heirloom treasures of Iorgu removed for the ceremonies.'

'They're after the treasures?'

'No. They're after what lies under the Mound. What the treasures hold in check.'

Priad rose. 'If there's anything that makes me want to crush a man's head, it's riddles, Mabuse.'

'The first settlers of Iorgu, the first monarchs, bested something here. Something they encountered when they first landed. The truth of it is lost in the veils of time, and only appears to us through the world myths. Some great evil was here... had been here since before the rise of man. The Iorguan first comers vanquished it and built this mound over it. The treasures are the components of a stasis system that keeps it dormant.'

'It?'

Mabuse shrugged. 'What's the worst thing you can thing of, brother-sergeant?'

Priad didn't answer.

'Worse than that,' Mabuse said. 'It's locked away, slumbering, and so it's safe enough to remove the treasures for a few days each time there's a coronation. But this coronation has been forced, and the moment the hierarchs removed the treasures, the cult made its way into the unprotected Mound to stage the rituals of awakening.'

'What do we do?' asked Priad.

Mabuse opened his knapsack so Priad could see inside. The sceptre and orb and all the other precious treasures were tumbled together inside.

'We put the relics back and re-engage the stasis system. Before it's too late.'

## VII

THE INNER BURROWS of the Mound were cased in stone: floor, walls and roof. From the atrium, they spiralled down into the belly of the hill, lit by fluttering light reeds and caged glow globes. At regular intervals, other down-spiralling tunnels spoked away from the main run. Mabuse led Damocles down in the half light, often taking choices at junction spurs that to the brother-sergeant seemed to defy logic.

'Trust me,' Mabuse said. 'The inner structure of the Mound is built like a triple helix, and is full of dead ends and liar-paths.'

'Liar-paths?'

'Artful diversions designed by the Mound builders. Fake tunnels and curves meant to outwit tomb robbers.'

They're outwitting me, Priad thought.

Reality had become unkempt in the lower levels. In one section of slowly sloping tunnel-curve, it was raining and lightning flashed. In another, the walls bellied and swayed like the wall of a tidal wave. In a third, every wall-stone became a chattering human skull. None of the skulls had eye sockets. The bone bowls were smooth down to the snapping teeth.

Mabuse seemed oblivious to it all.

Around another wide bend however, he faltered and paused.

'I've made an error,' he told them. 'Go back. We should have taken the left-hand turn.'

They retraced their steps back to the last junction.

'No,' he decided suddenly. 'I was right. It's trying to fool me. You're trying to fool me, aren't you?' He yelled the last phrase at the walls, which rippled and sweated.

They went back the way they had come. Fleshless rat-dogs the size of small horses blocked their way, eyes like yellow coals, exposed muscles and organs glistening in the light. Aekon cried out in surprise and fired his bolter.

'Glamours!' Mabuse said. 'Just walk through them.'

Following the inquisitor's lead, Damocles waded through the semi-corporeal beasts, feeling them leave a sticky trace of ecto-plasm on their armoured legs. As they touched them, the skinned things dissipated into steam.

'They're just ghosts,' Mabuse assured the Iron Snakes. 'Phantoms generated by the psychic birth pangs of the Sleeper. All of them, symptomatic phenomena like the storms and the auroras and the corposant.'

What they met around the next bend wasn't glamour at all. Cultists rushed them from the division of another spiral, weapons blazing. Khiron and Pindor took the brunt, reeling back. Aekon, Dyognes and Scyllon met the attack with a broad-side of bolter fire that sprayed the tunnel wall with blood and bone shards.

More cultists charged them from the depths. They carried a mix-ture of las weapons and autoguns. One had a flamer.

The gout of fire wrapped itself around Priad and his armour sang out an imperilled series of alarms. Priad strode through the flame and laid in with his bolter and his power claw. Three cultists fell to the spitting gun and two more to the venerable claw-weapon.

Andromak pressed in beside Priad and extinguished three more cultists with his plasma gun.

Others fell back, firing as they went, chased by Priad's punishing fire.

'The inquisitor is down!' Khiron voxed.

Sending Andromak and Kules ahead at point, Priad hurried back to where Khiron and Natus stood over the crumpled body of Mabuse.

He was a mess. At least three auto-rounds had hit him. His pale face was paler than ever as he held out the knapsack to Priad. When he spoke, blood gushed out of his mouth.

'Finish it, brother-sergeant.'

'Stay with him,' Priad told Khiron as he took the knapsack. 'You too, Aekon, Xander.'

'The rest with me.'

THEY PRESSED ON, ignoring the glamours that rose at them, fighting back the cultists that tried to stop them. For thirty-five minutes, they battled down the last stretch of tunnel-curve into the heart-chamber of the Mound.

Priad lost count of the cultists they had killed. The tunnel slope was awash with blood.

He could hear a frantic ticking, like the stridulation of insects, getting louder with each passing moment. It sounded like a billion bugs clattering their wing-cases in the darkness.

The heart-chamber was wide and high, a chapel in the bowels of the Mound. They struck in from the left, gunning down a dozen cultists in a rattling blaze of fire. There was a podium and an altar of greasy pink stone. The cultists had laid out the most appalling offerings on the altar.

Sacrifices. Butchery to turn even the strongest stomach.

The fritiniency of chattering bugs increased in volume. Unseen elytra in their double-millions crisped and rubbed against each other. The air was thick and sour, and the environment sustainers in the Astartes' suits began to struggle as they worked harder.

Apparitions of goat skulls fizzled in the air around them. Kules head-shot a cultist that they had presumed dead but was now reaching for his weapon.

The Sleeper was almost awake.

A noxious smoke, the vile stink of aeons, furled out around the altar. Despite his suit filters, Priad smelled grave-mould and the corrupted rot of deep tombs, locked away from air and light for thousands of years. There was a sickening taste they could sense even in their airtight helmets. A numbing dislocation. A kaleido-scope of nauseating colours.

Priad knew his nose and ears were bleeding. The suit vents jud-dered as they tried to cope with the liquid welling out of him. He saw Kules and Andromak fall to their knees. Natus and Scyllon started shooting at shadows. Dyognes and Pindor wavered in con-fusion.

Bugs, stridulating bugs, were crawling all over them. Priad saw their clicking forms scurrying across his visor-view, antennae waving.

He tried to wipe them away. He tried to reach the altar.

The Sleeper began to form in the air of the heart-chamber. Its shape was made up of swirling insects, slowly coalescing into a solid.

Eyes... vast ocelli in compound form... skull cheekbones... slowly swaying palps as long as a man's body. Yellow light began to froth up in the monstrous compound eyes as they resolved.

The swarming insects coated the members of Damocles, forcing them to their knees. Priad saw the tide of insects eating the flesh from the cultists' bones. Living and dead alike, the cultists were consumed.

The glowing yellow ocelli stared at him as they became more real. The monstrous palp mouthparts reached for him.

Priad fired a bolter round into the Sleeper's gummy, salivating maw for good measure and reached the altar. He had to wipe blood and entrails away to find the age-smoothed recesses designed for the relics.

Swarming carnivorous bugs weighed his limbs down and spilled in fat squirming masses into the knapsack as he opened it. He took the treasures of Iorgu out, one by one, and slotted each one back into place.

As he reached the last one, the sceptre, the writhing weight of insects blotted out his visor and swamped his vision. He wiped his visor with his hand.

'Sleep again!' he bellowed through speaker grilles clogged with insect parts and still-wriggling, shorn off legs. 'Sleep again forever!'

## VIII

AFTER THE CALAMITY, Iorgu City smoked like a kicked-over bonfire. The storm roiled away into the north and left the sky bleached of all colour except the yellowish sulphur dioxide trailing from the fires.

A great, wounded outrage lingered in the city.

'Message from Lord Militant Farnsey's officio,' said Kules, transferring the vox-squirt to Priad's data-plate.

Priad logged it with the others. Fifteen formal communiqués of denouncement, from Farnsey, the Princess Royal, even the king elect.

'Damn them all,' he said. Damocles had purged and sealed the Mound, but had not yet made a report to anyone. Perhaps it was better if the Iorguans remained ignorant of the fate that had almost befallen them.

'They will send petitions to Karybdis,' Khiron said softly.

'Let them,' said Priad. He took the golden digit from his belt pouch and activated it. A tiny holoform of Mabuse appeared. 'Exalted Chapter Master Seydon,' the holoform began. 'With my dying breath, I commend Damocles to you. They will undoubtedly receive rebuke and censure for abandoning their duty of care to the Imperial nobility. However, there are certain facts that must be made known to you–'

Priad snapped the holoform off.

'I don't think we have anything to be ashamed of,' he said.

Far below, the flash of their landing ship reflected off the muddy plains and temporary seas of Iorgu. Bright as a serrated knife from the daylight winking off its ridged bows, the Imperial barge loomed ahead of them like a rising star in the eastern sky.

# PART SEVEN
# GREENSKIN
# Undertaking to
# Ganahedarak

# I

THE SOFT BANK of sediment sand shelved away before him and sloped down into the darkness of the trench. Above him, the world was a pale blue vista where the sunlight penetrated. It was a serene place, and Aekon felt he might have been standing on a sandy beach under a clear blue sky. Except for the vicing pressure, the enveloping cold and the booming roar in his ears.

He took another weightless step down the bank, his bare feet lifting slow mists of sediment around his ankles. He was naked but for a thong and a strap-belt around his broad torso that supported a small, draw-string bag.

How long now? Sixteen minutes. He'd been counting carefully, but those in the phratry who knew such things said it was easy to lose count. After seven or eight minutes, despite the closed function of an enhanced pulmonary system, despite osmotic oxygen exchange, despite metabolic toxin dispersal, the mind would begin to cloud. Poison accumulated in the bloodstream, adding to the effects of temperature and pressure. Errors would start to creep in.

If he had miscounted, even by a half minute, if his mind had clouded, then it was already over, and he was dead. And a fool.

Some in the phratry had warned of the narcosis dreams. The calm serenity that overtook the unwary or the ill-prepared. The dreams were comfortable, they said. Beautiful. They made a man believe he was fine, and that he could last down there forever. They were the symptoms of a death already half-complete.

Aekon kicked off from the bank, and reached out with his powerful arms to drag himself further down into the weight of water and the darkness of the trench. He felt the slowly increasing burn deep in his lungs, the lactic acid in his muscles, the profound pressure stretching the skin of his face and chest. His limbs seemed leaden.

Just a little further, a little deeper. Sixteen and a half minutes now, by his steady count. His secondary heart began to thump harder. The blackness of the trench embraced him. From the soft lip of the bank, the trench dropped away, virtually perpendicular to the upper seabed. The water became colder almost immediately. Too far from the sunlight, ten or twelve degrees cooler than the water above. He kicked with his legs, head down, arms cleaving the water like oars. His head felt like it had been wrapped in metal, and that metal wound tight. A few pearl bubbles escaped the corner of his lips.

He was down in the blackness now, in the cold bosom of the trench. The trench. It had no other name, even though it had been a special site for the phratry since the earliest times. A place of self-testing, of endurance and courage, of risk and bravado. A place where a man might literally leave his mark.

A place where a man could make a testament of his own strength that only those others as strong – or as foolish – could see it.

Seventeen minutes. His eyes, rendered responsive to optic-therapy since his fourteenth year thanks to the occulobe, read shape and form in the lightless depth. He resolved the first of the offerings scattered in the mud at the base of the trench. Blades, shields, cnokoi, the tips of sea-lances, beads, bones, slivers of armour plate, totems and charms, icons and trophies, all ghost-pale in the gloom, fronded with the sugary white filigree of lime and algae. Each offering was inscribed with a name or mark, though some were too sea-smoothed to read any more.

Seventeen twenty. Aekon crawled forward, and chose a likely place, a smooth curl of mud between a bronze figurine and three lance-heads. The lance-heads had been planted cup-down into the mud so they grew like a little crop of sprouting blades. The bronze figurine, which may have once been the great primarch but which had lost all likeness, stood askew, its face turned to the azoic darkness of the trench, as if it had no desire to be a witness to the foolishness of men.

Aekon kicked his legs to stay in place, and pulled open the drawstring bag. It flopped slowly and heavily in his numb fingers as the current took it. He reached inside and removed his offering. It was the munition clip from an autorifle, still packed with live shells. He'd taken it from a cultist he'd slain during the assault on the Sacred Mound on Iorgu. That had been his first undertaking as an Iron Snake, and as a member of Damocles. The cultist had been his first battlefield kill. It was a good offering, appropriate, and he'd marked it with his name and the symbol of his squad.

He placed the clip on the mud, and pressed it down with his hand so that it wedged in far enough not to be dislodged by the trench current. Then he made the sign of the aquila across his chest.

He thought of Iorgu for a moment. His first undertaking, all right and – aside from two uneventful sentry missions – his only undertaking in the two years since he'd been inducted to the phratry and Damocles. Certainly the only one in which they'd been blessed with combat. He ached for combat, ached for–

He blinked. He ached, full stop. Thinking of Iorgu, he'd let his mind slip for a moment. He'd stopped the count.

Was this it? Was he already clouding? Already dreaming? He longed to draw a breath.

He rubbed his eyes with his white, shrivel-tipped fingers, hoping to coax some clarity back into his vision and his mind. He was done here. He had done what he had come to do. All that remained was the return. Back to the surface.

For a moment, in the blackness, Aekon could not remember which way that was.

He sank a little, and his toes touched the mud. The sensation made him flinch. He looked down, saw the trench bottom, and his straining, pounding mind performed the simple logic of up and down. He bent his thick, powerful legs and kicked off the sea floor.

It grew lighter as he rose, straight up the cliff of the trench. A pallor invested the sea above, a cyan glow. He kicked his burning legs. The water grew warmer as he passed the lip of the trench and came up into sunlit bottoms. Beams of light, golden, shafted down through the blue, like ladders from the surface far above. Fish glittered by in patterned formation. Going up was faster than the crawl down. How long? Five minutes? Four?

Could he last that?

Aekon began to think he couldn't. He was kicking still, rising, occasionally sweeping with his weary arms, but his mind was drifting. He thought of childhood friends, of a hound he'd once owned. He thought of the small village house where he'd grown up, before his selection and induction. He thought of a woman who might once have been his mother. He thought of his first sea-lance, half-size, a boy's model. All these things, like fast-changing picts on a viewer. He couldn't concentrate or focus. He was seeing things.

Things like the merman who had come to claim his life, and carry his soul away to sleep in the Endless Ocean. Tall and broad, beads of air trapped like quicksilver in the contours of his musculature, his legs kicking together like a beaknose's flukes. The old god of the sea, bearded and grey, a sea-lance in his hand.

The merman came closer, powering down through the light. His face was grim, his eyes narrow, his jaw jutting, like Khiron's face wh–

No, not *like* Khiron. It *was* Khiron.

The Apothecary of Damocles surged towards Aekon and reached out his hand. Aekon's mind woke up at once, shocked into clarity.

He recoiled from Khiron's reaching hand and shook his head. Khiron frowned at him. Aekon shook his head again. *No help. I'll do this alone.*

He began kicking again, head back, almost convulsing his way towards the surface. Khiron swept in behind him in a graceful turn, sea-lance at his side.

From the blue of the mid-range into water that was silver and yellow in the sun, water that teemed with bright shoals and drifting sea-ribbon.

So close now. So close.

* * *

THEY CAME ASHORE, up the white-gold sand of the empty beach. Beyond the crescent shore, the forests rose, green and thick and lush around the headland. The Ithakan sky was a delicate blue, the sun fierce.

Aekon saw nothing of it. He splashed up through the breakers, bent double, gagging and choking, his head pounding. He tried to force the sphincters of his multi-lung to relax, but his chest was burning and they had been locked tight for too long. His skin was pimpled white, drained of colour, and the sun burned his back.

Khiron waded in after him, his sea-lance across his shoulder. He was breathing cleanly, clearing his throat and lungs.

'Relax your throat,' he said.

Aekon fell onto his knees on the hot grit of the sand. He retched and brought up a small amount of sea water.

'Relax,' Khiron said again. 'Untense. Your lungs will unlock if you stop forcing them.'

Aekon nodded. The constriction in his chest was just beginning to fade, and the fire in his heavy limbs was going out. He looked up at Khiron.

The Apothecary had stuck his lance into the sand and was leaning on it, standing on one foot. Every few seconds, he switched to the other foot, sparing himself the painful heat of the sun-cooked sand.

'Shade,' Khiron said.

Aekon became aware of how much the sand was burning his knees and shins and the tops of his feet. He rose unsteadily and followed Khiron to the dark shadow of the tree-line. It was cool there, and smelled of wet vegetation. Bird calls rang out of the deep forest.

Aekon sat down on a log and forced himself into a relaxation exercise, the *limbus*, that eased muscles to the extremities and calmed the mind.

'You think I'm a fool,' he said at last.

Khiron shrugged. 'I think you're young. I think foolishness and courage are sometimes different faces of the same coin.'

Aekon looked around abruptly. 'Priad...?'

'Is not here. And knows nothing of this. Nor will he, unless you choose to tell him.'

'He would hate me for it.'

'Brother-Sergeant Priad does not hate. Hate's a strong poison, Aekon. You know that. There's no more room for hate in the mind of any phratry member than there is fear. Hate clouds and muddles the mind. Like deep, cold water.'

Aekon looked down at his own feet.

'No warrior needs hate or fear, son. They get in the way of efficient warfare. Priad would not hate you. He might even understand. But he would cast you out of Damocles.'

Aekon groaned.

'He'd have no choice. You know that.' Khiron had leaned his lance against a tree and was carefully tying his grey hair up in a pleat across his crown. 'Phratry rules. Trench offerings are a forbidden test. You'd be bounced back to petitioner.'

'But you don't agree?' Aekon asked.

'Because?'

'Because… you said you wouldn't tell Priad.'

'I obey the edicts of the Chapter without question,' Khiron said. 'But I am an Apothecary, and so I have some latitude. I came to the beach and went for a swim. I saw nothing.'

'Thank you,' Aekon said.

'Don't thank me with words,' Khiron said, dismissively. He walked a few paces away and gathered up his kit from where he had left it: his leather training cuirass and greaves, his knife-belt and carrying pouch, his red linen chiton, and his sandals. He began to get dressed.

Aekon watched him. 'How did you know, Brother-Apothecary? How did you know I'd do this?'

Khiron pulled the chiton over his head, shook down the hem of it, and began to strap on his cuirass.

'We come on a nine dayer to the remote Cydides Isthmus, a place of good forest country and hills for cross training and exercise, and fine sea-inlets for swimming trials. But every soul in the phratry well knows that the Isthmus is also the location of a certain bay and a certain trench, celebrated in the informal lore of the Chapter. On long exercises like this, there's always one young buck who slips away to try his strength and become a member of that secret honour club. I kept my eyes open. It's usually one of the younger

men, so I figured on you or Dyognes, or perhaps one of the petitioners. I decided it was you.'

'Why?'

'Because the petitioners are an unimpressive rabble, and not
one of them has the wit or guts to try it. Because Dyognes, in my
opinion, has nothing to prove. Because you are the youngest of
all, and feel you are in the shadow of the whole squad, including
Dyognes.'

'Am I so transparent?' Aekon asked. 'So... weak?'

Khiron smiled. He was lashing up the cords of his sandals. 'That
was just a guess. In truth, it was one little thing. On a nine dayer
like this, the order is for basic kit. Bare minimum. Training armour,
shield and lance, oil and whetstone in one pouch, vox relay in the
other. I noticed you carried an extra pouch, inside the rim of your
shield, small, but heavy. Your offering.'

Aekon laughed. 'I should know better than to try and hide something from the likes of you.'

'You really should.' Khiron fitted his greaves around his calves
and then stared at Aekon. 'Well? Did you make it?'

Aekon pulled off his strap belt and held out the little, sodden
bag, empty. He couldn't stop himself from grinning.

Khiron raised his eyebrows. 'Well done. So, you're a trencher
now. One of the foolish few.'

'It didn't feel foolish,' Aekon said. 'It felt like a proper test. We're
too safe in our war plate, too safe in our augmented bones and
muscles. Every day, we wake and feel like gods. It was good not to
feel invincible for once. To find the limit of even this post-human
flesh. To feel danger, pure and genuine.'

'And fear?'

Aekon shook his head. 'Not fear. Not for a moment. But I felt I
was being tested as a man might be tested, not a superman.'

'Medes,' Khiron said, hefting up his combat shield and fitting his
arm to the grip.

'What?'

'That's not you, that's Brother-Captain Medes talking. Don't
bother denying it, I've heard him. Medes of Skypio squad, bravest
of the brave. It's said that Skypio himself started the honour club
and to this day, they practise the rite, in defiance of the Chapter

edicts. By merit of being the foremost, the elite of the elite, Skypio is allowed some freedom by our Chapter Master. Don't get drawn in by their recklessness.'

'I wouldn't, brother.'

'Yet you made the dive. In the history of our phratry, Aekon, thirty-seven brothers have died swimming for the trench. That's why it's forbidden. It's a waste of good men.' Khiron paused. 'Also,' he added, 'I imagine that's precisely why young men persist in doing it. Would you rather have made Skypio, son?'

'Of course not.'

'Is Damocles not good enough for you?'

'No!'

'Then we'll speak no more of this. Get your kit. We should rejoin the others before our absence is noticed.'

Aekon rose. He balled up the empty bag and threw it into the undergrowth. Khiron followed him down the beach to where Aekon had left his kit, wrapped in the bowl of his shield and hung from a low bough where the ants couldn't invade it.

'How long?' Khiron asked as Aekon was dressing.

'How long what?'

'You must have made a count. How long?'

'Twenty-six,' Aekon said.

'Not possible.'

'I'm fairly sure. Twenty-six. Give or take ten seconds. My count did slip, but it couldn't have been less than that.'

'Your count was wrong,' Khiron said. 'No one manages over twenty-three.'

## II

THEY MOVED THROUGH the sunlit jungle depths, silent as glaciers. Andromak twenty paces to his left, Pindor twenty more to his right. The air was close and clammy, and mottled flies drowsed in the creeper-swathed gloom. Shafts of sunlight speared down through the canopy, as straight and firm as the lances they gripped across their right shoulders.

Shields up, rims to their eyes, shield-shoulders tilted forward. Priad flexed his fingers around the hardwood haft of his lance. They'd removed the blade tips, and fixed those razor-sharp warheads inside the dishes of their shields for safety. In place of the blades, their lances wore blunt, bronze practice heads.

The glade was quiet, except for birdsong and the drip of moisture. Priad looked across at Pindor, and the old warrior gestured with his eyes. Ahead, to the right.

They took up positions, becoming statues, entwined in the root systems of ancient trees. Now Priad himself heard movement. Something approaching, quiet, but not quiet enough.

Wait... *wait...*

A searing pain shot through the meat of Priad's left calf. He breathed in, not making a sound, and slowly turned his head to look. In amongst the roots around his legs, a green-back viper, two metres long, had made its hidden nest. Disturbed, it had sunk its fangs into his leg under the back of his knee where the sides of the greave met. Its bite was still in place, pumping venom into his flesh.

Priad did not move. His leg began to burn, as if a heated poker had been rammed into the marrow of his shin-bone. A pulse began to thump in his throat and in the base of his skull. Local hunters in the Isthmus used green-back venom to tip their ape-arrows. One scratch would kill a full grown simian big enough to feed a village for a week.

The pulsing and the fire grew worse. Priad remained still. The viper disengaged, its sacs spent, and coiled away into the root bole. Priad could see the glistening red puncture wounds where the blood was weeping out, refusing to clot. He remained calm, allowing his enhanced system to cope. His implanted haemastamen began its rapid ministry of his enhanced blood, altering its constituent make-up to fight the venom. His secondary heart and oolitic kidney started their conjoined detoxification work, pumping and filtering his tainted bloodstream. Larraman cells sped to the wound and, on contact with the air, formed a skin substitute to close it, overwhelming the anti-coagulant properties of the snake venom.

For a long thirty seconds, Priad felt weak and nauseous, deafened by the blood thumping in his ears.

Then the burning discomfort eased. The pain passed away. The only signs of the injury that remained were the scab-tissue on his leg and a swelling of the Betcher's glands in his hard palate. Rather than neutralising the deadly toxin, his sophisticated body systems had captured it and taken it for storage to the glands of his mouth.

A good omen. Now, for a time, this Iron Snake brother could bite like his namesake. As a rule, the Chapter did not actively practise use of the glands, deeming it unmanly and crude. But when accident made it possible, it was considered a benediction from the God-Emperor. To be envenomed by snake bite was lucky, a singular omen craved by every member of the phratry.

Priad slowly turned his gaze back to the clearing ahead. The noises were closer now. He could not see or sense either Andromak or Pindor, even though he knew they were there. Their skill was as good as ever.

The petitioners came into view. There were eight of them, all youths of seventeen or eighteen years, in the final months of implantation and induction. This wasn't their first field test, but it was their first nine dayer in the wilds with actual battle-brothers. They were young, but full-grown: massive figures whose skeletal and muscular structures had been amplified to post-human size by the long rigours of their genetic enhancement. In greaves and cuirass-plates, armed with blunt lances and shields, they looked like full members of the phratry, except that their chitons were novice white instead of red.

They moved well, Priad noted, but their noise discipline was imperfect. Two of them – Lartes and Temis – carried their shields too low, leaving their throats exposed. Aristar held his lance badly, the grip too far back on the haft for a balanced pivot or strike. But they were wary, observant. They came forward.

Priad had set the day's drill three hours earlier. He called it the cheese run, for that's what it had been called when he'd been a petitioner, dodging through these glades on exercise thirteen years earlier, under the watchful tuition of Veii squad. He'd taken a small curd of goat's cheese, the highlight of the day's meagre camp-feast, wrapped it in muslin, and handed it to Klepiades, the leader of the petitioners. The petitioners, all twenty-five of them, had been assembled at Starchus Rock at the peak of the headland. The task was to get the curd of cheese safely to the anvil stone, eight kilometres away in the thinning jungle at the tip of the Isthmus. If the petitioners succeeded, by any means, they would win the task. The brothers of Damocles squad vanished into the forest, and lurked there to stalk the petitioners and prevent them from accomplishing the drill.

The eight youths edged closer. Priad began to count to himself. Five steps, four, three, two...

On one, he came out of hiding. So did Andromak and Pindor, who had been making the same mental count in perfect unison. The three battle-brothers of Damocles burst out of cover, raising the ululating yell of attack, lances raised.

One of the petitioners squealed aloud in dismay. Another turned to run and tripped over.

Priad and his brothers fell upon the rest.

Priad thrust his lance and cracked a combat shield in half, the blow landing so heavily, the petitioner behind the shield dropped on his arse, winded. Rotating, Priad crunched his shield boss into the guard of another, and took the boy's legs out from under him with the flat of his lance. Andromak smashed the side of his blunt lance-tip across Aristar's ear, pulping it, knocking the boy over. Aristar hadn't been able to pivot his own lance up in time.

Pindor broke a lance shaft with his shield edge. The crack of wood was as loud as a lasgun discharge in the enclosed glade. His lance-tip stabbed in and winded Temis, doubling him up, gasping and gagging. Then Pindor, oldest of them all but as fast as a darting fish, swung his lance about and jabbed again, smacking another of the petitioners between the eyes. Nasal bone broke. Blood spluttered out of the petitioner's nostrils and hung in long, sticky ropes as the boy went down, clutching his face.

A lance-tip came at Priad, and he knocked it aside, spinning on his left foot to swipe with his shield, slamming a boy clear across the glade. Priad turned, saw the youth who had fallen as he tried to flee. He was still trying to get up.

Priad placed the tip of his lance on the youth's shoulder. 'Yield,' he said.

'I yield, sir!' the youth yelped.

Priad nodded, then struck his blunted lance tip across the youth's scalp to reinforce the lesson.

He looked around. All eight of the petitioners were writhing on the ground, broken and hurt. Andromak shouldered his lance and kicked Lartes in the rump. 'Keep your shield up next time,' he scolded.

Priad found Klepiades, the leader of the petitioners, the youth whose nose had been broken by Pindor's quick jab. He dragged the young man to his feet. Despite his painful injury, Klepiades was laughing. It was a snotty, snorting sound.

'Something funny?' Priad asked.

'Yes, brother-sergeant,' Klepiades choked, spitting blood.

With a terrific howling roar, the rest of the petitioner company came charging out of the undergrowth around them, shield-rims to their eyes, lances back over their shoulders for thrusting. They rushed the three seniors of Damocles together.

Priad took three glancing blows from lance tips before he got his shield up to guard. He smiled as he counter-struck. He was almost impressed. Klepiades, who had been chosen as leader because of his quick, cocky manner, had almost outsmarted the veterans. He'd set a trap, with himself and his party as bait. He had thought to give Priad and his seniors a stiff beating, taking them by surprise.

Almost, that was the key word. No petitioner, no matter how smart, got the better of a brother-sergeant, especially not a brother-sergeant as gifted as Priad, whose innate grasp of tactics had elevated him through the ranks faster than most. Priad seldom considered how he had come to take Raphon's place on Rosetta after only three years in the squad. He hadn't ever questioned it. He did what was expected and asked of him, and had never really appreciated the trust and admiration his superiors had shown him. In truth, all the phratry seniors, from Great Seydon himself on down, had seen in Priad enormous promise from the very start. The fact that Priad himself was oblivious to his own talents was a key part of his worth. He had no arrogance, no vice of ambition. He was the very model of the selfless Astartes.

And he could think two or three moves ahead of just about any-one.

As the petitioners came in, cracking lance-tips and shields, trading blows, and relishing the opportunity to thrash their drill masters with impunity, Priad gave out a yell.

The petitioner he was engaging stumbled back in alarm at the cry and the smile on Priad's mouth. Priad swung his lance and felled the boy with a skull-crack.

Damocles appeared. Rushing from cover, Kules and Natus, Scyllon, Xander and Dyognes. They landed blow after blow, free hand, on the backs and arms of the petitioners, forcing them down into the yield position. Those that fought back got their fingers broken, their noses too, their shields and their shoulder blades. Priad watched Klepiades's face fall in dismay.

'Your trap,' Priad said, 'out-trapped.'

'I submit, sir,' Klepiades said, falling to one knee. 'The petitioners submit. I bow to the might of Damocles.'

'I should think so!' Xander yelled, running past, thwacking a flee-ing petitioner across the buttocks with his lance.

'Stand down!' Priad shouted over the cries of pain and the sound of blows. 'Let them be! They did well, bless them. Spare your fury!'

Laughing and joking, the brothers of Damocles shouldered their lances and grouped around the cowering petitioners.

'Nice try,' Scyllon said.

'Bold try,' Andromak agreed. 'Setting a trap. Gutsy. I like gutsy.'

'Still got their arses whipped, mind,' Kules said. The brothers laughed again.

'Payment where due,' said Pindor.

'That's how you learn the lesson,' Natus added.

'And have you learned, boys?' Xander called aloud. The petition-ers, most of them down and in pain, moaned an assent.

'Have *you*?'

Priad turned. Khiron and Aekon emerged from the undergrowth.

'Meaning what?' Priad asked his Apothecary.

'Have you learned from these boys, brother-sergeant?' Khiron said.

'Have they got anything to teach us?' Priad asked. 'By the way, where were you two?'

Aekon shrugged, a little furtive. 'The lad and I swung west, pre-suming they might come along the shoreline,' Khiron said. 'We were wrong. We got here as quickly as we could.'

Priad nodded, not really interested. 'What did you mean, old man?' Priad had come to call Khiron 'old man', fully aware that Khiron despised the label.

'I mean, brother-sergeant… have you counted heads?'

Priad frowned, and did a head count. Twenty-four petitioners.

'Little bastards!' he hissed.

'Who's missing?' Pindor asked, annoyed.

'The lanky one,' said Xander. 'What's his name…?'

'Pugnus,' said Dyognes.

'That's the bastard!'

Priad stared at Klepiades. 'Where's Pugnus, boy?'

'Pugnus, sir?' Klepiades asked, as innocently as a youth with a shattered nose could. 'Do you mean our Brother Pugnus, also called *flight-foot*, the fastest runner in the petition class?'

Praid nodded. 'You know who I mean, you rat-pellet.'

'Well, sir, I believe he went running. You out-trapped our trap, but even that was just a diversion. We decided to keep you occupied. Right now, Pugnus is sprinting towards the anvil stone.'

'Little bastards!' Scyllon exclaimed. 'They're going to win this bloody drill! That's never been done!'

'Yes, it has,' said Priad, quietly.

'Damocles will be the laughing stock of the Chapter House for this!' Kules cried.

'Letting petitioners pull a fast one!' Andromak cursed. 'Throne alive, we'll never live this one down!'

'Relax,' said Priad.

'But they've bested us, on a cheese run!' Natus protested. 'That's never been done!'

'I think you'll find it has, brother,' Khiron said.

'I say we beat them some more!' Xander said, hefting up his lance. Many of the petitioners quailed back. 'A few more broken bones will take the sting out of this shame for Damo–'

'Wait, wait,' Pindor interrupted. He looked at Khiron. 'What were you saying, Brother-Apothecary?'

Khiron grinned. 'The cheese run. It's been done. Once. Isn't that right, brother-sergeant? I believe Veii squad still nurse that hurt.'

'They do,' admitted Priad.

'You did it?' asked Kules.

'I did. On my third nine dayer. Second proudest moment of my life.'

'What was the first?' asked Andromak, his eyes wide.

'Take a guess,' Priad said. 'Damocles! Up and ready! You petitioners too, no lagging! Double time! We're going to race this
*flight-foot* to the stone! Now!'

OUT OF BREATH, burned by the sun, the battered petitioners trailing
behind, Damocles reached the anvil stone in the wiry thickets at
the end of the Isthmus. There was no sign of petitioner Pugnus.
Priad had half expected to see a muslin-wrap of goat's cheese sitting on top of the stone.

Hardbills whooped in the thickets. Out beyond the point, where the
ocean broke against the trailing rock in white ripples, scale-birds circled
and called. The air was cool and fresh, and they could smell the sea.

'No sign of him,' Pindor reported.

Priad waved the hobbling, panting petitioners up close, and
grouped them around the stone.

'Five minutes' rest,' he ordered. Khiron went to treat wounds and
bind cuts. He took his beak-nose pliers from his pouch to tug lance
splinters from their flesh.

Klepiades sat down beside the stone, put his hand against it, and
began to laugh again.

'What's funny now?' Priad asked, getting tired of the youth's
insouciant manner.

'We win,' Klepiades said.

'How do you figure that?'

'We brought the cheese to the anvil stone. By any means, that was
your instruction. You brought me here.'

'And?'

'I ate the cheese this morning.'

Priad blinked. 'You ate the...' He started laughing himself, breaking out in great guffaws. One by one, the men of Damocles joined
in. They started clapping their hands against their bare thighs in
the mark of recognition.

'Well played,' Priad said.

'Can't we at least beat them again?' Xander asked.

'No, brother. Full rations. And wine. They deserve this win.'

Priad went and stood with Khiron. 'Smart boys.'

'Yes. I didn't think they had it in them. My mistake. I was telling
Aekon I didn't think they had guts, but they've got brains instead.

Maybe that's the future, my friend. An end to brawn and the rise of brains.'

'Let's hope not, old man,' Priad said. 'Brawn is all I have.'

'You sell yourself short.'

Priad shrugged. 'A good day. And the petitioners will have the bruises to prove it.'

'I'd say so.'

'I just wonder…'

'What?' asked Khiron.

'Where's Pugnus?'

They walked back into the group around the stone. Most of the youths were passing the wine skin and easing their aches and pains. Some lay down to doze in the sun.

'Where's Pugnus?' Priad asked Klepiades.

'Surely, I don't know, sir,' the youth said, his voice muffled by his badly swollen nose.

'You told him to run here?'

'No, sir. I just told him to run. As far away as he could. Run and hide.'

'Or go swimming,' one of the other petitioners muttered with a smirk.

'What was that?' Priad snapped.

'Nothing, sir.'

'Say it again. What's your name?'

'Tokrades, sir.'

'Say it again, Tokrades.'

'I… I said Pugnus was a good swimmer, sir. A good runner and a good swimmer. That's all I said.'

Priad turned away. 'He wouldn't be fool enough…' he began.

'What?' asked Khiron.

'The trench,' Priad murmured.

Khiron saw Aekon stiffen. 'No one would be fool enough to try a stunt like that,' Khiron said firmly. 'Not on a nine dayer under your command.'

'Pugnus is ambitious, anxious to prove himself. When we looked over the lists, you said that much yourself. Him and Klepiades. Hot-heads and triers both. Klepiades has proved himself today. Pugnus may wish to do the same.'

'He wouldn't be that stupid,' Aekon said.

A sharp chime sounded. It came from all of them, every member of Damocles, every petitioner. The chime came from the vox-relays in their belt pouches.

Khiron took out his relay and read the display. 'Immediate regroup. The exercise is cancelled. We are summoned back to the Chapter House. Shall I assemble the–'

'Not yet,' said Priad. 'We all go back, or none at all.'

## III

THE BEACH WAS empty. Priad grouped the petitioners under the tree line, with Kules and Andromak to watch over them. The rest of Damocles fanned out, covering the length of the shore.

Priad read the sand: the scuff-marks and the prints. 'Someone's been here,' he said. 'Today.'

'Yes,' said Aekon solemnly. He was about to speak further when he saw Khiron make a surreptitious throat-cut gesture.

'Priad!' Scyllon's voice rang out down the beach. He was standing at the edge of the trees, holding something up. A leather cuirass and a white chiton.

'Oh Throne damn it!' Priad snapped. He stuck his lance in the sand and began to strip off his training armour. The vox-chimes sounded again, insistent.

'Brother-sergeant,' Khiron began.

'It will wait,' Priad growled, unthreading his sandals.

'Just so. I am, however, obliged to remind you of our duty.'

'Duty?' Priad made a hollow laugh.

Khiron put his hand on Priad's arm. 'Let me go.'

'No.'

'Have you dived the trench, Priad?'

Priad glared at the Apothecary. 'Of course not. It's forbidden, and I'm no glory hound. But I'm not diving the trench, am I? I'm going after a bloody fool.'

'With respect, brother, the dive is difficult. For safety and sense, I'd recommend you let someone go who's done it before.'

Priad dragged his red chiton up over his head. 'And is there any such a fool in my squad? I trust not! Tell me now, for shame!'

There was a pause. Aekon was about to step forward when Kules raised his hand. Then Natus raised his too. A moment later, Andromak's hand went up, Pindor's, Scyllon's and Xander's. Hesitating, Dyognes lifted his palm.

Aekon put his hand up. He blinked when he saw that Khiron's hand was also in the air.

'All of you?' Priad murmured. 'Am I the only one not seized by this madness? I should cast the lot of you out of Damocles and start again!'

'Priad...' Khiron said.

'I've seen enough! Glory, how the hell do you follow me when you're all so much braver than me?' Priad demanded. His sarcasm was acid. All of Damocles winced at the disappointment in his voice. He turned to face the water.

'Let me go,' Khiron called.

'No! It seems I've got something to prove, Brother-Apothecary, if I'm going to keep up with the valorous fools in my command!'

Priad ran forward, the huge muscles in his bare back bunching as his arms came up in a spear-tip above his bowing head. He plunged into the waves, and ploughed out into the open water with powerful, windmill strokes. They watched as he paused, raised his head to fill his lungs, and vanished.

'Emperor help us, he's furious,' Xander said bleakly.

'We'll not hear the end of this soon,' said Kules.

'He hates us,' Aekon muttered. He blinked and corrected himself. 'I mean–'

'No, son,' said Khiron. 'You may be right.'


'How long?' Khiron asked.

'Twenty-two,' said Pindor. Xander nodded, agreeing with the count.

'I see h–' Andromak began to call, then shook his head. 'No, just a scale-bird.'

'Twenty-three and you're dead,' said Natus.

'Not always,' said Aekon. The older brothers looked at him.

'What would you know?' Xander asked.

'Nothing, brother.'

Khiron began to strip. Scyllon and Xander started doing the same.

'Twenty-three!' Pindor called.

'I'm going in,' Khiron said, handing his greaves to Dyognes.

'Will you shame him further?' asked Aekon, quietly. The squad members glared at him once more.

'You've got a mouth on you today, youngster,' said Pindor.

'Our brother-sergeant's not doing this for fool's glory like we all did,' Aekon persisted. 'He's doing it for the boy. But if he takes glory in it too, I think it might soothe his mind.'

'Rubbish!' spat Xander.

Khiron stared at Aekon. The sea breeze caught at his loose grey hair. 'You think he'd prefer to do this without help?'

'I think he'd rather die than show weakness after what we've told him.' Khiron glanced at the others. A few nodded.

'Twenty-four!' Pindor called out. Scyllon and Xander began to run down the beach towards the water.

'No!' Khiron yelled. They faltered and turned.

'No,' Khiron repeated.

'But–' Xander began.

'That's an order, brother. No one goes in.' Scyllon and Xander trudged back up the beach. As he passed Aekon, Xander growled 'Fine counsel you give, brother. If Priad dies–'

'He won't,' said Aekon.

'He's dead already,' Natus said. 'Twenty-three and you're dead. No one's ever bettered twenty-three.'

'That's enough,' barked Khiron.

They waited, past the call of 'twenty-five'. The sun burned their skins. The waves broke, and breezes stirred the treeline where the pale-faced petitioners waited, watching the veterans on the sand. Scale-birds circled and called overhead.

'Twenty-six,' Pindor whispered.

There was a splash, far out, and they all stepped forward. Racing sail-fish broke the water again, scales glinting like glass. Some of Damocles turned away, not wanting to look any more.

'Twenty-seven.'

Aekon looked at Natus, knowing the brother was about to pronounce his doom-laden rule yet again.

'There! There!' Andromak yelled.

They saw head and shoulders break the surface thirty strides from the shoreline in a puff of spray and foam. The form vanished again, then resurfaced and began swimming slowly to the shore.

The men of Damocles, all except Khiron, raised a lusty cheer. Xander punched the air with his fists.

'Priad! Priad!'

Priad struggled ashore. As he came up through the shallows, they saw why his swimming had been so laboured, and their cheer died away. Priad was half-carrying, half-dragging a limp, white form draped in sea-ribbon like a victory garland.

This was no victory.

The men ran down to him, and helped him to bear Pugnus's body up onto the sand. Khiron knelt over the petitioner, pulled away the slippery wreaths of sea-ribbon, and began to pump his chest. He opened Pugnus's mouth and cleared the airway, but there was no breath.

'His third lung's seized and locked,' Khiron said, pressing deep with his fingertips. 'It's a solid mass. No heartbeats.'

'He might have deanimated,' Kules said.

'He's not had the tutoring,' Andromak said. 'Besides, you think he could put himself under while he was drowning?'

Khiron pressed harder. Pugnus gave a long, moaning gasp as air squeezed out of him.

Khiron shook his head. 'Not respiration. Just the multi-lung relaxing and opening. He's gone.'

No one spoke. Their eyes turned towards Priad.

'Pick him up,' said Priad.

## IV

SOMETHING WAS GOING on. The urgent summons had already told them that much. As their transport descended into the great landing vault of the Chapter House fortress, they could see full scale preparations for war under way. Loaders and munition carriers milled about parked lift ships, and fighting vehicles were being marshalled up the deck ramps into yawning carriers. Service personnel bustled everywhere, taking orders from the equerries. Martial banners had been unfurled along the bastion wall.

This was no commonplace undertaking.

Priad led the company off the transport. Captain Phobor, dressed in plate and carrying a pair of marshalling flags, came over to their landing deck. In his gargantuan case of armour, he towered over all of them. His head was bare, his hair oiled and bound up to receive the war helm.

'You're late,' he said. 'Lagging behind all the others by two hours. I expect better of Damocles.'

'I stand rebuked, brother-captain,' said Priad, taking Phobor's steady gaze. 'I await censure.'

'No explanation? No excuse?'

'We are late answering the summons. I cannot hide that. There is no reason to excuse it.'

'Twenty stripes for your back, Priad. Ten for each in your command. But first, you–'

He halted. Six of the petitioners, in their white chitons, were carrying Pugnus's body down from the transport on a bier.

'A death?' asked Phobor.

'Yes, brother-captain.'

'Make your report to the lexicania. Make it good. But first, as I was saying, report immediately to the strategoi.'

'What's happening?' Priad asked.

'War's happening. Now get on.'

PRIAD SENT THE petitioners to their dorms, and his men to the barrack hall to ready themselves. Clad only in his red chiton, Priad walked the marble colonnades of the fortress moon and attended the strategoi.

Sweet incense had been lit in the censer bowls to propitiate the spirits of war, and petitioners were raising a slow, heartbeat pulse from kettle drums behind the awning. The armoured roof of the chamber had been closed, though that was merely symbolic.

In the vestibule of dark brown and black tiles, squad officers were gathering, most in full plate, to listen to the news and cast their ballots in the ancient, chipped kylix that stood ready on its plinth in the centre of the chamber. The officers were taking carved faience tokens from the wall rack and tossing them into the old toasting cup. Priad heard the stone tokens drop with a plunk. Each token denoted a phratry squad, and by placing it in the kylix, an

officer declared his squad battle-ready and eager to be considered
for the honour of selection. At the end of the period, the two-
handed cup, wide-dished upon its pedestal foot, would be taken to
Seydon and the selection made.

Priad saw Strabo, heavy in his armour, placing Manes squad's
token in the pot.

'Brother, what is the number?' Priad asked as his comrade came
over.

'Twenty-five squads,' Strabo said, unable to disguise the excite-
ment in his voice.

'Twenty-five?' Priad had not known the Chapter field such numbers in his lifetime. Not in one place. In the great age of the Reef
Wars perhaps, but in modern times? Even at Eidon they'd raised
only six.

'For what undertaking?' Priad asked.

'Full war with the greenskins,' Strabo smiled. 'War with the swine!
A mass incursion, so they say. A plague. It is reckoned Seydon himself will lead the order. We are sent to Ganahedarak to pitch
combat with them there.'

'*We*, brother? Are you so confident?'

'Manes squad is due selection,' said Strabo. 'We deserve a slice of
this glory, and Manes has not been in such fettle for years.'

'I send you luck,' said Priad.

'And Damocles?' Strabo asked. 'Surely your brothers are itching
for a taste of this? Cast your ballot. Let it be Manes and Damocles,
shoulder to shoulder, like the old days.'

Priad half-smiled and nodded. He stared at the casting kylix for
a long time.

THE GREAT BELL of the Fortress was tolling. There was no chamber,
no hall, no basement in the Chapter House of Karybdis where it
couldn't be heard.

To Priad, walking the shadowed hallways of the western barracks,
it sounded like a dull gong, but that was merely due to his distance
from it, and the thick bastion walls that stood in between him and
it. The Great Bell was the size of a drop-pod, and a team of twenty
servants in the belfry were hauling on the geared pulleys to move
the striker.

The toll announced that the period was over, and that the Chapter Master had made his selection for the order of battle.

In the ante-room of the barrack hall, Damocles was gearing. The brothers stood amid the trestle frames, anointing and casing themselves. Klepiades and the other petitioners were serving them, working as earnestly and devotedly as regular Chapter House attendants. Hair was being oiled and braided up; hands, forearms and torsos bound tight with straps of leather and linen. Plug points were being lubricated, feed lines fixed across skin with flesh staples, armour plates dutifully connected and locked into place. The petitioners were polishing every segment of armour with oil cloths, burnishing the surfaces to an almost mirror-quality gleam. Each segment was ritually blessed before it was clamped in place. Myrtle leaves and camphor burned in dishes around the alcoves, filling the air with perfume.

All activity ceased as Priad came in. The brothers rose to their feet to face him, most of them half-suited in their armour. Priad saw his own case of armour supported ready on a trestle, polished to a spectacular finish, his power claw on a smaller trestle to the side.

'Twenty-five squads, so we were told,' Khiron said at last, breaking the expectant hush. 'Damocles is battle-ready.'

'What is the undertaking?' Xander asked, his golden eyes bright.

'The Chapter makes war on the greenskins,' Priad replied. There was an eager mutter. 'The Master himself leads the battle chosen to combat.'

'A momentous day,' said Pindor, old enough to remember the last time such a grand muster had been made.

'What are our orders, brother-sergeant?' Andromak asked. He was holding the squad standard in his huge, gauntleted hands. 'We are ready for you to begin the rites.'

Priad did not blink. 'Damocles has not been selected,' he said.

The silence that followed had a heavy, painful quality.

'Damocles has not been selected?' Xander repeated slowly, as if he could make no sense of the words.

'We have not been selected for this undertaking,' Priad said.

'There's been an error made!' Andromak spluttered.

'An error?' cried Natus. 'An insult more like! Damocles is one of the Notables! This spits on our honour!'

The others began to add their voices to the complaint. Khiron remained silent, watching Priad with hooded eyes.

'Twenty-five squads, and we didn't rate?' Xander raged. 'This is a joke! To think the Chapter Master would select even the ten best squads, the five best, and Damocles not be one of them!'

'The Chapter Master did not select Damocles,' said Priad, 'because I did not cast our token into the kylix.'

Khiron sighed. Xander looked fit to strike at Priad, his face seething with uncomprehending fury. Scyllon placed a firm hand on Xander's arm to stay him.

'Why?' asked Kules.

'An officer casts his ballot to announce his squad is battle-ready.' Priad stared at them all. 'Damocles is not battle-ready. Not at all.'

'The hell you say!' Xander exclaimed.

'Watch that mouth,' Khiron growled. 'The brother-sergeant's word is law in this room.'

'You feel cheated of glory?' Priad asked them. 'Good. By your own admission, all of you have revelled in the empty glory of the trench. You have given in to your own weakness and pride. You are not fit to advance under the standard.'

'That's nonsense!' Andromak cried. 'It may be forbidden, but the trench is an old, respected honour test! There will be dozens of battle-brothers selected today who have done it!'

'But they have not openly confessed to their officers. Besides, each and every squad leader commands by the terms of his own conscience. I do not expect a high standard of behaviour from Damocles. I expect a *flawless* standard of behaviour. Strip off your armour, and make ready for practice drills. Expect at least a month of primary regimen. And there will be stripes to take before the day's end.'

'Is this punishment?' asked Aekon.

'No,' answered Priad, 'it's atonement. When I think you've restored your honour, and mine, then I might approve you as battle-ready.'

## V

THE MOON KARYBDIS seemed to fill half the night sky. It shone with a glassy, perfect clarity through the cold air.

Priad perched on the top of an outcrop of dark blue ice, the bronze cleats of his ice-boots chipping into the surface, and pulled his furs around him. He gazed up at the fortress moon, and fancied he could still see the light wakes of the departing battle-barges, making way on their undertaking, bound for glory.

Imagination, of course. By his estimation, the battle company had left at least five days earlier. He hadn't even allowed Damocles the consolation of attending the embarkation parade.

He rose to his feet, his lungs full of biting winter air, and looked back down the white glow of the glacier with his night-adjusted eyes. This was Kraretyer, greatest and mightiest of the glaciers that snaked their gigantic bulks out of Ithaka's southern pole into the frozen, ice-littered seas.

There was no wind, but the temperature was eight below due to the emptiness of the sky. In the far west, above the Oikon Ramparts, snow-bearded frost giants that formed the central massif of the polar region, the twinkling stars were hazy, as through a fine mesh. An ice storm was brewing, fillings its cheeks with the purest, lethal cold of the polar heartland. It could be on them in an hour, cutting like a swarm of blades.

He jumped down from the outcrop onto the rink-flat surface of the glacier itself, smooth violet ice dusted with a skin of powder snow that seemed almost luminous in the moonlight. His cleats kicked up flurries of it in the still air, and he steadied himself on his blade-pole. He waited for Damocles to come into view.

Priad was clad in an insulated bodyglove, boots, mailed ice-gloves and a hooded mantle of snow-leopard furs. The brothers of Damocles enjoyed no such luxury.

They came in sight, jogging hard across the flatness of the glacier shelf. Bare feet, aching from contact with the ice, bare legs and arms and hands, simple chitons of thin, red linen. They wore frost-shawls, tied like sashes around their waists, supporting small pouches of simple utility items and bronze ice axes. They were panting, cheeks raw and pinched, sweat freezing on their upper arms and brows. Each man was lugging a thirty-kilo block of ice on his shoulder.

Priad watched them approach. He struck his blade-pole into the ice, and unhooked the sling scales from his waist-belt, shaking out the canvas loops.

The men came closer. As Priad expected, Xander was in the lead by some distance, Andromak and Dyognes behind him, then Kules, with his odd, almost waddling manner of running. The rest of them played out behind. This was the sixth time in three days they had run this drill, and each time Xander had made the best showing.

Xander ran up and came to a halt, his bare feet, blue-numb, scuffing in the snow. He slid the block off his shoulder, leaving the folds of the chiton there clinging with meltwater.

'Brother-sergeant,' he gasped, supporting the glistening block in his hands.

Priad fitted the canvas loops around the block, supported the scales by the brass hook, and let the weight swing free. The gauge read thirty-one and a half kilos.

'Pass,' said Priad, letting the block fall out and smash on the ground. 'Go dig your burrow.'

Xander nodded, too cold to speak, and limped away, pulling out his ice-axe. He headed for the snow banks on the far side of the glacier.

Dyognes arrived next, outrunning Andromak for the first time. Andromak was close behind, and had to wait as Dyognes's block was weighed.

'Thirty-one and one hundred, a pass,' Priad said. Dyognes nodded, grateful, and respectfully waited while Andromak got his reading.

'Thirty and seven hundred. You pass too.'

One by one, the men reached Priad. The drill was simple enough: each man had to hack out a block of ice with his axe, then run with it down twenty kilometres of the glacier. Who came first and who last was not the question. The block simply had to weigh in excess of thirty kilos by the time it was measured at the finish. There was no weigh-in at the start. Each man had to gauge the weight of his block by eye and common sense, allowing for that part of it that would be lost to melt during the course of the drill. Underestimate, and the block would be less than the crucial thirty kilos by the time it was delivered. Indeed, on the first day, Aekon's inexperience led him to cut a slab that couldn't have been more than twenty-seven kilos to begin with.

But overestimation was a handicap too. Cut too much of a margin of error, and the runner would be labouring under far more weight than he needed to manage. On his second run, Aekon compensated for his initial error, and brought back a block that was over thirty-eight kilos. He had barely been able to stand by the time he arrived.

Failure to meet the thirty-kilo cut-off required a candidate to repeat the drill, alone if necessary, as many times as it took for him to get a pass.

Pindor and Khiron, the oldest men, were the last to finish. Pindor's slab weighed in at a fraction over thirty, the lightest load, but legal. Priad passed him, and he went to join the others, digging resting holes in the snow bank with their axes.

Khiron's block weighed twenty-nine and nine hundred.

The Apothecary tossed it aside, so that it splintered on the ground, and turned away, taking a deep breath. Though he was as aggrieved with Khiron as with the rest of them, Priad had felt it unseemly for the Apothecary to participate in the common drills. But Khiron had rejected any notion of favoured treatment. He had demanded to be tested on a par with the others. As a result, he had re-run the drill twice in the past two days.

'Pass,' said Priad.

'It was not,' Khiron replied, without turning round.

'I say it was. Get to your burrow.'

'I was unsuccessful. I am required to repeat the test.'

'Brother, there's a storm coming in...'

'Let it bite.'

'Damn it!' Priad said. 'Do as I tell you! Your blasted stoicism–'

'It's not a matter of stoicism, brother-sergeant. It's about dignity. Did my slab weigh thirty kilos?'

'No.'

'Then I'll see you again in three hours.' Khiron shook out his arms and began to run. Priad watched as the lone figure tracked away down the river of ice.

Priad crunched across the glacier to the snow bank where the men were digging in. Most had untied their frost-shawls, and draped them around their shivering bodies as they curled up into the insulated dens they had scraped out of the drift. Priad had a habitent, a single-occupancy module with a thermal cell. He got inside without a word, took off his mailed gloves, and chafed his hands beside the glowing heater.

Outside, a wind began to stir.

HE HAD BEEN in a self-induced catalepsean state for an hour or so, sleeping yet awake, allowing portions of his mind to close down and rest in sequence while his forebrain stayed alert. All the while, he had controlled and conditioned the flow and exchange of blood in his system, preserving and distributing heat. All of Damocles was doing the same, though it was easier for him in a secure habitent with a heater source.

Priad snapped sharp at a sound outside that the rising moan of the wind couldn't disguise. He took up his blade-pole and left the tent. There were snow bears in these latitudes, massive creatures that could shear a man in two. He scanned the area, sniffing the cold air for scat or odour.

The men were dormant in their burrows. The moon was still huge, but it had fogged and blurred, as if a dust was in the sky. The wind was stronger, gusting slightly, winnowing snow down the slope and rippling the loose flakes out across the surface of the glacier like eddies of fine sugar.

Something was here. Something close.

Pole in hand, he climbed to the top of the slope, from where he could see the ice storm rising in the distance, still two hundred kilometres away, a ghost shroud across the lower sky.

'Mine was a gold figurine of Parthus,' said a voice behind him.

Priad wheeled, his pole raised. He lowered it slowly. Facing him was a huge Ithakan male wrapped in a cloak of snow bear skin.

Petrok.

'What are you... sir, what are you doing here?'

'Visiting. Observing training. How goes it?'

'Well,' Priad said, still off-guard and confused. 'The men are fit. A few rough edges.'

Petrok nodded. 'That's good. You'll knock the roughness off with a winter regimen like this. How long have you been drilling?'

'Eight days.'

'And you'll keep at it?'

'For another eight. Then twenty days in the dune wash, basic endurance.'

Petrok smiled. 'They really must have pissed you off,' he said.

'Regimen is necessary. So the Codex states. Even the best must work to preserve their edge.'

'Eight days?' Petrok mused. 'So you missed the embarkation, then?'

'Yes.'

'A splendid sight. The like we hadn't seen in decades. Seydon was so damn eager to taste war again. Like a boy warrior. Sharpening his own blades, oiling his own hair. He had to blow the cobwebs off his armour.'

Priad snorted, but felt ashamed at the disrespect.

'Don't worry, brother,' Petrok said. 'Seydon made the joke himself. "Come help me with these cobwebs, Petrok," he said. "I'm sure there's armour in here somewhere." War, my brother. It was good to see his appetite back. Advancing out, at the head of his Notables.'

Petrok looked up at the occluded stars. 'Not all his Notables, of course.'

'It is only right the Master is served by the best and the ready,' said Priad.

'He was disappointed, you realise?' replied Petrok. 'When he found you hadn't voted, he asked for it to be checked. Thebes, Veii, Parthus and Skypio in his front rank, and no Damocles. What would Raphon have made of that?'

'He would have made the same decision, I believe,' said Priad.

'Of course, brother. Or he wouldn't have named you his heir.'

'I still don't understand why you're here, sir.'

'Petrok, remember? I thought we'd cleared this up. Eidon, wasn't it? You call me Petrok, unless I tell you otherwise.'

'I understood you'd been left in command, in the Master's absence.'

'I have. Locum master of the Chapter House Karybdis. You know how dull that is? No wonder Seydon was itching for war. It takes me away from my other work. Mandates to approve, parades and exercises to observe, petition selections, all manner of inventory to consider. The equerries, by the Throne! They'd drive a man mad with their fussing and their lists. I can't bear them. I've killed four or five of them already.'

Priad said nothing.

'It's all right, I've hidden the bodies well.'

Priad blinked.

'Funny, you can spot a tracer round flying at your head in time to duck it, but a joke...'

'That was a joke?'

'I haven't killed any equerries. It's frowned upon.'

Priad smiled.

'There, you see? And they say the Astartes has no place for humour.'

'Why are you here?'

'Ah, we're getting philosophical now, are we?'

'Sir... Petrok... please.'

Petrok shrugged his heavy shoulders under the furs. 'I was bored. I fancied a taste of unprocessed air. Rodos told me that Damocles had gone down to Ithaka for some winter training, so I thought I'd run an inspection. There's nothing sinister or devious about it. Besides, this is good bear country. I fancied I might claim myself a new pelt.'

He pulled something out from under his furs. Priad expected a bolter, or at least the mighty blade Bellus. Instead, he saw Petrok was holding a stabbing knife with a saw-tooth edge. It glittered in the darkness.

'You think we'll find one?' Petrok asked cheerfully.

'I hope not.'

'Ah, well.' Petrok looked west and sniffed the air. 'Storm's rising. A bitter one. Where's your tenth man?'

'How did you–?'

'One tent, and eight burrows. One less than I have fingers. Who is it?'

'Khiron. He's repeating the block drill.'

'Poor bastard,' Petrok said. 'Overdue?'

'Not yet.'

'Let's take a walk and see how he's doing. If the storm catches him, he'll be dead. You don't want the bother of finding a new Apothecary, do you? I mean, after the trouble you went to getting this one?'

Petrok slithered away down the snow bank. Pole blade in hand, Priad followed him.

## VI

THEY TRUDGED ALONG the flatness of the glacier, side by side in the filmy moonlight.

'What did you mean, a gold figure of Parthus?' Priad asked after a while.

'My offering,' Petrok replied.

'Offering?'

'To the trench. I was young, foolish. I believe only the second of those two things is a requirement, but the first helps.'

'You dived the trench?'

'During my first year, with Parthus squad. On exercise. It was all the fashion back then, more than it is today. Positively encouraged by the upper ranks, but discreetly, of course. You weren't of the phratry unless you'd taken a wyrm and done the trench. A test of personal skill and fortitude. Customs change, I suppose. The frequent deaths didn't help.'

'So you're a trencher?'

Petrok shook his head. 'Not me. I dived down, the figure of Parthus in my fist. I chose Parthus because he was my squad-founder. I never made it. Missed my count, ran out of breath. Barely got back to the surface alive. I was sick with the narcosis fever for days. My brothers covered up for me. It's a hard dive. But you know that. You're a trencher too.'

'No, I'm not,' said Priad.

'You went into the trench…'

'And I didn't bring any glory back. Just a dead boy.'

'I've heard about it. I read the lexicania report. And I spoke to Khiron. He told me what had been left out of the report.'

'He never said anything to me.'

'He wouldn't. He's a proud man, diligent. He told me how every last man in Damocles had owned up to diving the trench at some time or other. He told me how horrified you'd been to hear it. I guess that's why you didn't vote, and why you're driving them so hard now. Penitence.'

'Atonement. We have rules for a reason. Guilliman didn't compose the Codex for his own entertainment. I am ranking squad officer. It's my duty to punish and admonish.'

Petrok was silent for a while. 'Priad, have you not thought why they told you? Why they all confessed to you, there on the beach?'

Priad didn't answer.

'They didn't want you to dive and risk your life. They didn't want to lose you. For all the dishonour they knew their confession would bring upon them, they wanted you to know that every one of them was ready, willing and able to take your place. You know what I think that is?'

'They openly admitted to breaking the Chapter rules.'

'I think it's called loyalty. But I make bad jokes about murdering staff, so what do I know?'

The wind was picking up again, abrading their cheeks with its touch, and leaving a dust of ice crystals in their hair and the furs they wore.

'This is why you've come, isn't it?' Priad said. 'To counsel me and show me my error.'

'You've made no error, brother. Work them as hard as you like. Break their backs. Whatever glory they get to take in their lives, it's yours to determine. If you'd let them off, you'd have weakened your command. What you're doing here is right. I just wanted to make sure you appreciated the whole picture.'

They strode on.

'By the way, that's not why I've come here.'

Petrok stopped short. He pointed. Far away, a kilometre or more, they could make out a tiny figure struggling towards them along the glacier. It wasn't running so much as stumbling.

'Khiron,' said Priad.

'On his way back. Throne, look at the size of the block he's humping. You won't need your scales.'

Priad didn't reply. He was looking up at the snow bank to their left. Three hundred metres distant, something had moved, white on white. Priad touched Petrok's arm and pointed.

They stood for a minute, still as kouros statues in the fortress atrium, until it moved again.

'Oh, that's a big one,' Petrok whispered. 'A big female, I'd bet. She doesn't make us, we're up wind of her. But she's hunting.'

'She's hunting my Apothecary,' Priad whispered back. 'They like stragglers. When they chase a herd of long horn, they target the weak and the slow. She's upwind of Khiron as much as we're upwind of her.'

'You've hunted snow bear before?' Petrok asked.

'No. Raphon used to, for sport. He had a necklace of claws. He told me of the ways.'

'She's leading Khiron all right, staying ahead, choosing her moment. Terra, look at her move! Ah, lost her again. Behind that ridge.'

'What do we do?'

Petrok smiled and drew his knife.

THEY MOVED UP into the snow banks, low and quiet. Priad turned his pole around so that the metre-long, single-edged blade was slung forward, like a sea-lance.

Petrok stopped and stripped off his boots, motioning Priad to do the same. The cleats were crunching in the brittle, crisp snow, but bare feet would make no sound. They both scrubbed their hands, faces and armpits with handfuls of fresh snow to mask their pheromones.

The wind stilled again, sudden and ominous, letting go of the particles it was carrying. Ice shards settled like smoke around them.

They climbed the ridge, keeping the moon at an angle to minimise their shadows. Priad caught traces of animal warmth and breath-stink on the air.

Petrok signalled Priad to go left, and disappeared from view along the right-hand edge of the drifts. The air was so clear. The stars seemed to tremble with the distant booming of the storm.

Priad came to a halt, his feet ankle deep in the snow. The moon glow lit the whiteness all around. He was close now, surely? It couldn't have moved away so fast.

A snow drift rose up and assaulted him.

Ice-white, the skulking bear had been invisible until it moved. It let out a huge, shuddering roar as it came up. Priad glimpsed the yawning red cavity of its mouth, the massive yellow teeth. He smelled rank breath, polluted by saliva and seal blubber, and saw two diamond-black eyes.

He tried to raise his pole but it flew out of his hands as the gigantic fore-paw struck him. Claws the size of fingers ripped through his mantle and cut deep gashes in the flesh of his left tricep.

The impact was stunning. He felt like he'd been run down by a land raider. The arctic world turned over and over, dazing thump after dazing thump. He realised he had rolled clean down the slope onto the face of the glacier, limbs flailing.

Winded, bruised, he tried to rise. He saw spatters of his own blood glistening like rubies on the face of the ice. He looked up. The she-bear was coming for him.

She was gigantic. Two thousand kilos of rippling muscle and fat, coated in white fur. Forepaws the size of power-claws. A muzzled skull as massive as a thirty-kilo ice block. A gaping mouth as broad as the dish of the Strategoi's ballot kylix.

Priad rolled. The colossal predator crunched down on the glacier top, cracking the surface sheet beneath it. She began to turn, bellowing again.

Petrok landed on her, straddling her hunched back. The knife flashed and the bear whined in pain. She thrashed around, throwing Petrok off. The locum master cartwheeled across the ice, bouncing hard.

The bear was lunging at him before he'd even slithered to a halt.

Priad's pole was gone. He groped for a weapon, any weapon, and found the sling scales. He ran forward, feet slipping, lifting the scales like a huntsman's noose. The bear was mauling Petrok, pressing him into the ice as she tore at his furs.

Priad got in behind her and threw out the canvas loops of the scales. He got one of them down around the bear's throat, and began to drag back with every shred of his upper body strength, drawing the loop tight into a choking collar, yanking the bear's head backwards.

She writhed up, clawing at the constriction, and almost crushed Priad by sitting on him. He dragged tighter, scrambling away and tugging at the scale's hook. The bear began to make a deep, gurgling rasp as her windpipe closed.

Priad maintained his grip, pulling even tighter, his powerful arms quivering with the effort. The bear shook again, trying to find him with her paws.

He jerked the loop tighter, ever tighter. The bear tried to rise onto all fours.

Petrok appeared in front of her, his face and chest smeared with blood. As the bear reared again, Petrok rammed his knife up between her front limbs. It stuck fast in the bone. Blood steamed like boiling water as it poured out onto the ice.

The bear flicked a paw and swatted Petrok aside. She fell forward, Priad still cinched around her throat, dragging him off his feet. He pulled again, trying to wind the loops now to constrict them further, frantically holding on.

She wouldn't die. She simply wouldn't die. Nose down on the glacier, crawling forward, her inhalations stuttering and clamped, she fought on with impossible vigour. She dragged him twenty metres, like a rider clinging to the reins of a bolting mount, and left a dark stream of blood behind her.

There was a brutal, crushing impact. Priad heard bone break, and the bear went still.

Slowly, he relaxed his grip and slid off the sprawled monster. She was dead, or at least in the final, fluttering seconds of life, inert, broken.

Her skull had been half-crushed by a thirty-kilo block of ice that had been driven into her head from above with inhuman force. Bent down, hands braced against his thighs, Khiron stood nearby, panting hard and trying not to be sick from the effort.

'Sit down,' Priad said. Khiron nodded, and curled up in a heap to recover his breath and his wits.

With a last whimper of escaping gas and fluid, the animal expired, a hoarse, phlegmy rattle issuing from its ruptured throat.

Priad limped across the ice to where Petrok lay in a puddle of blood. The great warrior looked as dead as the bear, but he roused as Priad bent over him.

'Where are you cut?' Priad asked.

'All over,' Petrok replied, lisping through a sliced lip. Still, he managed to grin. 'But it's worse than it looks. Fine sport, eh, my brother?'

Priad shook his head and laughed. He gazed back at the bear's corpse, fascinated by the sheer size of the jaws and teeth, now exposed by the rictus of death that pulled the pink lips back in a snarl.

'The bite on that thing,' he muttered. 'So damn big...'

'A massive set of jaws,' said Petrok, rising slowly to a sitting position and holding a deep laceration on his chest together. Priad realised he wasn't talking about the bear.

'There was a reason I came here tonight,' he said slowly, his respiration ragged. 'Beyond the reasons I gave you before. I had a dream. I get them from time to time. It's part of my nature, and I've known enough of them not to ignore them.'

'A dream?'

'When a Chapter Librarian dreams, brother, you pay heed. Especially when they dream of you.'

'You dreamt about me?' Priad said, gingerly testing the gashes on his arm to check they were already healing.

'Yes, Priad. I dreamt about you. I don't know what it means yet. I was hoping you might help. I dreamt a scene. A place. A woodland. You were there. Others too, but I haven't remembered that part properly yet.'

'Damocles?'

'I don't think it was. But you were there. And there was a massive set of jaws. As big as the bear's. But the teeth weren't sharp. They were blunt. Does that mean anything?'

Priad shook his head.

'Think on it. It's important.'

Priad nodded. He looked back over his shoulder to find Khiron. The Apothecary was walking away from them.

'Where do you think you're going, old man?' Priad called.

'To repeat the drill,' Khiron replied. 'I lost my slab.'

'It was thirty kilos. You pass, you old fool.'

'I lost my slab,' Khiron repeated.

Priad helped Petrok to his feet. The wind was picking up again, raising powder snow in swirling loops from the facing bank. The storm was inbound now, closing fast.

'Khiron?' Petrok called out above the rush of the wind. The Apothecary turned.

'Drill's done,' Petrok said.

## VII

GANAHEDARAK HAD SUFFERED miserably at the hands of its invaders.

They had come, not swift and vicious in the night as was the way of the malign primuls, but bold and loud and slow. Their ships, if such cumbersome machine monstrosities deserved the name ships, had arrived like lost moons, slowly tacking in through the outer magnetic fields and taking up low orbits like wayward, lumpen meteors, visible to the naked eye.

They made no effort to conceal themselves, or even to effect a fast deployment. Surface batteries around some of the northern cities began firing on the menacing objects, but though hits were recorded, no damage seemed to result. The greenskins didn't much seem to care if a few fresh pits and craters were scored into the hulls of their lumbering craft.

It had been a long time since the greenskins had let slip their particular brand of horror on the worlds of the Reef Stars. For thirty centuries, their kind had not been seen, and the memory of them had dulled.

Ganahedarak had its memory refreshed on the sixteenth day after the new moons arrived in its skies. The greenskins began to descend to the planet's surface, their transports dropping like heavy comets. They did not fall upon the cities, but deposited themselves on the wide northern plains, forming up great hordes upon the flats there, hiding their numbers in the dust they kicked up. Then, raucous and loud, their braying and roaring audible from fifty kilometres away, they began to move.

One fifth of Ganahedarak's eighty cities burned on the first night.

THREE PRINCIPAL BATTLES took place. The first, at Aarple's Plain, lasted a day. Thirty thousand men, led by the glittering, armoured warriors of the King's Legion, marched out to meet one of the dust clouds. None returned.

Three days later, eight thousand men massed on the lowlands outside Kubrisa City, a fortress town in the Lower Cates. Supported by regiments of pike and musket, and retinues of the militia, the vanguard of the human army was composed of the Cates Dragoons, riding their great, crested lizards, and the Immortals of the Queen's Summoners. Their pinions were gold and blue and green. Their swords shone like mirrors in the sun.

The enemy arrived, a droaning wall of dust and noise, clashing their weapons against their shields, roaring into the sky. They advanced as slowly as a lava tide. A smell came off them, putrid and rank, like vegetation rotting in the bottom of a sump. As they came into view, they didn't seem very green at all. Body paint, black and red and white, caked the massive, shambling figures, and they were shrouded in animal skins and cloaks of chainmail.

The Summoners broke in fear, and were cut down as they attempted to flee across the brook at Litern. Such butchery was done, and witnessed by the remaining ranks, that fear spread. The smell of blood was in the air, like heated copper.

The Dragoons engaged then, driving their lizards into the lines of the foe. Lance-tips and lizard beaks became wet and glistening with ichor. Trumpets sounded. For a brief moment, victory seemed to taste stronger than inhuman blood.

Then the greenskins – or the Painted Ones, as they had become known by that time – rallied. In fact, they didn't even seem to rally as such. The line of them, thirty deep, towering monsters twice as tall as a man and thrice as broad, just seemed to flex, like a muscular arm, and throw back the Dragoon files. By the time the city fell, witnesses reported seeing lizard mounts, some weighing half a tonne, carried forward as trophies, skewered on the pikes of the foe.

Routed, the human soldiers fell back to Chessely, where they were reinforced by twenty companies of rifle and some two hundred cannon sent up, in haste, from the trading towns around the Gulf of Loomis. There, in the shallow valley of the Quibas River, the third battle took place.

The cannon teams barraged the Painted Ones for three hours after daybreak, then the rifleman infantry pressed forward into an enemy line punctured by the force of the artillery. For two hours, a running fight played out amongst the valley woods.

By sunset, there was no human left alive in the valley, or at least none that would still be alive come the following daybreak. The woodlands burned. The Painted Ones, so it was said, feasted through the night on human flesh torn from corpses that had been cooked simply by hanging them from the boughs of the burning trees.

TWO DAYS AFTER that, Chapter Master Seydon led his Snakes down onto the surface. By then, the Northern Hemisphere was lost to humanity, reduced to a trampled, ashen waste of scorched bones and fire-stripped cities.

The kings of the south had prepared the way for the Iron Snakes. They were fearful men, their armies traditionally weaker than those of the north, those that had already been vanquished. The kings of the south were relieved to see the bold warriors of Ithaka arrive.

In the grassy, wind-blown uplands, great roundhouse halls had been erected to shelter the Iron Snakes. Stone-built, with roofs of peat, they had been built out of respect and gratitude, the kings of the south expecting the Snakes to require bastions in which to sleep and feast prior to the war.

It had taken Seydon some time to persuade the kings that his warriors needed no such comforts. In their cases of armour, polished to a steel-glass finish, the Iron Snakes seemed like gods to the local men. Their voices and manners were strange, their weapons and wargear frightening. They smelled curiously of oils and unguents, and each one of them was twice the size of a regular human.

They assembled to begin their war-making. The greenskins approached: a vast, rowdy horde that covered the land. Sighting the Ithakan phratry, the enemy began to chant and mock, goading a response.

Seydon gave none immediately. The greenskins were numerically superior, five to one. Seydon formed his Snakes into a battle line around the ramparts of the uplands, and waited. He had reduced planets into cinders in his time. He would choose his moment. Such was the luxury of an assured commander in formal war.

After three days of bellowed mockery, the greenskins began an assault. Most of their charging front echelon died, pulped and split like over-ripe pumpkins under the steady bolter fire. Bruised, and thwarted for the first time since making planet fall, the greenskins set up a keening lament long into the night.

The next day, they tried again. Captain Phobor, hero of Ithaka, led the line to deny. In the space of fifteen minutes, the squads under his command, including two of the Notables – Parthus and Thebes – took the lives of eight hundred orks. The low-lying heather was rendered flat and wet with ichor for many acres. Huge, misshapen corpses littered the slopes.

The greenskins renewed their attack. Veii met the brunt of it, around a stand of tall trees known as Hessman's Copse beforehand and the Glory Hill ever after. Ork bodies were piled five deep in the heather, and virtually all the trees in the stand were shorn off at hip height by gunfire. Five Space Marines perished, including Lexicanium Nocis and veteran-hero Rubicus, champion of Syrakuse. The latter was found, decapitated, at the top of an earthwork bank after the battered enemy lines had retreated. The cadavers of sixty orks littered the bank beneath him, tumbled and torn in the undergrowth.

Phobor took the news hard. Rubicus, he said, deserved a better end than this. He advocated a revenge assault into the command lines of the enemy. Seydon refused, until he saw how deeply Phobor grieved and how lack-lustre the men of Veii had become without their most famous champion.

He approved the assault. It fell to lots, as was the practice at such times, and Parthus squad won the honour of avenging the loss of their noble brothers in Veii.

Brother-Sergeant Xeron of Parthus led the attack. Moving more rapidly and directly than the greenskins expected, he sliced into their command group at the summit of a low hill west of the copse, and made great slaughter. Xeron personally took the head of a swinekin chieftain, and raised up the grisly mass on his lance. Over four hundred greenskins died in the attack.

But that didn't seem to matter. Across the plain, the numbers of the enemy seemed without end. As the wind changed, Seydon saw in dismay that a second horde had appeared from the west, unannounced. More extraordinarily, this new force went to war with the existing mass of greenskins. Ork fought ork, two screaming, rampaging tides that clashed and locked into one another. This onslaught lacked all sense or reason. Seydon was forced to pull his forces back before they were overwhelmed between the twin opposing tides of shrieking monsters.

Parthus squad, extended and alone, was cut off. On the low hill, they were caught up in the internecine bloodshed as the greenskins murdered one other. Locked as on an island, they fought to the last, slaying huge numbers in the thundering chaos.

One by one, they fell, consumed in the sheer tumult, fighting off greenskins from every side. They were ground to atoms between the clashing fronts of the rival ork armies.

He saw it all.

He saw Xeron, last to fall. Xeron, his old squad commander, his trainer, his mentor, staggering from multiple wounds, slashing and stabbing with a broken sword, his bolter spent, his polished armour wet and gleaming with ichor.

He felt the blow land. An axe, sharp-toothed, cleaving through the back of Xeron's helmet, caving in the skull and spilling out all that made Xeron Xeron in an inglorious spatter.

He saw the lenses of Xeron's helm fill up with blood, saw the trampled heather rush up to meet his face through the wine-dark fluid.

He felt the chopping blows rain down on his unguarded back, breaking plate, breaking shoulder blades, breaking spine.

His legs went numb, without feeling. He saw the world through blood, and saw only blood.

And woke up.

PETROK WAS CHILLED with sweat. His limbs quivered. He had to touch his own face, bare and helmet-free, to believe there was no blood upon it. The Chapter House was silent.

'Rodos!' he called, hoarse.

Rousing, the lexicanium came to him.

'Find Priad,' Petrok told him. 'Tell him to make Damocles ready, ready or not. The Chapter Master needs us.'

'SELECT FROM THE others,' Priad said simply.

'I have and I will,' said Petrok. 'But I want Damocles. I want at least one squad of Notables in my phalanx, and Seydon has all the rest.'

'With respect–' Priad began.

'Then show me some!' Petrok snapped, rising to his feet. His private chamber was dark and cold, lit only by a few tapers and sour with the reek of burned herbs. He had been making offerings to the spirits of war and guidance. Bronze bowls full of pungent ash sat along the ledges of his wall shrine.

'I apologise,' Petrok said quietly. 'My friend, I was too sharp just then. My mind is troubled.'

'I can tell,' said Priad.

'Seydon is in danger. The undertaking is in danger.'

Priad tensed. 'I have heard nothing–'

'No word has yet come, Priad. But a dream I have had, a bloody dream. There was warning in it, faster and surer than any despatch. I aim to raise a force of at least five squads and journey to his aid.'

'But Damocles is–'

'If you say Damocles is not battle-ready, Priad, I swear I'll strike you down! I don't care! I admire your strength of command, and your duty. Perhaps your men do need stern punishment. That's your rule to lay down. But these new concerns outweigh them. I require Damocles to form the heart of my force, whether you deem them ready or not.'

'I see,' said Priad. 'If you command, sir.'

'Back to sir again, are we? Fair enough. I spoke harshly. But I'm not Phobor. I won't command you and then give you no good reasons. I want Damocles along for two very good ones.'

'Which are?'

'I trust you. I believe Damocles is just about the best combat squad the Chapter has to offer. Your presence will help keep some of the less experienced units in line. Secondly, and far more important, I dreamed about you, Priad. Remember?'

'I do.'

'What do you know of Fate?' Petrok asked, fixing himself a cup of wine. He offered the jug to Priad, who shook his head.

'Fate, sir? It's the will of the Emperor. It's the marrow of our lives.'

'Spoken like a true petitioner,' Petrok smiled. 'Consider this, my friend. You prevented Damocles from accompanying the Chapter Master, though they would most surely have been chosen if you'd put them forward. Because they disgraced themselves in your eyes? Perhaps. But perhaps, instead, it was Fate's purpose. Perhaps Damocles had to disgrace itself so they would still be here at Karybdis for me to call upon now.'

'Your mind works in wonderful ways, master,' Priad smiled. 'Truly. I see no such sense myself. My men broke phratry rules, and I have confined them for it until they know better. I see no great scheme of Fate. Just warriors who must toil until they understand discipline.'

Petrok nodded. 'For argument's sake, let's pretend I'm right. In the name of the Golden Throne, Priad, I've never met any soul as pragmatic as you. I believe that's why Raphon chose you as his successor.'

'Do you question Raphon's choice?' Priad asked.

'Not at all. Raphon and Memnes, Emperor love them, were quite right about you. Now summon your squad for me.'

'I will, sir. If that's an order.'

'Consider it so. Fate is expecting us.'

## VIII

THERE WAS A meadow, sunlit. A bright blue sky. Summer heat in the air. Something moving in the corn.

A meadow, golden in the sun. Blue sky. There, in the stirring corn, something black.

Meadow. Sky. Something.

Meadow again. The sky as blue as the waters of a certain bay on the Cydides Isthmus. The moving something brushed through the yellow corn.

A meadow. A something.

A black dog. Trotting through the corn, jumping in sport at passing corn flies.

His heart began to beat.

Priad woke.

THE IRON VAULT was so cold, wet frost had coated the walls. The lumen strips had been turned down to their lowest setting, and the vault was full of green shadows. A deep, slow rumble came from behind the bulkheads.

Stiff and slow, Priad got up from his brass cot. His mind felt as numb and pinched as his body. He flexed his bare hands in front of his face, saw the vapour of his breath break around them. Sense was slowly returning. He'd been dreaming.

Something about a meadow, over and over again.

He took a look back down the rows of brass cots filling the vault, and then padded, barefoot, to the chamber door, pushed it open, and went through.

Sensing his movement, lights in the adjacent compartment flickered on. It was warmer here, a dull, dry artificial heat. He took one of the chitons hanging from a line of pegs and pulled it on, then walked across the rush matting to the shrine.

The shrine was a simple alcove in the metal wall. The motifs of the phratry were inscribed around the arched recess. Within, taper pots and offering dishes sat on the ledge, along with other charms: figurines, shells, fish scales. In the centre of the ledge sat six copper flasks, banded with zinc.

Priad knelt down before the shrine, lit two of the tapers, and then bowed his head, his hands planted against the rim of the ledge. He murmured his devotions, his thanks and his blessings, his requests for good fortune in war, guidance, and success.

'Brother?'

Priad looked up. Khiron stood nearby, holding a bowl of steaming broth.

'When did you wake?' Priad asked, rising to his feet and accepting the proffered bowl with a nod of thanks.

'Two hours ago.'

Priad sipped. The broth, invigoratingly warm, was a revitalising fluid, concocted from herbs and plant extracts to ease the distemper of animation. Apothecaries were always woken first, to prepare such draughts for their silent comrades.

'How far out are we?' Priad asked.

'A day, perhaps a day and half. I sensed you were close to animation, so I prepared the draught. The others will wake in an hour or so. There's food too, if you desire it.'

Priad shook his head. He was still muzzy.

'Anything to report?' Priad asked, sipping again.

'I did not ask and have not been told,' Khiron replied. 'Simple matters require attention first. But I can tell you Petrok is awake, and the armourers too. The embarkation hall sounds like a smithy.'

'Petrok's awake?'

'In truth, I don't believe he's slept this voyage.'

'It wouldn't surprise me,' said Priad. 'How long?'

'Nineteen days.'

'A good time.'

'The barge captain saw the look in Petrok's eyes when we boarded,' smiled Khiron.

Petrok had ordered the squads to deanimate for the duration of the voyage. It wasn't standard practice, except for long hauls, but he'd told them he wanted them sharp for the moment they arrived. Priad knew the real reason was more complex. Of the five squads selected by Petrok, two – Laomon and Ridates – were composed of recent inductees, most of them without any real battle experience. It was a technique Petrok favoured, mixing veteran warriors – in this case, the men of Nophon, Pelleas and the Notable Damocles – in the line with newcomers. The inductees would receive invaluable experience as a result, and the veterans would overcome any complacency by compensating for the fact that some of the men around them were relatively inexperienced. It was an alloy that often brought out the best in a fighting company.

But Petrok had ordered them to deanimate to keep the newcomers fresh. A voyage of undertaking, especially one such as this where combat was inevitable, could fatigue the spirits of the inductees, and encourage them to over-train and overstretch themselves as they battled the twin menaces of tedium and anticipation. Better they should sleep and awake on the eve of war than spend nineteen days pacing and fretting and impatient. Such worn-out souls were no use in war.

'Is your heart clear?' Khiron asked.

'My head isn't,' replied Priad. 'I dreamed.'

'You dreamed? Of what?'

'I'm not sure. The same thing, over and again, like a pict transmission on loop play. I don't usually dream. In fact, I can't remember the last time I did.'

'And you can't remember the content?'

Priad shrugged. 'A dog in a meadow.'

'A dog in a meadow? What colour was the dog?'

'Does it matter?'

'I hardly think so. I have always held that there are dreams and dreams. Some are like the ones our master Petrok has, true dreams, carried to him by the spirits of beyond, full of potent meaning and profound significance. They are the dreams that count. The rest of us, with our poor blunt minds, if we dream at all, we dream of nothing and no one that matters. What colour was the dog?'

'It was black.'

'A black hound? Brother, that's an ill omen!'

Priad looked at his Apothecary and realised the older man was joking. He grinned back.

'Now I'm happy to see that,' Khiron said. 'Too much glowering from you of late.'

Priad raised his eyebrows and Khiron tutted. 'Don't start,' Khiron told him. 'When I asked if your heart was clear, I meant clear of disdain. Damocles wronged you, Priad, and you were right to whip us up and down that glacier. And maybe we're still not clean enough in honour. But we're sailing to war now, for better or worse. In the fire of combat, Damocles will need you clear hearted and strong in leadership. No grudges, no ill will.'

'I hold no grudges,' Priad said.

Khiron shrugged. 'Yet, if you do, set them aside, Take them up again when we return to the fortress, for all I care. But leave them here for now.'

'Your counsel is appreciated but unnecessary. I am clear of purpose, black dog or no black dog.'

Khiron nodded. There was a sound of bare feet on decking, and two more figures emerged from the deanimation vault, naked and stretching. Eibos and Laetes, Apothecaries of Ridates and Pelleas squads respectively. They nodded to Priad and Khiron as they dressed and set about the business of preparing for their men.

'It's good to see Ridates re-formed,' Priad said.

'It pleases me,' Khiron replied. 'The name should not fall into disuse. Brother-Sergeant Seuthis has wrought those men into a good unit.'

'Speaking of ill will...' Priad murmured. Khiron smiled. He had been Apothecary to the old Ridates squad, and in that service, his career had almost ended in disgrace.

'There's none at all,' he said.

ONE BY ONE, the Snakes returned to life, ministered to by their Apothecaries. Priad left Khiron in charge of the animation, and wandered down to the barge's embarkation hall, where the teams of armourers and servitors were laying out the preparations. In long, burnished rows, the cases of Mark VII power armour stood on their racks, gleaming in the lamp light. Weapons were being cleaned and oiled, and munitions laid out across the scuffed deck to be sorted and counted. Boy slaves ran the munition lines, marking out tallies in chalk on the floor.

Hammers and drills sounded along the wide bay as final refits and alterations were made to plate sections and mechanisms. The Techmarine Suprema and his apprentice checked and blessed every item of wargear, from the smallest digital components of gauntlets to the massive Rhino transporters as they were cradled up onto the deck, klaxons hooting from their hoists. From hidden practice ranges came the rattle of test firings. Servitors ran back and forth, conveying each man's weapon in turn to the practice ranges for certification.

Steam presses thumped, and sparks billowed in the heat-wash of portable forges. The air was filled with the scents of hot metal, coals, oil and pumice, thermite, exhaust fumes and human sweat. Priad breathed it in. It was the smell of war, and he revelled in it. He walked over to his own armour, and ran a bare hand across the polished grey ceramite. It shone like glass, and in its surface, he saw the bustling activity of the embarkation deck reflected. A small, dark shape flickered across it, and Priad turned, expecting to see a black dog running in and out of the armour rows, chasing corn flies. But it was just a boy slave with an armful of munition caskets.

Petrok appeared, talking with the Suprema. The Librarian was clad in an ice-white chiton, but his face was pale and his eyes dark. He noticed Priad and came over.

'Fit for war?' he asked.

'If war awaits,' replied Priad.

'Most certainly. I'll brief all the sergeants presently, but this you should know. All hell's shaken loose on Ganahedarak. I've been monitoring the transmissions. Our brothers are cut off, and surrounded. The greenskins number more than we can imagine.'

'How can twenty-five squads of our phratry be cut off?' Priad asked.

'Like a swimmer in mid-ocean,' Petrok replied. 'Unfathomable as it seems, the greenskins are at war with themselves. This is not the incursion Seydon assumed. This is something else. A civil war, if the swinekin have enough civilisation in them to deserve the term. Two hosts, uncountable, out for blood. Humankind is merely caught up in the middle.'

'What is the purpose, the cause?' Priad asked the Librarian.

'My friend, I do not even begin to understand what makes an ork an ork, or why such a thing exists in this cosmos, or what his living purpose is. They are xenos and inscrutable. But this war of theirs will take many human worlds into the furnaces of hell with them unless it is checked.'

'And can we check it? With only five squads?'

'I'm working on that,' said Petrok. 'Let's get to the soil fast, and taste things there. Once I'm in vox-range with the Chapter Master, perhaps we can evolve a plan.'

Petrok paused and looked into Priad's eyes. 'I dreamed about you again. You and the jaws. It's most perplexing. There's a meaning there, but I'm damned if I can draw it out.'

'I dreamed too,' Priad said, slightly embarrassed to be mentioning it.

'You did? What of?'

'Nothing significant. Khiron says I'm not to worry about–'

'Let me be the judge. What was in your dream?'

'A meadow, and a black dog.'

'And?'

'That's it. A meadow, and a black dog.'

'Does that mean anything to you?'

Priad shook his head.

'Have you ever owned a dog? Have you ever trained dogs?'

'I've used dogs in war a number of times. Against primuls, as we were taught. But…'

'Think on it,' Petrok said.

## IX

THE BATTLE-BARGE *Temerity* put into high anchor and surveyed the bright face of Ganahedarak and the multitude of dark satellites that drifted like beetles in its lower orbits. Upwards of twenty hulks and crag-craft circled the planet like vultures.

At Petrok's command, the relief company made the drop in Thunderhawks, screaming down low across the southern continent. In the north, smoke had spread out to stain vast regions of the atmosphere, striating the sky with lho-brown slicks of soot.

There was no way in to the north. Communicating with the kings of the south, Petrok arranged for his force to set down on the plains outside an ancient city called Pyridon, some two hundred kilometres west of the main warzone.

The climate there was brisk and bright. It was planting season. They marched from their landers into the city, seeing vast crowds gathering outside the walls as if in welcome.

These were not adoring masses, turning out to rapture the coming heroes. This was overspill, millions of ragged refugees fleeing the war, congregating around the city in their plight. The crowds looked at the gleaming armoured giants with dull, uncomprehending eyes as the Snakes marched through. Some screamed prayers or benedictions, others hurled abuse and jeers. Some threw missiles of trash and gnawed bones.

The city was a ramshackle place of terracotta towers and clay-built slums. The narrow streets were teeming. The warriors, reduced to a double line to push through the stinking press, had to activate their guidance locators to make sense of the place. The only landmarks were the occasional looming temples, brick and clay edifices in great disrepair that were filled with statues and crumbling shrines. No one seemed to remember who the temples had been raised to. The identities of gods and dignitaries had long faded, yet no one had considered demolishing them.

The thoroughfares were packed with wagons, contractors, citizens, beggars, priests and mourners, mules, servitors, merchants and soldiers. The soldiers were beaten, broken men in threadbare armour, their speartips blunt and twisted, their laslocks out of charge. They were survivors fleeing the End War.

That, the Snakes of Ithaka learned, was what they called it. The End War. A catastrophic combat that would split the sky and the world and bring an end to Ganahedarak. This was the finality of fire the elders had long prophesied. This was Ur Maggedon.

Only the broken soldiers seemed to notice the Ithakan file. They saw the gleaming Snakes and turned their faces away, ashamed of the fortune that had washed them up in that place. Petrok stopped a number of times to converse with officers and take intelligence, but little was forthcoming.

Like all the others, Priad was used to being noticed, especially when he went abroad in his full case of plate. Now he towered over the passing crowd and drew not one look. No one was afraid or impressed. They had all seen too much, too much exhaustive horror, and their capacity for fear or even awe was wrung out of them.

Three of the kings of the south awaited Petrok in a decomposing palace at the heart of the city. Weeds sprouted from the flagstones of the courtyard, and the sumptuous plasterwork was flaking from the walls. Empty windows stared out like skull sockets. The kings were slovenly men, attended by dirty slaves and sullen womenfolk. They had nothing to tell, except that they repeated the fact that roundhouses had been built to accommodate the phratry. Directions were given, with no little urgency, as if the kings longed for the Iron Snakes to leave. They seemed unduly preoccupied with the roundhouse halls they had constructed in the open country, as if that was their part of the bargain over. They had built bastions to house the warriors, now would the warriors please rid them of this menace? Wasn't that how the undertaking worked?

Petrok dismissed the kings of the south, and they shuffled away with their miserable retinues. Alone in the courtyard, Petrok gathered the five squads and conducted the Rite of the Giving of Water, dripping Ithakan brine from his tubular copper flask.

He had almost finished when a great commotion broke out in the city around them. Pyridon itself seemed to quiver and shake at the din of voices and running feet. Horns sounded above the clamour.

The enemy had been sighted.

The city trembled. Stampedes boiled down the winding streets as people attempted to flee to the south. Beyond the teetering walls, dust rose as the hosts of refugees broke and ran into the farmland outside the city.

Petrok, the very flagstones beneath him vibrating from the shock of a million running feet, studiously completed the rite.

'Plans can wait,' he said, refraining from mentioning that he was still unable to raise the Chapter Master on the vox. 'War visits us, and we must make it welcome.'

IN THE DRY, stubbled fields north of the city, a wall of dust was approaching. In it, hulking shadows shambled and plodded. Howls echoed across the valley, accompanied by the rumble of motors and war engines. There was no estimating numbers or context.

Petrok brought the relief force out in front of the city's clay wall, and fixed a position along a trackway at the head of the cultivated land. A single line: Pelleas, Ridates, Damocles, Laomon and Nophon. The Snakes stood like steel statues in the hard afternoon light, watching the dust approach. Inside their armour, the brothers flexed massive limbs tight-bound with straps of leather and linen, dusted with fine powder and anointed with oils. Apart from those men who bore specialised weapons, every warrior carried a bolter and a combat shield, as well as a sheathed warblade. The teams of armourers and attendants, all in loose, light armour, waited behind the line with munition reloads and bundles of sea-lances sharpened for war.

The dust line drifted closer. The roar and cry grew louder.

At Petrok's command, the armourers' boy slaves ran the line, planting a sea-lance, base-spike down, into the earth behind each brother. Some had pennants fluttering from them. The squad standard bearers raised their double-looped crests and fixed them to their shoulders. Aekon made sure Andromak's standard was fitted correctly in place.

Five proud double-snakes glittered in the sunlight.

Squad channels clicked open, each unit on a separate frequency, with a command override on the common channel. The sergeants spoke to their men, coaching, assuring, priming. Goront of Pelleas told his men of past glories and of glories yet to come. Seuthis explained to the jittery, eager newcomers of Ridates that this was the day they had been born for. Ryys of Nophon reminded his squad that Nophon had never left a battlefield in defeat. Lektas of Laomon, reining in the enthusiasm of his own inductees, told a story about the primarch that made them clap their shield fists against their leg plates.

'Damocles,' Priad said over his link, 'the Emperor knows why we're regarded as one of the Notables. According to the trench, you're all much, much braver than me. And I say you'd better prove it to me now, or even that damned trench won't be deep enough to hide you from my displeasure.'

He raised his lightning claw, so they could see the electricity spark and crackle off its burnished talons.

'For Terra, for Ithaka, and for Damocles!'

## X

THE GREENSKINS CAME into view, swathed in their dust cloud.

They were charging, pounding forward across the dry fields, shaking the ground with their leaden footfalls. They were vast creatures, every bit as big and robust as the giants facing them. Priad felt a knot of wonder that for the first time in twelve years, for the first time in his life, he was squaring up to an enemy that matched him, kilo for kilo, muscle for muscle.

Everything about the greenskins was oversized. Their paw-like fists, their shoulders, their snouts and yawning, howling maws. Fat lips, slabby cheeks, rotten teeth like pegs, ears as twisted and frayed as bat wings, laced with studs and rings. Some wore pot-black horned helmets, iron caps encrusted with antlers or ox horn or the curled spikes of rams. Others sported tusks the size of short-swords, curving upwards from slavering lower lips. They snorted and grunted and roared as they came on, hunch-backed, billowing rank breath and spittle ahead of them.

And they weren't even remotely green. Their rushing bodies were draped in pelts and animal skins, or shawls of mauve fibre, or cloaks of rusting chainmail. Crude armour of hide and tin cased their limbs and torsos, and bangles and necklaces danced along with their momentum. Some wore scalps and teeth and even clattering skulls as trophies. All of them had caked their flesh with war paint, with dyes of red and black and a sugary pink that dazzled in the sun. They were gaudy and bright, black and red like glowing coals, like the embers of a still-burning fire tipped out of the grate, rushing out across the hearth stone.

In their beringed fists: cleavers and axes, pikes and halberds, mauls and bitten blades rank with dried blood, the pommels and hilts streaming chains of beads and human fingerbones. Some carried firearms – crude bolters and broad-nosed cannon. As they closed in, a ponderous avalanche of metal and meat, they began to fire.

Shots tore past the waiting Snakes. Missiles shrieked in the air. Hard rounds burst and shattered off armour and shields, denting and tearing the smooth curves of perfect, polished plate. The random flash and spark and crack resembled a munitions store accidentally touched off.

Twenty metres. Ten.

'Aim for the heads! And fire!' Petrok cried. The fifty ready guns of the phratry let rip into the oncoming tide.

Bolters chattered. Plasma guns whined and spat. Flamers retched and spewed.

Death rushed out to greet the storming greenskins. The front of the line went over, tumbling, thrashing, ichor spurting into the air from bursting bodies. Those in the second rank trampled the bodies of the first underfoot until they too were brought down by the relentless fire and met the same fate under the hobnails of the third rank, and the fourth.

The bodies piled up, limp and wet, crushed to an oozing pulp by the weight of numbers behind. Ork feet slipped on compressed corpses, struggling for purchase. A wall began to build as the greenskins, the Painted Ones, scrambled to ascend the growing litter of dead to get at the shining human line. A stench of death, a cloying mix of decomposed vegetation, slime and stomach acid, filled the air. The feral enemy warriors clawed through the dead limbs and entrails of their fallen comrades in a stupefying frenzy to meet the human foe. They hacked through the blubber and flesh of the dead, only to be killed by the next salvo of bolter fire.

Centimetre by centimetre, this wave of the dead, the dying and the still alive was crawling towards the Ithakan line, until there was no longer any time for the phratry to reload again.

'Close combat!' Petrok ordered. He stood at the centre of the line, the mighty warblade Bellus raised in his mailed fist.

The Snakes tossed their bolters onto the ground behind them, where the armourers could reach them, and plucked their sea-lances from the soil.

'Address!' Petrok bellowed.

The lances, all fifty, swung forward, glinting in the bright light. and lowered as one to face the enemy, staves clattering and clink-ing. The brothers brought their combat shields up and hoisted their lances above their right shoulders.

'Strike!' Petrok yelled.

The flowing torrent of swinekin, breaking the air with their howls and violating it with their odour, reached the Ithakan wall. The Iron Snakes began to stab forward with their lances, repeating pow-erful overhand thrusts that punched their lance tips into chainmail and leather hauberks and meat. The hafts shivered from the multi-ple impacts. Dark blood the colour of rubies jetted into the roiling dust.

There was a jarring moment of impact, an actual crash of bone and metal, as the ork horde piled into the Iron Snakes. The shock force caused a few of the brothers to step back and brace them-selves, but the line held firm. The lances began to jab and jab with renewed vigour. It was impossible to miss, so dense was the press of orks at their shields. Lance tips gouged through shoulder plates, through helmets, pinned limbs to bodies, burst gore out through backs. It became increasingly hard to wrestle the lances free.

The pressure increased. Greenskins at the back of the torrent shouldered in to reach their enemies, impelling forward those ahead of them with their shoves. Many corpses remained upright against the Ithakan shields, pinned by bodyweight and unable to topple. Some orks began to clamber over the heads of the front ranks in their enthusiasm to sample combat.

As the line of brothers milled the foe with their lances, the boy slaves and armourers rushed in at their heels, ducking to dodge stray missiles and wild shots that penetrated the line. Bolters, hot and smoking, were gathered up from the dust and reloaded, and fresh sea-lances planted in the shadow of the human wall.

For each Iron Snake, there was no sense of general battle. The combat was so close that the only concern was the space immediately in front of him, a space permanently filled with screaming, wriggling hostiles. No man could see further than his own arm's length. It was like fighting alone, except for the arm plates and shields on either side.

An almost tropical heat gathered in the close quarters of the front line, generated by bodies and blood and explosives. The line of dispute, the slender bloody thread where the killing was focused, sweltered like a butcher's shop in summer. The fronts of the Iron Snakes' armour were slippery with alien gore.

The veterans accepted this tight, frenzied combat. Their breathing and pulses slowed as they closed focus, concentrating only on the next jab and the next, expertly determining the vital order of priority with which the raving targets needed to be addressed. Not simply the closest, but the ones with the longest reach. Orks with firearms or pikes took precedence over frontrunners with cleavers. Their visor displays selected and prioritised targets, flickering and switching.

The newcomers fought to remember the tenets of their training. Nothing could prepare a man for this claustrophobic fury. Some began to sing to concentrate their minds, and fend off the whirling blur of violence that could entrance the unwary with its chaos. Their voices crackled tinnily from their helmet speakers.

Shields deformed as blows rained upon them. Hatchet blades broke and remained stuck in place. Impacts glanced off chest plates and shoulder guards, leaving great dents and gouges. The first lances began to break and crack.

Priad felt his lance shaft give, and he stabbed out with the broken end to make a last impale before letting the weapon go. Raising his scored shield higher, he began to lash and strike with his lightning claw, spilling greenskins onto the soaking earth, slicing them asunder and causing them to spasm and contort with the searing charge. One huge beast, unarmed, lurched at him, biting, and Priad brought his shield up. The ork bit into its lower rim with its huge tusks, and Priad ripped his claws through the meat and gristle of its neck, unleashing a cascade of arterial fluid. A chain-axe mowed at his head, and he raised his power claw to block it, splintering the weapon out of the air.

He wondered how much longer the enemy could maintain the pressure. He was waiting for the ebb, the slight relaxation. He knew Petrok was waiting too. It would come, as surely as the tides of the sea came and went.

He felt it. The weight against his front relaxed. The greenskin charge had finally lost momentum and was leaking backwards like a spent breaker. The enemy was not fleeing or even turning, but it was recoiling as a mass to renew its fury. Corpses held upright by the pressure keeled over or slithered to the earth. Steam rose. A mangled pile of bodies sprawled at the feet of the Ithakan warriors. A moment's hiatus, part of the natural punctuation of warfare.

'Arms!' Petrok shouted, knowing they had to capitalise on this break at once.

The Snakes turned, those still bearing twisted and bent lances tossing them aside, and accepted their reloaded bolters from the waiting slaves. They swung back into place, freeing breech blocks with a staccato clatter. The greenskins were already surging back, their voices rising again.

Petrok didn't need to give the order to fire. The phratry, even the newcomers, knew precisely when to commence. Muzzle flashes lit up like starbursts down the gore-drenched rank, punching heavy shots into the returning mob. A second shooting blitz began, mowing down the greenskin numbers like corn before the scythe.

Munitions spent once more, the Snakes threw down their bolters where the armourers could recover them, and drew up their second lances. The Painted Ones were coming into reach again, stomping and sliding over the mounds of the slain.

'Address!' Petrok commanded, and the fresh sea-lances rattled up over shoulder plates, razor-tips aimed forward in the stabbing grip.

'Step!' Petrok ordered, and the line took a step forward on the left foot, meeting the crush head on and smashing their lances into the face of it.

'Step!' Petrok echoed, and the line took another step, left foot again, bringing the right up to meet it. Another flurry of stabbing lances, another shiver of impacts on their shields.

'Step!' Again they moved, shoving forward into the mass, puncturing faces and throats, elbowing bodies off their shield guards. By sheer force of arms and backs, they had carried the line forward well beyond the original clash point, leaving the heaps of cadavers behind them.

'Step!' Fifty sea-lances smote down, stabbing high and over, spearing through chests and disembowelling bellies. 'Step! Step! Step!'

The second batch of sea-lances was reaching the end of its usability. Blade tips were blunting, breaking or twisting out of true, and hafts began to snap and fracture. The weight on the brothers' shields was immense. They were no longer standing to resist, they were forcing back.

'Hold the line! Blades at will!'

The necessary order, before all advantage was spent. The Ithakan line, like a dam in a river, locked up tight again, shoulder to shoulder, and the brothers finished their lance work, discarding their broken spears as it became necessary and switching to their fighting blades, squealing the swords out of their scabbards, metal against metal.

The sound of combat altered, another natural sea-change in the flow of war. Predominant now was the ragged, arrhythmic noise of swords hacking, of blades hammering and chopping into bodies, each brother slicing and tearing with his short combat sword.

The murderous, chopping effort lasted for twenty minutes, the Snakes bludgeoning into the foe wall like woodcutters assaulting a thicket, severing and decapitating, shearing trunks and splitting shoulders. The edges of their swords began to dull and chip.

And then it was done. The host of the Painted Ones dwindled, and then disintegrated.

The greenskins had not broken, at least not en masse. Such practice was as alien to their mindset as they were alien to the humans. A few stragglers capered and limped away, some dragging bodies, most dragging pilfered weapons of value from the slain.

The Iron Snakes had cut their way through the entire mob of them, chewing the ranks apart from front to back, consigning to death every monster that dared to face them. Each wave thrown at the peerless wall of human warriors had suffered, their numbers eroding down further and further until their tidal force was all spent and their strength expended. The greenskin host that had chanced upon Pyridon had been exterminated in one solid, brutal clash.

The Snakes came to a standstill, gasping and sore, flushing ichor out of their helmets' valves, clearing optic slits of blood and shreds of meat. Slowly, they realised what they had accomplished. Behind them, for a distance of about three acres, the earth was piled six or seven deep with the enemy dead, stinking slopes and mounds of carrion, gurgling as waste and fluid leaked out and turned the ground beneath to a quagmire.

They heard distant cheering. The armourers and slaves were yelling and rejoicing, brandishing lances in the air, banging plate hammers on fresh shields. One by one, the brothers of the Snakes raised their fists, raised their blood-smeared, nicked short swords. Helmets were unlocked and cast onto the ground, exposing faces ruddy and sweaty with effort and confinement, hair plastered to scalps, fierce bright eyes.

The brothers raised a howl of their own, their first of the battle and the end note of victory.

Priad, alternately whooping, and spitting stale phlegm from his mouth, looking up and down the disjointed line. There were wounds, torn armour cases, shields splintered down to the boss nubs, red blood mingling with the moss-green cake of ichor on everything and everyone.

But not a single man in the five squads had fallen.

He raised his tattered shield, shaking it aloft in triumph, and felt it heavy and unbalanced. The severed head of the biting ork was still attached to the rim, its tusks and peg teeth locking to the shield in the rictus of death.

He prised the great jaws free with effort, and tossed the mangled mass onto the dirt.

Then, unbidden, he thought of a black dog in a meadow and turned to find Petrok.

## XI

'IT WAS OVER a decade ago. In my first year of induction.'

'That's over twelve years ago, brother,' Petrok corrected.

'Your memory is more precise than mine, master,' Priad replied. 'However long ago, it was my first year. To test my individual skills, Raphon sent me on an undertaking to a world called Baal Solock. There had been a visitation of primuls, a downed ship, actually. I purged the place.'

They walked side by side across the smouldering battlefield to the makeshift camp set up by the armourers. Behind them, those brothers with flamers had begun the chore of heaping up the swinekin corpses and making a cleansing pyre. The rest of the company was assembling around the campsite. There was an air of jubilation, especially from the newcomers. Priad and Petrok passed Brother-Sergeant Seuthis, and Priad clasped the man's hand tightly.

'Ridates lives again,' Priad said.

'Long may it,' replied Seuthis, clearly proud of his virgins' performance.

'They'll be Notables yet,' Petrok said, clapping the man's shoulder. Seuthis laughed and moved on to muster his men.

In the camp, the Apothecaries were mending wounds while the armourers serviced weapons and set to the repair of damaged plate. All around, brothers were being stripped down by the slaves, damaged segments of case unbolted and handed to the warsmiths to be hammered true again, or patched and heated back into form with fusion lamps. A smell of hot metal filled the air.

Attendants hurried to Priad and the Librarian as they came in, removing their weapons and fussing over their suits. Bellus was carried away to be washed and anointed. Priad's lightning claw was decoupled and unlatched. An armourer tugged at Priad's right vambrace, which was buckled and punctured. Priad hadn't even noticed that damage.

'Sit,' said Petrok, and the pair sat down on a raised hillock of earth as the attendants worked around them. 'You purged this place?'

Priad nodded. 'It was a minor thing, over in a day or so. But there was a dog, as I now remember. A black dog.'

Slaves were sponging the blood and sweat off Petrok's face with dishes of watered vinegar. The armourer had now removed Priad's vambrace and gauntlet. The shorn teeth of a chain axe or some similar weapon had torn entirely through it and punctured the flesh of his forearm. Clotted blood drained out of the armour segment as it came away.

'Apothecary!' the armourer yelled, as he turned to set the damaged vambrace on his mobile forge to beat out the deformations.

Khiron was busy patching a deep gash in Pindor's side, but Laetes of Pelleas came over at once, and took his beak-nose pliers to the axe shards in Priad's flesh. He offered Priad a leather strop to bite on.

'I'm too busy talking,' Priad said, and resumed his tale to Petrok, oblivious to the Apothecary's digging. 'A black dog.'

'Was the dog significant?'

'No. It had had all but gone from my memory. But here's the thing. The primuls were guarding a trophy of some sort. A set of huge jaws with blunt teeth.'

Petrok's eyes narrowed. A slave was attempting to apply skin wrap to a laceration on Petrok's cheek, but the Librarian brushed him away. 'That'll heal by itself,' he said. He stared at Priad. 'A set of jaws?'

Priad nodded. 'A massive set. With blunt teeth. The jaws of some greenskin, I'm sure of that now. Now I've seen them in the flesh. Like the bite of the things we've slain here. But bigger. Bigger than any beast we met today.'

Petrok was silent for a moment. 'It pains me to ask, Priad, but why do you only remember this now? I told you of my dream weeks ago.'

'Because,' said Priad, 'I never saw the jaws in question. I was told about them by a witness present at the time.'

'Reliable?'

'Completely, I believe. The jaws themselves were destroyed before I saw them. But they were evidently of importance to the primuls. Significant in some way.'

'They were destroyed? You're sure of that?'

'Incinerated by a grenade.'

'Humour me, brother. Can you be certain of their nature and scale if you didn't actually see them? Witnesses, even reliable ones, are prone to exaggeration.'

Laetes had finished his work, and had sprayed skin wrap on Priad's torn and bruised forearm to assist the natural healing process. The jagged saw-teeth lay bloody in a steel bowl beside Priad. Laetes had been trying desperately not to overhear the conversation.

Priad flexed his arm. 'Fine work,' he said.

'Rest it a few hours, if you can,' Laetes said, wiping his tools and packing them away. Other voices were calling for the attention of the Apothecaries. 'The shards were dirty, so you may experience sweat fever as your body cleans out poison. If that happens, go steady and let it run its course.'

Priad nodded, and Laetes withdrew, accepting a grateful nod from the mighty Librarian.

'Two teeth survived,' Priad said. He held up his bare right hand and splayed the fingers to suggest size. 'Just two teeth, but enough for me to know that there was no exaggeration.'

'What did you do with the teeth?' Petrok asked.

'I left them on Baal Solock, as trophies for the locals. They seemed unimportant at the time. I was young. It was an age ago.'

Petrok got up. The slaves still washing his armour stepped back hastily, some spilling their murky dishes. Priad rose quickly. Petrok smiled at the brother-sergeant, then clasped him by the shoulder plates. 'It makes no sense yet, Priad, but what you've told me makes some pieces fit together. I will consider this further, now I have details to contemplate. The spirits want me to know about this, and, though it took some time for them to guide you too, you've given me the key. I'm sure of it.'

'I hope so, master,' Priad said.

'Petrok,' Petrok reminded him.

Priad walked across to where the brothers of Damocles were assembled. Their armour had been scrubbed clean of the worst filth, and they were already refitting and checking weapons. Kules was waiting while an armourer worked a fusion lamp over his left shoulder plate on an anvil. The shoulder plate had been almost torn in two by some monumental blow. Attendants were approaching, bearing fresh combat shields to replace those ruined in the battle. Others collected up the brothers' short swords to take them to the squealing whetstones grinding at the edge of the camp.

Priad greeted each brother in turn, clasping his hand and speaking private words of congratulation. When he took Aekon's hand, Priad drew the youngster close.

'Proper combat, eh? Better than Iorgu?'

'Yes, brother-sergeant. My heart is full.'

'You acquitted yourself well, Notable,' Priad said. 'And proved everything the trench couldn't.'

Aekon blushed.

'Khiron told me all about it,' Priad whispered.

'I wish he hadn't,' Aekon said. 'He told me he would not.'

'There should be no secrets between the men of Damocles,' Priad said. 'But to be fair to Khiron, he would have respected your confidence had things not turned out the way they did. No more diving for glory, all right? Prove yourself to me and the God-Emperor, not the sea.'

'Yes, sir.'

'Damocles!' Priad called, and the men roused and got to their feet, looking at him. He turned a full circle, catching each man's gaze, one by one, nodding in satisfaction. 'More where that came from,' he said.

The brothers roared their approval.

Brother-Sergeant Lektas hurried by, nodding to Priad. 'Gather in, brother,' he urged. 'Petrok wants us. The vox has found our Chapter Master at last.'

## XII

THE INFORMATION WAS threadbare. Somehow, the greenskins, possibly by means of crude devices in their orbiting hulks, were jamming general transmissions across most of the vox bandwidth.

But contact with Seydon and the twenty-five squads had been established. Scratchy, broken voices crawled out of the relief force's vox-caster, like phantoms searching for release.

Petrok gathered the five sergeants and their Apothecaries. As was the custom, each sergeant nominated one of his squad to accompany him to the briefing, as a safeguard should he fall in battle. Priad brought Xander as his second.

The men of Damocles nodded quiet approval to this selection. Since Priad's elevation to sergeant, there had been no talk of succession. But Xander, hothead though he might be at times, was the obvious choice. Only Priad, by feat of arms, and Pindor, by dint of age, held finer battle records. Pindor showed no bitterness. As a true veteran, the chances were that at some point he, like the similarly venerable Seuthis, would be drawn out of Damocles to whip into shape another squad of virgin pups. The bloody tally of Ganahedarak made that all the more likely. Once this war was done, whole squads would need to be rebuilt from the ground up.

Petrok had brought no lexicanium nor any servant Chapter serf with him on this undertaking. He prepared the hololithic display himself, ordering two of the slaves to split open a fresh white chiton and hold it out like a banner so that the machine could project upon it.

The afternoon light was fading, and a blank grey dusk was falling on the fields without Pyridon. Light was further choked off by the immense black smog lifting from the funeral pyre of the enemy dead. There was a harsh stink of burned roots and gristle on the slack wind.

Petrok showed them the coloured display against the flapping chiton, a patchwork chart composed of the interlocked unitary scans made by their descender ships on the passage down. The sergeants and their seconds saw plain land, hills with graphic contour overlays, the white threads of rivers and water courses.

'What is the blackness there?' asked Ryys. 'A forest?'

Petrok shook his head. 'The enemy, brother-sergeant.'

Even the veterans present made a sharp intake of breath. The mass of the ork swarms made a stain like pooling blood across the majority of the chart. The Iron Snakes dealt in superhuman magnitudes: of strength, of speed, of endurance, of commitment. This superfluity was beyond even their minds to accommodate.

'Our beloved master is embattled here,' Petrok explained, indicating a cluster of white pimples on the display. His gauntlet moved through the coloured light like a hand through sunlit water. 'They have fortified themselves in a group of roundhouses on this hillside.'

Petrok looked up. 'Yes, ironic, I know. The very roundhouses these southern dogs raised for us. Pointless halls of convenience, ignorantly constructed by the locals. Now fundamental to the survival of our twenty-five squads. As I understand it from Phobor, with whom I spoke earlier, the situation is grave. Greenskin hosts of incalculable strength are swarming around them, waging war upon themselves. From the writings of our illustrious brethren the Ultramarines, experienced as they are in the habits of the orks, we know our enemy to be miserably internecine. They wage war upon themselves, and apparently delight in that mindlessness. Now our home, our Reef Stars, is churned underfoot by that calamity.'

'Is not the word "waaagh", or somesuch?' Laetes asked.

'That, my friend, is how we understand their term for holy war, for jihad,' Petrok relied. 'This is not "waaagh".' He spoke the word, not like Laetes, faltering and human, but full throated and fluent, as if conversant with the elocution of the Painted Ones. 'This is mob on mob, horde on horde. This is a species committing suicide by war. And taking us with it.'

He looked at the officers. 'We won't win here. Seydon knows that. Phobor too. I know it. Perhaps not even with the entire phratry could we begin to make a dent in their numbers, though we slaughter a thousand each. We must find victory in some other manner.'

'What other manner?' asked Goront, sergeant of Pelleas.

Petrok glanced at Priad. 'I have plans in mind. Strategies that are too fledgling and weak to be revealed here. But we will win. We have undertaken this, and we will see it to victorious conclusion.'

'But surely!' Ryys exclaimed. 'With all the Notables here, with twenty-five squads plus our numbers–'

'There are no twenty-five squads,' said Petrok, his voice stiff and bleak. 'Parthus is gone, entirely. Proud Veii at half numbers. Across the units in Seydon's command, more than fifty of our brothers have been sent on to the next world. Virtually all that remain are wounded to some degree. The fighting has been ferocious.'

'Fifty…' Lektas murmured.

'At sunrise tomorrow,' Petrok said, 'Seydon intends to lead his squads in a break out along this valley. If our brothers can reach this table land here, we can effect an extraction. We can salvage our numbers, and compose ourselves for another effort.'

'Here?' asked Priad.

'Probably not,' Petrok replied frankly. 'I have sent to Karybdis and to the Sector Governor to raise fleet strengths. This nightmare might be finished in the void, ship to ship… or ship to hulk… if we're lucky.'

Petrok turned back to his chart. 'We have to safeguard the breakout. Overnight, we'll go cross country to the valley head here, and begin an assault before first light, aiming to sting the greenskin hordes into confusion. Then we hold that valley head until the Chapter Master's forces have come through.'

He glanced round at them. 'Make no mistake. This will be bloody. This will be hard. This will be overwhelming. If we fail, if we let the line falter, the greenskins will mass in and our twenty-five squads will be as nought.'

## XIII

THROUGH THEIR LOCKED visors, the pre-dawn read as luminous green. Ahead stood the crags of the valley mouth, registering cold and black to their sensors. Beyond, a sea of heat showed up as lime green warmth, interspersed with hot points of white. The ork hosts, filling the land from horizon to horizon, spread out around their pit fires.

Above, in a black-green heaven, the stars stood out painfully bright like static tracer shells. Every now and then, the sharpest stars would be eclipsed as another hulk silhouetted by, tracking on its own, ponderous orbit.

The relief company scaled the head of the valley in single file, following the thin track. They had sent the armourers, slaves and all the other attendants back to the landing site at midnight. Now they continued alone, Petrok at the head of the fifty men. They carried double munition loads, explosives, fresh shields, and two lances apiece.

Sunrise was a suggestion warming the clouds to the south. Petrok struggled to find a suitable territory to compose a decent fighting field out of. The chart scans had been imprecise. The valley terrain was sheer and formidable, hard crags dropping away three thousand metres sheer into the valley base. They shouldered on, trudging the narrow path, boltguns armed.

THE PATH BEGAN to descend. They came out onto a plateau overlooking a vast camp of greenskins, so close they could smell the cookfires and rank stink when they opened their helmet filters.

Petrok waved them down to a crouch on the lip of the plateau. In less than thirty minutes, mayhem would explode ten kilometres to the north-west as Seydon began his exodus. There was no doubting that, whatever the outcome, the day would witness one of the Chapter's most brutal and infamous combats.

'This is a good enough place,' Petrok told them. 'This is our fall-back point. We sow from here, and take them as they sleep on foot.'

The instruction was understood.

Petrok drew Bellus and tested the weight of it in his hands. The blade was impatient for the killing to begin. He soothed it softly.

There was no fear in the fifty. They knew no fear, for that was part of their conditioning. But there was anxiety, frustration, eagerness, anticipation.

Petrok walked his line and squatted down beside Priad.

'When we're done,' he said, 'I'll need you and Damocles to escort me to Baal Solock.'

Priad turned his helmet's face to look at Petrok. As usual, the Librarian was bare-headed. His psychic hood had been implanted into his crown by the armourers before their hasty departure. A strange light seemed to suffuse the Librarian's eyes.

'To Baal Solock?' asked Priad, his voice a quiet crackle through his mouthpiece.

'I dreamed again last night,' Petrok said. 'A waking dream as we marched into these deathlands. I have seen the truth of this. The spirits were kind enough to unveil it for me. Baal Solock is the answer to our prayers.'

'Then let's hope we're alive to get you there,' said Priad.

Petrok smiled. 'Let's hope.'

PETROK ROSE TO his feet. He lifted his warblade, the edges of it smoking like coals in the cold night air. 'Time to sting them,' he said aloud, pitching his voice just enough for his five squads to hear him. 'Lance, bolt, blade, then as you will. No quarter, if that needs to be said. Order to withdraw will be the name of Parthus. Hear that, and break… if you can. The ships await. Seydon needs us. The Emperor protects. And I…'

He paused, grinning like a bull wyrm about to strike. 'I… expect.'

\* \* \*

## XIV

WHAT FOLLOWED THEN was a dream, the sort of dream that every man of the phratry experiences once or twice in his life. A tumult, but unreal. A frenzy, but somehow divorced from life and blood and the solid matter of being.

Most of the fifty had known war before, and even the newcomers had been baptised by the splendid brawl outside the walls of Pyridon.

This was something else. A chaos, an adventure into catastrophe. A dream, worse than all the bad dreams they had ever woken from. Solid, yet phantom, stunning the senses by the sheer clangour of it.

A nightmare of battle. And one they could not simply rouse from and laugh away as the monstrous fantasy of their denied fears.

Combat shields up, lances across their shoulders, the fifty brothers of the relief force chose a shallow incline and came down upon a foe that outnumbered them one hundred to one. For the first two or three minutes, the killing was easy. Surprise was with them. They picked up speed, running like gods, and charged through the picket line, thrusting lance heads into meat and bone. Ork sentries pitched and fell. In full frenzy, the striking Snakes overran the outer skirts of the enemy sprawl and launched into the mass of the greenskin camp. Lance tips started to draw blunt as they stabbed and smote.

The Painted Ones began to rouse, throwing up a disjointed holler of dismay. Even alert, the hulking beasts discovered that it was no small thing to face a full-fledged warrior of the Adeptus Astartes when he was travelling at a charging sprint, fully cased, lance in hand. Orks were smashed aside by the charge, knocked flat, skewered, trampled underfoot. The brothers utilised shield skills as much as lance tactics in this initial phase, slamming away those beasts that rose up to confront them, cracking tusks and faces with glancing blows of their shield-bosses, breaking necks with their shield rims. All the while, they were finding fatal targets with the slicing heads of their sea-lances too.

And then they were in the thick of it. Petrok led the way, reaping down the Painted Ones with his famous sword. Bodies began to pile up in his wake, split and severed. Ichor gushed out onto the ground and transformed it into a pungent marsh. Psyker light strobed and crackled around Petrok's hood, screwed down tight as it was into the bones of his skull. Every few steps, he convulsed and expelled a sizzling bolt of power from his left hand, decimating the enemy, frying them to charred bones.

As each gout of power left his fingertips, it was pure and bright and white. As it lanced into the greenskins, it was hot and yellow, and it set them ablaze, shrieking like pigs.

The fifty rushed in as a V around him, breaking collarbones with their shields, stabbing faces with their lances. Every brother carried his second lance in the grip of his left hand, and his weapon – bolter, flamer or plasma gun – anchored to his chest plate by magnetic couplers.

The momentum of the Iron Snakes' charge began to ebb, as the momentum of the orks had done the previous day outside Pyridon. A wall of monsters rose up to block them, blasting with firearms and swinging blades. The first man fell. Braccus, of Pelleas, his head exploded by an enemy missile. He fell on his front, down in the slick mud, still and dead.

'Cast!' Petrok bellowed, taking off the head of a whooping war-boss with his blade.

The brothers broke step and hurled their lances, and thirty or more greenskins toppled, transfixed and split through. Each Snake, running forward again, then snatched his second lance from his left fist into his right and smote on with the fresh blades.

A terrible steam billowed up in the pre-dawn air, the steam from entrails and blood and ichor, hissing hot and fresh into the cold atmosphere. It rose like a mist.

Priad struck an ork down with his shield, then drove his lance into the skull of another. He ripped it free, but the tip was bent over and cracked. He made his second cast, plunging the lance deep into the belly of a gargantuan greenskin, that rolled over, spitting ichor.

Priad snapped his boltgun off its magnetic couplers and began to fire. His first shots made sure the gargantuan ork was dead. Then he dispensed head shots, a flurry of blasts, walloping ogres over onto their backs.

Heat gushed. Bearing the Damocles standard, Andromak raked the ground with his plasma weapon, turning orks into dust, into vapour, into stinking piles of cooked meat.

Pindor vaulted two mortally wounded orks, and cast his second lance into the chest of a raging chieftain. The thing died messily, yowling as it tried to scoop up its own spilled entrails. Bolter freed, Pindor fired two blasts into the oncoming rush of orks, splattering meat and fluid. He began to laugh at the glorious insanity of their act.

Khiron kept his second lance up. He loved the sea-lance more than any other weapon. He drove the tip of it into the left eye socket of a particularly massive brute, and cursed as he had to let go of the shaft. The weapon was wedged fast in the monster's head-bones. He grabbed his bolter and blew apart a gaggle of smaller ork-things that were menacing him with pikes and catcher-poles.

Scyllon, lance master, cast his second spear long and hard. It whistled over the heads of the nearest rising rank, and struck clean through the body of a towering creature that had reared up, a chain sword in each fist. Scyllon watched in dismay as the creature got back onto its feet, and dragged the lance out of its chest. By then, Scyllon had his bolter freed, and he blew the thing's head off.

A swinging cleaver took away Xander's boltgun before he'd even expended his first magazine. He drew his blade instead, and lacerated the ork who had denied him firepower. Then he began to hack, merciless and unforgiving.

A thrown axe brought Aekon down, knocking his legs out from under him. He rolled in the mud, frantic to rise. Blasting one handed with his bolter, Kules dragged Aekon upright, and covered him against the onrushing greenskins until Aekon had drawn his own bolter.

Smoke wept around them. Ork gunfire sliced the air.

Dyognes cast his second lance, then found himself grappling with the enemy as he tried to bring his bolter to bear. He broke heads open with his shield, but the swinekin were mobbing all over him.

'Brother!' Natus cried out, firing as he ran in close, pulling limp bodies off Dyognes. 'Get up! Get up!'

Dyognes rose, bolter in his hands. An explosive round streaked in and blew Natus's bionic arm away at the bicep. Natus yelled out, and staggered aside, sparks kicking out from the shorn-off wires and useless armature.

He turned, firing with his good hand, and quickly took two more rounds in the breast plate.

Stumbling backwards, blood seeping from the blackened craters in his chest, Natus kept shooting, kept screaming 'No! No! Nooo!'

A massive ork, fully three times the mass of a Space Marine, pounced on Natus, mashing him back, flat, into the mud. Pinning his remaining arm, the ork bit down with its gigantic jaws, crushing Natus's helmet with such awful force that the visor lenses shattered.

Screaming, Dyognes blasted ten rounds into the ork's torso and smashed its corpse off Natus. Natus's helmet came away with it, clamped in the ork's mouth. Revealed, Natus's face was bruised and torn, the cheek and brow bones shattered and malformed. He had lost both eyes.

'Get up! Dyognes yelled. 'Get up!'

'Where? Where are you, lad?' Natus asked.

Dyognes reached for him, grabbing his gauntlet and hauling him up out of the muck.

'Come on, old man!' Dyognes shouted.

His voice cut off. An ork pike suddenly transfixed him from behind. The tip of it had splintered out through his chest plate and his blood was now gushing out around the shaft.

'Dyognes? Dyognes?' Natus yelled, blind and frantic, aware that something was wrong simply by the stink of human blood.

Dyognes sank sadly to his knees, snapping off bolts at the orks enclosing them. He found Natus's remaining hand and forced the smoking bolter into it.

'Keep shooting!' he gurgled. 'Keep shooting!'

Sightless, Natus began firing wildly. Dyognes held onto his waist and aimed him as best he could. Slowly, inexorably, Dyognes sagged, slumping to the ground, awkwardly propped up by the pike that had been pushed through him.

Still calling his brother's name, Natus continued to fire until his clip was out.

### XV

HALF-HEARD, THE signal came through. To the north-west, Seydon and the twenty-five had begun their breakout. Fighting there was savage, but the greenskin host had been properly misdirected by Petrok's daring assault. The sun was rising, back-lighting the smoke-filled air above the valley and turning it blood-red.

Spreading wide in a fan formation, the five squads cut a deeper and yet deeper wound into the flank of the greenskin host. Petrok skilfully kept the spread as wide as possible to maximise the Iron Snakes' attack, yet tight enough so that each squad formation could overlap and cover its neighbours. As befitted their status as Notables, Damocles was placed at the most demanding section of the formation, at the left-hand edge of the fan, furthest from the valley slope, where the numerical strength of the rallying orks was at its strongest.

The fighting was too thick, too intense, for any comprehensive grasp of the flow to be perceived, but Priad quickly became aware that his squad was in trouble. He was missing men. Had brothers fallen, unnoticed, in the rage of combat?

'Anchor us here!' he yelled to Xander. 'Follow Petrok's lead!'

'I will!'

Priad broke formation, gunning his way through the seething mobs of greenskins, his bolter pumping. The enemy host, goaded into fury by the dawn attack, was congregating on that small patch of hillside, and it seemed as if the entire world around him was made of orks. As far as he could see, the howling host stretched away, surging towards them. Amongst the waves of foot troops came war machines, steaming armoured transports, clattering gun-platforms, wagons wrapped in spikes and chains, smoke-stacks belching.

Struggling forward, he found the ominous fault in his squad line. A breach, through which the greenskins were piling forward like a flash flood, threatening to cut the composition of Damocles in two.

Ahead, through the chaos, he caught sight of Natus, bare-headed, his face a blind mask of gore, his bionic arm torn off. The worthy brother was firing off his last shots, wild and hopeless, as the baying greenskins encircled him, jabbing with their spears and pole-hooks.

'Ithaka!' Priad bellowed, and launched into the mass of it. His boltgun hammered on auto, shredding ork-flesh out of his path.

Weapons crashed at him, crunching off his armour. Explosive rounds detonated against his back and shoulder plates. One caught his combat shield, disintegrating it, and spinning the wreckage of it clean off his arm.

Clenching his bolter in his right fist, Priad blasted onward, tearing at the foe with his lightning claw, adding a new catalogue of glory to its ancient martial history. He cut his way through to Natus, and saw to his dismay that Dyognes was with him, face down at Natus's feet, his body half-raised by the pike transfixing it.

'Natus! Natus!' Priad called. Natus jerked his mutilated head around at the sound of the voice.

'Brother-sergeant?'

Priad reached his side, fending off the brutal assaults from all quarters.

'Help Dyognes!'

'I can't see him?' Natus shouted. 'I can't see!'

'He's at your feet, brother!'

Natus stooped down, dropping his empty weapon and groping blindly with his one good hand, finding the young Ithakan's collapsed form.

'Does he live?'

'I can't see his life sign!' Natus wailed. He yelled Dyognes's name out in despair, over and over.

Priad wanted to turn to help him, but there was no break in the onslaught. As fast as Priad shot or smashed a greenskin warrior down, two more filled its place. Priad reeled from the concussive force of a cleaver that shattered against the left side of his helm, leaving a bare-metal gash ruched in the metal from ear to snout.

A massive ork was upon him, a chieftain by his bulk and tusks. His massive arms and torso were painted black and gold, and wrapped in an armour of oily chains. He wielded a twin-headed war-axe, whirling it like a quarter staff. Priad ducked under one lethal swing, then dodged the return, blasting down a smaller greenskin chancer that tried to dart in and stab at him while he was occupied. Holding the thick haft of the double-headed weapon across his massive chest, the chieftain surged at Priad, aiming to run him down. Priad threw out his lightning claw and viced its grip around the centre of the cross-wise haft, splintering it. The chieftain staggered back, salvaging the broken halves of the war-axe so that he now spun a battle-cleaver in each paw. He raised them both overhead to split Priad like firewood. Priad jabbed the muzzle of his bolter up under the chieftain's sagging dewlap and blew out the back of his skull.

As the huge ork fell, blood splashing out as he hit the ground, bolt rounds slugged into the greenskins at his heels. Dozens went down, maimed or slain by the crossing firepower.

Khiron appeared, shooting his way into the heart of the melee to reach Priad, white flash-flames sizzling from the barrel of his weapon.

Roaring his approval, Priad emptied his own clip into the enemy waves in support of his Apothecary's daring run.

Khiron reached them, laying down further fire while Priad re-armed his weapon. His munition supply was perilously low.

'Keep them off!' Khiron ordered without ceremony. As Priad renewed his blasting, ripping defence, Khiron clamped his bolter to his chest and looked to the two wounded men.

Khiron tore open his narthecium, and brought out instruments of brass and toothed steel. He had feared he would need his reductor to unceremoniously recover Dyognes's precious progenoid glands, but the boy was miraculously alive. The pike had ruptured Dyognes's secondary heart and both his natural lungs, as well as cracking his ribcage front and back. But the worst problem was blood loss.

With the injuring weapon still in place, Dyognes's struggling metabolism was failing to seal the wounds. Khiron drew his short sword, braced the pike, and lopped the head of it off with one sure stroke. Dyognes groaned aloud. Without hesitation, Khiron yanked the headless shaft of the pike out through Dyognes's back. Blood gushed free in a ghastly downpour, and the boy rolled limp. Khiron levered open Dyognes's chest plate, used sterile clay from his narthecium to pack both entry and exit wounds, and then sprayed both with skin wrap to expedite sealing. He took out an inoculator and fired potent doses into the young Ithakan's bloodstream to stimulate coagulation and spike Dyognes back to consciousness.

Dyognes began to tremble and jerk.

'Quickly!' Priad yelled, keeping the enemy at bay as best he could. Khiron unlocked Dyognes's helmet and pulled it off. Dyognes sat up, coughing out a matted flow of dark red blood and bile. His face was sallow and pale. He blinked as he woke up to the maelstrom of noise and violence around him. Khiron helped him to his feet. Dyognes seized his fallen bolter, reloaded it, and began to stutter shots out in support of Priad.

'Keep strong!' Priad told him. He could see how weak and unsteady Dyognes was. Khiron turned his attention to the miserably maimed Natus. He strapped bandage tape around Natus's broken skull, and glued it tight with skin wrap, then he locked Dyognes's helmet over Natus's head. For the most part this was an effort to brace Natus's skull and keep it held in one piece, but Khiron adjusted the headgear settings as he reconnected the suit systems.

Natus raised his gloved hand to the side of his head.

'I can't give you eyes, old friend,' Khiron yelled above the din of fighting, 'but I can boost your hearing.' He'd notched the helmet's auditory systems up to maximum gain. Though it now plucked at his pain threshold, Natus could hear every excruciating detail of the war around him. Sounds assailed him. He could distinguish between the grating hum of Astartes power armour and the jangling ring of greenskin mail. He could hear and feel howls and thundering footfalls as they washed in. Khiron pushed a reloaded bolter into Natus's hand. Immediately, Natus shot two charging orks apart.

Priad took Dyognes's left hand and planted it on Natus's right shoulder. 'Lead him!' he yelled. In a tight, blasting group, the quartet formed close and began to drive back into the press to fill the broken line. Ahead they could see the blue light of Andromak's plasma weapon, and hear the screams of its victims.

They closed the rank. To their right, Andromak stood his ground, bellowing obscenities at the heathen masses, his armour covered in gouges and his standard tattered and frayed. To their left, Scyllon fought with bolter and sword, his shield long gone, just a useless, broken boss swinging around his left vambrace like an oversized bangle. He had taken a wound to his right hip, and his thigh was glistening with streaks of crimson blood.

'Damocles! Damocles of Ithaka!' Scyllon shouted as he saw them.

'Parthus,' Natus gasped hoarsely.

'What?' Priad asked.

'I hear… Parthus,' Natus answered. The order to break. It had been broadcasting for several minutes, but none of them had been able to make it out over the cacophony. Only Natus, with his hearing alert to every shred of noise.

'Break! Damocles! Break!' Priad ordered.

Iron Snakes do not run, but this was not flight. This was part of the battle scheme as Petrok had planned it. Once word had come from Phobor at the head of the twenty-five squads, Petrok's relief company was supposed to pull back up the slopes, to hold the head of the valley. The legions of the enemy swarmed after them as they worked their way backwards, channelling into the narrowing defiles of the canyon mouth like water rushing into a drain.

The way was treacherous. Petrok's Snakes were forced to move backwards, literally. They could not risk turning from the fight for even a moment. The terrain was steep and littered with rocks, and long-range fire from ork heavy weapons, mounted on vehicles back amid the ork horde, raked across them, pulverising boulders and heaving geysers of loose earth up into the air. A wind picked up, driving banks of smoke sideways across the valley, building great, choking rafts of cloud in the upper flues of the valley heights.

The squads covered one another as they retreated. Laomon, under Brother-Sergeant Lektas, reached the designated plateau first, and knelt down, offering sustained cover fire to the others from the higher vantage. Lektas had lost two of his brave inductees that hellish morning. Pelleas, with Brother-Sergeant Goront at their head, came up next. Goront had lost his helmet to a warboss's chainsword, and part of his scalp hung away in a grotesque bloody flap. He whipped his seven remaining men up onto the plateau, and in those final moments of retreat, that seven became six as Brother Meglos was blown limb from limb by a screaming rocket. Laetes, the Apothecary, leapt down the smouldering slope to the devastated body, his reductor in his fist and tears in his eyes.

Nophon squad, the right wing of the fan, backed up the slope, their munitions all but gone. Brother Baccys fired single-handed, his other arm wrapped around the waist of Brother-Sergeant Ryys, holding his beloved commander upright. Ryys had lost his right arm and terrible wounds disfigured his chest and back. Still he was yelling encouragement to his men, blood leaking from his helmet's filters.

The swinekin gathered in vast numbers around the throat of the valley. Horns sounded, trumpeting a premature victory, the orks believing they had put their attackers to flight. War machines churned forward, crushing over the piled corpses of fallen orks, trundling onto the slope foot amongst the front runners of the greenskin horde. Rockets dazzled in the air, leaving streamers of smoke. Heavy shells pounded into the valley walls. An echo like the wrack of doom rolled up and down the precious canyon.

Priad brought Damocles onto the slope, firing as they came. Andromak at last had to dump his beloved plasma weapon, for it had become so overheated it was in danger of critical misfire. He blessed it as he set it down, smoking, on the steep incline, then drew his bolt pistol. Twenty metres back, he put a bolt-round into the abandoned power cell and blew the ancient weapon up in the faces of the advancing greenskins. A ball of blue light engulfed them, hurling painted bodies into the sky, some of them fused or scorched or denuded of flesh by the extreme heat.

'Where's Petrok?' Priad barked. There was no sign of their master on the slopes, nor any sign at all of the fifth squad, Ridates. Priad searched the clamouring mass below for some clue.

'There!' cried Xander.

Petrok had been delayed in his retreat by a massive warboss, with whom the Librarian had squared in mortal combat. Petrok had driven Bellus deep into the warboss's sternum, but not before he had received two savage wounds to the chest and stomach. Ridates, inductees all, and fired with the will to prove their valour on this, their first ever undertaking, had closed in a circle around the stricken Librarian instead of falling back as per the design.

'We can't leave them!' Khiron bellowed.

'We can't leave Petrok!' Priad agreed. 'Xander, get Damocles to the summit! No arguments! I want two men!'

Fate, and the simple disposition of the men, decided that the two would be Andromak and Aekon. They were the two closest to Priad, though every brother, even Natus and Dyognes, would have volunteered.

'Come on!' Priad urged them. Khiron made to follow. 'Do as I ordered!' Priad yelled at him. 'Help Xander form the others tight!'

'Priad–'

'Do it! Help Xander!'

Khiron knew what this meant. It wasn't simply an order for now, it was an order forever. If Priad didn't return, Xander would be in command, and he would dearly need the Apothecary. Khiron began to scramble back up the slope.

Priad, Andromak and Aekon slaughtered their way back down the rocky rise, driving a path into the brute squadrons of the Painted Ones. They were no longer figures of grey, plastered as they were from head to foot with blood and gore. They were giants washed wet with the blood of their foe amongst the whirling phalanxes of black and red and sugar pink.

Priad's trio broke in behind the circle of Ridates, forging an exit by force of arms. Priad and Aekon fired their boltguns, Andromak supporting with shots from his heavy pistol and blows from his notched sword.

'Come on! This way!' Priad shouted.

Seuthis saw him, and snapped his squad around, pulling them back under the boom and whistle of the falling shells. Three of his inductees were gravely wounded, one badly. Seuthis ran to his stricken brother and began to guide him clear, hacking with his short sword at the closing press of greenskins.

Petrok stood his ground, defiant to the last, whirling Bellus two handed and squirting out forks of jagged light from his brow. Priad reached his side, firing the last of his shots. He clamped the empty bolter to his chest and drew his combat sword, striking out with it and his lightning claw together.

'Quite an hour, this,' Petrok muttered to him as they fought side by side, holding the tide back long enough for Ridates to filter away onto the clearer stretches of the slope.

'This must be what Fate had in mind for us, master,' Priad answered.

Petrok snorted, felling an oak of a greenskin with a single, bone-breaking blow. 'So, at last my friend Priad takes Fate seriously?' he retorted.

'I know this much,' said Priad, slogging and slicing, his limbs so fatigued they felt as if they were on fire. 'If this is Fate's purpose, Fate doesn't like us very much.'

## XVI

PETROK, WHO SEEMED to find amusement in all things including doom, was still laughing aloud as they reached the plateau. Seuthis had brought Ridates squad onto the summit half a minute before them. Now the remnants of the five companies employed the gained advantage of height and cover, and teamed that to the narrowing of the valley, which forced the swinekin below them into a compressed formation as they poured up the slope.

Such a narrow, defined profile made the orks an easier target to contain, as long as munitions held out. The Painted Ones thundered up through the canyon mouth, and each rising wave was cut down as it came into range. A wide embankment of ork bodies began to form as the phratry guns found them. The embankment became a wall, a bulwark, as orks clambered over it only to be cut down to add to it.

'Swineguard!' Seuthis yelled in warning.

Below, the greenskin mass was edging back and parting to allow the enemy elite a chance to try for the plateau. The swineguard were true monsters, each one of them a giant the size of a mature warboss. They wore polished mail linked with black gold and human bones, some of them carrying murder trees of black iron spikes on their shoulder harnesses. Clusters of human skulls, glowing white in the smoke-stained sunlight, rattled and clattered, pinned on the iron barbs of the murder trees as career trophies. The swineguard warriors were daubed in white body paint, banded with streaks of pink and red. Their throats were deeper, their roars more gut-shaking and bellicose than anything the phratry had yet heard. They eclipsed the war horns with their howling. Natus shuddered and stepped back, fumbling to remove his helmet, one handed.

The swineguard began to assault the slope. Every one of them carried a chainblade of some description and a heavy bolter. Priad knew just by looking that some of those weapons would have been a true test for even him to lift, but in the ghastly, oversized fists of the swineguard they seemed like toys. The boss leaders, larger even than the elite warriors they commanded, wore barbed helmets, or bronze skull-pots adorned with magnificent antlers four metres in span.

'I think you were right about Fate,' Petrok said. He was no longer laughing.

Behind the swineguard came the formations of war machines, the fortress trucks and battlewagons of the ork host. They chugged and clanged like steam engines, exhaling soot, driving saw-edged dozer blades into the mounds of the dead to plough them aside like snow drifts. Chain cannon on the foremost wagons opened fire, and the Iron Snakes ducked as tracer rounds streamed over the plateau like luminous hail.

'Time for our last gift to them,' Petrok announced. The five squads had carried as great a quantity of explosives as they could bear with them over the pass the night before: just about every demolition charge they could muster from the landing ships. As they had advanced into the fight, they had seeded the explosives in their wake, inert but primed.

The charges had been prepared for sowing by Pindor, whose skill with such materials was without peer. The devices were on a lapse trigger that would be keyed by the detonation of marker charges.

Priad beckoned Pindor to his side. 'Your privilege.'

'Are you sure?' Pindor asked.

'Quickly, brother!'

Pindor raised his boltgun to his chin and took aim. He knew as well as any of them that he was not the best marksman in the phratry. He targeted the lead marker charge.

Pindor fired. The bolt crumped off the rock a metre wide.

'For Throne's sake...' Xander growled.

'Oh, shut up! I'm just getting my eye in,' Pindor grunted back.

He aimed again, and fired.

The marker charge, struck cleanly, ignited. The force of the blast showered stone chips into the air. The gravel went scattering down the depth of the slope into the faces of the advancing swineguard.

Harmlessly.

'Bloody hell!' Xander exclaimed. 'We–'

Pindor turned to face Xander and held up one hand for quiet. 'Two… one…'

The slope came apart in a shockwave of fire and dirt. The magnitude of the backwash was so fierce that some of the Iron Snakes on the plateau were thrown over. Below them, swineguard monsters were torn apart, or hurled into the air, or simply vaporised. A retching column of boiling fire and smoke rose up above the plateau in a mushroom cloud.

In shuddering series, the lapse triggered charges continued to fire, detonating right back down the slope and out onto the plain where they had been sown. Whole phalanxes of greenskins were obliterated in blooms of flame, and war wagons hurled over, disintegrating in showers of sparks and outflung scraps of metal and armour plating.

With a noise like the Emperor's own thundering voice, part of the valley face came away in a colossal landslip, and buried thousands of greenskins under a tide of churning rock that obeyed no master except the force of gravity. An inferno retched up the slope, consuming the few, struggling ork survivors in the canyon. Torched ork munitions, some of them the payloads of fighting vehicles, exploded sympathetically, adding to the holocaust.

As the booming echoed away and the veil of dust and ash began to clear, the five squads saw that an almost endless sea of raging greenskins still occupied the plains below, screaming and howling in outrage. But in the canyon slope and the foreland beyond, only devastation remained, a wild storm of fire and swirling smoke, lifting embers into the air. Vehicles, smashed beyond all recognition, burned and collapsed, their chassis disintegrating. Thousands of scorched corpses littered the incline at the mouth of the valley.

'Move out,' Petrok said, 'back up the valley. Now, while they're reeling.'

Priad looked at him. 'What of the Chapter Master?'

'Phobor reports that the twenty-five squads have broken clear. They're heading for the landing sites,' said Petrok.

'Fate loves us after all, Priad. It's time to join Seydon.'

* * *

## XVII

BY THE EVENING of that day, the Iron Snakes had left the surface of Ganahedarak. Despite their losses, the extraction was a notable achievement. Several of the senior officers made it known that the action at Ganahedarak would stand proud amongst the attainments of the phratry.

To most of the brothers, it felt like defeat. To most of the brothers, it felt like running away.

It felt that way to Priad. He had never been so conflicted about an undertaking in his life. The warfare Damocles had weathered had been about the most intense he'd ever known, and the two battles they had fought had been unequivocal victories. Now, the phratry was simply consolidating its forces, and shifting its tactical emphasis to a more viable footing. It was the pragmatic and sober thing to do. Any commander believing otherwise was committing unit suicide.

But still, they had met a foe so vast in numbers they could not overmaster it in formal war. Their achievement had been simply staying alive. And they were leaving Ganahedarak to its fate.

On the wounded world below them, the human cities and townships had been abandoned, the populations fled into mountain fastnesses and hinterland retreats. Woeful, lingering doom was all they could look forward to. The kings of the south, and other potentates of Ganahedarak, as they became aware of the phratry's forced withdrawal, sent raging, indignant messages after them, which became more and more venomous and, when no response was sent, faded into desperate, begging pleas.

The greenskins had also witnessed the extraction of the Iron Snakes. Though they had lost perhaps tens of thousands of warriors during the undertaking, no obvious reduction had been made in their sprawling hosts, and they gleefully celebrated the feat of turning the vaunted human champions to their heels. Across the ragged, pummelled continents, war horns and battle drums sounded out, raucous and frenetic. Huge vox-casters droned their triumphant trumpet blasts at the sky. Millions of swinekin voices ululated at the heavens, as if to shake the firmament down in pieces.

The embarkation halls of the battle-barges stank of blood. Not a brother amongst Seydon's twenty-five squads or Petrok's relief force had come back unmarked in some manner, and many were gravely wounded, as were many of the ancillary forces of armourers and attendants who had supplied Seydon's warband. Great quantities of armour and materiel had been damaged, some beyond the point of repair. Several vehicles in Seydon's complement had been abandoned or destroyed, and most of those recovered were crippled and broken.

The Apothecaries worked triage on the decks, stripping off armour to treat wounds, often ignoring their own injuries to work on the critical cases. Their efforts were bolstered by the physicians aboard the barges.

There were the noises of movement and activity, and the moans of the wounded, but over all, a strained silence hung around the returning squads, the numbing ache of total fatigue and ground-down spirits.

Seydon held counsel in the reclusiam of his barge, summoning all the captains and the squad officers. The Chapter Master had refused all attempts by his hand servants to wash him or bind his wounds. In his pitted, buckled armour, he sat on the central podium, caked in a drying residue of blood, both human and ork. Much of the human blood was his own. His face was a pale, drawn ghost inside the darkness of his cowl, and his breath came sharp and irregular through his exchanger tanks. His jigsaw cloak of polished wyrm-horn pieces had been ripped and torn, and loose fragments dangled from unravelling golden threads. His great lance, Tiborus, lay across his knees.

As Priad entered the reclusiam, bare-headed, with the other officers, he mourned the distressing appearance of the great master. Seydon seemed so dreadfully bowed and hunched. The blade tip of Tiborus was nicked and buckled, and deep cuts had been gashed into its mighty shaft.

Priad stared, for it was so seldom any brother apart from the highest ordinates got to see the Chapter Master in person. As he took his place in the ring of warriors, he found himself captivated by Seydon's left hand. Seydon had removed his gigantic gauntlet, and allowed it to fall onto the deck at his feet. His bare hand, so very large but so very human, was the first proof Priad had ever seen that Seydon was sheathed in flesh and blood like the rest of them. Priad hated himself for noticing that Seydon's left hand trembled slightly, as if palsied.

How Ganahedarak had reduced them! It had forced even the Chapter Master, the legend that bound the phratry together, to expose his mortality.

Slaves had lit myrtle, orub and camphor in the burners around the reclusiam, and perfumed smoke drifted through the cold air. Starlight twinkled in through the stained glass of the towering arches.

The ring of warriors around the podium filled in and became complete. In their broken, gouged armour, the officers stood at attention. Some, like Priad, carried their buckled, scored helms under their arms. Some dripped blood upon the deck. The odour of sweat and filth and body matter, and the coppery stink of blood, quite overwhelmed the sweet smell of the incense.

Every surviving officer was present. From Petrok's force, even Ryys had come, leaning weakly against Seuthis, his upper body wrapped with dressings bound tight and red-wet around the shreds of his missing limb. Others were just as mangled. Kryto of Aegis had lost his left hand and the flesh of the left side of his face. He carried half of his helm, a cloven half, in his right gauntlet. Mikos of Lakodeme, victor of Penses and Tribulation Rex, nursed a terrible stomach wound. Iklyus of Thebes, great hero of the Berod Fray, had suffered an amputation below the right knee, and leaned with effort on a sea-lance. Priad felt ashamed of his minor scratches and cuts, even though he was aware of the bruised tissue swelling and throbbing across his face from his left ear to his cheek.

Seydon made a gesture, and Cyclion, the Master Chaplain, conducted the Rite of the Sharing of Water. Tall and mournful in his power armour, Cyclion's silver skull mask seemed entirely in keeping with the mood. At a gesture from him, boy slaves brought forth the eusippus, the copper death urns, and set them on the deck before Seydon. They were empty as yet, but soon they would confine the ashes of the fallen for the voyage home to Ithaka.

There were sixty-one of them. Ten for Parthus squad alone.

Priad swallowed hard.

'Good counsel,' said Seydon after a long silence, 'is the backbone of any phratry. We are victorious, yet defeated, valiant, yet disgraced, alive, yet broken. Like beloved Ithaka, this undertaking has a bright face and a constant darkness. I salute every one of you for your efforts and your courage. I order you to impart that salute to every brother in your commands. Any shame of failure is mine and mine alone.'

'Not so, master–' Phobor began. The veteran captain looked like a vagabond, so torn and frayed was his once-proud plate.

Seydon raised his bare left hand to hush Phobor. 'Mine and mine alone. Brothers, since the foundation of our phratry, there have been eighteen Chapter Masters, an illustrious lineage that it has been my duty and my honour to follow. Under them, and under me, the Chapter has won sterling victories and many laurels, and has suffered its defeats and routs, like any good company of warriors. Just as we relish the triumphs of Falling Star, Presarius, Ambold Eleven, Cornak or Far Hallow, and etch those deeds upon our fortress walls, so we regret such disasters as Beriun, Outward Kalenk or Forbrium. But never before have we seen a day like this. Never before have we taken victory and defeat in equal measure. Never before have we relinquished an undertaking, and left behind us a people crying out for our aid.'

He rumbled into silence, murmuring 'Never before...' one last time. No one spoke. Seydon stroked his bare hand along the notched haft of his beloved lance. 'This drives against our oath, our ancient compact. This disgraces our bold claim of undertaking. For that error, I blame myself. Only in the time of Seydon has such a calamity befallen our order.'

The Chapter Master lifted his lance and threw it onto the deck with such vigour that the weapon rolled away from him and came to rest at the feet of the ringed warriors. 'I must make amends, my brothers. I must find a way to turn this infamy into glory, for the sake of our spirit and our name. But I am at a loss to know how. We are the greatest warriors of our age. We can meet and squarely best every monster that rises against us in formal war. But we cannot match an endless foe. And the greenskins are without limit or end. Though we heap their corpses to the heavens and beyond, still they will come.'

Seydon lifted his head to look at his men, so that the light fell in under his heavy cowl and caught the line of his chin and cheek. There were beads of blood upon the white flesh.

'So I look to you now, my warriors and my brothers, for counsel and answers.'

No one spoke for a moment.

'We have to think,' said Petrok finally. All eyes turned towards him. He was standing in the ring, his back hunched with pain. The wounds to his chest and stomach delivered by the warboss urgently needed attention.

'So I have said, Librarian,' Seydon answered. 'Perhaps time to reflect—'

'No, master,' Petrok cut in. 'I mean we have to think our way to victory. We have reached a place where every scrap of our martial prowess is worthless. We have to use our brains instead.'

Several of the officers, including Phobor, sniggered in disgust.

'Might is all we have,' announced Myrmede of Ankysus. 'Might is what we do so well.'

'This is no longer a matter for warrior brethren,' said Seuthis. 'A fleet must be gathered. This is a duty for warships, in formation.'

'Seuthis is right. Where infantry has failed,' said Sardis of Lystra, 'we should take our vengeance by fleet action!'

'Burn the orks and the worlds they tread upon!' cried Phanthus.

'Should we burn Ganahedarak?' asked Petrok.

'If that's what it takes to rid the Reef Stars and fulfil our undertaking!' Sardis replied curtly.

'Burn all those people…?' Petrok sighed.

'They're dead anyway!' Phobor muttered.

'Let the orks suffer the Chapter whole!' cried Medes of Skypio, drawing assent from his brothers. 'Twenty-five squads? Thirty? Let them face one hundred and flee to the dirt that spawned them!'

'Aye!' Iklyus called out. 'Turn the phratry loose and burn them to hell!'

'Would you magnify this misery, Brother Iklyus?' Petrok asked quietly. 'Thirty squads and we take home sixty-one urns? Would there be anyone left alive to carry the urns home to Ithaka if we turned all one thousand of us upon the greenskins?'

'You repudiate our skills,' snapped Medes.

'If such fatality is where your thinking gets you, Petrok,' Phobor tutted, 'I'll stick by my muscles.'

'You do that,' Petrok snarled back, earning hisses from the ring of warriors. 'The orks are strong and hardy, resilient to injury, and countless. Are we not swift and clever? Are we not beings of culture and ingenuity? Must we descend to their level and play them at a brute game we cannot win?'

'Give me the Chapter at arms and I'll show you how we can win!' Medes exclaimed.

'If I gave you the Chapter at arms, dear brother,' Petrok replied, 'you would show me a thousand dead heroes.'

Medes, bullish and heavy-set, the master of celebrated Skypio, the finest warrior in the phratry and captain of the finest squad, took a step towards Petrok. The officers around him dragged him back by his arms.

'Not here!' Cyclion warned, pointing the haft of his thunder hammer at the pair the way a school master would point with his cane at unruly pupils. 'Bite your tongues and hold your rage, or I will drive you from this holy place!'

'My apologies, Master Chaplain,' Medes said, cooling.

'As Brother Medes says,' Petrok smiled, 'his apologies.'

Medes surged forward, stung by the insult, and only the strong hands of Phanthus and Phobor restrained him.

'That's enough!' Seydon growled. 'Bad enough we reel from the orks, I'll not have us fighting ourselves. Petrok, my kind brother, retract your slur to Brother Medes.'

'I will not, master,' Petrok said. White fury gripped the still-restrained Medes. The other officers glared in dismay at Petrok's insubordination.

Seydon rose. 'The devil is in you, boy,' he said, stepping towards Petrok.

'Then let's hear what the devil has to say for himself,' a low, grating voice echoed from the shadows. Seydon looked round and sighed. He sat down again. 'You're awake, then, master Autolochus?'

'I'm always awake,' the voice replied. 'Noise you idiots make, it's hard to slumber.'

Hydraulic pistons hissed in the gloom, and the warrior ring parted respectfully to admit the new figure. He towered over them, clomping forward on his thick bionic legs, his huge grey chassis casement draped with ancient, flaking pennants. The venerable dreadnought Autolochus took his place in the ring of warriors.

'I say, let's hear Petrok,' Autolochus said, his voice gusting dry and toneless from the synthesisers in his bodywork. A veteran captain in his age, Autolochus's battle-mutilated remains had been cased, with honour, in the dreadnought mechanism for perpetuity. An ultimate weapon, like all dreadnoughts, Autolochus was kept in hibernation for most of the year, woken only for triumphs, or ceremonies.

Or crises.

'Yes,' said Medes, shrugging off the hands restraining him, 'like master Autolochus, I would be intrigued to hear the complexities of Petrok's scheme.'

Autolochus pivoted his huge metal bulk around so that his ocular sensors regarded Petrok. 'Let's go, Librarian. Make it good.'

Petrok nodded to the huge, sentient war machine. 'I have been plagued with dreams this last month. Pivotal dreams, in which the manner of our deliverance... excuse me, the deliverance of the Reef Stars... has been foretold.'

'When a Librarian dreams,' Autolochus rumbled, 'it pays to listen. If I'd listened to Nector, I wouldn't be four tonnes of scrap metal.'

Some of the officers laughed.

'The dreams of a Librarian count,' Medes offered, 'but all I've heard from Petrok is rubbish about using our brains.'

'Rubbish is all I have,' Petrok assured the company. 'Disjointed, dislocated nonsense about... about a set of jaws and about Priad.'

'Who's Priad?' Medes asked, pretending not to recognise the name.

'Brother-sergeant of the Notable Damocles,' Autolochus rasped. 'Your arrogance does you no favours, Medes.'

Priad felt a sudden fluff of pride. Autolochus knew him, knew his name and station.

'Oh, *that* Priad,' Medes said. 'Speak up, Brother Priad. Tell us how you feature in these dreams.'

'I–' Priad coughed. 'I... well, there was a meadow, and also a black dog...' He paused. His voice sounded pathetic and thin.

'Now we're getting somewhere,' Phobor mocked.

Petrok held up his hand to gently silence Priad. 'My dear brother and friend Priad doesn't understand this. I don't understand this. But I declare to the band of warriors here, if you let me go from here, with Priad, to Baal Solock, we will secure a victory for you. For the Reef Stars.'

'How?' asked Iklyus.

'I don't know,' replied Petrok. 'Not yet.'

'You'll be doing something there, will you?' taunted Medes. 'Using your minds?'

Many of the warriors in the ring laughed.

'Just a while back,' Priad said quietly, 'on Ithaka, out on the Cydides Isthmus, my Apothecary, Khiron, ventured to me that the time of brawn and force of arms might be waning. The petitioners we were training lacked all martial vigour... lacked the guts, as Khiron put it. But still, and I admit this with a happy heart, they outsmarted us and won the drill. They bested Damocles squad.'

'Not hard,' Medes crowed.

'Don't make me come over there and hurt you, brother,' Priad said. 'The petitioners bested Damocles squad, and I'm proud to confess it. They outplayed us with their minds. Weaker than my brothers, they out-thought us. We were playing a simple, martial game, a physical exercise. The cheese run, you remember that, don't you, Brother-Sergeant Bylon?'

Bylon, sergeant of Veii, nodded.

'The petitioners couldn't match us, muscle for muscle, so they changed the rules and won. Khiron said to me that maybe brains represented the future. The rise of brains and the fall of brawn. I said I was sorry, as brawn was all I had.'

This raised a sympathetic laugh from most of the officers.

'I don't know why I'm telling you this. Gods, I don't even know why I'm speaking aloud in the presence of our Master and Lord Autolochus. But I know battle, and I know how the most curious patterns can form out of the randomness of war. I believe Petrok is right, and I believe I am somehow part of that pattern. Me, and the meadow and the black dog. I don't know how, but I'd like to go to Baal Solock and find out. I'd like to use my mind for once. I envy Brother Medes for not needing one.'

'You bastard, Priad!' Medes spat.

'Oh, *now* you remember my name,' Priad smiled.

'You little–'

'Shut up, Medes,' said Seydon, rising to his feet again. 'Petrok, undertake this with Damocles. The *Bullwyrm* is yours to command. If you come back empty-handed, then don't come back at all. That's my word on this. The rest of you, see to your wounds and your men. We'll counsel war again at the edge of the system. I will consider full deployment in–'

He paused. 'How long to Baal Solock and back, Librarian?'

'Forty days,' replied Petrok.

'Forty-five,' contradicted Autolochus.

'Fifty days, then. After that, I raise a fleet to full deployment of the Chapter House, death or glory.'

'We will not fail the phratry in this,' Petrok said.

'I'll make sure of that,' Autolochus grumbled. The dreadnought clanked around to face Petrok squarely. 'It's been a long time since I last did anything useful. I'll be coming with you.'

## XVIII

DRIVE ENGINES FLARING, the fast cruiser *Bullwyrm* ploughed on through the airless winter of the stars.

Every man of Damocles had accompanied Priad, even Natus and Dyognes, weak from their wounds. Dyognes was a shadow of his former self. Once a virile youth as robust and energised as Xander, he now walked with aching steps, his breathing chopped and curtailed, his skin sickly. It would take many months of recuperation, as well as augmetic and bionic surgery, to restore him to battle prime, and even then that recovery was not guaranteed. There was a chance that Dyognes's career as a phratry warrior was done, and he would spend the remainder of his days amongst the ancillary staff of Karybdis.

'Let me come,' he had said to Priad, when the brother-sergeant offered him the chance to return to the fortress moon with the main force. 'This may be the last undertaking I make with plate upon my back.'

Natus was in better spirits. There was something eternally vital about Natus, a wellspring of vigour that had seen him through many wounds in the past, including the loss of his original arm. No augmetic refit had been made yet, but a skull cap of grey iron had been cased around his head, surgically screwed to the bones, to preserve the integrity of his healing skull. Before scar tissue could cover the ruptured nerves of his ruined eyes, Khiron began a preliminary round of reconstructive surgery during the first few days of the voyage, installing the neural plugs and socket brackets for augmetic implants. The eyes themselves would be connected on Natus's return to Karybdis, once the initial work had healed favourably. For the rest of the voyage, Natus wore a blindfold of bandages around his eye sockets. But Khiron had run relay leads from the nerve meshes inside the sockets and connected them to a simple ocular scanner, providing Natus with basic monochrome vision and depth perception.

Natus wore the scanner on his forehead, attached to his skull cap by a magnetic coupler. He looked for all the world like a cyclops of old myth.

With Petrok withdrawn to his quarters for meditation and further probing of the spirit domain for answers, Priad took charge of preparing Damocles. There was a body of armourers and fitters aboard the fast cruiser, and they set to work on the squad's wargear, so much of it mangled or ruined. The brothers themselves put the strength of their arms into the repairs, under the supervision of the master armourers. Weapons were stripped down entirely and every part of them cleaned and blessed. Blades were re-edged, or in some cases replaced. The damaged functions of power armour were repaired.

Andromak had been brought an old but functioning flamer from the ship's magazine stores to replace his lost plasma weapon. Priad hoped that on their return to the fortress moon, Andromak might be granted custodianship of another heirloom plasma gun, and thus restore Damocles's heavy bite. Andromak spent many days of the voyage sitting apart from the others in the corner of the martial deck. Like all of Damocles, he wore a simple chiton or himation, for the plate cases were undergoing their refurbishment.

Andromak was working on the squad's precious standard, the emblem he always carried between his shoulder blades. It had come through the two battles on Ganahedarak the worst for wear. Andromak was patiently repairing it, patching it back together with pieces of chiton and storm cloaks, using tough fishing twine, silver thread, and long sailcloth needles.

Great Autolochus roamed the hold decks and empty hallways of the fast cruiser, brooding and unsettled. It was as though once roused from his mechanical dormancy, he could not abide being still. Often, as the brothers of Damocles took their exercise runs around the ship's corridors, they would encounter his trudging, clunking form.

On the eighth day of the voyage, when Priad was on the martial deck observing the industry of the armour smiths, Autolochus appeared and called to him. Priad withdrew with the dreadnought to a far corner of the deck.

'Tell me about your undertaking to Baal Solock,' Autolochus said.

Priad recounted the venture, as best as his memory would serve. He spoke of the ruined land, the downed primul war party, the cruelty inflicted upon the people of Baal Solock. He spoke too of primary clerk Antoni and the purging he had dealt out.

Autolochus listened, then questioned Priad repeatedly, closing in on certain points of the story and urging Priad to recall more and more of the specific detail.

Priad found that the careful interrogation prompted him to remember tiny fragments that he was surprised he could dredge up after twelve years. He remembered aspects of the countryside, his munition tally, even the name of the black dog that had run through his dreams.

'Princeps,' he said. 'The dog was called Princeps.'

Priad wondered why Autolochus was so concerned with the details, presuming the ancient warrior intended to build the most complete tactical picture possible in his mind. But before he could ask, they were interrupted.

Scyllon appeared, with an agitated look on his slender face.

'Khiron needs you,' he said.

A GAGGLE OF boy slaves and attendants were waiting around the entrance to Petrok's quarters, and they scurried away as Scyllon brought Priad and the lumbering war machine to the place.

Within the lamp-lit chamber, Khiron was kneeling beside a cot on which Petrok lay, so pale and still, Priad feared he had been carried off to the other world.

'The attendants found him,' Khiron said quietly. 'Our Brother-Librarian has neglected treatment for the injuries he took on Ganahedarak, and that neglect has caught up with him.' Khiron lifted the blanket he had placed across Petrok's torso, and revealed the ghastly wounds the greenskin warboss had handed out. They were deep, much deeper and more significant than Petrok had pretended. Despite the superhuman resilience of his body, septic corruption had set in. Petrok was in a feverish stupor.

'Infection, perhaps even poison, raked into the wounds by the filthy ork,' Khiron said.

'Is he dying?' asked Priad.

'Yes,' replied the Apothecary. 'Yet he may live. At this time his life hangs in the balance. If his body and my salves can fight the infection, he will recover. But if they can't...'

Khiron glanced at Priad. 'His survival is in Fate's hands.' Priad thought about that, and didn't like the sound of it very much.

'This means you have command,' Priad said to Autolochus.

Autolochus's voice rumbled out of his hull-casing. 'By dint of age and experience, yes. But I'm no squad commander, not any more. You should have seniority here, Priad. Consider me your ally, but don't expect me to lead.'

Priad stared at the huge machine, at the graven images of war and the purity seals that decorated the front of his hull. There was no arguing with a thing like that.

IN THE SUBSEQUENT days, Petrok's condition grew steadily worse. He did not wake or become lucid, but was given to fits of raving and convulsion, accompanied by a dripping fever. Khiron began to fear that there was more at work than simple wound infection. Some evil influence seemed to have Petrok in its grip, and would not let him go. Rites were performed, of cleansing and purification, to banish evil spirits and daemons from the echoing halls of the *Bullwyrm*.

To no avail.

\* \* \*

ON THE SEVENTEENTH day of the voyage, with Baal Solock within reach, and Petrok relapsed into a profound coma, Priad had a dream.

It was as strange to him as the last, for dreams visited his pragmatic mind so seldom. Stranger in fact, for from the start of it, he knew he was dreaming.

He was standing in the sunlit meadow, under a wide blue sky, surrounded by golden corn. He could feel the breeze on his skin, though he was clad in his full power armour. He felt weightless, as if he could take off and, with one bound, touch the harvest moon.

Looking down, he saw his armour was as new, polished like a mirror. He took off his war helm, and realised with some mystification that it had the laurels of a captain marked around the crown.

'Why am I dreaming?' he asked. The corn stooks hissed. Familiar hills rose white and clear above the far edge of the meadow. He looked around for the black dog, and it appeared, as if on cue, trotting through the corn, snapping playfully at spiralling corn flies.

It came up to him, tongue lolling from a grinning snout, and cocked its head.

'Princeps?' Priad said, remembering the name from his conversation with Autolochus.

The dog barked, twice, then turned away and took off into the corn, running from him on a zig-zag path, slowly disappearing from view in the nodding gold. Three times, it stopped and looked back at him, barking again on the final occasion, until he responded and began to follow it.

The black dog led him up through the meadow, through the hissing corn.

'Slow down!' he called out once or twice as its lead on him increased.

It was a pleasant enough dream, he thought, engaged by the rarity and reality of it, and especially by his lucid participation. He knew it was a special dream, and wondered if it was like the true dreams Petrok and his kind experienced.

By the time he had followed the dog to the far end of the meadow, clouds had run into the sky, and the sun went in, hidden behind them. The light became grey, the corn white rather than gold. It grew colder. The black dog, still black, barked again. Shadows were forming in the edges of the meadow, beneath the stands of olive trees and under the mountain woods.

He realised each footstep he took made a crunching sound. He looked down again, and saw that he was walking on a crust of ice. The corn stalks were frozen and brittle. The dog's breath made little clouds in the frosty air.

Priad realised he was stepping out onto the great glacier Kraretyer, that giant of Ithaka's southern pole. He looked behind him and saw the overcast meadows of the Pythoan Cantons, and ahead, the blue ice and air fronts of the polar glacier. Dream logic, he supposed, laughing aloud and half-enjoying the impossible segue between landscapes, between worlds.

He stepped out onto the ice. The black dog had gone. Mean winds shrilled along the glacial crags, and surface snow, wind-carried, smoked off the cusps of the drifts. There was a storm coming.

He walked onwards, anticipating something, but only sure of the fact he should anticipate. He wondered if he could wake up if he willed himself, but dared not try. This was a true dream, and he was loath to break its spell.

The great snow bear waited on the ice shelf ahead of him. He could not say where it had come from, for it had not been there a moment before. Instinctively, he reached for a weapon, but there was nothing in the loops of his harness except a golden figurine of Parthus. Priad looked at it in surprise for a second, and the figure became ice and melted in his hand.

The snow bear came closer. Priad realised it wasn't a snow bear at all. It was a man, swathed in white fur pelts. It was Petrok.

'Fit for war?' Petrok asked. The great Librarian smiled, but his face was as white as a death mask, and his bright eyes sunken in dark circles like bruises.

'If war awaits,' Priad replied. 'Why are you in my dream?' he asked.

'I'm not,' said Petrok. He was limping, and his arms were pulled tight around his body, as if for warmth. 'You're in mine.'

'I don't understand,' said Priad. 'How can I be in your dream?'

'Because I sent for you. It was the only way to make contact.'

'You sent for me?'

'I sent a psychopomp.'

'A what?'

Petrok sighed, as if the explanations were a struggle. 'I sent a guide to bring you to this other place. It probably took the shape of that black dog of yours.'

Priad nodded. Then he frowned. 'I still don't understand…'

'And I don't have time to explain,' Petrok said. He glanced at the skies behind him, the cold black vault of the polar night. 'There's a storm coming. It's been chasing me for days. You can't be here when it comes.'

'Come with me, then,' Priad said. 'There's a sunlit meadow just a few steps behind me.'

Petrok shook his head. 'Not for me, there isn't. That's your dream, the one I summoned you from. This is mine, and I'm stuck here. Do you know where I am?'

'Kraretyer,' said Priad.

'No, my oh so literal friend. I am on my cot, in my quarters aboard the *Bullwyrm*, dying and insensible. I fashioned this polar dream so you would recognise it as a meeting place particular to us.'

'I still don't understand this,' Priad said.

'Then just listen to me.'

'But this could all be my dream, and you a part of it, and I'd just be listening to myself, wouldn't I?' Priad asked.

'I can't convince you otherwise. But that's no reason not to listen anyway, is it? I need to tell you things. My consultations with the darker places have brought me answers that I must convey, and cannot in the waking world.'

'Because of the wounds you suffered?'

Petrok chuckled, and opened his furs away from his naked chest. The mortal gashes were there, but he bled not human blood but ork ichor. 'This is not the greenskin's doing. Those injuries just weakened me, made me susceptible.'

'To what?'

'To our enemies. Listen to me, brother. Listen. Hear the things I would speak to you in life, if I could only return there, sensible and awake. This effort I've gone to is the only way I can make myself heard.'

'I'm listening.'

The pitch of the wind rose, and crystal ice danced in swirls around them, carried up off the blue-glass face of the glacier.

'The greenskins cannot be defeated in formal war. Not even if our Chapter was multiplied a thousandfold. This bloody truth the spirits have revealed to me. But there is a way to drive them from the Reef Stars. They are at war with each other, tribe upon tribe, mob on mob, host on host. And this war has been engineered.'

'Engineered?' Priad echoed. 'By what means? By whom?'

'Who is so cruel and malicious they would use the carnage of others for their own ends? The primuls have done this. Unable to muster enough force to take the Reef Stars out from under our protection themselves, they have fanned the flames of hatred in the greenskins. They have triggered the orks' fury, setting the swinekin loose to do their dirty work for them, and achieve what they could not.'

'How does anyone, even a primul fiend, force an ork to do anything?' Priad asked, almost amused at the notion.

'By stealing that which is precious to them. An ancestral trophy, a relic of great consequence. The jaw-bones of an ancient and revered warboss, a champion leader sacred to their species.'

'The jaw bone…' Priad said, beginning to shape the truth in his mind.

'The primuls you purged on Baal Solock, twelve years past, had accomplished the theft, but their damaged craft was forced to set down on that world. Their intention was to carry the relic into human space, and leave enough provenance behind that the orks would blame mankind for the crime.'

'But it was destroyed!' Priad said.

'That only aided them, in the long run. Their traces were covered.'

'No wonder that bastard laughed before I killed him,' Priad said, remembering at last the one detail that had previously escaped him.

Petrok shrugged, and took another anxious look back at the encroaching storm. The horizon at his heels had lost definition as the distant blizzards fogged the air. Above their heads, the bright stars were fading from view.

'For over a decade,' Petrok said, his words slower and more halting, as if pain was wracking his innards, 'the warp-witches and carrion lords of the primuls have been casting suggestions into the minds of the greenskin tribes, goading them in dreams and visions, showing them lies about where their prize has been taken to. It has caused mob-wars, faction fighting. Whole worlds in the swine territories have burned out in the heat of hate-inspired violence. Now that frenzy has spilled into our protectorate. Needled by the mystic urgings of the primuls, the orks are pursuing their relic into the Reef Stars, slaughtering each other for the honour of recovering it.'

'What do we do?'

'We give it back to them.'

Priad roared out a bark of incredulous laughter. 'But it is lost! Destroyed!'

'Not all of it.'

'But–'

'Any true scrap will contain enough genetic trace,' Petrok cried, having to raise his voice now against the moaning of the wind. 'Enough to prove its truth to the greenskins. Ask Khiron. Such work is not beyond our flesh smiths. We–'

The glacier shuddered. Pelting ice whipped across them in a brutal flurry, driving from the darkening south. They were forced to shield their eyes against the deluge.

'Time's up!' Petrok yelled. 'The storm's found me again! You must go!'

'But–'

'Get out of here, friend! Get back to the meadow and the waking world!'

Petrok turned, huddled in his furs, and began to trudge away into the teeth of the storm.

'Wait!' Priad shouted. 'I need more!'

'Go!'

'I can't leave you here!'

'You must!' Petrok bellowed, turning back for a moment. 'Go! Don't you understand, brother, the primuls have become aware of my probings! They have touched me through the warp and know my purpose and intention! They mean to silence me forever before I can undo their scheme!'

'Petrok!'

'Get gone from here before all my efforts are wasted! Priad, please! Go!'

The lethal blizzard rushed in around them, and Priad lost sight of his beloved Librarian almost at once.

'What did you mean? About Khiron? What did you mean?'

Petrok had gone. In dismay, alarmed at the dream that had appeared so pleasant to begin with and now seemed beyond his means to control, Priad stumbled backwards. The raging ice ripped around him, seeking, as it seemed, to cast him off his feet. He understood now why Petrok had cased him in his armour plate.

There were dark shapes inside the storm, fluid black things with sharp edges that whipped and coiled around him, spectres in the gale.

He turned, hoping to see some shaft of daylight that might lead him back into the meadow. There was none. Only the desolate landscape of the nocturnal glacier, spread out endlessly before him. He heard a sound like slicing blades behind him. He heard feral cries in the storm. Ice shards pelted past him, the splinters wet with human blood. He heard laughter.

The black dog was at his side, looking up at him, frost upon its glossy pelt.

'Lead me!' Priad cried.

The dog trotted away, and Priad followed, crunching over the blue ice, fighting against the force of the wind.

He stepped into cold daylight. He stepped into the meadow. The sun had drained away and left a grey sky and a field of hissing, ash-white corn. The dark shadows under the trees at the limits of the meadow had pooled blacker, like ink. The dog ran off ahead of him. A few stray snowflakes fluttered in the air around him.

He began to walk down the meadow, through the nodding corn. A strong wind blew, and the corn hissed louder. The distant valleys and mountains were obscured by low cloud and the fog of rain. Great sections of the corn field had been reaped down, the stalks sliced flat by scythes or other harvesting blades. The dead corn lay piled beside the cut stubble.

'I want to wake up now,' Priad said aloud.

The black dog turned, whined mournfully, and then began to bound away, heedless of his calls, vanishing into the distance.

'I want to wake up now,' Priad said again, looking around.

He froze. The dark shadows under the trees had moved out into the open, becoming tall, sharp silhouettes, grim figures that steadily cut their way towards him, swinging scythes through the corn.

He started to blunder on. The corn he strode through chimed and clunked off his thigh plates. Looking down, he saw that it was no longer corn. Every stalk was made of iron, fashioned into a snake. Every stalk hissed.

'I want to wake up now!' Priad cried. 'Let me wake up, in the name of the Throne! Let me do this!'

The figures closed in, glossy black and skeletally thin, their reaping blades cutting down sheaves of snakes that hissed and bled on the meadow ground.

'Let me wake up!' Priad yelled. He felt the chill of death creep over his shoulder. He dared not look around. He heard the steady, slithering swish of a scythe, cutting through the stalks, close behind.

'I want to wake up!' he demanded.

And he did.

### XIX

THE BULLWYRM, WEARY and spent, made orbit over Baal Solock, and set to high anchor. The entire world below was silent. No response came to the signals of the phratry warship.

Priad had said nothing of his dream, though the content and sensation of it had lingered in his mind in the days since. Petrok had still not woken from his death-sleep. Priad had sat at his cot-side for hours, searching the still face for some sign that his dream had been more than just a dream.

Finally, as the brothers of Damocles dressed in their wargear and prepared for descent, Priad had taken Khiron to a private part of the vessel, and told him all that had visited his slumber.

'You must tell this to Autolochus,' Khiron said.

Priad shook his head. 'The old warhorse will have enough trouble dealing with the rest of my intentions. You tell him, after I'm gone.'

'What does that mean?' Khiron asked.

\* \* \*

DAMOCLES SQUAD HAD assembled on the martial deck, gleaming in their repaired and refurbished plate. Autolochus stood with them.

Priad entered the deck, and allowed the attendants to case him in his armour. They bound his limbs and torso with linen and leather straps, anointed him with oils, and carefully locked the segments of the armour into place, connecting feed lines as they built the suit around him. It had been finished to a rare degree of wonder, buffed and polished to a glassy brightness. The armourers had worked with consummate skill. He half expected to see a captain's laurels around the crown of his helm.

Priad sat on a dressing block as they fitted his lightning claw. Slaves oiled his black hair, and coiled it up around his scalp, ready for the helmet fit. Others brought him his blade and his boltgun. Munition spares were strapped around his waist.

The lightning claw was connected. Priad test-clenched it, watching the finger blades work, and the blue energy crackle, fierce blue, like the ice of the Kraretyer glacier.

He rose to his feet as the armourers and their servants withdrew, nodding his thanks to them. He took his helm from a waiting slave.

He crossed the deck to join the others.

'The rite, Apothecary,' he said.

Khiron nodded, and withdrew the flask – tubular, copper, banded with straps of dull zinc – from a sheath strapped to the thigh-plate of his power armour.

This was the Rite of the Giving of Water, and none of proud Damocles looked away. Nine armoured warriors, the entire assault squad, along with the looming dreadnought, surrounded the kneeling Apothecary as he unscrewed the stopper, and tipped a few drops out onto his segmented glove. The armour they wore was gunmetal grey, edged with white and red, and the armourers had burnished all the suits to a gleaming finish. The threads of water made stark black streaks on the shining metal of Khiron's gauntlet. As the brothers intoned the sacred rite, voices toneless as they rasped out through visor speakers, Khiron dribbled the water onto the deck. It pooled there, and the rite was made. Water had been given, precious drops from the raging salt oceans of their home-world, Ithaka.

They were born from a world of seas, raised from it like the great horn-plated water-wyrms they named themselves after. To them, it was the embodiment of the Emperor, who they voyaged space to serve. Wherever they went, on whatever undertaking, they made this offering, the life-water of Ithaka, the blood of the Emperor.

They were Iron Snakes. Just for a moment, this rite of compact reminded them of their solemn, eternal oath. The double-looped serpent symbol glowed proudly on their auto-responsive shoulder plates. They were Tactical Squad Damocles, charged with a holy duty. They stood in the ring, as Brother Khiron rose to join the circle, warrior-gods in the form of men, armoured and terrible. They sang, a slow ritual tune, and beat time in deadened clanks, slapping right hands against their thigh plates.

Their weapons had been made safe for the Rite of Giving of Water, as ready weapons would be disrespectful. The chant over, they moved with smooth precision, clicking sickle-pattern clips into bolt pistols. Brother Andromak lit his flamer. Blue lightning crackled back into life around Brother-Sergeant Priad's lightning claw. He nodded. The circle broke.

'I go alone,' said Priad.

'I had a feeling you would say that,' Autolochus grumbled.

'Twelve years ago, as a virgin inductee, I came here. I made an undertaking that I believed was done and finished with. I was wrong. I have to finish what I started. I have to complete the task I failed to complete then, or I am no better than an inductee, with no right to lead this band of Notables. And I must finish it as I started it, alone.'

'Brother,' Xander began.

'No argument, Xander,' Priad said. 'No discussion. I go on ahead. They know me here. Wait for me, for my summons. I'll call for you if I need you.'

'Then may the Emperor protect you,' Autolochus growled, and the brothers of Damocles murmured their assent.

Priad walked to the air gate and settled himself into the cabin of the lander. The flight systems were fully automated, and governed remotely by the skill of the *Bullwyrm*'s chief pilot on the cruiser's bridge.

Priad sealed the hatches, blew the air ducts and fuel pipes, released the clamps, and settled down as the cabin lighting dimmed and his arrestor chair rotated back into descent mode.

'Clear for descent,' the vox crackled.

'Drop me,' Priad replied.

There was a bang. A multi-G lurch. A rush.

The lander fell sharply away from the belly of its mothership, corrected attitude in a torch-flare of burners, dipped nose-down, and rushed away towards the bright sphere of Baal Solock.

## XX

PRIAD HEADED FOR Fuce, scoring the cloudy sky above the old city and made landfall in water meadows that seemed familiar.

It was dawn, and the air was grey. Hefting up his wargear, Priad descended from the lander. No one came to meet him. Beyond the water meadows, the piles of the ancient city rose up, silent and unforthcoming.

He made his way up out of the water meadows. His memory told him of a state park, a formal woodland, but that had long gone. Barrier walls of rockcrete and mesh encircled the outer flanks of the High Legislator's palace. Within the barrier walls, tall palings of wood and flint tiles had been erected, and earthwork defences had been built. They were old, he noticed. Moss and lichen clung to the tiles and coated the wood.

'Hello!' he called, amping the volume of his helmet speakers. His call echoed around the empty place, rebounding from the stern, defensive walls.

Unopposed, he climbed the walls and the paling fences, and came up the stone apron of the palace.

His auspex read heat signatures ahead, and automatic target crosshairs lit up across his vision. He blinked them away. The hot spots were pockets of body heat, and the glow of gun batteries, concealed in the bastion wall ahead.

'Unless you mean to be my enemy,' he called out, 'stop aiming your weapons at me.'

The heat traces melted away. Priad heard hasty footsteps retreating from him along the platforms of the bastion. He walked in under the gate. The courtyard was empty. Glancing up, he saw how the sun was losing its battle with the weather. Clouds rushed across the sky, as if in a hurry to be somewhere else.

He reached the palace door, a heavy timber thing, and raised a fist. Then he stopped, amused at the notion of knocking. He pushed the door open and stepped inside. Cold stone. Rush lights. Again, that vacant sensation that human life was hiding in the corners of the world, just outside of his perception.

He strode down the hallway, his footsteps loud, passing under great windows full of sky, and oil portraits of significant men, long dead. A mechanical clock chimed somewhere, far away down one of the quiet halls.

'Hello?' he called. 'Anyone?'

He heard a soft, padding sound. A dog appeared.

For a moment, he was disappointed it wasn't black. It was a large attack dog, its coat a woolly grey. It glared at him and growled.

Priad knelt down and issued a command whistle.

The hound balked, then ran to him, snuffling at his greaves.

'Show me,' he said.

The dog turned and ran ahead, down the lonely hallway, to a set of massive doors. Priad pushed them open. The room beyond was huge, a vaulted chamber glazed with candle smoke. A hundred tapers flickered around the edges of the chamber. A thin figure was seated in a wooden throne at the far end of the lofty room.

'I have come to meet with the High Legislator,' Priad said, the dog running off ahead of him.

The figure rose. 'You've found her.'

Vocal recognition templates flashed across Priad's visor. 'Primary clerk?'

Perdet Suiton Antoni, slender and grey-haired, rose to her feet. 'Priad?'

'The very same.'

'Terra in the heavens! I thought you were my death, coming to claim me.'

He stepped towards her. She looked very old and delicate.

'You are the High Legislator of Fuce?' he asked.

'Can't a woman hold such an office?' she replied. There was a vigour inside her, despite her frailty. 'Great gods, Priad? Is it really you? I... I didn't send for you.'

'I wasn't summoned,' Priad replied. He walked down the length of the cold chamber, and removed his helmet.

'Gods!' she gasped. 'You haven't changed!'

He was close enough now, face to face with her, to see how time had eroded her looks and shrunk her frame. She was an old woman. The sight shocked him.

'I mean it,' Antoni said. 'You haven't changed a bit since I last saw you here. Do you remember that? It was an age ago. You've probably forgotten, the life you lead.'

'I remember. Twelve years ago, on this soil, summoned by you.'

She blinked, and went over to a nearby table, pouring herself a cup of wine. As she drank it, Priad saw how her lined hands trembled.

'It's not been twelve years,' she said. 'More like... forty. Forty years, by the calendars of Baal Solock.'

'That's not right...' Priad began to say, then stopped. He recalled what small learning he had about the complex ways time and the warp moved around each other, indifferent and unaligned. He had followed the path of his life along its own measurement, travelling from world to world, undertaking to undertaking, but it was entirely possible that dislocated places away from that path might have advanced through time at different rates. He had been gone for twelve of his own years, but Baal Solock had moved on at its own pace. There was no definition to the process of the galaxy, no fixed mark, no absolute degree of period. Even sidereal time, by which he'd measured this return, had no governed meaning.

'You haven't changed,' he said, believing that was the thing one was supposed to say.

'Not true!' she snapped. 'I've grown old and paper-thin. You're the one who hasn't aged a day.'

She put down her glass and came over to him, staring up at his face. 'Not a day,' she said, and hugged him, stretching her arms around the broad case of his armour.

'You haven't changed,' he said, truthfully. 'You might be older, Antoni, but you're still the same.'

'You smooth talker,' she laughed, gamely, and playfully slapped his arm. 'I've become an old woman on an empty throne, watching over a frightened world. And now you arrive, fresh as the day you left, and confirm that all our fears are founded.'

'How is that?'

'You wouldn't be here, Priad, if Baal Solock wasn't in danger.'

'That's not why I've come, primary… High Legislator. I'm here to finish some old business.'

'What old business?' she asked, limping back to her throne to sit down.

'The teeth. The trophies I left you with. From the jaw bone.'

She frowned. 'Teeth? Yes, I remember. The teeth. Funny peg things. Throne, that was long ago. A long time. I must have been pretty then. Young and pretty. Is that how you remember me, Priad? Is that what you expected?'

'I expected Perdet Suiton Antoni, and that's what I've found. The teeth, Perdet. Please, where are the teeth?'

She thought about that and shrugged. 'I can't remember. I haven't seen them in years.'

Priad looked around. 'Try to recall…'

'I have had other matters to contend with,' she snapped. 'Ruling the cantons and what not. We have lived in fear since your passing, Priad.'

'Does that fear explain the new walls and palings?'

'New? I had them raised thirty-five years ago, on my election. For which I must thank you, by the way. I'd never have reached this rank but for the celebrity of adventuring beside the Iron Snake hero who saved our world. '

'What are you afraid of?' he asked simply.

'That they'd ever come again. The primuls. Baal Solock has lived in fear and watched the heavens every day since you last set foot here.'

'The primuls are gone,' Priad said. 'I drove them out. You won't see them again.'

'You're wrong,' said the aged High Legislator. 'They've come back. We've seen the lights of their ships in the sky.'

'That was my vessel, on descent.'

'Not today. For the last three weeks. Why do you suppose the city is empty? My people have fled to the hills. The primuls have come back, Priad. The primuls are here.'

Priad looked up at the huge windows. Rain clouds had darkened the sky. There was a peal of distant thunder.

'Are you sure?' he asked.

'Oh, completely,' she said.

## XXI

SHE SUMMONED SERVANTS. Half a dozen appeared, unwilling and scared. They had evidently been hiding in some basement or cellar. She made them take up tapers and light the way for them.

'Where are we going?'

'The museum,' she declared.

Surrounded by the bearers with their fluttering candles, the two walked side by side along the dark and empty corridors of the palace, passing staterooms and apartments where the furniture had been covered with dust cloths.

'It is a curious thing,' she began. 'When you came to us, you brought us salvation from a very real and very terrible threat. It was a historic moment for the Legislature. But there's always a price, isn't there?'

'I would imagine so,' he said.

'Your salvation left us with a legacy of abject fear. It has quite become a national condition over the years. Before the primuls, we were innocent. Wary of the stars, perhaps, and sensible to such hazards that might come. But we lived our lives in peace and calm, and never jumped at shadows.'

She waited while one of the servants unlocked a heavy set of wooden doors that glinted almost black with varnish.

'Now we do,' she said. 'We live in fear, paranoid. The visitation of the primuls proved the existence of true, cosmic horror, and showed us that we needed the help of gods to rid ourselves of it. It showed us our place in the galaxy, Priad, showed us how weak and insignificant and vulnerable we are.'

'I'm sorry,' he said.

'Don't be! It wasn't your fault. It changed people's spirits, though, changed character. In the years after the visitation, resources were taken up with the construction of fortification, with the improvement of our soldiery, with the development of new and better weapons and finer detection systems. Fear made us hard and untrusting.'

She led the way through the open doors, down a long flight of marble steps into a grand room lined with columns. The floor space was filled with rows of display cases, and the lights of the candles reflected off the lead glass.

'The teeth were popular, at first,' she said. 'In the months after the visitation. I was popular too, and so were the stories I had to tell. I was feted throughout the Legislature, invited to attend the salons of many rich and influential lords. I was even sent on embassies abroad. Everyone wanted to hear about the monsters and my great adventure. Everyone wanted to hear about you.'

Priad smiled. 'And how many primuls did you slay in the end?'

'What do you mean?'

'Surely a tale like that would have grown and flourished in the retelling?'

She looked hurt. 'Do you inflate the tally of your deeds, warrior?'

'No, I do not.'

'Neither do I. I have prided myself on a life conducted with proper honesty and decorum.'

He thought that he might have offended her, but then she said, 'I may possibly have killed one or two more of them, by the time the invitations started to become less frequent. And you were a lord general, not a man-at-arms.'

She looked at him. 'You wear insignia now.'

'I am brother-sergeant of Damocles.'

'Only a sergeant?' She turned away and began peering at the display cases. 'I should have brought my spectacles. These labels are old and hard to read.'

'Is this the museum?' Priad asked.

'The state museum. I kept the teeth with me to begin with, but there was great interest, as I said. People would come from leagues away to see them. I had them set on display here in the museum, where the public could visit them without bothering me, and they were quite a draw for many years. I haven't thought about them for such a long time. I suppose they're still here, somewhere.'

The servants spread out, helping her to search. She sent one off to locate a curator, or some index or catalogue. Priad wandered the hall, inspecting the displays. Old coins, medals, maps and manuscripts lurked in the dim glass boxes. Rain began to beat against the high windows of the museum, and outside it had become very dark. Priad began to fret at the time it was taking, but Antoni seemed much more impatient.

'My damn eyes! So weak and old.' She rubbed her hands together. 'I have lived a very long time, by the standards of my people,' she said. 'Did you know that? The physicians are at loss to explain it. I've outlived two husbands. I never bore a child. The physicians suspected that the exposure to contamination left me sterile. That has been a sadness to me. How could that be, though? Left barren by the poisons of the enemy, yet cursed with a long life?'

'I protected you,' he said.

'With drugs. I remember that very well. They made me awfully sick. But they can only have been temporary.'

'No,' he said. 'I gave you a measure of my own blood, so that you might share my immunity.'

'Oh,' she said, and thought about that. 'That would have made a very good addition to my story. The blood of Ithaka, in my veins.'

'Where is Princeps?' Priad asked.

'Who?'

'The dog?'

'Great Throne, he died years ago. He was only a dog.'

The servant returned, lugging a dusty catalogue of the museum exhibits. After much discussion and page turning, Antoni and her servants determined that the teeth had been removed from the exhibition twenty years earlier.

'Where to?' Priad asked.

'Into storage,' Antoni replied. 'Oh dear. They could be in the museum archive beneath us, or in the Treasury. I wish this damn book said, one way or another.'

She clapped her hands, and sent one of the servants off again to gather more servants out of hiding and begin a full search of the museum archive. The rest would accompany her to the Treasury.

'This is most annoying,' she said to Priad. 'With so few servants left in the palace precinct, this hunt could take weeks.'

This did not sound encouraging to Priad.

They left the museum, and crossed a wide courtyard in the rain to reach the sulking basalt edifice of the Treasury building.

Out in the open, Priad paused. There was something in the air, a feeling more pernicious than the lowering storm and the downpour.

He felt his unease grow.

WIPING HIS HANDS upon a cloth, Khiron came out of Petrok's chamber and allowed the attendants to reconnect his gauntlets. Autolochus was waiting for him.

'Well, Apothecary?'

'Petrok is awake, praise be the Emperor. His fever has broken. He is still weak, and can barely move or even speak. But he is returned to us. He made me put my ear against his mouth so he could dredge up some small words. He said something about advising Priad.'

'What exactly did he say?' Autolochus asked.

'He said "They're here. Tell Priad that they've come to stop him." This much he repeated twice.'

'Prepare Damocles for descent,' said Autolochus. 'I believe that at last I might get something useful to do.'

## XXII

INSIDE, THE TREASURY building felt like a mausoleum. Within the thick walls lay a series of rooms and vaults in which the Legislature had stockpiled bullion, fiscal records, taxation archives, art treasures and many other objects deemed valuable or worth safeguarding. The items and the bundles of files were stacked willy nilly and without method, like the clutter of an attic, sometimes spilling out into the hallways from overstuffed chambers. The interior walls and floor were dressed with tiles of red and black marble, and what windows existed were mere slits. There was no real daylight outside to seep in.

Several unshaven and distracted guards were discovered and put to work with the servants sorting through the rooms of junk and paperwork. Tapers and lamps were lit, creating little yellow pools of light in the sepulchral dark. Priad felt they were like tomb robbers, looting the funerary offerings inside some dead king's vault. He hoped it was simply the nature of the place that made him think so: his sense of foreboding made him worry that

the Treasury might soon take on the most fundamental prerequi-
site of a tomb.

He idly looked through piles of old paintings and stacks of dusty
ledgers, wondering how involved he ought to become. These were
not his treasures to ransack. Antoni directed the servants to clear
shelves of bundles of exchequer rolls, old edicts, and the manuscripts of ancient laws. Strong boxes were opened and searched,
filing drawers rifled, old coins of long withdrawn issues scattered
on the red and black floor. Occasionally, Antoni would pause to
examine something, as if wondering why anyone had ever kept it,
or murmur 'so that's where that went,' until she noticed the look
on Priad's face and got on with her business.

'Why do you need these damn things anyway?' she asked, rummaging through a small metal casket.

'To save many lives,' Priad replied.

She waited to see if he would elaborate, and when he didn't, she
set the casket aside, and pulled back the dust sheets curtaining
another shelf.

'Look at this now,' she said. It was a painting. It was her, in regal
gowns, upon a gilded seat. She looked much as she had done when
he had last been on Baal Solock.

'My official portrait. I sat for it the month after my election.'

'What's it doing here?' he asked.

'I never liked it,' she replied. 'Rather too glamorous, I always felt.
I hated having it in the palace. An image of me I could never live
up to. I sent it away for cleaning, and managed to have it interred
here. Hmm, look at it. Look at her. So proud.'

She lifted the painting and studied it with squinted eyes. 'I fancy
I will hang it again. In the palace, above my throne. I may not have
looked like that then, but who's going to argue with me now that
I wasn't ever so beautiful?'

A servant came over, and she put the painting back down. The
servant had found something. Priad moved forward, eager, but
heard Antoni snort derisively.

'Do these look like teeth?'

The servant shook her head.

'Then why did you think they were teeth?'

The servant shrugged.

'Get along with your work and stop being silly,' Antoni said. She looked at Priad and smiled. 'Buttons,' she told him.

They could hear the rain pattering off the roof and walls of the Treasury. 'What a miserable day,' she sighed. 'Shall we stop for lunch?'

He was about to reply when all the candles blew out at once. Priad stiffened, adjusting his eyes to the darkness and making to strap on his helm. He heard some of the servants moan in fear and surprise.

'It's just the wind,' Antoni chided them. 'Light them again. Tinder, someone.'

Sparks chinked in the darkness. One by one, the tapers were relit, illuminating fearful faces with wide, startled eyes.

'Carry on with the work,' Antoni ordered. She looked at Priad and whispered 'That was just the wind, wasn't it?'

'Stay here,' he said. 'Keep looking.'

He left the inner vaults and the bobbing lights of the candles and made his way back along the main hallway, his helmet display reading and graphing the topography in the gloom.

He heard something, and moved his hand to the grip of his bolter. Targeting graphics lit up across his vision and hunted for something to condemn. He was cautious. He didn't want to execute some blundering servant or Treasury guard.

Something moved, down a side hall to his right. He turned that way, feeling the delicious engagement of his honed combat instincts. Whatever it was had disappeared out of sight beyond the next corner of the hall. Astonishingly silent for someone so large and heavily armoured, he turned the corner.

Alone, in the middle of the sub hallway, the black dog stood looking at him. It wagged its tail stump, and cocked its head slightly, its tongue dangling from its dog-grin.

Priad had faced many things in his life, many things that would have congealed a mortal soul in abject terror. But this made his heart skip.

'Princeps?' he said, then felt like an idiot. The dog was ages dead. This was just another black dog, lost in the ill-kempt halls. Except that look, that cock of the head...

At the sound of his vox-filtered voice, the dog growled slightly and backed away. Priad removed his helmet so his own voice would issue.

'Princeps?'

Stump wagging again, the dog trotted forward and sat down at his feet, gazing up at him. He knelt. The dog was real. He could smell its wet coat and its sour breath.

'Why have you come to find me, Princeps?' he whispered, silently adding 'all this way'.

The dog got up again and began to trot off down the sub hallway. It looked back at him once and yapped a little bark, twice.

Priad didn't need to be told. He followed the dog's lead, down the hallway into a gallery that led through into the Treasury's second principal hall, which extended to the rear exit of the building.

The dog vanished. He took his eyes off it for a moment, and suddenly it wasn't there anymore.

He was alone in the rear hall. He stopped still, and slowly slid his helmet back on. The visor systems lit up as they came down over his eyes.

He wasn't alone at all.

There were shadows in the shadows, dark shapes that resolutely refused to become visible, even when subjected to the amplified scrutiny of his visor systems.

He heard a chittering noise, like rats or grinding teeth.

Time slowed down.

Priad ripped his bolter out and up, freeing the lock, and began to fire as the shadows rippled towards him. He blasted one shape to his right, and heard it bounce with recoil and fall, then swung round to slam two more shots into the shadows to his left. Two more shapes flew backwards in the darkness, flailing and writhing. Dark blood splashed across the red and black marble.

Something struck his chest plate hard, and drove him back a step. Then a second object plunked heavily off his shoulder guard and ricocheted into the wall beside him, chipping the stonework. He heard the unmistakable buzzing of splinter weapons.

They came for him. Shadows coiled forward out of the walls, out of the darkness of the ceiling. He squeezed his trigger and kept it squeezed, firing a sustained burst, ripping the darkness to pieces wherever it moved. His aiming graphics jumped and flickered, delineating target after target. The muzzle flash of his weapon was so bright, the after-image became a slow-fading ghost on his optic systems. Enemy fire chopped and tore into him, gouging his plate and leaving craters and gashes of bared metal.

His clip ran out far too soon. He made to reload, but the primuls rushed him, clawing into him and hacking with their blades. He smashed one away with the weight of his bolter, tore another in two with his lightning claw, then slammed his own body backwards into the wall, crushing something that had jumped onto his back.

Another daemon-shadow lunged at him, driving a lance-like weapon with a long, wicked blade. The blow forced him back against the wall, and he felt pain, as cold as glacial ice, explode across the left side of his gut as the razor-tip plunged through his plate and into his torso.

He thrashed out with his empty bolter again, and split the skull of the thing that had stabbed him. It fell backwards, jerking in its death spasms, and the blade tore out.

Priad rammed a fresh munition load home. The next things that moved were cut down in swift flashes of gunfire.

He ceased fire, scanning, hearing his own breath rasp inside his helm. A commotion had risen in other parts of the Treasury, and in the palace quarters outside. He wondered if Antoni's guards had any real combat skill. He doubted it.

Dark bodies sprawled, mangled and twisted, along the hallway. Primul blood steamed in the chilly air. He moved towards the thin daylight, towards the rear entranceway, executing two more shadows that rose up at him from the darkness.

He was onto his third clip. He could feel the slippery warmth of his own blood leaking down from his gut wound into his groin and thighs beneath the armour.

He emerged into the grey morning. The rain was sheeting down. A wide courtyard lay behind the bastion of the Treasury, flanked by wings of the palace. Four sleek raider craft sat on the yard, hooked and menacing like giant anthracite scorpions. They were uncrewed, but as he watched, three more swooped overhead, banking out across the roofscape of Fuce.

He heard distant screams, gunfire, and clanging bells. Smoke fumed up from the city.

Baal Solock's long-held fears had become reality.

The primul lord must have been waiting for him. Too late, Priad swung round at the warning pulse of his senses. The blade's blow caught him across the shoulder plate and threw him down the wide stone steps of the rear entranceway.

Priad landed hard, but rolled immediately on the soaking flagstones, in time to see his enemy leaping down towards him, his long-bladed spear stabbing low. The primul lord was quite the most magnificent example of his species Priad had ever seen. Tall and slender, his lithe form covered in a sharply segmented body armour of black and gold metal. Priad knew it was a lord, for only the most elevated of the dark eldar race would rate armour so fine, and a war-mask helmet so tall and cruel and spiked.

He tried to raise his weapon to fire, but the primul was faster. The whistling spear tip flashed down and pinned Priad's right wrist to the ground. He felt his wrist bones crack and shatter as the blade ground through them. He kept hold of his weapon, but the enemy's spear was power-charged with a shock field, and agony seared through Priad's arm.

As the primul, standing astride Priad, gleefully drove the spear deeper, electrical discharge danced up the brother-sergeant's pinned limb, triggering involuntary neural spasms. The bolter fell from his limp fist.

Priad cursed and kicked upwards, driving his armoured foot up between the primul's legs. The force of the blow threw the primul over, taking his spear along with him.

Priad leapt to his feet, aware of how encumbering his belly wound had become, and how painful his skewered wrist was. He shut those feelings down. The primul lord landed smartly on the flagstones, legs splayed, hunched over in a fighting posture. He circled his lethal spear in his hands. The falling rain glittered on his armour like diamond beads. His eyes were yellow slits in the sculpted mask.

Priad lashed out with his claws, ripping at the foe, the rain crackling and fizzling off his charged gauntlet weapon.

The primul lord side-stepped and dodged each powerful strike as it came, agile and light, dancing away from the heavy Ithakan warrior. Priad lunged furiously.

He hit rain and empty air. The primul lord had hopped back, turning delicately to swing in with his spear. Priad managed to parry the strike. The primul danced away again, pivoted, and then gripped his spear with both hands by the centre of the haft. There was a clicking whirr, and the metal spear extended, doubling in length.

Whirling the long weapon, the primul re-addressed, and struck in at Priad. The Ithakan dodged the first strike, deflected the second, and then took two heavy blows to the upper body from the butt-spike end that sent him staggering across the yard.

The primul lord did not spare him a second's remorse. He closed again, smashing a haft blow into Priad's face, before ducking under the grasping lightning claw and drawing the spear back like a club, two handed.

He swung from the butt of the shaft. The long weapon's blade, like an oversized executioner's axe, slammed into the side of Priad's head.

## XXIII

BODIES LAY IN the echoing halls of the palace. Human bodies: guards and servants, murdered as they tried to flee. Hall tables and candle stands had been overturned. Drapes had caught fire. Screams resounded from the heart of the palace complex.

The primuls moved forward, lingering over the strewn bodies. The fiendish warriors cackled as they found humans that were still alive, those injured or playing dead in their terror.

Blades were drawn and abominations performed. Shrieks filled the air. Blood spread out wide across the tiles. One of the primul killers discovered a servant girl cowering behind a wall hanging, and cast her out into the main body of the hall. She wailed. The primuls mimicked her distress in hideous fluting voices, then laughed again as they closed in to have their sport.

One of them suddenly burst in an explosion of gore that misted the air with blood droplets. Another, turning, lost his head to a howling bolt round. The others buckled and twisted as they were cut down.

Xander strode down the hallway, boltgun smoking. To his right came Aekon, to his left Kules.

'Damocles and Ithaka!' he cried. The servant girl, down on her hands and knees, looked at them uncomprehendingly. To her, these grey giants were as terrifying as the laughing daemons.

'Help her up,' Xander barked.

Aekon moved forward, holding out a hand. 'You're safe,' he said. 'This site is now under the protection of the Ithakan phratry.' She blinked at him.

'Hide yourself, or get clear of the palace,' Aekon said, lowering his hand, aware that he was intimidating her. 'Go on, now.' She understood that much. With a squeal, she got up and ran.

'Contacts, side staircase,' Kules said. A hail of splinter rounds chipped and whined down across their position, shattering against their plate and pinging off the stone floor.

'As I was saying,' Kules remarked sourly.

'Damocles and Ithaka!' Xander answered, opening fire. Aekon and Kules moved in beside him, raking the marble staircase with their shots, killing the shadows lurking there. Aekon swung to his left, calmly exterminating two primuls rushing out of a side apartment. He paused, and bent down, wrenching the helmet off one of the eviscerated corpses.

'What are you doing?' Xander snapped, his voice curt and metallic over the comm.

'I always wanted to know what they looked like. What their faces looked like, I mean,' Aekon said.

'Any the wiser?' Kules asked.

'My curiosity is satisfied,' Aekon replied, repulsed. He tossed the empty helm aside.

'Contacts, far hallway,' Kules called out. They slammed home fresh clips and opened fire again, swabbing white smoke into the lofty roof of the hallway.

'Xander to Damocles,' Xander called. 'Sound off!'

'SECOND SECTION!' KHIRON replied, hearing the call via his link. 'Some resistance in this area.'

At Khiron's side, Dyognes smiled to himself. The Apothecary was underselling the situation. The three of them – Khiron, Dyognes and Scyllon – had stormed the palace compound via the garrison gate, and come up through the kitchen wing. Every step of the way had been haunted by primul skirmishers. He had tried to keep a tally, but had honestly lost count when the number passed forty. They had expended most of their allotted munitions. Soon it would be down to blades and shields, the bloody grunt work.

There was a very good chance they would die if it came down to hand-to-hand. The primuls had numbers on their side. But the idea somehow lifted Dyognes's spirits. After Ganahedarak, he had believed his life as a phratry brother to be over, and that he would never taste action or glory again. He had been convinced that, although Priad had allowed him to accompany the squad on this undertaking, it was a matter of sympathy alone. There would be no action. It would be a last, symbolic function before his long and shaming retirement.

And he had only just begun.

But now, marvellously, they were in war. Combat resounded and blood flowed. Their ancient and particular enemy was about them, seeking victory in their deaths.

If he lived or if he died, he couldn't have wished for a more fitting final undertaking.

He was Damocles, cased in his plate, boltgun in his fists, alongside his brothers, death all about them. There was no finer destiny than that.

THE THIRD SECTION of Damocles had penetrated the south wing of the palace. Andromak's flamer had scoured the marble chambers and undercroft stairs. At his flank, Pindor and Natus picked off the stragglers.

'For Ithaka!' Andromak shouted as he gusted fire along the stone hallways.

'And for Priad,' Natus suggested.

'That's right,' said Pindor. 'For Priad, our heart and soul.'

'Sections!' Andromak called. 'Has anyone made contact with the brother-sergeant yet?'

'Negative!' Xander replied, his voice distorted over the link. 'Heavy fighting here!'

'And here,' Khiron's voice cut in. 'No trace of Priad's whereabouts yet.'

'If he's dead…' Pindor began.

'If he's dead, what?' asked Andromak.

'If he's dead, these xenos scum will pay.'

Natus laughed. 'How can they be made to pay more than they are paying now?'

'I'll find a way,' said Pindor.

AUTOLOCHUS CLUNKED INTO the main courtyard of the palace. Through his ancient, cracked ocular sensors, he read the heat lifting from the human bodies that littered the yard. Beyond that haze, he detected the warm shadows laying in wait.

'Show yourselves, then!' he boomed, his voice resounding off the high walls on every side.

Nothing stirred.

'If that's the way you want it,' he growled. 'Coming, ready or not.'

The weapon mounts on either side of his bulky torso cycled up into place, and he let rip with his lascannon and storm bolter. Whole sections of wall exploded and collapsed, bringing stone facings down like an avalanche. The hidden enemy discovered what slaughter meant.

Autolochus stomped over to a dying primul, sprawled in a lake of blood at the side of the main steps.

'Where's Priad?' he asked.

The primul gurgled some obscenity.

Autolochus lowered his storm bolter. 'Wrong answer,' he remarked.

## XXIV

PRIAD FELL, PAIN flaring through his skull. His visor went blank, scrolling only the malfunction symbol. He heard the primul lord crowing in triumph.

He tore off his ruined helmet, and hurled it at his foe, forcing the primul lord to back-step and deflect the flying helmet with his spear.

As it left his hand, Priad saw how deeply his helmet had been damaged. The side of the helm was folded in and crushed. It had only barely spared him from the primul lord's blow.

He half-rose, the rain streaming off his bare face, but the primul assaulted him again, and knocked him back. Priad swung his lightning claw, and made the primul lord jump aside. He regained his feet, then staggered as the renewed blows of his dark foe drove him back against the prow of the nearest raider craft.

He summoned his willpower, and put the strength of his back into one devastating swing of his gauntlet weapon.

The primul lord parried the stroke with the blade of his spear, and rammed Priad backwards, skewering the lightning claw against the raider craft's elegant prow. Pinned and helpless, the claw flickered with discharge, blades moving uselessly.

The primul lord kept the claw pinned hard with his spear, one handed, as he drew out a bite-dagger to finish Priad off. The twinned blade rose up.

In the final second, Priad remembered his benediction. He was still envenomed from that lucky omen on the Cydides Isthmus. He was a striking snake. He tensed the Betcher's glands in his hard palette, where the green-back viper's toxins had been contained, and spat into the primul lord's eyes.

The primul screamed and fell back, clawing at his mask.

Priad tore away the dark eldar spear staking his left hand and hoisted it up in his crippled fists. It felt remarkably light, as if it was barely there.

'Ithaka!' he grunted, as he drove all his weight behind the blow.

The primul lord's magnificent helm bounced off the rain-swept flagstones and his beautifully armoured body toppled slowly onto its side, blood jetting from the neck stump and splashing on the yard, where it was diluted by the downpour.

Priad sank to his knees and cast the odious spear aside.

He heard a slow, heavy tread approaching him.

'Done?' asked Autolochus, towering over him, a grim monolith in the dismal rain.

'I think so. Is Damocles here?'

'Purging the palace as we speak. They are fine men, Priad. You should be proud of them.'

'You presume I'm not?'

'I'm certain you are. Notables. What glory to be called by that rare name. I was a Notable once.'

'You still are, Autolochus,' Priad said.

'Thank you. But I was. I truly was. Skypio was my squad. Notable Skypio. How well we wore that title. Ah me. Happy days.'

Priad shook his head and laughed. He tried to rise. Autolochus extended his cannon mount for Priad to brace against.

'Look to your wounds, lad,' Autolochus said, 'or you'll end up in a combat chassis like me.'

'There are worse places to be,' said Priad.

'Are we finished here?' asked the ancient dreadnought.

'I think we are.'

'And was it worth it? Was Petrok right?'

Priad nodded.

## XXV

IT TOOK TEN years, ten years by whatever measure of time a man cares to employ, for the consequences of the second Baal Solock undertaking to have any lasting effect.

Using the dark and calcifying teeth – which High Legislator Antoni had finally discovered, two days after the end of hostilities, in the bowels of the Treasury, locked in a small casket labelled 'other' – the Apothecaries and flesh smiths of the phratry fashioned a copy of the relic. They crafted it from inert organic matter, lacing the artificial bone with the genetic codes extracted from the original teeth. This work, though ingenious, was a simple extension of the genetic applications they had mastered through the ritual creation of altered humans. The relic was grown in a vat, fed with minerals, its shape slowly defined by the template writ within the teeth.

Later, it was conveyed into disputed territory, and displayed during a number of conflicts, so that the greenskins could identify it. Several worthy squads of the phratry undertook these dangerous actions: Veii on Banthus, Manes on Triumverate, Thebes on Calicon. Twice, Damocles carried the relic into war to goad the orks.

Once the lure was set, the phratry's Librarius, working under Petrok's instruction, and aided by the massed astropaths of twenty-eight worlds, reinforced the ploy, saturating the greenskin horde with psychic propaganda, stirring their loyalties and their hungers, forcing them to turn and seek the holy relic.

A final mission, conducted by the reconstituted Parthus squad, who won the honour after a drawing of lots, carried the relic far outside Reef Star territory, and secured it on one of the primuls' own raid worlds.

Eight months later, the swinekin hosts descended on that world, and reclaimed their trophy. The primuls suffered a terrible fate at their hands, ultimate victims of their own deceit.

By that time, the inexorable ork muster had turned away from the Reef Stars, drawn off by the ruse. The green host receded into the darkness of the outer systems, chasing the recovered relic and making war with their own kind to claim its ownership.

The greenskins did not return to the Reef Stars for a thousand years.

The primuls did. But the phratry was always there to greet them.

ON THE MORNING of their departure from Baal Solock, the brothers of Damocles assembled in the palace yard at Fuce. They stood in a line, with great Autolochus at the end of it. The rain still fell, with unseasonal vigour.

The corpses of the enemy had been cleared from the palace and the city, and burned in a quarry pit to the west of Fuce. Fires had been put out. It would, however, be a long time before the devastated palace and the city surrounding it were fit for comfortable habitation again.

High Legislator Antoni came out to review the squad. She walked the line of them, leaning on a cane, for the past few days had been hell on her back. A servant scurried alongside her, holding up an umbrella to shield her mistress from the rain.

Antoni studied the bare faces of the Iron Snakes carefully, one by one, as she went along the line.

'I'm sorry if I appear inquisitive,' she told them, 'but I've only ever seen one of you before. Ten of you, like this. It will make a damn good new story. I'll be the toast of the Legislature for years to come.'

She glanced at Priad. 'They all look alike,' she whispered.

'They're not,' he assured her.

'I'm sure they aren't, but they all do look so very much alike. Except him, the one with the funny eye.'

She pointed at Natus.

'But only,' she continued, 'because he has a funny eye. It's a nice feature. It makes him stand out.'

Priad couldn't immediately form a decent response.

'And as for that,' she said, nodding at Autolochus. 'I don't know what to make of that.'

'You're quite a piece of work yourself, lady,' Autolochus grumbled.

'It heard me!'

'It can hear a pin drop on the other side of the mountains,' Priad said.

'Have I offended it?' she hissed, her voice as low as it could be.

'Only by referring to me as an "it",' Autolochus croaked.

Antoni turned and looked up at Priad. 'Will you not stay? We do a nice line in celebratory feasts, and you missed the last one.'

'We have to go.'

'Well, here they are then,' she said, and produced the peg teeth from the pocket of her gown. He took them from her carefully. 'Are you sure you won't stay?' she asked. 'There's a very fine artist on his way up from Caddis. I had fancied to have a glorious portrait of you made, if you'd sit for it. It could hang beside the one of me looking young and beautiful.'

'We have to go,' he repeated.

Antoni shrugged. 'Off you go, then.' She reached up with a thin hand and ran the tips of her fingers down the side of his face.

'You are such a very beautiful man, Priad,' she said. 'For a giant, I mean. You look just like a hero should.'

'I don't know what to say,' he replied.

'A simple "thank you" will suffice. Will you ever come back?'

'I don't know. I hope I won't ever have to. Will you still be here if I do?'

Antoni grinned. 'I should expect so. There's no killing me. I'm immortal, you see. I have the blood of an Ithakan in my veins.'

'I'm not sure–' he began.

'I was joking,' she said. 'You don't really do jokes, do you, Priad of Damocles?'

'No,' he admitted.

'Get going then,' she said. She limped away towards the palace, and did not look back.

PRIAD TURNED the squad and marched them out through the palace gates. Their lander was waiting in the main square. Priad watched them board and lift away in a shower of spray, then walked alone back through the palace complex to recover his own lander from the water meadows.

There was mist in the air. A watery sun fought with the clouds to be seen.

As he passed through the outermost gateway, he heard a sound behind him. He turned.

The black dog was following him, trotting eagerly at his heels.

He sighed, and knelt. 'Go home,' he said.

The dog dropped onto its belly and looked up at him with doleful eyes. 'Go on!' he gestured. 'Go home!'

The dog whined and wriggled its crouching body towards him.

Priad rose to his feet. 'Go on home, Princeps,' he said.

The black dog rose and turned. It ran back to the gateway and stood there, watching as Priad continued on his way.

When he was almost out of sight, it barked twice.

He turned to look, but the dog had disappeared.

## XXVI

THE WORLD ENVELOPING him was warm and blue and crushing. Priad dipped his head against the current, and pulled with his bare arms. The wounds on his palm and wrist were healing, just dark bumps under the skin wrap.

How long now? Twenty-one, twenty-two?

He'd lost count, but he didn't really care.

The cold gloom of the trench enclosed him. He saw the offerings, spread out across the base of the trench, so many, so fine. Some of them were so old their nature had been worn away by the sea.

He pulled lower, and hooked his own offering out of its pouch.

Pressure roared in his ears. He planted the grey, blunt peg of the ork's tooth in the soft sediment, between a munition clip and a golden figurine of Parthus. It seemed like the right place to leave it.

It felt liberating to be foolish for a change.

Rite done, he turned and kicked out, planing the water with his arms.

He swam upwards, into the warmer, sun-pierced waters, towards the surface, where the brothers of Damocles waited for him on a golden strand in the endless light of Ithaka.

# ABOUT THE AUTHOR

**Dan Abnett** lives and works in Maidstone, Kent, in England. Well known for his comic work, he has written everything from the *Mr Men* to the *X-Men*. His work for the Black Library includes the popular strips *Titan* and *Darkblade*, the best-selling *Gaunt's Ghosts* novels, the Inquisitor Eisenhorn and Ravenor trilogies, and the acclaimed Horus Heresy novel, *Horus Rising*.

# GHOSTS

THE FOUNDING
A GAUNT'S GHOSTS OMNIBUS

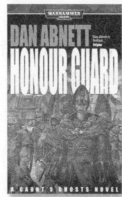

DAN ABNETT
HONOUR GUARD
A GAUNT'S GHOSTS NOVEL

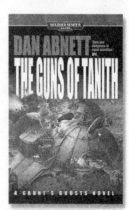

DAN ABNETT
THE GUNS OF TANITH
A GAUNT'S GHOSTS NOVEL

DAN ABNETT
STRAIGHT SILVER
A GAUNT'S GHOSTS NOVEL

DAN ABNETT
SABBAT MARTYR
A GAUNT'S GHOSTS NOVEL

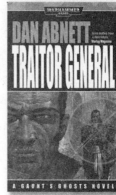

DAN ABNETT
TRAITOR GENERAL
A GAUNT'S GHOSTS NOVEL

DAN ABNETT
HIS LAST COMMAND
A GAUNT'S GHOSTS NOVEL

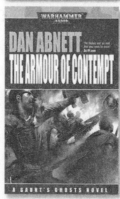

DAN ABNETT
THE ARMOUR OF CONTEMPT
A GAUNT'S GHOSTS NOVEL

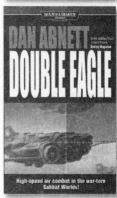

DAN ABNETT
DOUBLE EAGLE
High-speed air combat in the war-torn Sabbat Worlds!

⊢ READ TILL YOU BLEED

# A MIND WITHOUT PURPOSE
# WILL WANDER IN DARK PLACES

## Also by Dan Abnett

### RAVENOR
ISBN 13: 978 1 84416 073 0 • ISBN 10: 1 84416 073 4

### RAVENOR RETURNED
ISBN 13: 1 84416 185 0 • ISBN 10: 1 84416 185 4

### RAVENOR ROGUE
ISBN 13: 1 84416 460 8 • ISBN 10: 1 84416 460 8

*Visit wwww.blacklibrary.com to buy these books,*
*or read the first chapters for free! Also available*
*in all good bookshops and games stores*